BLEEDING OUT

Book Three in the Tranquility Series

TANYA ROSS

For my parents, who taught me the joy of reading and encouraged me to follow my dreams.

The heart has no tears to give, it drops only blood, bleeding itself away in silence.

— Harriet Beecher Stowe

Prologue

FIND a chapter by chapter soundtrack for this book by following this link for Youtube.

https://music.youtube.com/playlist?list=PLLcTI8CSSQ-ncsRi-8xsjgpXSy_Ac2lNF&si=9Ax8pgTv4F3-rOHE

Or search "Bleeding Out Soundtrack" on Youtube.

Preface

Book Three, *Bleeding Out*, begins immediately after *Facing Off* ends. In case you don't remember...

In Book Two of the Tranquility Series, *Facing Off,* the story of Ember, Will, and Xander return to the city to begin their revolution to bring down Serpio Magnus, Tranquility's Magistrate, they are immediately renegades on the run. As they separate to conceal themselves, Will is captured by the Sciolists, Tranquility's police force. Ember must make her way to the Plauditorium alone where their main rebel force, Phoenix, is in a self-imposed lock-down. Along the way, she must use her untapped time-bending powers to escape capture, but also receives a message from beyond the grave from her mother.

Xander, too, is challenged during his escape when he meets with foul play. The Magistrate has arranged for an unfortunate accident meant to kill him. When Xander is saved by a Medic named Ava, who is sympathetic to their cause, he is able to join the others at the Plauditorium to plot plans for the future.

Ember finally arrives safely at the Plauditorium, where she finds a group without leadership, as Xander has not yet arrived, and Will has been captured.

Will is tried and is only saved when he insists he has actually been spying on his friends for the city. He undergoes multiple challenges and torture from the Magistrate to betray the whereabouts of his friends and is then used as a pawn by the Magistrate to do things that this pure-hearted soul would never do. (He remains a prisoner throughout most of the book, and the reader is given his story in parallel form).

The Phoenix rebels launch a few bombs on City Hall to gain access to the library where the Magistrate's journals are kept. These will further implicate him in the murder of Ember's mother.

After Ember, Xander, and the rest of their rebel group Phoenix are threatened with poisoned gas, they must escape underground into tunnels, most notably an abandoned subway tunnel. There they devise elaborate plans to infiltrate the city by escaping the subway just before they are discovered.

In a dream, Ember gets information again from her mother. After several forays into government buildings with Ava's help, she and Xander discover her mother is actually alive and is being held prisoner in a horrible area outside the city known as The Outside, where the government sends emotional resistors.

Xander and Ember go on a quest to The Outside to locate and rescue Ember's mom. During this time, they experience a number of adventures. Xander, who has always been in love with Ember, forges a relationship with her, and she returns his feelings as they journey on, as she believes Will has turned traitor to the rebellion.

Ember and Xander rescue Talesa, Ember's mom. While the reunion is great, Ember learns that not only does she have paranormal abilities, but her mother does also, and there are others in the city that do as well, due to a genetic program unbeknownst to the government when it was happening.

The reason why the Magistrate has been killing people is because they are the ones with extrasensory abilities, but he doesn't know the identities of all of them.

When they return to the city, Ember and Xander are captured.

In a final sadistic spectacle, the Magistrate pits Xander against Will in an arena to fight to the death with spears. Will shows his true colors when, instead of throwing his spear to kill Xander, he throws it at the Magistrate, where it enters his chest, killing him.

Ember immediately realizes that Will has always been on their side, and that she is now in love with two different guys.

Ember, Will, and Xander are able to escape to set up the scenario for the next book in the series, which will push the rebellion into full swing and use the genetically altered people to help them.

At the very end of the book, the Magistrate does not actually die, but is able to revive himself because he, too, has been altered genetically. He is immortal.

ONE

Ember's Message

The Magistrate is dead.
The Magistrate is dead.

THE WORDS CYCLED through Ember's mind, keeping time with the wild heartbeat thrusting against her ribcage.

In a stolen MediCar barreling down the road, Ember's chest heaved as she tried to catch her breath. Less than ten minutes had passed since they'd raced out of Amity Arena, where Xander and Will had faced off against each other in a fight to the death ordered by the city of Tranquility's leader, the Magistrate. Now, not only were they fugitives, but Will was an assassin.

She grasped both boys' hands. Their emotions poured into her psyche, almost overwhelming her. Fear, yes. But also desire and love.

The rush drenched her. She abruptly dropped their hands and took a deep breath.

Xander's voice exploded. "Damn!"

Ember shrank back. "Sorry, I had to let go. I—" She felt his anger now instead of his ardor. The emotion rippled out like a lightning bolt connecting with a metal pole.

"No. Not that. Behind us! Sciolist vehicles. Two of 'em." Xander gritted his teeth from where he sat in the control seat.

In the aftermath of the chaos in Amity Arena, someone had finally realized they'd escaped and alerted the Sciolists, the city's police.

Multicolored homes, modern city structures, and floral borders whizzed by like a blurred abstract painting, but not fast enough.

A dozen shadows tossed darkness onto Ember's face, only broken occasionally by approaching red lights from their pursuers that flickered with demonic convulsions. She grabbed a blanket from the floor and held it tightly around her shoulders, hoping this was just another nightmare; but she knew it couldn't be.

"Any way to speed up?" From his position in the back, Will peered over Xander's shoulder.

Xander's gaze flickered across the front panel's minimal controls. "Yeah, looking … This is a MediCar. Should have some sort of hyperdrive for emergencies. Don't want to activate any sirens, though."

Will's face took on the pallor of white porcelain. "The wheels … they're totally up?"

"No way to know, but I think so. I'm not feeling any bumps. Are you?" Xander gave the few buttons on the dashboard a cursory glance.

"Can you find a higher speed?" Ember twisted in her back seat to look out the rear window. The Sciolist's distinctive red cars blazed behind them less than one hundred yards away. Terror ripped through her. *How are they so close?* They couldn't be caught! Not now. Not when they'd celebrated escaping just moments ago.

Her eyes settled on Xander in the front, his shoulders glistening with perspiration. She was sure sweat was running down his chest, too, still bare from his face-off in the arena. Will also wore only shorts and shoes, his torso marked with bruises and his ankle crusted with dried blood.

"How'd they know we're in a MediCar?" Ember wondered, her frustration palpable.

Xander huffed. "The Medics aren't stupid. They know how many MediCars were called to the arena for the Magistrate's injury. And we're missing. So …"

"We're already at seventy miles per hour," Will noted as he pointed to the sparse dash instruments. "Can Sciolist vehicles go past seventy? If they don't, we'll leave them behind in no time."

Xander brushed long locks of his black hair from his forehead. "Yeah? We can't count on that. And we can't go to any of the warehouses. Too risky."

"The *warehouses*?" Will frowned and tilted his head.

Ember waved her hand dismissively. "Can't explain now, Will."

Will nodded before he moved further toward the rear of the vehicle, positioning his back to his friends. "I'll watch behind us."

Xander ran his hand back and forth under the dashboard. "I'm finding nothin'! There's no way to get this buggy goin' any faster." Xander brought his fist down hard on the middle console.

"Ouch. That hurt. Please, do not damage my interior," a female voice said from the center speaker.

Xander stared down at where he'd just slammed his fist. "What the—!"

Ember gasped. "Of course! We don't need a device. It's a voice command. MediCar, speed up!"

"Yeah!" Xander yelled.

But nothing changed. The car behind them sped up, but their MediCar didn't. The distance between them shortened, and the Sciolists' silhouettes were visible through the windshield of the car behind them. Panic rose in a wash of stomach acid into her throat. If Sciolists captured them now, Will would face murder charges for killing the Magistrate. She and Xander would be accessories, on top of their other crimes against the city—insurrection, kidnapping, escape …

Will's voice was like a drill, jerking Ember out of her thoughts. "Xander! You're in the navigator seat! Give the car commands!"

"Speed up!" Xander yelled at the top of his lungs. "One hundred miles an hour!"

"One hundred miles per hour. Are you sure this is your requirement?" the MediCar's sweet voice inquired.

"Yes. *Yes*! And—and turn right! Next street!" Xander gripped a foot-long metal bar riveted to the dashboard. "Hang on, Ember!"

As the car slid into the turn, Ember grabbed the back of Xander's seat with both hands but lost her grip and crashed against Will. Not unlike the race cars at the Fun Zone Ember remembered as her favorite ride, the meteoric velocity was a rush. This, though, was no fun zone. The hair on her arms stood up. Her knuckles blanched as the MediCar continued to gather speed. It ripped around the corner and through the red light. A massive yellow van crossing their path escaped destruction within inches of its taillights.

She screamed as the MediCar rolled to the outside of the curve before flying into a straight direction and careening down a broad avenue. Will's head jerked back with the surge, and he grabbed on to Ember's arm like a drowning man.

"Will—do you think we lost 'em?" Xander glanced into the side mirror and then at the camera on the dash.

"No Sciolists now. Few cars. It's almost curfew." Will grinned before his mouth shrank back to tight lips. In the dark, his face held shadows that disappeared when the next car drove by.

Having spent the last few hours in an adrenaline haze, Ember had lost track of time. The typical welcoming calm of curfew, marked by the moon's mid-position in the sky, was as evasive as blown bubbles in the wind. And if she didn't know the moon's surface was pocked with craters, she would have sworn it mocked them with its smile.

Instead, she noted each intermittent car that went by, wondering how everyone else could simply be going about their normal routine when their lives hung in the balance.

"MediCar, turn right at Nirvana Parkway." Xander's voice carried a newfound confidence.

"Xander, if we see no Sciolists, shouldn't we just keep on a straight course?" Will's question was laced with confusion. "Nirvana Parkway has tons of curves! A scenic route's not what we need." He dropped his hand from Ember's arm to wipe the sweat off his forehead.

Xander kept his eyes on the road, his tone as assertive as the street was straight. "I'm going to try a zigzag. A straight course is too easy to follow." He clipped his words toward the end of his response.

The car careened around another corner, and the motion gave Ember a sudden throbbing in her forehead. She'd never tolerated motion well.

Just ahead, a white neon streetlight revealed a crimson flash of paint. Oh no. A Sciolist vehicle crossing their path.

"Frikkin' Shazz!" Xander yelled, pounding the console again.

"Anger is a forbidden emotion," the MediCar was quick to respond. "Please, check your Alt points."

"Stupid car! Stop it," Xander groaned.

"They maybe—maybe didn't see us?" Ember breathed her words out in a rush.

"They're looking for us. Of *course* they saw us." Xander's words were wrapped in his characteristic sarcasm.

Ember shook her head. "Geez. Turn around, then."

"Not that easy," Xander complained as he scanned the road ahead. "MediCar—make six alternating turns up ahead."

"Very well. Where is the emergency? I have no GPS coordinates," the vehicle's voice crooned.

Will held tightly to a stretcher separating him from Ember.

"We'd better decide where we're gonna go, Xan. We can't drive around all night. Ideas? Ember?"

"Right. No warehouse …" Xander ran his hands through his hair. "I got nothin'!"

"Ember, can you freeze time and get us out of here?" Will asked, training his questioning eyes on her face.

Ember laughed bitterly. "No. Even if I could generate the energy, it would only take me out of the time loop, and I can't do anything by myself to stop the Sciolists. There are too many."

Another sharp turn had them leaning to the right like warped statues before they shifted to the left with the next.

"Scrambling my brains here," Will complained in a serious drone.

"Where is the emergency?" the car persisted.

"Another Sciolist behind us!" Will's hand went to his forehead. "Pulled out from that alley! Gah!"

Dark fear weighed on Ember like an iron apron. What were they going to do? Should they pull over and take their chances on foot?

A voice pierced Ember's consciousness: *"Turn left!"* She shook her head and glanced around. Her skull throbbed. It didn't sound like the car talking.

"Turn left!" The second time, she knew. Sure enough, the voice was in her own head.

Her mother's voice! Talesa was using her special gift to communicate with her.

Ember pressed her fingers to smiling lips. "Xander—tell the car to turn left."

"What? Why? I've already told it six alternating turns …"

"Xander! *Listen* to me. My mom's speaking to me—in here." She tapped her head. "Turn left at the next block!" She leaned forward and jammed her hands hard into Xander's shoulders.

"Yeah, yeah. Okay! Last turn was right, the next turn will be left anyway. Then what?" Xander's words pressed.

"Uh … your … *mom*?" Will's mouth opened a second time and then abruptly closed.

Ember shut her eyes. "Shhh." She concentrated, listened to her mother's voice in her head, and nodded. "That left is Bliss Avenue. Then go straight for three miles."

"Three miles? Ember, what if we can't shake the Sciolists?" Will's hand trembled slightly before he grabbed on to the stretcher again.

"They don't have the speed we do." Ember, her own fears suffocated by hope, reached over and patted Will's arm. "We're gonna follow my mom's directions."

Will frowned. "I didn't think you believed in ghosts …"

"Oh, Will. My mom's alive—sorry. So much to tell you."

Will blinked back at her, the rest of his face a stony mask.

As the MediCar approached Bliss Avenue, the Sciolist car behind them gained speed and matched their change of direction as if boosted by an unseen force. A booming voice on an exterior loudspeaker demanded they pull over.

"What the—! They're right behind us!" Will scooted closer to the back, almost smashing his face against the glass. "We've gotta turn—throw 'em off!"

Ember's eyes flared. "No! We stay on course."

Xander turned slightly in his seat to make quick eye contact with Ember. "I trust you—and your mom—but Will's right. By now, every Sciolist in the city knows our whereabouts. They'll converge at any moment. Then we'll be blocked in with no escape! Or they'll throw pylons up. That doesn't end well. I should know."

"Shhh!" Ember closed her eyes and tried to wall everything out. The emotions she received were Will's and Xander's, but also her mother's. And Talesa was calm. Ember could trust her. "She's telling us where to go. We need that."

Xander clenched his jaw and nodded. "MediCar, *emergency* speed. Three miles."

"Emergency speed is only for people who are dying. Are you confirming emergency speed?" The MediCar's dashboard lit up.

Xander extended his hand in a victory V. "Yes! Dying! Emergency speed. Three miles."

"Emergency speed. Three miles," the electronic voice validated.

"Perfect." Ember high-fived Xander before a sudden jerk.

The MediCar's speed leaped, and the three renegades gasped. Ember held on to the side door, white-knuckled.

"How fast can this thing go?" Ember's eyebrows connected in a frown.

"We're at a hundred and twenty!" Xander threw his hands up before clenching the bar on the dashboard again.

"You guys seeing this?" Will gasped.

"What? I'm *feeling* it." An enormous grin slid across Xander's face as a vibration buzzed through the vehicle.

Will jabbed at the back window. "Hey … hey! Smoke! Our ride's literally smoking!"

"Oh, crap! What the—!" Xander's eyes widened. "We're gonna have a problem."

"You are approaching three miles. *Where* is the emergency?" the car pleasantly queried.

"Ember?" Xander demanded.

"Right turn on Purity Place."

On the dashboard, a yellow light suddenly flashed off and on with words accompanying it. "Warning. Functionality declining. Warning. Functionality—"

A loud pop interrupted the MediCar's alert, startling all of them. The puffs of smoke Will announced became a steady stream that billowed in waves from the back of the car.

"Shazz! Frikkin' Shazz!" Xander yelled.

"I can't see anything behind us with that thick smoke," Will groaned.

"MediCar, right turn. Purity Place." Xander's wide eyes darted back and forth.

The vehicle turned but dramatically slowed. A clicking sound accompanied a dragging sensation coming from underneath them.

"What's happening?" Will demanded.

"Heck if I know," Xander said.

"Energy is failing. Be advised. *Energy is failing.*" A red light pulsed on the dashboard. "The reactor capacitor is blown." The car's words were a death knell. The acidic smell of burning electronics filled the cab as the whine of the motor died down and silence replaced wind noise.

"This car is gonna be our doom! Why is it stopping?" Will's panicked words set Ember on edge.

Xander pumped a bright red knob to his right. "I'm trying everything …"

"That's not doing a damn thing, Xander. Stop it." Will clambered forward, his direct momentum adding an aggressive weight to his words. "The car's done! We need a plan. Now!"

"Okay, okay. I say we bail outta this car and take our chances on foot. Ember?"

"See that open door up ahead?" Ember pointed across the street.

"That garage?" Will asked.

"That's the one." Before the MediCar fully limped to a stop, Ember released the hydraulic latch on her side. "Get ready to jump ship. We're here."

TWO

Ember's News

SHROUDED BY DARKNESS, the three bolted from the car and ran for the open garage door. The building was massive and painted a rainbow of colors, all the hues of Tranquility's Status designations. A neon sign read "Obviators."

"What is this place?" Xander called out as they hurtled toward the shadowy opening. He barely missed colliding with Ember as he rushed ahead. He slowed his pace then and grabbed her hand.

"Something to do with CommuteCars. Look." Will pointed at a few cars lined up outside the place. His breath came in heavy heaves.

"C'mon!" Ember yelled. "Duck inside." Her pace quickened as she became used to the grainy pavement on her bare feet. She wished for a split second that she had shoes, almost regretting leaving her heels behind before remembering they weren't meant for running either. She jerked Xander along with her, squinting into the darkness.

Upon entering the open garage door, they flattened themselves against the closest interior wall. Ember panted from the sprint, and her heart seemed to grow in her chest with every move. Fleeing the Sciolists as often as she had should have turned her into an expert, but the now familiar inner scream never quit rattling her psyche.

Xander squeezed her hand. "We're in. So far, so good." His eyes connected with hers in a warm, all-absorbing gaze before they darted around their new environment, dark except for a widespread golden illumination across the floor.

Just as Will had determined, the place was a CommuteCar paradise. Two vehicles, one brown and the second pink, sat spaced apart on the floor; a third, a brilliant yellow, was up high on a hydraulic pedestal.

The garage door closed, and a voice seemed to come straight out of the floor. "Ah! You're here. Talesa told me you'd be coming."

Reclined on his back atop a wheel board, a man rolled himself out from under a white CommuteCar, pushed himself off the trolley, and stood up. His mop-like head of messy black hair, narrow, nearly black eyes framed by thick, black brows, and scruffy goatee in a deeply olive-toned face made him look more like a mad scientist than a mechanic. Ember, though, also noticed his physique. This guy's muscles protruded underneath his kelly-green uniform, and his arms looked capable of lifting all three of them at once.

Blindly following a complete stranger was dangerous in their position, but Ember perceived the guy's innocent eagerness, verified by the pink in his aura. She absorbed his emotion, the sympathy that arced up around him. When the boys still hesitated, Ember nodded and bestowed affirming glances on them.

"Come." The man motioned frantically. "Quickly! They'll be searching for you."

The mechanic darted over to a cupboard and opened it to reveal a dozen overalls matching the kelly-green ones he wore, all hung on a rail. Roughly pushing them aside, he reached in with his arm. Ember had no idea what he was doing, but something activated an immense dull metal plate spanning twelve feet on the floor in front of them. It slid away to reveal a platform suspended a foot deeper below.

"Hurry now. Jump on. We're goin' below."

Ember had a fleeting thought: What if she'd misinterpreted the message? A hiding place underground could be as much a prison as a safe harbor. They would be at the complete mercy of this individual, whom they'd never met before.

Outside the building, sirens screamed like enraged banshees, becoming louder by the second, before they stopped cold in an abrupt silence. Had the Sciolists seen them and were now checking the building to see where they'd gone? Had they spotted the MediCar and tracked them somehow? She tried to peer beyond to a point outside. Was that a flash of red out of the corner of her eye? She could swear she even heard the mechanical voices of Sciolists drilling pockmarks in the shadows close by.

Her own blood pulsed in response, as if one red wave could negate another. If they were caught now, already inside this place, they would be trapped with no escape. She gawked again at this stranger who seemed an unlikely savior. His dirt-streaked overalls and intense stare sent ripples of uncertainty into every nerve ending.

The stranger's face softened, as though he'd realized how frightened they all were.

"Hurry! Come with me," the mechanic urged.

At this point, she had no choice but to trust.

Will shrugged and led the way. The three bounded onto a wide steel base, large enough to accommodate a car, and grabbed its surrounding support bars. Like an oversized open-sided elevator, it descended into the space below with the hushed hiss of hydraulics.

Their escort turned to Ember and shook her hand. "You, for sure, are Ember. I'm Kamar. Good to meet you." His broad smile disarmed her, and her fears started to melt away.

When she grasped Kamar's hand, though, Ember felt an

unfamiliar snap similar to static electricity. She could have sworn she had even seen a spark. Could her empathic ability be giving her a warning? She flinched before she shook off his hand and pulled her own back toward herself.

"Everything okay?" Kamar cocked his head before giving Ember another quick smile.

"Oh—oh … yeah. I'm … fine. Just a little overwhelmed, I guess."

Ember ran a hand through her hair, surprised that whatever she'd felt didn't also make her hair stand on end. The man himself made her feel strange, too, almost like they were physically connected, even after she let go. The buzz from their touch lingered, but a burst of renewed energy coursed through her veins.

Will stepped forward. "Kamar, I'm Will." Out of habit, he initiated the Tranquility salute before dropping his arm back down by his side.

Recognition dawned on the man's face. "Well, of *course*, of *course* you're Will! You're the one who just killed the Magistrate in the arena!" Kamar grinned before putting his hands on Will's arms and shaking him. "The hero of the day—of the world!" Kamar chortled. "Welcome, welcome!"

Will flushed before a smile crept out. "Yeah, I—that's why we had to run."

Ember continued to assess the emotions emanating from Kamar, and they were, thankfully, only positive and caring. An additional rush in her senses simultaneously signaled both Will's self-conscious modesty and Xander's jealousy.

Ember watched a green wave radiate off Xander's chest and then dim. "I'm Xander," he said as he initiated a fist bump. "Thanks for giving us a place to hide. We'll be fried if they find us. Especially Will." Xander shook his head and blew out his cheeks.

The platform at last reached the bottom, and Kamar stepped off, motioning for them to follow. "No one knows this is here. You'll be safe." A wink added more comfort to their welcome.

A musty smell—a combination of moisture, mildew, and whatever else might be stored in this unexpected basement—forced Ember to wrinkle her nose. Kamar clapped his hands, and the room lit, if you could call it that. Primitive light fixtures hung from the ceiling, providing illumination fit only for bats. Any length of time down there, and they'd crave sunlight.

Her eyes swept the space. "It's … giant!" She estimated the underground area spanned sixty feet in length and thirty feet in width. The walls were thick granite, giving the vast space a tomb-like feel in spite of its size.

An oversized cupboard spanned a section of one wall. Several worktables sat in the center of the room, littered with unidentifiable tools. The only noteworthy item in the chamber was a standard-sized flat monitor mounted on the wall, surrounded by a primitive workbench with an array of pieces of dull metal, multicolored wires, and assorted junk. In the center of the room stood one lonely chair.

The floor looked like concrete, but Ember noted its reddish hue and wondered why Kamar would have spent the extra time making a colored floor with a smooth, almost shiny finish.

Kamar caught Ember's examination. "You like the floor? It's adobe—a clay found in the ground. Not used here in Tranquility for anything, so I helped myself." He crouched down and knocked on the surface. "Came out better than I'd hoped."

Xander began to walk around, his eyes sweeping the vast room, as if he could uncover its mysteries in a thorough perusal. "What *is* this place?"

"It's a panic room of sorts. I built it for myself. No one knows it's here. I'm the only one who can access it because I'm the only one who works here.I can keep up with the repairs and not have anyone else nosing around here. I created this underground structure alone." Kamar puffed his chest out, and his eyes glittered.

Ember's lips parted in disbelief. "All by yourself? How?" She didn't know whether to be more surprised by the fact he'd done it single-handedly or by his ability to keep it all under wraps.

Kamar moved his entire head back and forth, even glancing over his shoulder, as if looking for anyone else who might have suddenly materialized in the room. "Well … I have … special talents."

"What does that mean?" Will narrowed his eyes and squared his shoulders. His suspicion hit Ember like a pile driver.

Xander answered in a matter-of-fact tone, which came off slightly patronizing. "It means he can do stuff we can't. Like Ember with her time time-warp talent. There are a few people like that around. In fact, that's exactly who Serpio's targeting. People with freaky abilities." With a nod at Ember, he clenched his hands into fists by his side.

"I know about that," Will snapped. "I haven't forgotten that Serpio is on a witch hunt."

Xander shrugged as if to give a grudging acknowledgment.

Ember's eyes grew wide. "*That's* why I feel strange around you, Mr. Kamar. We have a connection." She stepped closer to the mechanic, swept both of his hands up in hers, and closed her eyes. "I can feel it—your energy. It flows into me like water. You're just like me. Altered DNA. And that's why my mom knows who you are and where to find you."

She dropped his hands but fought the desire to put her arms completely around him. Not only because, other than her mom, she had finally met someone like herself, but also because he was another person who'd lived his life in hiding. She knew that situation all too well.

Kamar's cheeks dimpled, and the corners of his eyes creased. "That's right. I'm genetically altered, just like you and your mom. Talesa sent me a message to be ready to house you and your two friends. I didn't get details, just instructions to be ready when you came."

Will's left eye squinted, and his mouth grimaced in confusion. "Okay … Ember. Your mom's not only alive, but she's an Empath like you?"

Ember dropped her hands from Kamar's and shook her head. "Not exactly. She has different abilities than I do. She can telepathically communicate with anyone who is like us." *And thank the stars for that,* she thought. *Otherwise, where would we be right now?*

Xander grinned with unsuppressed amusement at Will's answering deer-in-the-headlights look. "We're the basic ones, Will. We have to get by on our good looks and personality. You're a little handicapped in those areas, but you might get by," he joked.

Will rolled his eyes and crossed his arms. "Yeah? At least I'm known for my modesty, Xander. That's a plus."

Xander laughed before turning back to Kamar. "So … you built this underground warehouse. How'd you dig out all the dirt?" He put up his fingers as if they were a measurement tool, placing them throughout the air in front of him. "Gotta be two thousand square feet."

"I can move physical things like earth around quickly. The ability is called geokinetics. I can manipulate soil and rock in every form."

Xander gave a low whistle, while Ember's head moved back and forth, skyward and down, sizing up everything from ceiling to walls to floor. Building this was an extraordinary feat. Kamar had to be incredibly gifted to do it. The thought of his DNA having been tweaked to provide him with this kind of ability? Nothing short of miraculous.

The mechanic waved off Xander's whistle with his hand and a shake of his head before changing the subject. "Talesa conveyed that you and your two friends needed shelter and a perfect place to hide out." He walked over to the wall six feet away and pounded on it with his fist. "This cellar is secret and impenetrable."

"Impenetrable? Impossible." Xander shook his head before

he wandered over to the same wall and pounded his fist against it as well. Barely a thud.

"Why not? The dome around the city is impenetrable." Will said. "The dome is made from a chemical. Aluminum oxynitride powder that's baked and molded. Made in a lab."

Xander's eyebrows shot up. "Really? I didn't know any of that." The edge in his voice was more than just grudging respect. It might as well have been a compliment.

Ember chuckled. "Is that from the Plauditor's Handbook?" she teased.

Kamar's voice carried deep pride. "No point in creating a place people can get into. That steel plate that slid away above us?" He swept his hands through the air. "It's four inches thick, bulletproof, unbreakable, and boasts a ten-gauge carbon steel inner plate secured with eleven bolts and a defensive perimeter. It also features electronic latch guards to protect the door against lock manipulation."

"How'd you get that kind of steel?" Xander jerked his thumb upward. "It's not like it's just lying around."

"When I pronounce a CommuteCar 'dead'—obsolete or unrepairable—it goes to the recycling center, where the steel is regenerated into new vehicles. Let's just say I've spirited some pieces out of there. Then all I had to do was melt them into a unit, which is another special talent I have." Kamar pulled his sleeves down and looked at the floor. He seemed suddenly self-conscious about sharing so much information.

"Seriously? You melt metal, too?" The words fell out of her mouth before she used her brain. She stopped just short of asking him for a demonstration but then realized doing so might offend him. She didn't like her own freakishness on display; she couldn't assume he would.

Xander sauntered back over and dropped the million-dollar question. "But something opened the floor up …"

Kamar hesitated before answering. "Yes. Located in that cupboard upstairs. I programmed a series of buttons that open it.

Not entirely hack-proof, but 99.9%." Wiggling his fingers before tapping the fingers of both hands together, he said, "That part doesn't take any special ability—just a little understanding of technology."

Will gestured toward four vehicles sitting a distance away. "And those are down here because …?"

Kamar grinned. "Another secret of mine. Not all Commute-Cars that die go to heaven. I always take parts from the cars labeled unfixable before they go to the recycling center, and I've been able to build new ones with the pieces. It's taken a long time, but it's worth it. These don't have the tracking devices the CommuteCars have. I wanted a safe place to hide and to assemble my own transportation. If I'm in a tight spot, I can't depend on stealing a fully equipped CommuteCar. A stripped-down model can stay under the radar. Literally."

Ember drew her eyebrows together. "We've needed one of those on multiple occasions." Her eyes settled on one of the junkers Kamar had pieced together. It was the only one that looked patchwork, a work in progress, the sections not matching in color, with places where the body was incomplete. "You're a real visionary."

"How many do you plan to build?" Xander asked.

Kamar shrugged. "I made this place big enough to construct a half dozen of 'em. Don't know if I'll ever make that many. I have to build 'em slowly over a long time, gathering materials I can use. It's a hobby, but if I ever have to leave the city, I'll have a way to do it. And maybe other people'll need 'em, too." He pulled a couple of wires out of his pocket, showing them off. "I save everything. You just never know."

Xander shook his head and gave a dismissive wave of his hand. "You'd have to be desperate to leave the city. The Outside is brutal." His lips tightened, and a faraway look passed like a shadow over his eyes.

"Better than dying," Kamar said. "I've kept a low profile all my life, but if my abilities are ever discovered …"

"I understand." Ember laid her hand on Kamar's arm. "You're in mortal danger if the Magistrate discovers you. Many of those who are gifted like us are dead. The Magistrate uses undetectable ways of eliminating us. He's never been able to get a complete list of everyone, though. Not yet anyway." As she said the last words, she could have sworn her heart trembled inside her chest.

Kamar shifted from one foot to the other and slipped the multicolored wires back into his pocket. "I don't know who the others are. But your mom told me in my mental message that *she* does. And she says the time has come for us to come together."

"Yeah." Ember dropped her hand. "We need you, and others like us, to become members of Phoenix." Her mind conjured up a vision of a hundred people, all like herself, standing outside City Hall, ready to fight for their freedom, never to fear being discovered, never to worry about their emotional highs and lows.

"Phoenix?" Kamar's bewilderment brought Ember back into the present.

"Phoenix isn't a name you'd know unless you're a part of it. No one knows us by that name. The Magistrate has labeled us 'rebels,' 'criminals,' and 'REMs.' We're the desperados who took over the Plauditorium." Ember nodded toward Xander, wishing he would have time to tell his entire story. "Phoenix's mission is to create a city where we can think and feel without fear. My mom and the 'missing' Plauditors are all part of the movement."

Kamar's mouth dropped. "No kidding? I had no idea. I've only heard that the Plauditors were missing and REMs were responsible." He slapped his knee and grinned. "You guys must be pretty magical to pull that off." His gleeful expression faded to rueful lips and a cocked eyebrow. He paused before adding, "You're in more trouble than I thought. You're not just escaping the arena … You've drafted a small army. But even that might not be enough."

THREE

Serpio's Resurrection

HOW DOES a person feel after coming back from the dead? Serpio knew.

The spear tearing through his body in the arena had been excruciating, equal amounts searing, sickening, and spasmodic, a visceral torment beyond human tolerance. He had felt the blood leave his body like the relentless rush of a violent storm— the instant release, the unquenchable torrent, and a pulse, like thunder, in his ears. It had been horrible, and he never wanted to feel such pain again.

Very soon, though, the pain had faded. A two-hour descent into darkness followed, where he was no more—no thought, no warmth, no feeling. And then, a glimmer of light dawned behind his eyes before a breath tore through his chest.

The promise of resurrection was always there in the back of his mind. He had counted on it. And yet, as he blinked his eyes and heat returned to his body bit by bit, he hugged himself in total amazement. With a slow, disbelieving shake of his head, he pressed his palms to his cheeks before laughing out loud. The formula had actually *worked*!

As his body regenerated, minute by minute, he was tougher. Better than he was before. The extra effort it took for his cells to rally would become a formula for increased endurance. Strong. Invincible. King. Superhuman.

The surprise announcement that would come on Tranquility News would be a triumph. Instead of the city's inhabitants facing the difficulty of mourning his demise, he could lift their spirits and show himself to be a Magistrate of unprecedented power. But more than that, they would venerate him for his worth; he would never fail them. Even death could not take him away. *As it should be,* he mused. He smiled at his secret—the Vitality that led to his immortality. A mystery, unsolvable to anyone in the city, allowed him to endure. He had never breathed a word of its origins to anyone.

Only one other person had known about his power—the person who'd engineered it. And that person was dead. Truly dead.

As he entered the Elite Chamber, he took note of it as if seeing it for the first time. The gold tables, so elegant with their shiny, laminated surfaces, placed in neat rows in front of plush armchairs, upholstery patterned with metallic strands creating geometric shapes. A screen and a small stage occupied the focal point at the fore, directly facing the chairs; that was his domain, a place to be seen and to command his council.

He found Feren reading, her demeanor calm and focused, Of course, a person of her Status would never indulge in grief; a Level Eighteen was way too conditioned for that.

The giant tome of Tranquility Law lay open on the desktop in front of her.The government stored everything in the Cloud, but emergency procedures, governmental guidelines, the Accords, and his journals also occupied several volumes of hardback books kept at City Hall.

"Hello, Feren." Serpio made his voice warm, casual, as if this were merely any other day. He kept his distance, choosing to step into the room and wait just inside the doorway. After all, he didn't want to creep up on her; the shock of his unforeseen fleshly presence would be enough.

Turning in her seat, Feren gasped at the sight of him, catching herself from a likely faint with a quick grab onto the back of the chair. "Wh-what?" Her face paled to the shade of a moonbeam, and her eyes glistened with the terror of a hunted fawn. As if her bottom lip became too heavy, it separated from its mate, to drag down her entire head until it hung, suspended. A slap of her hand to her mouth did nothing to quiet the shock in her eyes.

Now on her feet, she backed up, her hand to her chest, her eyes bulging. Blinking rapidly as if to dissolve the hallucination, she tore her gaze away, her eyes darting from ceiling to floor to the colored fixtures on the wall.

Serpio stepped forward a few paces and held out his hands. "It is me, Feren, dear. Don't fear. I'm alive and well."

Swaying slightly, Feren squeezed her eyes shut and shook her head again as if to dispel the apparition before her. "No. No! You —you can't be real," she said to him, her voice cracking and warbling with emotion. Then, putting her hand to her forehead, she mumbled to herself, "I must still have trauma. I need to call a Plauditor … seek help."

When she moved to press the emergency icon on her Alt, Serpio advanced to her side in giant strides. "Stop!" he commanded, putting his hand on her wrist. "You're not having a breakdown. I am really alive! Not a ghost. See?"

He wished there had been another way to reintroduce himself to Feren. She was the one he'd been seeking, though, when he came this way. Grateful to have avoided anyone else in the hallways, he had underestimated the hysteria and confusion his appearance would generate.

"Oh! Oh my! You are real!" She collapsed into his chest in a spirit of relief before removing herself in the space of two seconds and stepping back to look at him. "How—?"

"My dear Feren. It doesn't matter how, does it? I am here."

With his political, physical, and spiritual power, he hoped she would take his return as a matter of course and leave the questions in the grave instead. Even though she was Elite, there were certain things she wouldn't dare probe. He was the Magistrate, after all.

"I'm so—so happy! You have no idea!" Feren threw her hands in the air and waved them around, now celebrating this victory over death as if it was the single most important news she'd ever heard. "Here I was, studying the next steps for choosing a new Magistrate. And it was all unnecessary. I can't wait to share this news with the city!"

"Yes. A broadcast is in order right away. We don't want any citizen's Alt points to suffer. Could you reach out to the Plauditorium and release the news at once? I'll follow up with another announcement in the morning."

Serpio's heart fluttered at the lightness in his chest, his insides vibrating in anticipation of his upcoming appearance. Already, he was dreaming up the most dramatic reveal possible. Everyone in the city would glorify him and put him on a pedestal.

"Of course, Serpio. I am thrilled to do it. The people of Tranquility will be overjoyed." Feren's snowy smile and nearly palpable euphoria made her look more radiant than her usual self, and that was saying something, as Feren was quite beautiful.

Much like the spear going through his body, a nightmarish recollection suddenly pierced Serpio's buoyant spirit. He had been so busy "coming alive" that he hadn't given himself a chance to remember the events leading up to his death.

Will Verus. The kid had assassinated him! Without a sound, he pulled his lips back and gritted his teeth, baring them like a wild animal ready to attack. Adrenaline blazed through his chest, arms, and legs, making him want to crush something large nearby. Muscles and veins strained against his skin as his fury threatened to break free. Cracking his neck from side to side, he closed his eyes.

With Feren present, he had to control his temper. She would understand his fury—after all, Will's betrayal had been epic—

but he couldn't afford to lose his composure. It wouldn't do. He had no obligation to stay within the realm of positive emotions since he was the Magistrate, but putting his best foot forward kept his Elite under the impression that he was the most caring and joyful person in the universe.

"I'm sure you're wanting to go home and rest after your … ordeal," Feren said as she rubbed her hand down his arm, an affectionate gesture that made him give her a wry smile. "If I get the announcement out for you, you'll be able to take some time for yourself. I'll make sure it includes the warning for our citizens to be on the alert for Ember, Will, and Xander. And now that you're back," she added, "the Elite must meet to discuss how best to handle the arrests and the searches for the Plauditors and REMs as well."

"The hunt must be the highest priority. We must find them!" Anger climbed up the ladder of his spine until it reached his face, where it inflated his cheeks until the pressure threatened to blow his eyes from their sockets. His fingers coiled into tight balls. "Tomorrow we will meet and activate sweeps on every street."

FOUR

Ember's Letdown

EMBER FELT the weight of his Kamar's words: "Even that might
not be enough." Yes, they were indeed in trouble, even with an
"army," and they'd need more than just Kamar's basement to be
protected. They'd need vindication.

Xander, as always, met danger and complications head-on,
blurting out, "You and this place are the answer to a huge need.
If we can relocate our entire operation here, we'd have a
protected base for everyone, an advantage we've never had.
Right now, our group is separated into four sectors hiding out in
the surplus food warehouses. The Magistrate is dead, but the
Sciolists and the Elite will still want to locate the missing Plauditors and punish the REMs. So, it's not just the three of us. It's
only a matter of time before our groups are discovered."

Kamar extended his wrist to show off his Alt, its digital
readout blinking with an up arrow pulsing green. "The more
support I can give you, the happier I'll be. But isn't Phoenix's
work ninety percent finished? Will saw to that." Kamar turned to
Will and clapped him on the shoulder. "Serpio Magnus is *dead*.
Our lives as people with exceptional abilities shouldn't be in
danger anymore. Maybe you won't need any of the rest of us."

A smile bloomed on Ember's lips. "Kamar's right." She

looked from Will to Xander with shining eyes. "We don't have to fear the Magistrate anymore! It still hasn't sunk in, though, has it?" In a dramatic gesture, Ember pinched her right arm. "I keep thinking I'm dreaming, so I have to make sure. Thanks to Will, a monster was destroyed. Maybe all we need now is good PR."

Xander lowered his voice to a growl. "We don't have to convince the population that Serpio was a murderer, although they should know so they don't make a martyr out of him. And we don't know what the Elite will do. Serpio's closest advisors could know more than we think. They could hunt us down just as easily. Phoenix's main mission isn't finished by a long shot. We need to change our city into a place where we can be totally free. We need a new leader. Someone who can change everything."

"You're thinking of one of us?" Will cocked his head. "Or someone from Phoenix?"

"Someone who understands and is part of the movement, yeah." Xander rubbed his chin. "Ava would be ideal. She's one of us and is Elite. We trust her, and she's done amazing work for us."

Will's face went blank.

Immediately, Ember felt sorry for him. Since they'd been reunited, Will looked like he'd lost his mojo. And maybe he had, plus all the missing pieces of the life before his capture. There was so much he had missed during the time he'd been the Magistrate's prisoner. Hard to grasp that he didn't even know Ava, their incredible friend, savior, and government mole.

"This … Ava?" Kamar queried as he crossed his arms over his chest. "If she's Elite, you're sure she's solid?"

Xander's tone was emphatic. "More than solid. Authentic. Reliable." He tilted his head thoughtfully. "I wonder what she's doing now. Last I saw her, she was rushing to Serpio's aid in the arena."

Will rubbed his hands over his face. "Was that forever ago?" He dragged his feet across the floor and plopped into the lonesome chair parked several feet away next to a small table, his body reminding Ember of a sodden scarecrow. "I'm beat." Although his body slumped with exhaustion, his right leg vibrated with a nervous jostling, as if it were plugged into an electrical socket.

Ember winced at his aura, where frayed nerves poked through it like dead tree branches.

Xander snorted. "More like two minutes ago to me. My body feels like pulverized meat."

Kamar glanced at his Alt. "It's been almost two hours since the broadcast cut out from your fight. Someone at the Plauditorium will issue an official statement soon."

Ember ran her palms down her arms, as if she'd felt a chill. *These boys. They're suffering.* She felt it with every fiber of her being. They'd been through hell. Especially Will. She watched as he put his head in his hands and rocked slightly in the chair. It tore her up inside.

Ember nodded toward Kamar and hurried over to Will. "You okay?" She put her arm around his shoulders and squeezed.

Xander rolled his eyes and put his hands on his hips. "If Will needs to rest, fine. But he can do it while—"

"An announcement alert!" Kamar interrupted, shaking his Alt-bound wrist.

The elevated screen across the room sputtered, flashed, and buzzed before lighting up with a headline, which repeatedly scrolled across. "Good news, citizens of Tranquility!"

The group looked at one another, surprise illuminating their faces. Xander's words echoed the words on the screen. "What could be good news? The Magistrate being dead is only good news to us."

A high-ranking Plauditor newscaster, indicated by his indigo clothing, appeared as if to answer Xander's question. Adjusting his jacket, the anchorman smiled into the camera and gave the city's salute.

"Citizens of Tranquility. We apologize for the late hour of this announcement, but this story cannot wait. By some magic or miracle, our Magistrate has survived the brutal attack he suffered at the arena earlier tonight. I repeat. Serpio Magnus, contrary to our earlier notifications, is *alive*." The anchor clasped his hands as if in thankful prayer to some unknown deity and continued. "Stay tuned for further announcements as we receive additional updates." Then the screen went dark.

FIVE

Will's Aftershocks

"WHAT?" Will jumped out of his chair. "That can't be true! I saw the spear go right through him. And … And we heard the announcement in the MediCar at the arena. He. Was. *Dead*."

Something that felt like an anvil lodged in his throat, cutting off his breath. Gasping, he plopped down into the singular chair again, tilting his head back and splaying out his arms and legs to look at the ceiling, as if dying himself.

Ember cried out, a keening that sounded like a wounded animal. Then she stood stock still, not moving at all before chanting "No, no, no, no, no!"

Kamar let out a sharp cry before putting his hand to his head. "I witnessed the whole thing on the broadcast. No *way* he could be alive. No Medela in Tranquility could fix that wound."

In a warp-speed flash, Will replayed the scene at the arena in his mind. He had thrown the spear directly at the Magistrate. It had pierced his chest. He was bleeding out. Serpio had slid down and slumped over … he'd been pronounced dead. Had he done something wrong to mess up the assassination? He must have!

Although he'd been in some weird type of delusional state at the time, he couldn't have dreamed it, could he? No. His friends here saw it. But if Serpio was still alive, he'd truly failed. He'd been used, abused, and yet had nothing to show for it.

Ember inhaled a ragged breath before squeezing Will's shoulders, the force of which conveyed her angst. "It was way too late for any medical aid! I saw it happening right next to me. The blood loss alone would have been too great. It was pouring out of him like a faucet!" She tilted her head before her next words emerged in slow pieces. "The announcement. It might be propaganda. False news to keep the citizens pacified. You know our *dear* government wouldn't want to cause a panic or sadness across the town. People have to control their own emotions, but the Elite won't want undue stress on the people."

Xander moved in closer to Ember and put his arm around her, disengaging her grip on Will and assertively drawing her several feet away from him.

Will noted Xander's proprietary movement. *She's been touching me enough that he's marking his territory.*

"Well, look on the bright side," Xander said, snark invading his tone. "If it's true Serpio's alive, Will, at least you won't be facing murder charges."

"No. He'll just be around to fry me for trying." Will pushed his hand out forcefully in Xander's direction with an exaggerated thumbs-up before he rose from the chair and began to pace. A microscopic nerve twinge on the lower lid of his right eye began a second-by-second assault, a reminder of just how strung up he'd been for days on end.

Ember broke away from Xander and ran her hands through her hair. "Gah! Seriously, guys. This is nothing to joke about. Propaganda only goes so far. If the Magistrate's really dead and they're saying he's not, they can only keep that up for so long. He *must* be alive! But how?"

Will voice broke as he spoke. "It's some … magic. Some voodoo! Or maybe—maybe he has a twin!" The sweat breaking out on his forehead and palms was a moist reminder that he wasn't dreaming, as much of a nightmare as this seemed. "If he catches me, I'll be dead in minutes. I know him. He won't give me a second chance this time."

Ember gripped the back of the adjacent chair as if she needed it for support. "I agree. If Serpio's alive, this will mean death for Will, and we won't be far behind. We have to stay hidden. But this changes everything. What are we going to do, just try and communicate with Phoenix to do the dirty work? As if we weren't already in trouble, Serpio being alive is disastrous. We could have hoped that the Elite could have been swayed if we were caught. But this?"

Will's dread became an ever-tightening noose around his neck, and he struggled to breathe. Had he always been this weak emotionally? This fearful? He managed to croak out, "Whether Serpio is dead or alive, Phoenix is still ready to fight—to do whatever it takes, right?"

"That's right," Xander said, his voice smooth and controlled. "Really, if Serpio's alive, we're only back to square one, where we were before the arena, before Will was captured. Remember, we didn't set out to kill Serpio—well, I guess I've always hoped to—but to just unseat him with a public campaign."

Ember glanced over at the other two before locking eyes with Kamar. "Speaking of which, like Xander said, this place is key. Kamar, it *has* to be our new headquarters."

Backing up in mock horror and winking, Kamar said, "I never would have imagined that my panic room would be the headquarters for a bunch of criminals. But considering the options and what's at stake, I'm happy to help. Whether Serpio is alive or not, you'll still need this place."

With the shift in the conversation, Will tried to also adjust his emotional gears. Why did he feel like he was the only person in the room—or in the entire world—who was just a spare part? It seemed everyone in the group except for him was moving past the shock of Serpio's resurrection and back to practical matters. He needed to get his head on straight and participate, but the pounding pulse in his temple remained a superglued souvenir of the shocking news.

When your mind doesn't let go of your body, it's hard to act normal, he reflected with some resentment. He needed to get back in the game. He began to pace a nervous zigzag across the floor.

"Okay. So, we assume Serpio is walking around, big as life. We get down to business based on that." Ember's words snared the wisps of Will's wishes. She gazed around the room, as if seeing it for the first time. "We don't have food here like in the warehouses, but if we find a way to get food—"

"We have food. I've been stockpiling cans for years." Kamar pointed to a closet across the room. "I can't feed ten thousand people, but I probably have enough for Phoenix for a while."

"You just made my day, Kamar." Xander's broad smile and optimistic outlook buoyed Will's mood, in spite of his antipathy for the guy.

Kamar threw out a thumbs-up. "I must have had some sort of premonition."

"I can't believe I didn't have a premonition. I dream about future events all the time," Ember explained as she followed Kamar to the cupboard across the room. "They're not ever very good dreams, always about some awful problem coming, a warning of sorts. I dreamed about the arena before the boys fought. Didn't know exactly what it meant, but Serpio's bogus death … that's something I wish I would have known."

Will felt a memory stir. Why did Ember's dream ability seem familiar? Did he know that before? He hated the tease of notions just being on the edge of his brain, elusive. Will pushed the chair on which he'd sat earlier with his foot, sending it backward a few feet, as if the possibilities were generating mad energy. His mind was starting to work a smidge better, less wrapped up in what had felt like fuzzy socks.

Ember said she also could hear her mom speak to her in her head. Weird. The idea stuck then. He called out, "Ember, you said your mom can speak to your mind, right? Can you do the same with her?"

"I … I don't know." Ember shook her head. "I don't think so. I'm empathic, not telepathic like her."

"Have you tried?" Will put a finger up to his eye to stop the annoying vibration that continued to assault his eyelid.

Even from way across the room, Xander's gaze cut through Will like jagged glass. "What? You don't believe her? She's telling you 'no.'"

Will gritted his teeth. The last thing he wanted was to put pressure on Ember and alienate Xander, which he was already successfully doing, it seemed. *I'm having trouble remembering what's acceptable to say and do.* "Okay, okay. Sorry, Ember."

"No, Will—Xander, it's fine. I haven't tried. Everything is all so new with my mom's talents. I never knew I could affect time, either, before I did it." Ember shrugged. "It would be the answer to a lot of problems if I can."

Will completely ignored Xander and rapidly made his way across the room to Ember. "Yeah, like communication. Imagine how great that would be. No Alt! No danger of messages falling into the wrong hands."

Kamar flashed Ember a full-on grin, his teeth showing a measurable gap between the two front ones. "If you could do that, that would be the best news all day. I can't communicate with Talesa. She can send me mental messages, but I can't reply. It's frustrating. I've resigned myself to doing exactly what she says, though, so there's no glitch. When she mentally sent word that you were coming, it's a good thing I was here and could help."

Ember cocked her head. "She knew you were here. Each person with special talents is trackable with her weird radar."

Will nodded toward Kamar before saying, "Otherwise, we'd be the Sciolist's bragging rights by now. I'm really grateful."

To his dismay, his hands trembled as if they were wired to live electricity. He put them behind his back, clasped them together, and cringed. He caught Xander exchanging a weird, knowing look with Ember that made Will shrink down to a tiny speck inside himself. Will wanted to scream with frustration. *What's going on with my hands anyway?*

In spite of it all, Will managed to croak out, "When you do talk to your mom, please tell her I'm especially in her debt."

"For sure, Will." Ember gave him an encouraging smile. "After I tell her who you are, of course."

Talk about feeling invisible. Ember's mom doesn't even know who I am?

Standing next to Will, Kamar gave him a quick pat on the back before he gestured toward the lift. "I'm goin' up to check out the street. Problem with this underground place is you don't see what's goin' on right outside the door." He scrambled onto the platform and ascended, his arms dangling over the four-foot-high outer metal frame.

Trivial. That's how Will felt as he stared after Kamar rising into the air. How does a hero twice-over get reduced to insignificance?

SIX

Will's Claims

"SO, EMBER ..." Xander began, oblivious to Will's melancholy. "What do you need to try the 'mind meld' with your mom? Silence? Music? Anything I can do?"

Ember twisted her hair with her hands, pulling it up into a spiral with the ends on top. "I wish! Nothing any of you guys can do."

Will gave Ember a solemn nod, yearning to take her hand. "I'd be happy to keep you company and give you moral support. Maybe you just need some positive energy to make it work." He knew he didn't have any energy left to give, but if it would allow Ember some encouragement, he wanted to be there for her.

Instead, she shook her head. "I'm willing to try, but I'm going to have to be alone. I'll go over to the corner." She pointed. "If it's going to work, I can't be distracted." She gave a little wave and turned her back, letting her hair fall as she went.

Will watched her cross the room until Xander's voice brought him back. "She's beautiful."

Will swallowed, discomfort becoming an annoying shadow. In his head, curse words he'd never used threatened to find their way out of his mouth. That remark. What was he supposed to say to that? He wouldn't meet Xander's eyes but knew there had to be a conversation about their mutual feelings for the girl. It lay between them like molten lava, spitting random drops of fire in either direction.

But he still didn't even know why he felt such a strong attachment to this girl. Beautiful? Yes. But what exactly was his relationship with her? Whatever Serpio had done to his brain had diluted every experience from his past. He'd bet his life he'd had some solid history with her, especially by the way Xander was so defensive.

He closed his eyes, concentrating. *Think, Will!*

What snippets could he conjure up? He let his feelings gush over him as he opened his eyes and glanced Ember's way. He studied her as she sat in a zen-like pose, her hair falling toward her face and her body bent in concentration. Then, she raised her head to face the ceiling, eyes closed.

Flash. That face, that pose. A kiss. *I have kissed her!* And not just in the arena, either. He remembered that. This was a kiss from another time, and yet it felt fresh, like its magic had never left his lips.

He nodded to himself, and a smile spread across his face. Validation was sweet. He and Ember certainly had an attachment or attraction, although he couldn't recall how far their relationship had gone. With time, he hoped these mental fragments would come back faster and knit themselves together in a fuller tapestry of his past.

His mind snapped back to reality, and he observed Xander running his hands along the lower guidewires for the hoist, which still hummed with a gentle vibration from Kamar's exit.

"This guy, Kamar, is a genius. Putting all this together underground? And building the hydraulic platform? Talented!" Xander's caress on the parts was worshipful.

Will folded his arms in front of him in a defensive gesture. With Ember no longer within earshot, now was the time to clear the air. But he'd need to choose his words carefully. "Umm,

Xander. You know I've been under a lot of stress … and Serpio dumped a ton of weird crap on me."

Xander dropped his hands from the equipment, and they fell to his sides, as if in surrender. "I feel you, buddy. You had to have had a complete lobotomy with what I saw you do. And I wasn't there, and I wasn't you, so I can't have any idea of what all you went through. Sorry that happened, man."

To Will's relief, Xander sounded sincere. *Good. He's sympathetic. Move forward.* "Yeah. It was rough. Much of my memory is gone." He paused, letting Xander think for a moment he was too loopy to retrieve anything. "When I watched the interrogation, Serpio insisted you and Ember were '*lovers*,'" he said with a scoffing laugh. "But I'm sure about one thing. The last time I saw Ember before my capture, I remember we were a *couple*. So, I'm confused. You're throwing warning flags all over the place like I'm trespassing here."

Xander's left eyebrow lifted. "You say you're confused but not? How does that make sense?"

"I know I'm not under any mind-altering chemicals right now, so what I'm feeling this minute is real."

Xander squarely met his gaze and tossed his hair back before leaning in. "Your memory's correct. You were a couple. Emphasis on 'were.' Things changed when she thought you'd gone to the other side. Do you blame her? At that point, you no longer were her boyfriend. She just hasn't had a chance to tell you that yet."

Will opened and closed his hands, making fists. "She actually calls *you* her boyfriend, then?"

"The one and only." Xander rocked back on his heels. "We are together. Ask her. She'll tell you."

"Maybe so. But you know, Ember might have a change of heart about her relationship with you now that I'm back. I'm here, and she knows I'm loyal, unlike before. Whatever she's got going with you is only because I wasn't around. There's nothing that says Ember and I aren't still together if we never broke up."

Xander's eyes glittered under lifted brows, and the left side of his mouth curled up. "You did break up with her once. Or do you not remember that?"

Will squeezed his eyes shut. Had he? That sounded like a really dumb thing that he couldn't imagine doing. But better own it so he didn't seem so vapid. A flash of intense recollection with a crushing squeeze in his chest transformed Xander's words into an active truth. The memory exploded in his mind like a two-ton bomb as he relived telling Ember that they couldn't be together because the city would punish them for their relationship.

Opening his eyes, he confessed, "Okay, that might have happened. I think … I think I was under a lot of pressure. It's not like I wanted to break up because I didn't care about her. It was just the opposite."

"Right. But what you once had with her might as well be a million years ago. Too much has happened. Ember and I are … bonded."

The heat rose in Will's cheeks, and he was aware of the rosy flush staining his face that often accompanied his strong emotion. "What's that supposed to mean?"

"Let's just say some clothes came off." Xander winked and grinned before turning serious. "I'm leaving it up to Ember to fill you in about our relationship. I have too much respect for her to give you all the deets. It's up to her to tell you what she wants you to know. You can understand that." Xander turned his back, indicating that he was finished with the conversation, and strode over to the cabinet across the room.

Will put his hands on his head, his fingers interlaced, before throwing them off in a fit of frustration. He made a slight growl in his throat before booming, "You're lying!"

Ember's head jerk up from where she sat huddled in the corner. *Shazz!* Did she hear the words he flung at Xander? He clenched his fists into compact balls and released his fingers one at a time, gritting his teeth when the last two fingers quivered involuntarily. Could this claim be true? Or was Xander just lying to get the upper hand? One thing was clear: Xander was staking his territory.

Watching Xander jerk the cabinet door open and examine the contents made Will even angrier. *He doesn't even have permission to be poking around in there!* Luckily, the suppressed lighting in the room could hide his increasing stress level. Shadows in every corner, in every part of his soul.

Xander swiveled back around to look at Will. With a grin, Xander displayed two cans in his hands. "Potatoes in these. Do ya know how long it's been since I had a potato?"

"No." Will said with gritted teeth. The last thing Will wanted to think about was potatoes. He was churning inside, his celebrated emotional stability skewed by new horrifying possibilities. Was Ember lost to him, then? He never would have imagined it. "But I don't know if Kamar is ready to share those things."

"Livin' on a dream here, Will. We could ask." Xander shelved the cans again and shut the doors with a sigh. "We are gonna need to get something to eat. Last time I ate was yesterday afternoon, long before the fight in the arena. I'm starving."

The heart-wrenching words Xander uttered were tattooed on his heart. He had to talk to Ember. Until he did, he couldn't think about anything else.

Will's friend-turned-rival glanced over toward Ember as he ambled back over and stood within a foot of him, saying, "I can see how frustrating all this is for you," shaking his head as if giving someone the news of a terminal disease.

Will didn't want Xander's pity. Better to show he wasn't as devastated as he was. He'd let Xander think he'd accepted the situation so it wouldn't become a huge issue. They had to work together and get along for the sake of something way larger than their love lives. Besides, any conversation he had with Xander about Ember drained him of all hope and sank him into a deeper melancholy. At this moment, and all moments to come, he'd be the bigger man. He held out his fist.

"Truce?" *At least for now.*

Xander hesitated, looking back at him with doubt in his eyes, as if Will had promised him the moon for free. Then, with a wink, Xander slowly bumped Will's fist before giving his shoulder a playful punch and stealing a quick look behind him.

The boys turned to see Ember shuffling back from the twenty-foot distance she'd placed between them. Her expression was somber, her shoulders marked by a heavy slump.

From the look on her face, Will knew. *She failed.* He wanted to be the first to offer comfort and took a step forward. "Ember, if it didn't happen, don't worry. We'll find something else that'll work. Later, if you want, you can try again."

"I was close, I think. I kept feeling like if I tried harder—could concentrate harder …" Ember's face was flushed, as if she'd just run the fifty-yard dash.

Xander put his arm around her. "You know the saying 'third time's the charm'? Well, that wasn't the third. Only your first. You'll get it."

Will shoved the hair out of his face. After the arena fight and their run, it was still such a mess. "What did you feel, exactly?"

Ember's eyes met Will's. "When I thought about my mom, I heard a high-pitched ringing in my ears, but it kinda faded in and out, like something wasn't making a complete connection. I've heard that in my ears off and on through my life, but I never connected it to anything. Now I'm pretty sure it's a signal in my brain. After a few minutes of concentrating, though, it was exhausting. I had to quit."

Xander gave her arm a squeeze. "It's almost one in the morning. We're all tired. I bet if you get some rest, you'll break through."

Will rubbed his eyes. "What do you guys say we get some sleep? I'm barely standing."

"Yeah, I'm drained." Ember's eyes swept the room. "We need to crash."

The steel lift interrupted their conversation with a quiet, soothing hydraulic hiss. Kamar stepped off and sighed. "All quiet on the streets, being past curfew. But Sciolists are out. Not on foot, but in cars, just driving along slowly, shining high-powered lights out the windows. They're looking for you." In his arms, Kamar carried some uniforms and a couple of small boxes.

Will shivered. He couldn't help himself. "For the first time, I can say the light is not my friend."

"We've already hidden in the darkness underground a lot, Will. I'm starting to feel more like a gopher or a mole." Ember put her hands up in a caricature of little animal paws and scrunched up her lips to resemble a tiny mouth.

Will laughed at her face. "Can't wait to hear the whole story."

"I have car repair uniforms here. You all need clothes." Kamar gave a wry grin.

"Hate to cover all this up." Xander grinned and splayed his arms out at his side. "But you're right."

Will rubbed a streak of dirt on his arm with a hand. "Hey, a shower, too? Then the jump suits won't stick to the dirt and sweat."

"You'd look more like a mechanic with a little dirt, Will." Ember giggled and gave Will a little shove.

Laughing, Will conceded. "Yeah, you're right, but I don't want to smell like one."

Ember looked down at her clothes, the ones she'd been dressed in for the arena fight. "I'll be happier in one of those, too."

Xander chuckled, too, before turning to Kamar. "Anything here to sleep on? Even if it's just blankets, that's a help. We're gonna crash."

"One air mattress and a few blankets. I haven't collected too much yet. The blankets are more for covering cars, but they're heavy. You can roll 'em up, and they'll be a little soft. I brought down a box of cookies and a few protein bars, too. Water's in the cabinet."

The boys went for the food, diving in with rabid joy so eager Will had to scramble around, picking up cookies that sailed onto the floor. Once he rescued them, he stuffed a couple in his mouth.

Xander wrinkled his nose. "Those are dirty, you know."

Will ignored the statement.

Ember took the uniforms Kamar had hanging over his arm. "Anywhere I can change before I eat and sleep?" she asked.

Kamar nodded. "There's a bathroom upstairs. All the lights in the shop's interior are off. It's probably okay for you to go up in the dark." He handed Ember a petite flashlight. "Don't turn on any lights."

"Thanks." Ember smiled while tossing a uniform to each of the guys. She held hers up against her body. "I'm going to disappear in this thing."

Xander smiled wryly. "Isn't that the idea?"

"Ha, ha. Don't be such a smart aleck." Ember winked at Xander as if his remark was a term of endearment.

Will cringed at the exchange. They obviously had some sort of camaraderie that he and Ember had never shared. *Had never had time to develop,* he thought with some bitterness.

"Ready to go up, then?" Kamar gestured to the lift.

"Yeah. Shower, clothes, food, and sleep. In that order," Ember replied, gripping the uniform in her arms before giving a little wave to the others.

"Don't drown up there, baby," Xander teased. "Will and I'll make things all cozy for you for when you get back."

As the lift ascended with both Ember and Kamar, Will held out the half-empty package of cookies. "Want one?"

"Trade," Xander replied, handing Will a wrapped protein bar, which Xander seemed overeager to give away.

"If I weren't so hungry, I'd pass on those protein bars. Lived off 'em for a few days." Xander peeled off the cellophane and shoved the trash in his shorts' pocket.

Will wouldn't have cared if they were cardboard. He stuffed the cookies he held in his hand and the protein bar in his mouth almost simultaneously, his cheeks nearly bursting from the food inside.

Xander raised an eyebrow. "You *are* hungry."

"Aren't you?" Will said, talking through his bulging mouth. He cracked up, crumbs flying, which had Xander covering his head and face with his arm.

Will laughed even harder, tears starting to flow from his eyes, before realizing that Xander was not finding any of it funny. In fact, Xander's eyes held enough contempt to dampen Will's laughter until it morphed into an awkward cough, and the remainder of the cookie slid down his throat.

Will said, "We'll divide this up so we can save some for Ember." Xander's gaze softened the minute he said Ember's name.

They sat down on the cold concrete floor and separated what they had into piles. Silently, they devoured their feast before getting to work arranging the air mattress and blankets they found in another cabinet on the far wall.

"The mattress can go to Ember, but she sleeps between us, okay?" Will pumped up the mattress with a primitive air pump that he had to figure out.

Xander grimaced a little but nodded. "She'll be in the middle."

There are no truer words.

SEVEN

Xander's Endorsement

SLEEP HAD NEVER FELT SO good, even though they were roughing it on the hard cement floor. After eating, showering, and changing into a uniform, Xander had fallen into a comatose-like slumber beside Ember, right after hearing Will's light snoring on her other side. However, it seemed as though he'd just shut his eyes when he woke up with a start. Groaning, he turned over, adjusting his clothing and wondering why he was so bound up in his pajamas.

He rubbed his eyes, disoriented at first, before remembering where he was. Pajamas—no, the borrowed mechanic's uniform was twisted around his body in what seemed an impossible fit for his body parts.

"Wake up!" Kamar's voice boomed. "It's long past morning curfew!"

As Xander sat up, he moaned. He ached, mainly from sleeping on the stone floor. Cold, too—the subsurface held none of the regulated temperature of Tranquility.

He watched Ember stir, her long tresses tangled in her fingers. Immediately, his discomfort fell away. He'd never get tired of seeing her wake from sleep, her hair tousled and her face as sweet as a child's, the soft, microscopic freckles somehow more noticeable on her nose.

Will groaned as he rolled onto his back, blinking up at the ceiling.

"Kamar … really. What time is it?" Xander stood and groaned again, his body still protesting the strain of yesterday's fight to survive. Every muscle and limb hurt from.

Kamar enunciated each word. "It's eight. People are out." He headed for the food cabinet across the room and came back with a couple of water bottles and some protein bars. He tossed a few to Xander and then set the others next to Will and Ember.

Will stretched his arms over his head and then rocketed up off the floor as if someone had lit a fire under him. He turned and nudged Ember with his toe. "Hey, sleepyhead. That means you, too."

He held out a hand, and Ember put hers in his. He pulled her into a standing position. Ember opened and closed her eyes a few times before dropping Will's hand.

Xander cursed at himself for allowing Will to do that. *I should be waking her up,* he thought. *Will's chivalry will be the death of me. Better up my game.*

Reaching for Ember's hand himself and pulling her toward him, Xander gave her a radiant smile. "Hey, Em. How was that mattress? Did you sleep okay?"

Ember smiled back, melting his resentment away. "I was out cold," she replied.

"Any dreams of the future we should know about? If so, let's hear 'em." Xander didn't want to pressure her about her predictions—he cared about Ember's well-being and the rare times she could just focus on being a regular person—but in their situation, they needed her to be clairvoyant. Xander wished she would have had a dream—something they could start analyzing for what was to come. While Ember's dreams were maddeningly cryptic, they were never wrong.

"No. I don't even remember shutting my eyes."

Kamar shook his head as if the verbal exchanges were more

annoying than helpful and took a big gulp from the kelly-green thermos he now held in his hand. His next words made Xander wonder if it was coffee or alcohol fortifying his morning.

"Okay. Now that you're all awake and friendly, are you ready for this? I saw a Sciolist detaining a whole group of people right outside on the street. The Magistrate, if he *is* still alive, is stepping up his game."

Will's mouth fell open. "Stopping random people on the street like they're suspects? That's no happiness campaign." He glanced up as if he could see it for himself through the ceiling. "I never thought I'd live to see that."

"Yes, and you know those guys are not all warm and fuzzy either." Kamar seemed to stand taller and squared his shoulders. "I walked out to the street and saw 'em stopping pedestrians right on the sidewalk, checking Alts against facial recognition. I gave 'em a smile and the salute and went back in." Xander noted visible tension in Kamar's muscles.

Ember chewed on a fingernail before dropping her hand to her side in a heavy gesture. "If they're checking everyone on the street, Phoenix can't go out. At all. Facial recognition is fine because it will match the Alt. But if they dig deeper, they could be in trouble. The names on those Alts aren't theirs."

Will shifted from one foot to the other and leveled a question at Ember. "You gotta fill me in here. Why—what do you mean their names aren't theirs?" A furrow on his brow threatened to divide his face in half.

Ember blinked, her eyelids like hummingbird wings. "Oh, Will and Kamar … Our Elite friend, Ava … She changed the Alts for every Phoenix member. Their new IDs belong to dead people. Their personal profile pictures are on their Alts but they have an alias attached to the deceased's stats and details."

Xander noted Ember's voice shook a little and continued, "Except ours. Ember and I didn't have pictures 'cause we didn't have our own Alts anymore. We borrowed them. We were frikkin' lucky nobody checked for that when we were in and out of places with Ava. When we were captured, we crushed 'em under our feet."

Licking his lips, Will said with a tentative tone, "And I don't have one either. The Magistrate made sure I had one, but I didn't wear it in the arena."

Xander's typical fervent demeanor settled into a momentary lull as his thoughts churned. "None of Phoenix's Alts have GPS, so that's another problem. Sciolists will check all the functions." He pressed his lips together in a slight grimace.

Will crossed his arms. "This is bad."

Tapping his finger against his lips, Kamar replied, "Sadly, they're safer than you. You're criminals already, and your faces are everywhere. Without any Alts, that's worse. Even disguised, you'll be stopped and arrested without them. Then it's game over. Right now, you're underground and safe, but to stay here forever is useless. Any ideas?" He plucked at the pockets in his uniform before discovering a loose string that he broke off.

Xander didn't hesitate. "Ava is the only one I know who could have access. But she's already done it once. Another effort would probably be suicide." Ava was going to be indispensable for many efforts to come, but he was beginning to feel protective of her. His fondness for Ava was pretty much tattooed on his soul.

Will tapped his lip with his forefinger. "We really need some-body else on the inside besides Ava, then. Is there really no one?"

Ember wrung her hands, her eyes reflecting a glimmer of light from the glowing fixture overhead. "Not that we know of. Ava might have more people in her pocket than we know, though. At least two Sciolists are on our side, so there might be more."

Will sighed before giving voice to the obvious. "We'll have to communicate with her. There's no other way. But even Kamar sending a message on his Alt won't work. It's too risky." He hiked over to the solitary chair, dragged it over to the group, and sat in it backward.

Xander spoke quickly in a steady voice. "Kamar, how do you feel about being a live messenger? You're not under suspicion, so it's perfect. You alone can find Ava and tell her what's going on. And we'll need disguises if we're ever gonna be able to walk around above ground. Our Alt pictures will have to connect to those disguises, too." For a nanosecond, he fantasized about himself in a superhero costume before getting real again inside his head.

Will took multiple, rapid deep breaths, enough that Xander wondered why Will was stockpiling oxygen in such a hurry. When Will finally spoke, it was through puffs of air. "We'll need to disguise our faces, some incredible physical changes. Facial recognition could still defeat us unless it's foolproof. Tall order."

"My hair is a problem," Ember moaned. I'll need a wig or hair dye."

Xander scowled, her idea lodging like a thorn in his side. He knew she was right, but he'd be beside himself if she cut or dyed her hair. "Wig. We all need 'em. But Ava will for sure raise suspicion if she goes chasing around for costumes. Kamar, you up for doin' that?"

Kamar snickered before joking, "Looks like I'm going to have to be real creative, but luckily, the annual Alternity Gala is coming up in two months. I could search for costumes in the shops for that." He winked.

Ember smiled. "You're right! I was never old enough to go before this year, not that I ever wanted to be in big crowds. But I'd love to dress up as something I'm not, something especially diabolical."

"It's a bizarre event," Xander complained. "I know it's all about personifying the dark values and social mores Tranquility has 'eliminated.'" Xander air-quoted the word, snickering. "But I'm happy to represent those every day."

Xander heard Will mutter, "Who cares?" under his breath before Will's forehead creased. "Shopping for costume stuff should work. But Kamar, you sure you know what you're getting yourself into? You're gonna be a target sooner or later. And you're already at risk because of your talents. You sure you want to commit to all this?" He rubbed his right eyebrow so hard Xander thought he'd rub it right off.

Kamar leaned in. "For now, I'm clear. I keep a low profile, and no one knows me as anyone special or as any person of interest. My Alt points are good, so I'm in. I'm free to be your emissary." He made a tiny bow.

Xander flashed a thumbs-up. "Perfect. It might be better to see Ava at her house rather than at City Hall. I happen to know where she lives. I was there." The memory of when he was practically dead was not a pleasant one, but he'd do it all again to meet Ava. She had saved his life and become an integral part of their lives.

Kamar stared openly at Xander. "You were at her house?"

Xander let the memory wash over him and grimaced. "Yeah. I was almost killed before the arena. Serpio crashed my vehicle. Ava's a Medic and fixed me up. So, I know exactly where you need to go."

Will put a hand to his head. "When did that happen?"

Xander lifted his chin with a little jerk. "A while after we entered the city. When Wee and I jacked the spare transport vehicle."

Will's mouth fell open, and he slowly got up from the chair. "You and Wee were *both* in a crash? I thought you said Wee was at the warehouse doing fine."

Xander blurted, "Yeah, yeah. He's okay. He was hurt, but Ava fixed him up, too. Don't worry."

Will pressed a palm to his chest, relief written all over his face. "Can't wait to see him."

Kamar drained his cup, set it on the floor, and then spoke. "Guys! Glad your friend's okay, but we have more pressing matters. I'll make up some phony authorization for checking the safety of Ava's limo. That should get me through the front door.

If I get stopped and questioned on my way, I'll have some reason to be going there."

With wide eyes, Ember put out her hand. "Wait—before you go! You'll need to know the Phoenix hand signal. That's how we recognize each other."

"Good call, Ember." Xander glanced at Will before sauntering over to them. He put his arm and hand through the quick loop. "Like this."

Behind them, Will was weaving his own and grinning. "That's one thing I never left behind." An instant mental flashback to the arena when he made eye contact with Ember in the stands caused him to drop his smile. That moment … so full of fire and astonishment.

Watching Ember and Xander, Kamar followed the example. "Easy enough, and important, yeah. I've got it."

Kamar headed toward the lift. "Locking up the shop shouldn't be a problem. I don't have any notifications that any sick cars are coming in. Now, if one should break down in the meantime? I'll be notified and can deal with that."

Will trailed after Kamar as if wishing he could go. "Be creative! I'm looking forward to a new identity."

Ember giggled before tugging on the front of her mechanic's uniform. "I hope I can get at least something that'll fit me."

Kamar's response could have been for either of them. "You might not like what I get. But no complaints, right?" Kamar pressed the button to activate the lift and leaned on the railing, waving frantically as if he was giving them a final goodbye before a long journey. "All right! I'm off! See you when I get back."

Will ducked his head. "Wish we—I—could help more. I feel completely useless right now and out of the loop on everything."

Ember shook her head and blew air out of her mouth. "Will, don't feel that way. You don't dare show your face. Or any part of you, even in that uniform. We're dead men walking. I'll sit down with you and share everything you've missed. I'll tell you all about Wee and everything. It's a lot, so we need more than a few minutes."

Xander crossed his arms. She'd need an hour or more to fill Will in on all that happened, especially if she included all the details—Wee's narrow escape multiple times, the time in the subway, their journey Outside, their relationship … Right now, he wanted to focus on survival.

"Can't you share at least—" Will started.

Ember was rolling up her sleeves to uncover her hands, dwarfed from the oversized jumpsuit, when she stopped and tilted her head. "Hush!" Ember put up her hand in a stop gesture and closed her eyes.

Everyone fell quiet, watching Ember as if she'd just grown wings.

When their self-imposed reticence spilled into ten interminable minutes, Xander almost lost it. He'd never been a patient person, and as he watched Ember's face change from brief joy to drawn-out concern and then finally to misty eyes, he let out a restless, heavy sigh.

"My mom just spoke to me!" Ember's face was flushed pink. "And guess what? I actually 'talked' back! I asked her if she heard the broadcast, and she said yes, that the info came to their Alts. She heard about Serpio being alive. She was calm, as she always is, but she was shocked." Ember hugged herself tightly.

"And?" Xander could barely contain his eagerness.

Ember galloped the ten feet over to Xander. "I told her we were safe, of course." She settled down, and her face became serious. "But you remember … she has this weird radar about locating other people that have special abilities—the Easterners."

"Easterners?" Will queried, scratching his head. "I must have missed a lot."

Xander shook his head. "Nope. New to me."

"Mom named them that. EAST stands for Exceptional Abilities and Special Talents. Anyway …" She stopped speaking to squeeze Xander's arm. "An Easterner is now at the west warehouse!"

Xander burst out with "Holy Shazz! No lie? That's damn wonderful."

Will inhaled sharply. "What else did your mom say? Did she tell you what more is going on at the warehouse?"

"No, only that the warehouse is secure." Ember reached out her hand and touched Will's arm.

"And what help, exactly, does the Easterner give us?" Will took a step closer, his green eyes sparkling with curiosity.

Ember kept grinning. "She didn't say, but she said it was a huge deal and that we would have a lot of strength soon."

Xander bumped shoulders with Ember and then Will before stepping apart and meeting Will's eyes and then Ember's. "The real strength, though, guys, won't come from the Easterner. It will be up to all of us average joes—-and how much sacrifice we're willing to make."

EIGHT

Ember's Heart-To-Heart

"SACRIFICE." The word seemed to momentarily shift the world on its axis. Xander's solemn observation of their perilous circumstances shattered Ember's newfound optimism about the coming Easterners. She went mute, feeling her entire future spiral and distort in a dizzying wave.

Over time, she'd grasped at shreds of hope and stacked each particle of good news together as if building a normal future brick by brick—as if everything that had happened since her mother's illness and "death" was a movie that eventually would end, and life would go back to the way it once was, a lonely but sheltered life in a "perfect" world.

The boys, too, stood silent and spun darkened auras, their opaque thoughts diffusing from their bodies like smoke rings into the stale air of the basement.

Will fidgeted by turning both his pockets inside out and then putting them back in place. He turned, pensive, and wandered off, his hands now firmly in his pockets, making his way over to the most distant of the three work benches cluttered with what appeared to be small, silvery headlights.

She watched him go, the droop of his shoulders and the dimming of his aura making her want to follow. Once there, Will picked up a glass dome and held it up in a futile attempt to catch the light, nonexistent in the space they called safety. How much heavier was everything weighing on him?

Unsure of how her sympathy would be perceived if she shadowed him, Ember turned her attention back to Xander and found herself caught in Xander's gaze. In contrast to Will, Xander was ignited, the upcoming risks coupled with the anticipation of the arrival of their redeemers fueling his spirit.

The unexpected smolder within his irises delivered a warm flush to her entire body. How was it he could make her into melted chocolate in a moment?

Their lives teemed with sacrifices, but being stuck underground with Xander wasn't one of them. She longed to be in the moment, to forget the fight, the worry, and the horror of the man who had decimated their lives.

With a coy smile, she reached for Xander's hand, threaded her fingers through his, and began to lead him away.

Resisting her tug playfully, Xander said with mock horror, "Are you kidnapping me?"

Ember's laugh was throaty. "If have to." She'd missed him in the days after their capture. And she knew there would be only a few precious minutes before everything turned upside down again.

Behind her, Will's emotions permeated her aura and wrapped themselves tightly around her chest. A blend of wistfulness, jealousy, and pain, they were the stuff of faded photographs, thorny roses, and tiger teeth. The separation between her and Will after he was captured had ripped the arteries from her heart. But one look at him when she'd run to him in the arena had left her mind in disarray and her emotions fighting among themselves. And right now, she couldn't deal with any of that. Whatever she felt for Will—and she didn't know what that really was—had to be pushed away. She had assured Xander over and over that she was his forever.

Untangling those emotions would cause her to face her guilt

over Will once again and make her examine just how many of her feelings were just physical attraction or based on what each boy represented. Did she have a hero worship attached to each of them? She had needed them, and they'd stepped up, sweeping her off her feet like white knights. And what would happen if she discovered she had chosen the wrong one? What would she do? It was too painful to explore.

With Xander in tow, she rushed off, distancing herself from the blond hero as quickly as she could.

Where was privacy? In a room like this, the only place she could think of was in one of Kamar's cars. As if they had a mind connection, Xander flicked an eyebrow upward and tossed his head toward the jerry-rigged vehicle parked furthest away.

Perfect, Ember thought. The vehicle had a smooth bench seat with a white interior where they could lounge a little.

It wasn't until after Xander was inside and she sat down beside him that she began to quiver, as if her muscles danced on their own. Even with some distance between them, her stomach fluttered, and she avoided Xander's eyes. Why was she suddenly so nervous? This was *Xander*.

He took Ember's hand in his and gave it a gentle squeeze. She met his eyes, and the familiar spark of connection passed between them.

"Finally, a moment to spend together," Xander said, his voice soft and warm.

"If only we could just stay here forever in this little car." Ember closed her eyes and inhaled to calm herself.

With a smile that dazzled and then faded, Xander motioned her to move in, holding his arms open for her. When she hesitated for a second, he pushed the hair out of his face and tilted his head as if determining a way to break the ice. With a sigh, he reached out, wrapped his arms around her shoulders, and gently drew her to him. He leaned in, his breath warm against her cheek. "Are you still completely mine?"

Ember's voice caught in her throat. "Completely."

Without another word, Xander leaned in and gently pressed his lips to Ember's. It was a soft, tender kiss at first, as if he was remembering how her lips felt. He broke off before kissing her again, the all-consuming passion unleashed. One hand caressed her cheek, and the other wove his long fingers through her hair, pulling her head in tighter against his mouth. Leaving her cheek, his hand slid down her spine and under her rear, riveting her solidly against his body, sending shivers down Ember's spine where they gathered in a warm pool deep within her.

As they pulled back to mere inches from each other, Ember's heart frolicked in her chest. "Wow," she whispered, her eyes still closed.

"Just as I remembered, but maybe better. You," he breathed, kissing her forehead. "Make." He planted a kiss on her nose. "Me." He groaned, running his tongue across her lower lip. "Crazy." Xander touched her face, running his fingers along her cheek.

The silver lining of Xander's aura seeped into Ember's very bones, a warm caress, a bewitching effervescence that made her crave his touch. Like a magnet, she could not resist its pull. But she knew that even without his aura's sterling halo, his dark, wild hair, slow grin, and sultry laugh would melt her in a minute. And the swagger. The confidence was somehow pure heat.

Ember's earlier nervousness evaporated as he continued to kiss her, his mouth wide against hers. He gently pushed her down again, his tongue twisting possessively and his hands at long last pressing against her breasts.

She felt herself going over an edge she should not cross. "Xander."

"Yeah … I know." With a groan, he slowly sat up and tilted his head back against the upholstery.

They sat silent for a minute. Ember smoothed her tousled locks and adjusted her baggy uniform while Xander ran his fingers through his hair and looked out the car's window, as if there was a significant event going on outside it.

"So, how's life?" Xander laughed to himself, his eyes glinting at the idiocy of his words.

Ember gave a gentle puff of laughter before her face settled into a slight frown. "We haven't talked about the arena."

Slowly turning his right fist into his left palm, Xander let a few seconds pass. "It isn't something I really want to talk about."

"You … you had to think you were going to die." She laid her hand on his arm.

Xander clenched his teeth as he gazed out the window once more before answering with heated words. "I was not going to lose that fight. No matter what. I decided I would do whatever it took to stay alive in case there was a chance to get free. I didn't want to hurt or kill Will, but I would've if I had to." His eyes took on a faraway look. "I almost slaughtered someone who's been on our side all along. But that guy's eyes out there? Insane. He was not the Will you knew. At least not until the end."

Ember relived the blows, the blood, and the fear from that night. "Did you speak to each other at all?"

"Maybe once or twice. For some reason, Will thought if he won, it would be you and him together again. He was fighting for his life, but he was also fighting for you." Xander winced and shifted, shoving his hands into his pockets.

Ember's cheeks caught fire. To be the cause of someone's fight to live? It was humbling and embarrassing and horrifying all at the same time. "Oh."

Xander focused on the white fuzzy headliner above him and drew his fingers across it in an X. "Yeah. Not what I expected to hear at the time. But at the end, when you ran to him, I …"

Ember could have sworn she saw his eyes tear up.

"You thought I instantly went from being yours to choosing him?"

She raised her eyebrows and placed her hand on her chest. But her mouth went dry, and she had to look away. It wasn't that far from the truth. At least at that moment in the arena. She had been overcome with hero worship, ecstatic to see Will. And his victory kiss? It was sweet euphoria, burned into her heart like a tattoo.

Xander winced, grooving lines into his pale forehead, then smoothing back his midnight hair, the only way he ever showed his uncertainty. Then, adopting a forlorn expression she'd never seen, Xander admitted, "I didn't know what to think. But I knew what I felt. I was hurt and bleeding, physically and mentally. But my biggest fear? Not Serpio. Not even dying. It was losing you."

Ember met his eyes then and grasped his hands in hers. She hoped her bisected heart wouldn't beat out of her chest and fall in two pieces on the CommuteCar floor.

"Lose me? I remember the first day I ever looked into your eyes and felt my entire world flip. You found parts of me I didn't know existed, and in you, I found a love I no longer believed was real."

His dark eyes glistened to a luminosity that threatened to undermine his unbreakable persona. He looked out the window and blinked before turning to focus on Ember's face. As if to underscore his words, he gripped her hand more tightly.

"If I did anything right in my life, it was when I gave my heart to you." She pulled her hands from his and put her hand on his chest. "And I'll protect that choice with all I've got." The car's interior seemed to close in, and her lungs fought to find the breath within her.

But a voice deep inside taunted her. *Do you really mean what you said?*

She closed her eyes and ran her fingers through her hair as she crammed the reproach into a crevice in her conscience after answering back, *Of course I do!*

Xander could both challenge her and flex with her exaggerated emotions and complicated talents. She needed that, but it wasn't a small commitment. "You see me for who I am. Besides, you make me laugh." Her hand still on his torso, she gave him a little shove.

His tone changed abruptly to a lighthearted tease. "You know that's how I roll, baby. Now, what do you say we see what Will is up to? Other than pining over you, I mean." He laughed but met her eyes.

A few snarky comebacks in Will's defense lay on the tip of Ember's tongue, but after seeing Xander's vulnerable bravado, they took shelter in the back of her throat.

NINE

Kamar's Expedition

XANDER HADN'T REMEMBERED ENOUGH to give Kamar a house number for Ava. And Kamar couldn't blame him, him having been at death's door when he was there.

With a simple "stop" voice command on Ava's street, Kamar halted his vehicle, a compact van painted with multicolored stripes and the shop's logo. After exiting the car, he strolled up to the house Xander so perfectly described. At the entrance was a behemoth gold door carved with an intricate design of a Halcyon songbird among leaves. Beautiful. As he used the lion-faced heavy brass knocker to announce his arrival, he hoped Ava hadn't yet left for her duties that morning at City Hall.

Looking to his right, he saw her garage door was shut, housing the vehicle he was there to "check out."

The home itself loomed around him. There was no question this was an Elite residence. Aside from the garish, shiny metallic paint on the outer walls reflecting the morning's sun rays, the place was certainly over three or four thousand square feet, enough to house multiple families.

Too bad this can't be a headquarters, he mused.

A full minute eroded before the front door rolled up and

open, revealing a young woman dressed in a crisp brown skirt topped with an embroidered apron and matching blouse trimmed with a large, lacy collar. Her short, golden hair was poofy.

A lot like a dandelion's fluff, he thought.

She greeted him with a smile, her oversized mouth revealing white, spectacular teeth. "Hello. How may I help you, sir?" The woman's gaze rested on the auto shop's embroidered pocket logo. "Ms. Ava was not expecting visitors today. Or mechanics." The girl's blue eyes twinkled as if she had the most exciting job in the world.

Kamar didn't want to share his real purpose with the little maid, so he went with the preplanned lie. "Yes, I know she wasn't expecting me. I apologize for the surprise call. I'm here to check on Ms. Ava's limousine. I received an alert that the battery pack was expiring."

"Oh, dear. It's good these cars communicate, isn't it? Ms. Ava didn't mention anything about it, and it would be terrible if she were to be stranded somewhere." The cheerful house girl stepped back to allow him to enter. "I can show you the garage, and you can make yourself at home." She paused and put her hand up to her lips. "Oh, dear. I didn't mean—I didn't try to imply that you live in a garage, Mr ...?"

Kamar chuckled as he entered the foyer. "Name's Kamar. And don't be worried. You didn't offend me. I do sort of live in my garage. But I am going to need to speak to her. It's customary before a repair. I may even need to take the car to the shop."

"I see. Well, you may have to wait a few minutes. She's getting dressed for the day. She has an important meeting shortly at City Hall. Would you like to take a seat, Mr. Kamar?" The petite domestic maid ushered him into an area off the hallway, where a small sitting area shone with the gleam of precious metal.

Kamar sank into an armchair that was plusher than it

appeared and glanced around, taking in his surroundings, before he decided he looked overly creepy checking out the place too much.

"I'll let Ms. Ava know you're here. In the meantime, would you care for something to drink?"

When Kamar shook his head to decline, she nodded. "My name's Evangeline. I'll be back shortly."

"Thanks, Evangeline." Kamar gave her a smile and sat back, surprised to hear music suddenly come through some hidden speakers.

In his head, Kamar practiced his reason for coming so it would sound fluid and plausible before he dumped the real reason for his visit. He had to be cautious in case the surveillance in Ava's home was hyperactive due to her Status. She was in government, after all.

Tapping his foot to the music, he thought of all that had happened in the last eight hours. He should be nervous about housing wanted criminals, but he wasn't. And being a part of an organization to overthrow the government? Not a second thought about that. With his special abilities, he'd had enough of the secrecy and artificiality that made Tranquility "great." He was eager to become part of something bigger than himself. A lot of these thoughts and actions came right out of a spy novel, something he'd been allowed to read as a teen before Tranquility began censoring books.

At the sound of clicking shoes on the polished floor, he looked up to see a woman he assumed was Ava approaching. Dressed in a gold tunic with identically hued close-fitting pants underneath, she entered with a gracious smile, extending her hand outward in the Tranquility salute. "Hello. I'm Ava Validus."

Kamar returned the salute and added a quick bow for good measure. "I'm Kamar Sedulus. A pleasure to meet you, Ms. Validus."

"Please, call me Ava. My assistant explained you're here to

check out my car? I haven't noticed any malfunctions but am glad you're proactive. Of course you have my permission to look at the car." She glanced down at her Alt. "My concern is that I have to be at City Hall soon for a meeting. Do you think it will take long? And can you fix the problem right here?"

A knot in his belly formed. Here he was, hoodwinking a member of the Elite. What if she dismissed him quickly and he couldn't convey his information to her? After all, her car was perfectly fine. He might not feel like a traitor joining a revolution, but he felt like a real jerk about the deception. She seemed nice and appeared perfectly Elite-ish, not like a part of a rebel group at all.

"I'll have to look at the vehicle, ma'am. Could we go to the garage? I can answer all your questions there."

"Of course." Ava led the way down a hallway and to a door, which opened with a wave of her Alt.

Kamar stayed quiet until they stepped into the limousine's appointed resting place. The limo stood under gleaming lights, its glazed, metallic surface defining luxury. He allowed himself a few precious seconds to examine it, as they were seldom in the shop.

He gently touched the car's back exterior panel, which flaunted deeply accented grooves across an aerodynamic rear. His mental assessment more awe-inspired than purpose-driven, he noted the protective titanium shell for safety. With a surge of envy, he tapped his fingers on the broad moonroof, a feature nonexistent on any other vehicles in the city. Finally, he ran his hand down its length, a fluid, curved design with sharp, 3D triangular features encasing the hydraulic wheels on each side made it an elongated, structured, yet streamlined ride.

Ripping his gaze away from the car, Kamar glanced around the perimeter of the garage, narrowing his eyes, trying to locate the inevitable surveillance cameras. "Are your garage's cameras synched to the vehicle?"

Ava shook her head. "Negative. Is that a problem?"

"No, no. I have to check for those things before I look at what's going on with the vehicle itself. Wouldn't want to trip any alarms." He looked at her in a way he hoped would communicate why he was asking the questions. "You do have regular cameras in your garage, correct?"

"I used to. I removed them recently … when I had a breach. After that, I applied for a privacy order and was allowed to take them out of the interior of the garage."

Kamar cheered inside his head. He had to be careful, though, that the Alts they wore weren't "listening." At this point, though, he had no choice but to move forward with the real reason he was there. Without sound, he mouthed, enunciating each word, "I'm here for Phoenix."

Ava took a giant step back and covered her mouth before nodding. She lowered her voice to barely a whisper. "Oh— you're … *Phoenix*?"

Kamar nodded and responded by giving Ava the Loyalty sign.

"Are the kids all right? I've been blocking them from my thoughts so the worry doesn't show up on my Alt." Ava's words were more like puffs of air.

"Yes. All three are at my C-car repair biz."

Ava took a breath in and then expelled it, putting her hand on her chest. "Thank the stars they're okay! Escaping the arena— that fiasco! And finding your shop? How?"

"Talesa Vinata. She directed them there through Ember telepathically. Without that, they'd have been in deep crap."

In spite of the lack of cameras and listening devices, Ava moved within a foot of Kamar and whispered, "I knew Talesa was alive. But she's *telepathic*?"

Kamar hesitated, his tongue frozen with caution. He'd keep to the essentials. "Yes."

"That's wonderful news! Maybe we won't need to rely on our Morse Code so much."

Again, he short-circuited his answer. "Talesa can only speak mentally to others with altered DNA. Only a chosen few—not all of Phoenix." The crackled gold-colored cement beneath his feet to the very air he breathed, which was somehow scented with lavender to create a relaxed space even in the garage, reminded him of how much their Status differed. A key government servant of the administration, a puppet of Serpio. Despite Xander's assurances, he wasn't ready to share what he'd kept hidden his entire life.

Ava ran a finger along the top of the hood and then examined her finger to see if it had collected any dust. It hadn't. "How are they hiding there? They're just tucked in alongside the vehicles at your shop? And how did Talesa know you could be trusted?" Then, her eyes widened, and she took a step forward so that she was within inches of his body. "You're not just Phoenix. You're …"

He grimaced. "Right."

Confessing his deepest secret appeared to be necessary, but his stomach took a dive all the same. He leaned against the limo for support, noting its lustrous sheen even in the dim recesses of the garage. He couldn't keep from staring at the gleam, kind of like himself, hiding in the shadows for his entire life and now finding a way to shine. A light in spite of all the darkness. He could be that, even if he was more vulnerable than he'd ever been. Even so, he hurried to assure her the kids were safe and sound.

"I built a basement under the shop. They're there."

"Like, underground? You're lucky you didn't burrow through an existing tunnel."

"A what?" Things were getting stranger by the minute, and he didn't have time to fill in all these blanks. He was only to deliver the message and get on his way.

"Tunnels under the city. There's a whole network of those."

"You're seriously messing with me." He knew she wasn't,

and he had a moment of sheer panic, realizing what could have happened had he destroyed something like that.

"And you built that underground facility by *yourself*?"

Here goes nothing. Ava watched at him with a microscopic stare. He imagined she was indexing and assessing what nonsense he might be dribbling, but she would have to know and would have to believe.

"Yep. That's the only way I could keep it secret. I don't need to give you all the details, but the kids have decided it's the best new headquarters for Phoenix."

Ava's jaw dropped, but she seemed to accept his words as truth. "A new place to hide! In the nick of time, too. It's only a matter of time until those warehouses will be searched. Luckily, I'll be finding out more today at the meeting."

They quickly worked out a new code for communicating through their Alts using car repair jargon before Ava walked Kamar to the front door. As he left the garage, he caught something out of the corner of his eye. Was there a light blinking in the corner? What was it? He looked again but caught nothing. He shrugged. He was getting paranoid.

Kamar drew a card out of his front pocket and continued the ruse in case Evangeline listened in. "Ma'am, your limo could need further work at my shop." He handed her the card, the address vibrant in kelly green. Despite the high-tech options of the Alt, the city still recommended business cards, which, until now, Kamar thought was ridiculous. "In the meantime, it's safe, but feel free to message me if there's anything unusual."

"Of course. Thanks again so very much."

As he exited and admired the bright green lawn, Kamar understood why Ava was so special to everyone. Not only was she charming, she was willing to do anything for the cause.

And the cause was beginning to be an unexpected glut of challenges and rewards.

When the door closed behind him, Kamar had to quiet his

elation. Happiness was one thing, but being ecstatic after a trip to check on a car could be considered bizarre and come under scrutiny. He headed back to his car down the block, his steps light.

His quick scan took in the things he often took for granted—the children across the street, their innocent faces wide-eyed with curiosity; the crystalline blue skies over his head, crowned with pale morning sunshine; the sound in the distance of upbeat music, probably coming from a live band downtown; and the bright, purple blooms on the bushes lining the street. A perfect world. Almost.

A small group of four people lined up on the sidewalk. Behind them was the crimson blaze of a cloak. A Sciolist was executing a stop-and-question procedure.

The Sciolist and his detainees were just to the north of his car, so he'd have to pass them to get into his vehicle. Not that he had anything to hide—not yet. But the inevitability of him being stopped too soured his stomach.

As he approached in the most casual way he knew how, the Sciolist seemed to be checking one last ID. The citizens began to disperse, going their own way down the street. He breathed a sigh of relief, hoping the quick check proved that no one in that group was connected to Phoenix.

Sure enough, however, as he approached his van, the Sciolist, a pale-skinned specimen with contrasting dark brown eyes and short wavy hair, stepped directly in front of him and gave him the Tranquility salute. "Sir, what is your business in this neighborhood?"

"I was checking on a possible car malfunction. You can't expect the Elite to worry about their own vehicles. We watch them carefully."

"Yes. I'm sure that's true," the Sciolist responded with a condescending smile. "Before you continue, show your Alt."

Kamar returned the acknowledgment and forced himself to smile at the serious face before him. *They seriously have to be some-*

thing other than human, he thought. Sciolists were always so robotic.

He poured honey into his voice. "Of course. No problem at all. I understand you're looking for some very dangerous criminals. I'm happy to do my part." Kamar winked, trying to make light of the situation. He tapped his Alt twice, the first time to show his current points and Status, the second to bring up his photo and corresponding proof of identity, a number that had been assigned to him when he turned five.

The Sciolist said nothing in response but looked at Kamar's face in the Alt screen and then at his face in the sunlight. "Seems to be in order. Where do you work?"

"That's my shop's vehicle right there." He pointed to his multicolored car painted with the Obviators logo. "Nobody else gets to ride in that but me."

The Sciolist narrowed his eyes and then headed for the car, where he opened the doors to look inside and examine the trunk space. He pulled a device from inside his robe, a six-by-six-inch square, and clicked on a button. Facing the gadget toward Kamar, he said, "Have you seen any of these people?"

Ember's face stared back at Kamar from the screen. With a click, Will's followed, and then Xander's.

Kamar grimaced. "Ah. Those are the people you're hunting for. I've seen them on the news broadcasts. Not on the street, though. The … the girl is really beautiful. I wouldn't forget if I saw her." And it was true. Anyone who had ever met Ember would remember her. She had some out-of-the-ordinary elegance.

"These three are the most wanted. There are others we can't yet identify also involved in the rebel group. Just keep vigilant. They could be anywhere."

"I'll let City Hall know if I see any of these or have any suspicions of others I might come across, although I see very few people. Only CommuteCars in my job."

The Sciolist turned his back to walk down the street, his cloak fluttering in the breeze. "You be careful there, mister. Have a special day."

The added peppy adage made Kamar squirm more than the invasive check on his Alt. Nothing worse than one of these creepy red-caped freaks doing their job than having one wish you a good day.

TEN

Serpio's Elite

THE ELITE ENTERED the chambers with bubbling voices and beaming faces. As they hurried in, greeting one another with the Tranquility salute, each marveled over seeing Serpio before them, alive and well. They surrounded Serpio in a rush, reaching out with hugs, claps on the back, and the joy of a kid at Christmas.

Magistrate, sir, I'm so thrilled to see you alive and well! It's a true miracle!" said one as the others around him nodded.

"Just goes to show that positive thinking can help a person survive anything. Is that what it was, dear Serpio? Feren asked. She fluttered her long eyelashes and clasped her hands together before widening her lips in a beauty-queen smile.

Their murmurs and comments floated throughout the chamber like the whispering of a wave over dry sand.

As the group finally settled and took their seats, Serpio looked out upon his Elite from the podium, and his expression lifted. Each and every member of his governing body gazed back at him with something close to worship, although a few exhibited observable jitters as if they'd come face to face with a phantom. It seemed coming back from the dead was a feat that freaked out some of the older members.

None dared to ask for details, but the unspoken question was: What had happened to allow him to have survived? After all, they had been there in the arena. They had seen the carnage firsthand from those Elite seats—the pool of blood and the ultimate failure of the Medics to revive him. He had to catch himself from wondering these things aloud as he stretched his mind into the past. Was he ever this naïve? This trusting? He thought not.

Just as he had arranged, a beam of light suddenly shone down from the ceiling, giving him an angelic glow. "Ladies and gentlemen. Thank you so much for being here today. I apologize for making this a mandatory session." He paused, appreciating the graciousness of his own words. "I realize your time is precious and all of you have other jobs to attend to. However, the purpose of this meeting is to show you that I am not only alive, but doing fine. I am all right and will continue as your Magistrate." Stepping out from behind the podium, he bowed, a demonstration that was completely appropriate given the circumstances. After all, this was an accomplishment even greater than a theatrical performance.

Applause broke out, and then the Elite all stood while Serpio took a second bow.

Above the ovation, Serpio called out, "Thank you, my wonderful Elite! I appreciate your loyalty and warm wishes."

Pinpricks of excitement traveled down his spine. He had them in the palm of his hand. Returning to his space behind the lectern, he released some nervous energy by dumping his fingertips on the wooden surface. His notes were laid out before him, and he skimmed the page for his best hook. Persuasion was not so much magic as choosing the right words—the ones fraught with hypnotic suggestion.

Then an angelic-looking blond stood, and Serpio nodded in acknowledgment, all the while thinking about how lovely her clothes hung on her curves. "I propose in celebration of the Magistrate's survival, a party! Why should we be the only ones to see our Magistrate in person? We can spread the joy!"

Hurrahs and cheers followed.

Feren stood and smiled, clasping her hands to her chest. "This is a splendid idea, Serpio. It could be a street party! Oh! A Revelation Celebration!"

Ah, Feren, my pet. Leave it to you to lead the pack and come up with a seductive title.

An Elite male, one of the youngest and a favorite of Serpio's, added to the liveliness. "But one where we pull out all the stops! This is the most memorable event in Tranquility history—a real jubilee!"

All at once the meeting became a frenzy of ideas.

"Upper levels may attend, say fifteen and above. I suggest we make this a formal party where our community can dress up in elegant, chic clothing."

"And the rest of the city can watch it on Purviews!"

"It will be a wonderful morale booster for the entire cosmopolis! Such brilliance!"

Serpio put on his most humble expression. Touching his chest, he drew tears to his eyes. "Such a lovely idea. I am honored." And truly, he hadn't planned for this. But it would satisfy so many goals—buoying up the city after all the trauma with the traitors, allowing him to reassure people in the flesh, scout out turncoats, and cement his legacy. He wanted to break out in song and dance.

Enthusiasm rippled through the assemblage. Already, the faces transformed from the queasy shock at his resurrection and apparent sainthood into smiles and sparkling eyes. The conversation buzzed with the words "chic," "smart," and "lush." This would be an *event*, and no one would want to be left out.

Serpio raised his hand in the air to signal a stop to the conversation. "This cannot be delayed. The Revelation Celebration! I am most looking forward to assuring our fine citizens that I am very much alive and in charge. Of course, you all will be special honored guests, along with the Levels Fifteen and above.

Is there anyone opposed to this celebration?" He cast his eyes around the room.

Most shook their heads. The denial was a breath of fresh air for the man in charge.

"Excellent. The party will be tomorrow night in Town Square." He knew he was asking for a quick setup. It would be a lot to plan, but the hospitality experts of the city could put it together, he was sure. The Magistrate rubbed his palms together in anticipation and gave the Elite his most benevolent smile.

The room broke out in cheers once more. His eyes swept the assemblage, settling on Ava. His visual probe speared her to her chair. She gazed back, unwavering. Serpio was only setting the stage for what was to come. The deceiver had to be extremely versatile, trusted, and overly helpful. Many of the Elite fit that description, but he had narrowed it down.

Then he put on a serious expression and faced them squarely. "Now we must discuss more…unpleasant items. Knowing we are enriching and empowering the lives of our citizens, we can still be positive. We are the crusaders of the light, fighting against the serious problem still infecting our city. Our dear Plauditors are missing. Dangerous fugitives are in hiding. So far, they have escaped." Serpio stopped, allowing a generous pause. He inclined his head, trying to hold a congenial expression while every muscle under his clothes puckered with tension.

"I am convinced there is someone in this room who is helping them."

Silence draped a silhouette of shock over the listeners before Feren stood, waited for the nod from the Magistrate and spoke. "Magistrate, I can speak for all of us. We are so thankful you're here. And yes, the problems facing Tranquility, although temporary, are serious. But I am wondering…are you sure about this accusation?"

Serpio stayed quiet for a spell as if he hadn't thought about the issue before; then he arched his shoulders in a bit of a shrug. "I am not certain of who it is. And it grieves my heart to even think about it." Serpio paused again and put his hand to his chest.

A subtle, unexpected whisper erupted from the back of his mind. What if his suspicions were wrong? Or worse, what if there were multiple players in a conspiracy? He lifted his eyes to the ceiling, not asking for help from a higher power, but hoping to grasp comforting answers from remembered snippets of the Accords.

The pale blue ceiling stared back at him with an unforgiving silence. He never thought one of his Elite capable of betraying him, but the rebels knew too much, did too much. And they were *children* outsmarting him. He wouldn't stand for it.

Another Elite, a gentleman with fluffy, brown curly hair and a handlebar mustache, stood and gave Serpio the Tranquility salute. "Serpio, I agree with Feren. We're all thrilled you're alive and well! However, someone in the Elite would never think for a moment about betraying our city! With all due respect, sir, this accusation cannot stand."

Serpio stepped out from behind the glass podium, designed for transparency in communication, and off the mini stage. He walked to within inches of the front row, noting the slight frowns and shiny teeth. "Would I bring this to you if I wasn't finding evidence to back this up? I assure you, this does not make me happy at all. Information that can only have come from here has been leaked."

He narrowed his eyes and regarded each face along the rows of chairs as if he could uncover the guilt just by the looks on their faces. If only he, like Ember, could read the emotions of all who sat in front of him! That's where the Alt failed; it wasn't a tool he could use when these situations arose.

"Right now, none of you are above suspicion, but understand I come to you with the purest of motives. Not to upset you, but to finally get our beautiful city back to its former glory. The sooner we discover how our fugitives are operating so well, the sooner we can capture them and get back to enjoying our perfect lives."

A murmur went through the group, a few nodding in agreement and others shaking their heads. The council's voices became louder as the refined assembly began to bicker with one another, a sound Serpio had seldom heard.

He scrutinized their behavior, noting those who were shaking their heads. *This is why I have always been so careful with my Elite. Having anyone in my council who is not completely loyal puts everything in jeopardy. No one can have the power to go outside of my decisions or become more powerful. It creates havoc.*

A group of eight members engaged in heated discussion, and Serpio focused on them.

"First he comes back to life with no explanation, and now he's questioning our Elite?" And "I haven't felt comfortable for a while. I approved the match in the arena, but we're getting into dangerous territory. This is not what our city represents…"

Serpio gritted his teeth to contain his outrage and shut his eyes from the sudden friction. Things were more problematic than he thought. Opening his eyes again, he fixated on what he believed to be a sign from Tranquility itself. Being mid-morning, the sun shone through the windows, still lightly peppered with remnants of rain.

He'd always abhorred the engineered rain; it was dreary, and he hated the way it felt when it fell on his skin. But it was temporary, and an overnight thing, and always dried, fading away each day as if it had never been. This momentary disagreement would be the same. A fleeting blemish that would not remain. He mentally marked, though, all those who spoke the waspish words.

The Elite were no longer the perfect government. They were tainted, dulled, rusted, and he'd strip the traitor of their Status and life for daring to cross him.

After several minutes, Feren stood and asked to be recognized. "We have many here who are concerned with the very idea of an Elite coming under suspicion, but we also realize that if there truly is a member who's untrustworthy, it is a threat to our entire city. A vote is in order to allow interrogation if there is sufficient evidence. This would be with restrictions—that the Elite be involved with questioning and entitled to know all details about when, where, and how this is to be performed."

An Elite member new to the council said, "We trust your leadership. But we're also involved with all that happens in our city. We guard and protect our excellent Accords and philosophy of happiness. It would be easy to allow them to slip away. I vote that the Magistrate may question, but only on the basis of evidence that the Elite see and we are kept informed about each instance."

Feren had remained standing but exclusively addressed her soft smile and question to Serpio, as if he were the only one in the room. "Shall we vote on this, then? And I feel it is serious enough that we do it by secret ballot."

Behind Serpio, the screech of a bird followed by a heavy thud agains the building caused his heart to nearly stop in his chest. He jerked and spun around to discover the source of the assault, his body stiffly alert for mor strikes, a fog of fury swimming in his eyes. *The rebels!* The idea made his lungs as heavy as a heap of stones. A flick of his finger to his OmniCom sent signals to his Sciolists.

Gasps and murmurs from the Elite stirred the newfound serenity within the chamber. A few stood up, craning their necks, while others cowered at the noise, protecting their heads.

With his hero complex on full display, Serpio boldly approached the glass window. A bluebird had flown into the glass and lay dead on the grass below. A shame, but not an attack at all. He hadn't realize he'd been holding his breath, but expelled it in a plume of hot air and dropped his shoulders.

"My dear Elite. All is well. A bird flew too low, that is all. Please appreciate your moment of concern as unfounded fear."

The Elite quieted but thanked Serpio for his bravery as he cancelled the summoning of his protectors.

Dragging his lips into a forced smile, he sighed, as if the whole process of governing made him tired. "Now, we must move on to other issues, that being our monstrous and mysterious insurgents." With the click of his fingers, a holographic board materialized to his right. He waved his hand, and the letters DNA faded in on the screen. "In the past, we have never used DNA analysis against our own people. But now, the greater good is at stake. We must sift out the traitors who have set to destroy our utopia. I am calling for every citizen who is detained as a suspect to be subject to collection."

Feren waved a finger. "As long as this is not an invasion of privacy. Only those who are truly suspects must be tested."

"I suggest this effort have a name so our citizens do not become alarmed," Serpio almost sang.

The young man Serpio favored suggested, "The term 'Providence Project'? It has a positive connotation and rolls off the tongue quite well."

Again, a swell of conversation arose as the Elite turned to one another.

It was Feren again who asked for permission to respond. "This idea should come to a vote. First, whether the Elite agrees it is necessary to require DNA from suspected conspirators. And second, if the name is satisfactory to all."

An elderly woman, a lady well-respected for her advanced age and good cheer, stood up in the back. "I second that motion."

"Very well," Serpio conceded. "All in favor of conducting DNA analysis for possible criminal activity, please say 'love.'" A chorus of responses made Serpio's heart of stone rise within his chest. "If declining, can I hear 'doubt'?" A handful of voices echoed back, and Serpio took mental notes of those who objected.

Thirty seconds later, the Providence Project got a full endorsement, based on seventy-five percent approval.

ELEVEN

Ember's Stunner

EMBER LOVED TELEPATHICALLY COMMUNICATING with her mom, but learning a million details wasn't practical. If her mom said knowing extra information about the Easterner was worth waiting for, she would. However, she could barely contain her curiosity.

She chewed on a fingernail to quiet her restlessness. "I can hardly wait to find out who the Easterner is and what he can do."

"I hope it's someone who can take down Serpio with a blink of an eye," Xander responded.

As if saying Serpio's name stirred some dark magic, the screen on the adjacent wall sputtered. A pop and a hum interspersed with flashes of light streamed from the older device struggling for life. Finally, a burst of energy illuminated the screen as an instrumental version of the Tranquility anthem played, revealing the same news anchor they'd seen the night before. But now it was the regular morning news programming.

"Good morning, fine citizens of Tranquility! Here is your positive affirmation for the day. The quote this morning is from Benjamin Franklin, a very early leader of the nation of America, which existed beginning in 1776 and ending in 2041." The screen showed text read by the announcer. "'*Happiness depends more on the inward disposition of mind than on outward circumstances ...*' May each of you find happiness in your day today."

The anchor beamed at the camera before holding up his wrist, the camera zooming in to show his Alt's positive icons and pulsing green arrow. He then dusted off his shoulders and straightened his tie, as if each motion would give him moments to prepare himself. "Now, on to other important news. There is no cause for alarm, but each of you will receive a message after this broadcast. We have already reassured you that the Magistrate is fine and doing very well. But after the upheaval in the arena, the anarchists Will Verus and Xander Noble have disappeared." Their pictures flashed up on the screen, one by one, at a slow pace and then magnified.

Ember approached the monitor at a run until she was within six feet of it and placed her hands on her hips. The two boys, each bringing stormy faces, gathered behind her.

The newscaster steepled his hands on the table in front of him. "And right after the fight in the arena, Ember Vinata, our very special Queen of Hearts, went missing. We believe the enemy rebels have kidnapped her for evil purposes."

"Kidnapped me?" She snorted. "Now that's a stretch."

Will's head whipped around. "Shh. Listen."

The broadcaster pulled down on his sleeves. "Do not be alarmed. We are doing our best to locate these criminals and are fully confident they will be apprehended soon. They are right here, among us. So, please understand, we must randomly question citizens in order to hunt these renegades down. Simply cooperate immediately if you are detained. In the meantime, as always, use your emergency app if you see anyone suspicious so we may restore Tranquility's peace and happiness."

Xander pinched his lips together and yelled at the broadcaster on the screen. "No one knows where we are, stupid!"

Will lashed out. "Shut up!"

Ember's brows frowned at Will's vehemence. She placed her hand on his arm.

The announcer continued. "Furthermore, if City Hall determines someone to be a person of interest, their DNA will be collected to verify the person's identity. This information will ultimately be stored on the Alt. We regret this inconvenience and invasion of privacy, but please understand. It is for your personal safety."

With that, the newscaster displayed his cosmetically enhanced teeth, raised his arm in salute, and concluded, "For now, this is Atticus Adamo signing off. Have a perfect day."

Xander exploded. "What the f—"

Ember's voice ripped through Xander's expletive. "Holy Shazz! We're in trouble. DNA? If anyone who has special gifts is arrested, they'll be exposed!"

Xander grabbed fistfuls of air with his hands. "As awful as Tranquility is, this is really messed up! Required DNA scans have never been done before. And how much concern do they need to label someone a person of interest?"

Ember put her right hand in her left palm and squeezed. "Remember what Ava told us? The use of DNA analysis has been outlawed ever since the experiments during the time her dad worked for the lab. That's exactly how and why the people with DNA alterations have been protected so far." The thought of anyone's blood being used against them made her want to punch something.

Will's eyebrows drew together. "Even Serpio couldn't just arbitrarily reverse that edict, could he?"

Her look heavy with disappointment, Ember said, "Not without the Elite voting in favor."

"So the Elite are in Serpio's pocket." Xander raised his chin as if in challenge. "I'm curious if Serpio's been acting on his own at all. Did he find out about your talent using DNA analysis, Em?"

"No. When I went to Solace, the instruments picked up a weird, infinite vibration. Like the Alt, but way more sophisticated. It showed a psychic, extrasensory emotional response. That's how Serpio knew I could sense emotions in other people. If he'd have pulled my DNA, he would've actually seen mutations. Surprised he didn't check afterward. But he was too wrapped up in how he could use me and my emotional abilities."

Will put his hand on Ember's shoulder, and his eyes teared up. "I actually remember that! You gave me the news right afterward. Until then, I didn't even know about your gift."

Xander glared at Will. As if Will felt real daggers from Xander's eyes, he dropped his hand from Ember's shoulder.

Leaning forward and slowing his words, Xander said, "The thing is, Will, there was a secret list of people with DNA mutations. No one has had access to the complete list, though. The Magistrate has tried to get his hands on it for a long time. People, including Ember's dad, lost their lives protecting those names."

Will fanned himself before nervously unzipping the front of his uniform to reveal inches of skin and then zipped it back up a few inches and began to pace. "Shazz! And now he has justification for testing everybody. Because of us. Because of Phoenix and the rebellion. We just screwed ourselves."

A pained expression crossed Will's face. Ember's heart went out to him. He wasn't himself. His timidity and constant questioning were foreign to her. Before she could say another word, though, Will crumpled to the ground.

"Will!" Ember cried out.

"What the hell?" Xander yelled. He leaped into action in giant strides. He leaned over Will, pulling his eyelids back to look at his eyes. "He's breathing. Looks like he just fainted."

At the same time, Ember rushed to his side, kneeling beside him. *He's out cold.* She checked for a pulse. A slow but steady throb responded to her fingertips on his wrist. She put her hand on Will's forehead. "He's not hot ..." His aura went white, dimmed, and flickered. Emotions suppressed, as if they hid under a blanket of goo.

"Still—we need a cool cloth for his head. And water. He could be dehydrated."

Xander appeared in control, thank the stars. Someone needed to be levelheaded.

Ember's mind went blank, and her muscles tightened into what felt like square pegs in round holes. She asked stupidly, "Where's the water?"

"The cabinet! Over there." Xander pointed to the far wall. "I'll stay with him. I don't want him to stop breathing."

Stop breathing? Xander thinks he's dying? What if he is? The sting of words never said and a second wave of panic pushed Ember to her feet, and she dashed twenty feet to the closet. "This one?" she called out, grabbing one of the handles of the two twelve-foot-tall cabinets that stood like sentries flush against the wall.

"No! The other." Xander had lifted Will's head and torso and was lightly slapping his face and calling his name with the urgency of an emergency Medic. "Will! *Will!*"

Ember pulled on the cabinet door, expecting a quick release, but the door wouldn't budge. "It's stuck!" Her voice sounded like someone else's—screechy, loud. Was the cupboard locked? No … couldn't be. She mentally chided herself for her physical weakness. Was she too exhausted to open a door? No. Perhaps the moisture underground made the wood stick?

"C'mon. Pull harder, Ember! Look for towels!" Xander raised Will's head and supported it in his arms.

She tried to concentrate. Pull the door open. *Pull!* The door still not budging, she gasped to control her breath as what felt like tar lodged in her throat. Towels. Water. Hurry. Ugh! The door would not open!

"It's still stuck! Help!" she yelled out.

She thought about turning around and sending Xander instead, but the thought vanished as a thought washed over her.

Turning … turn back time … turn back time … She could prevent this!

But nothing engaged. The talent seemed as rusty and useless as a steel blade left out in the rain too long. She wanted to cry.

And what was wrong with Will? Breath was coming now but overloading her. She began to hyperventilate. *What if they couldn't wake him up?* Then a thought. Had the Magistate given him some long-acting poison to finish him off after his stint in the arena? Shazz!

Her fingers wrapped around the cabinet's U-shaped handle in a vise-like grip, the steel edges biting into her handhold. A moan from Will spurred her on, the pain of the Herculean effort bringing tears to her eyes.

She changed position, Tugging on the door from the right side with all her might, it finally flew open, knocking her backward against the wall. Her balance upended, she fell in a contorted heap, her elbows and back taking a violent hit. Surprised and mortified, she froze, the pain stunning her into submission.

Xander shot to his feet, his eyes pooled with panic. "Ember! You okay? What happened?" He crouched down again and then sprang up like a dutiful jack-in-the box.

The indecision Ember saw and felt from him distracted her for a moment from the throbbing waves of pain spread through her body. However, she couldn't eek out an answer. She had hit *hard*. She remained in place for another minute, allowing the pangs to subside and to regain her dignity and balance.

Finally, she stood up, embarrassed. Her ego, in addition to her body, was more than a little bruised. "I'm … I'm okay…"

Then she saw the wall. A crack had formed in the surface of it, spidering out into what looked like rivers on a topographical map.

Across the room, Will murmured something inaudible, moaned, and blinked his eyes.

Xander directed his full attention back to Will. "Good! You're

awake. You fainted, Golden Boy. You're okay, though, I …
think." He scrambled to his feet, now able to concentrate on
Ember. He ran to her, placed his hands on her forearms, and then
touched her face gently with his fingertips. "Are you okay? That
was quite a scene."

"Umm … yeah. I'm fine, but the *wall* isn't." Brushing herself
off, she tossed her hair to shake out particles.

"No way. The impenetrable wall? That one over—?"
Xander's gaze settled on the damaged stone. His eyes widened.
"*You* did that?"

"I … guess. C'mon. We need to take care of Will, not the wall.
I'll get the water now. Cabinet's definitely open." She grinned,
her soreness already dissipating enough to make a jest. She
swiveled to return to the cabinet, but Xander grabbed her arm to
stop her.

"I'll get it. Go check on the drama queen over there."

Xander's contempt for Will always showed through, but in
spite of that, Ember perceived actual worry radiating from him.

Rubbing her hip a little as she walked, Ember hurried to
where Will lay still as stone, looking dazed. She caressed his face.
"Poor Will. We're gonna get you fixed up."

Xander warily glanced again at the wall. "That's some crack
you made. Kamar's not gonna be happy." He grabbed a couple
of bottles of water from the cabinet. Running back, he knelt and
put a bottle to Will's lips. "Easy. Just a little." He then poured
some on his hands and splashed Will's face with it. "Sorry—no
washcloth."

Will sputtered, "I—thanks. I guess." With Ember's help, he
sat up and looked around the room. *Probably getting his bearings
once more,* Ember thought.

Will's confusion and unease flowed like a cloud around him,
manifesting gray, the color of low energy and self-doubt. She put
her hands on each side of his face and felt the warmth returning
to his cheeks.

"Feeling better?"

"Yeah. Don't know what happened," he said hoarsely. Without support, Will was able to rise to his feet. "All good."

"Better drink more. You probably need a lot of water." Xander held out the bottle to him.

The bottle shook in Will's hands as he took it, but he managed to get the liquid into his mouth in small sips. "Thanks." Taking more swallows, he finally said, "I am starting to feel better. You're right. I must have needed water. That fight in the arena took a lot out of me."

Ember wished she knew what was going on with Will. The sudden faint was bizarre. His aura disturbed her in the way that a flower in full bloom wilting in the sun would, the way a cloud could so quickly occlude the sun, or the way a stalwart stone wall unexpectedly shattered into pieces …

Rising to her feet, she doled out motherly advice. "You're going to have to take it easy, Will, and drink. You're probably dehydrated. But that's an easy fix compared to Kamar's earthwork over there." Ember gestured toward the scene of her awkward fight with the cupboard door. "That crack I made looks seriously bad."

She shepherded the guys over where her body had slammed against the masonry. Remembering the cartoons she'd watched as a child where a goofy character smashed into a wall and then walked away, she realized this scenario was much the same.

"You did that when I was unconscious?" Will asked. "Were you a projectile?"

Ember flushed pink and looked at the floor. "What am I going to tell Kamar?"

She shuffled over to the damage and ran her hands over the middle before stopping to outline a place with her hands. "This looks like an actual imprint of my shoulder." No sooner had the words left her mouth than the wall began crumbling in little pieces, the stone appearing to dissolve into a mosaic shimmy. Once-hard substances became fine, gritty powder, sifting through the air and landing on her hair and shoulders and the floor. "What the—"

She withdrew her hands as if burned and looked at the boys in disbelief.

"Damn! How'd you do that?" Running his hand across the damaged mortar and finding it solid, Xander whistled. "You suddenly super strong or something?"

Ember laughed. "Let's see." Where Xander stood caressing the wall, Ember threw both arms around him and tried to pick him up. "Ugh! You're heavy!"

Xander guffawed before play-acting a show of resistance, his arms pushing her back. "Please! Don't take me against my will, Superwoman!"

Not to be discouraged, she inhaled and pulled up with all the strength she had, but nothing she did from any angle mattered. Her muscles seemed more like liquid as she put all her might into lifting Xander. At his height and weight, Xander's feet didn't leave the ground. Shrieking from laughter and effort, after several tries, Ember gave up.

"So much for that theory. Kamar's wall has a definite problem."

TWELVE

Ember's Mystery

THE LIFT DESCENDED into their safe room.

Xander's head swung to the side, and he launched himself out of the chair on which he was sitting. "Kamar, you're back! You were gone forever!"

As Ember ran to Kamar, her lightheartedness made her wonder if she was glowing from the inside out. She eyed Kamar's armfuls of bags like a kid at Christmas. After weeks of her life being turned upside down, an imminent fashion party, albeit costumes to keep them disguised, would be a fun diversion from life-and-death drama.

"Did you have luck shopping? How about Ava? Did you find her? Tell us everything!"

Will sat up from where he'd been resting on the air mattress on the floor. Now his cheeks were flushed, and Ember felt Will's anticipation radiating into her like waves. Without a doubt, he was feeling better, his emotional equilibrium back to almost normal.

With one finger count at a time, Kamar named off each of his accomplishments." I saw Ava, got costumes, and dodged the Sciolists. Not bad for a day's work." Kamar grinned, setting his parcels down on the floor. "Did you guys make yourself useful while I was gone?"

Xander spoke up. "Will had a fainting spell, but he seems okay now. We can't catch a break." He turned and looked at Ember. "And … Ember has a confession."

"I leave for just a little while, and all hell breaks loose?" Kamar swung his head in a "no," looking like a disappointed parent. "Will, are you all right?"

"Yeah. I'm sure I'll be fine. But Ember—"

Ember lowered her head and cast her eyes to the ground. "I broke your wall." Although far from the scene of the crime, Ember stood in front of the area she'd decimated, hoping Kamar wouldn't see it right away. Apparently, he hadn't.

"What?" Kamar tilted his head and narrowed his eyes as if he were hearing Ember speak in a language he couldn't possibly understand.

"Yeah. Well, not all of it. A … section. I'm so sorry! I don't know what happened. I'll show you." *Not a good way to start a friendship—damaging somebody's place,* she thought.

She turned and surveyed the mutilation, putting herself in Kamar's shoes, how Kamar must be now seeing it and thinking a million negative thoughts about her, his workmanship torn apart. With her own emotions already churning, Ember absorbed Kamar's mystification internally. Her drooping shoulders broadcasting her sheepishness, she led the way to the damage, Kamar in her tracks. Will and Xander dragged behind, Will shaking his head all the way.

Kamar reached out with a delicate stroke, running his fingers over the broken pieces of stone and gaps in the structure. "Has this ever happened to you before?"

"What? Cracking a wall? No." For an instant, Ember wondered if Kamar's question was serious. *Who would damage the interior of buildings unintentionally?* "I'm so sorry. I slammed into it by accident when I was opening the cupboard to get water. Now I'm afraid to even touch the wall. Could the whole thing collapse?" Ember held her hands behind her back.

Kamar didn't take his eyes off Ember. "It won't totally collapse, trust me." Kamar seemed awfully sure of himself. "Push in another place again with your hands. Not too hard, but with some force."

"What? Are you sure?"

Ember's nervousness did the jitterbug up and down her body, but everyone was rooting her on. She allowed her fingertips to graze the stone before she pressed on an area unbroken by her earlier disaster. Will peered over her shoulder like a shadow. Xander leaned against the wall a few feet away like he was hoping to hold it up in case it fell.

"Nothing." Ember frowned and poked her tongue into her cheek. "I must have just found a weak spot in your 'impenetrable fortress.'" The remark came out more sarcastically than she'd planned.

Kamar shook his head. "Not so fast, girl. These walls don't break. If you damaged that wall, there's something going on."

Xander moved closer, put his hand on her shoulder, and looked into Ember's face. "C'mon. Get serious. Use your fist instead." He gestured to a spot in front of him.

The gray, dusty stone of the wall stared back at her, its black marbling across the vast expanse heavier than others and even swirly, as if the wall practiced making signatures all day.

Ember curled her fingers into a fist and punched the wall as hard as she could, but the resistance she expected never came. Her hand flowed through the wall's surface as if the stone was made of jelly and she gasped in surprise. She could only stand there gazing at it with wide eyes. What had happened to the unyielding slab Kamar bragged about?

Despite the squishy feel of the masonry, in front of her was a good-sized hole, its edges jagged with sharp pieces of granite. Fine dust swirled in the air, a party of particles dancing in the dimness. She sucked in a breath. Stranger still, her knuckles didn't hurt. She examined her fingers, twisting her right hand back and forth. No blood, either. What was this strange phenomenon?

Kamar whistled. "There's something going on, all right. But it's not the wall. It's *you*."

Ember shook her head, her stare boring into the wall almost as intensely as her fist had. "What? That's not … possible." Her thoughts popcorned into a plethora of alternatives, each completely implausible and absurd.

Will backed up a few steps. "Do I need to be afraid?" He put his hands up in front of his face before laughing.

Ember laughed too, grateful for some joviality to lighten what seemed like some dark magic taking a seat inside her.

Kamar approached the mess Ember had made earlier. "Watch."

Placing both his palms on the wall, he pushed, pressed, squeezed, and smoothed. The stone melted under his hands. The dry surfaces became just like wet clay, and he was able to shape the fragmented area on the wall back to normal.

Ember gasped as she watched the stone mend. Kamar did indeed have a special gift.

Behind her, Will breathed out, "Whoa."

"I've been dying to see that, truth be told," Xander confessed.

Dropping his hands, Kamar instructed, "Now you, Ember."

"What? I can't." She wasn't sure if she wanted this to work. With all she'd discovered in the last few hours, she was questioning her grip on reality. Everything was starting to seem like a dream or something out of the antiquated classics like *Alice in Wonderland*.

"Yes. I'm convinced you can." Kamar took Ember's arm and positioned her hands on both sides of the hole she had made with her fist. "Think about moving the stone and closing the gap."

He put pressure on her skin, then let go.

Ember's brow furrowed, but she did as Kamar asked. She felt

foolish, but when she concentrated on the task, the stone warmed under her hands until it felt like playdough. Her heart began to beat faster with the discovery. She blurted, "Now what?"

Kamar chuckled. "Just smooth it around like frosting and level it out."

Sure enough, the stone flowed and fused under her touch. Her fingers felt at one with the stone, as if she were some sort of elemental. With meticulous effort, she moved the liquid cement around until it became flat, transforming the former hole into a level surface.

The men gave Ember a rousing round of applause. She turned to the group, her face aglow. "How is this happening?" Never could she remember her hands feeling so powerful and yet so artistic.

Kamar pulled a slow smile. "Want my guess? Transference. Have you ever been around others with special talents? Other than your mom, I mean."

"Ah … no. Just my mom." Ember cast her eyes down. "I was very secluded before my mom got sick. I only had a few friends, and not close ones. My empathic talent made it difficult."

Xander stepped forward and draped his arm around her shoulder. "But you can send messages telepathically, just like your mom, so Kamar could be right."

Will still stared at the wall, bewitched by it. "This means you can do what Kamar can do? That could really help Phoenix."

Xander smirked. "Well, I don't know how. But what I see is Ember being a very serious threat to Serpio if she can collect talents like she does emotions."

Shaking her head, Ember admitted, "I don't know how that's even possible, but if it is, I want—need—to find all the others."

"Umm … yeah! You're a walking nightmare for Serpio if that's true." Will bestowed an awestruck look at Ember, looking like he'd just captured lightning in a jar.

"Serpio's like titanium, though. It'll take a lot more than that to bring him down." Ember clapped him on the shoulder to bring weight to her words.

Kamar leaned forward, rubbing his hands together. "Potential. That's what it is. And we need to get this party started." He drifted over to where he'd set down the bags of disguises. "As we figure out who's gonna look like whom, I'll tell you about Ava."

THIRTEEN

Ember's Agreement

EMBER SHIVERED. She still hadn't gotten used to the chill in the basement. The stone encompassing her had made her bones cold ever since she'd arrived, but the temperature made changing clothes especially uncomfortable. The boys, however, appeared to be unaffected, laughing and joking as they tried on their disguises.

Masks like their own skin, thin and realistic, made each one look like different people entirely. Kamar had done a great job with clothing, too, even remembering to find outfits that changed not only their typical everyday clothes, but ones with complex patterns that would further confuse the algorithms of the city's cameras.

Kamar crossed the room and dragged the chair over to the center, making scratching sounds against the clay floor. He sat down. "I'll tell you everything Ava said, and then we've got to engineer getting all of Phoenix here. Take off those costumes, and let's get a strategy in place. It won't be easy. The ability to move rocks won't get Phoenix here any quicker."

Ember opened her mouth to speak before she paused, collecting her thoughts. "We're not moving rocks. We're moving mountains. This operation has 'lethal' written all over it."

"Agreed." Xander grimaced before stripping off his funky shirt and wadding it up in his hands. He tossed it basketball style into the darkest corner of the room, a good fifteen feet away.

"Shh!" Kamar held up his wrist to indicate a notification. "Another announcement—"

Shadows bounced against the rock walls from the broadcast screen across the room as it sputtered to life.

Drowning out Kamar's next words, a loud fanfare and the Tranquility anthem blasted from the speakers attached to the modest monitor. Chased by a bright gold illuminated background on the Purview, Tranquility's brilliant animated mascot, the Halcyon, glided across the expanse with the words "Special Bulletin" throbbing behind it.

Seconds later, in contrast, a full-shouldered black silhouette of a man stood on a dais.

An unseen, excited announcer voiced words appearing on the screen in what seemed like a well-rehearsed blurb. "With the support of the Elite, we are proud to reintroduce our death-defying leader to the people of the city. In celebration, the Elite is sponsoring the Revelation Celebration, a street party held this Friday directly in front of City Hall. The Magistrate himself will be present to acknowledge his amazing recovery and continued benevolent governing of Tranquility. Those who are Level Fifteen and above are invited to attend. This will be a black-tie affair, gowns and tuxedos, and the party of a lifetime. More details will come through your Alt, including your invitations. Be grateful our Magistrate is alive and well! Have a wonderful day!" A virtual lightning bolt with accompanying thunder struck the dark male profile, briefly exposing Serpio Magnus holding a jeweled scepter.

"Frickin' Shazz! That was him! That was Serpio! Does he have some sort of secret we're missing here? Whatever it is, I want it." Xander fresh confusion and horror was written all over his face, a transformation that made him appear old beyond his years.

They looked at each other, stunned. Until now, they could sluff it off—pretend and hope the Magistrate's survival was all a big lie. But now, they had evidence Serpio Magnus was indeed alive. Unless there was some trickery to the broadcast, he was not only healed, but looked regal and in control.

Ember shook her head, her brain still scrambling to find a logical excuse. Each arm, leg, finger, and toe felt heavy, as if every nightmare, trauma, and heartache decided to take up residence in her limbs. "It can't be possible! I don't understand."

Xander's voice was raspy. "One thing's clear. Serpio is *not* just a regular person. No one could have survived that."

Will did a double take. "That's it! He's *not* a regular person!"

Ember gasped. "Oh! Oh no! Genetic engineering never entered my mind." Suddenly dizzy, she almost lost her balance, catching herself on Xander's arm.

"You okay?" Xander put his hands on both sides of Ember's face, the discussion halted until Ember nodded.

Kamar fired, "Well, it's the only explanation, right? How else can someone get impaled, bleed out, be pronounced dead, and then reappear completely fine?"

"You're flat-out right, Xander!" Then Will turned and lashed out at Ember. "How could you not know? Or your mom? She knows who all the special people are!"

Xander's aura looked like it suddenly crackled with heat. "Hey! Ember's not clairvoyant! Find somewhere else to stockpile that anger, Will."

"My mom obviously couldn't with Serpio! He must have a way to conceal it," Ember stammered. "And me? I never could tell who has anything out of the ordinary about them."

Will cast his eyes down, his cheeks blooming with their characteristic pink mottling. "I'm sorry, Ember. That wasn't fair. It was more my frustration coming out." He reached out and briefly touched Ember on the arm.

"I understand," she replied, and she meant it. Will's aura looked like tinsel, shiny and pink. His regret shellacked her.

All at once, though, Ember's thoughts validated Will's question. Maybe Talesa *wasn't* able to find everyone in the city with a gift? The possibility sobered and scared her more than a little.

Xander scoffed. "Immortality is the stuff of legends. If some genetic breakthrough was possible, we'd all know about it. You can't keep a secret like that under wraps."

Will shook his head. "You're wrong. He's been killing people, and no one knows about that. Only us. He's a master at keeping secrets."

Will's mouth quirked sideways in a wry bend. "Everyone has an Achilles heel. A weakness. We just have to find Serpio's."

The lights, dim as they were in the basement's vast space, flickered. White to yellow and then back to full strength. Will's eyes blinked along with them.

"Am I having a stroke, or are we losing power in here?" Xander half joked while he stared at the light fixtures that were barely putting out much light as it was.

Kamar "Don't worry. Sometimes that happens. I didn't do so great with the lights in here."

"That's it! It's fear! Serpio's weakness is the fear of losing power."

"We just add 'finding Serpio's weakness' to the to-do list, along with everything else." Xander made exaggerated multiple check marks in the stale, basement-bound air.

"Like worrying about this weird street party they just announced?" Ember tipped her head back. "It's too much," she moaned.

"Yeah," Will said, his head flinching back slightly. "Why would the city plan a big event like that right now all out in the open? It's weird."

Xander stroked his throat and grimaced. "Serpio's proving to Tranquility that he's alive and well. And he's enjoying the drama. A focus on him directly. It's not the same just having him pop up on the morning news. He's got to have people see him … touch him."

Ember's fury over Serpio's escape from death and his explosive, taunting image burned. It was just like the Magistrate, narcissist that he was, to make a huge deal out of surviving the attempt on his life.

Heat entered Ember's tone, rising from her chest. "It wouldn't surprise me if he's doing it for glory *and* to hunt people. Under the guise of a party, the Sciolists could be checking Alts right and left, patting people down. Collecting a huge number of citizens all in one place. What could be easier than an event to do that?"

"Hate to say it, but that's smart on his part." Kamar worked his jaw.

Ember's anger, along with the tension and anxiety emanating from her companions, did an electric dance down her arms. Finding out that something was true had never been as disturbing. Drawing herself up, a new strength within her soul emerged. "Whatever. We're going to need to stay far, far away. No party for us. And here's the thing, guys. Finding out the truth is only half of it. It's what you do with it that matters."

"That's right, Ember. When did you get so wise anyway?" Will winked, although his eyelid tic returned as if he'd flipped a switch.

"Serpio'll be kissing babies and shaking hands with people who are now going to see him as completely perfect and miraculous." Xander pressed his hands against his stomach, made a hurling noise, and ran to grab a bucket turned on its side a few feet away.

Kamar's and Will's laughter buoyed her spirits, and her shoulders released long-knotted tension. She, too, was glad she wouldn't be there. "I agree. But did I hear right? Only upper Status can go?"

Xander brought the bucket over, having finished his theatrical performance, and slammed it back down to the floor, where the metal made a sharp clink against the stone. He wore a serious expression, his eyes glittering. "Yeah. So, he's counting on having a safety zone in place while Sciolists try to find infiltrators."

"He'd have them in a heartbeat, but don't take it out on the bucket," Kamar added.

Ember reached out and grabbed Xander's arm, her eyes wide. "Will your parents go to the party? They're Level Fifteens, right?" The idea of anyone connected to them being at risk made her heart beat faster. She didn't know if having a criminal for a son would make them less likely to go or if, under the circumstances, they'd be specially invited …

Ember wrung her hands as a meteor hit her consciousness: both Xander and Will's parents were in acute danger. They had to be targets. Serpio would stop at nothing to bring the boys out of hiding or to punish the parents for the sons' crimes.

Xander made a light whistling noise. "Babe, I have no idea if they'll be there. I imagine. Who knows? And who cares?" His disobedient hair had dropped in front of his right eye, and he brushed it away.

Ember watched Xander's hair fall back down again, the four-inch strands heavy across his face. She brushed it back up. Then, putting her hands on Xander's arms, she shook him.

"You should care, Xander!"

Xander placed a hand over one of hers. "I don't. You know my story, Ember."

Kamar's green shoes traced an invisible design into the reddish floor. Will fiddled with his pocket, examining some lint from inside.

"These are your *parents*, and they're going to be in real trouble!" She swallowed, imagining the worst-case scenario of trying to help each other and the boys' parents but all of them getting captured.

Ember saw the stir in his aura. Xander's one-of-a-kind silver outline tight around his body, a base to his typical deep red, undulated, and she watched the silver morph to a dirty gray, indicating his skepticism. *He can be so stubborn!*

"You owe it to yourself to patch things up," she said softly.

He gazed down at her with an eyebrow lift before walking a few paces away, his back turned. "Pfft. Maybe someday. I'm sure they're super embarrassed right now—their son's picture on every billboard. And they had to have watched me sweat it out in the arena. Yeah, I'm sure they were proud." He forced out a laugh before turning back to face them.

Ember wanted to throttle Xander but instead gave the bucket a swift kick. "We need to warn them, at least! Then they'll know you're actually a good guy. Once we get Serpio eliminated once and for all, they'll see you're a hero."

"That's *if* we get Serpio eliminated. Then we'll see," Xander parried, a weak half-smile on his lips.

Ember turned from Xander and advanced on Will. "What about *your* parents?"

"Hmm." Will paused for what Ember found to be an uncomfortable stretch of the clock's hands, until she thought he'd gone into some sort of trance. Finally, he said, "I'm having a hard time remembering them. Are they upper class?"

Ember pursed her lips and raised her brows. Her eyes searched his. Will's mental state was beginning to concern her. His aura didn't flow naturally. It churned. "No, Will. You told me they were Level Ones."

"Oh. Well, they won't be at the party, then." His eyes seemed to fix on the chains of the lift. "And you know what? I don't give a hang. They hate me."

Will's words penetrated Ember's veneer. "What? Hate you? Why would they hate you?"

Will rubbed his right shoulder with his left hand. "I know they do. Who wouldn't hate their kid for trying to kill the leader of the city? But they didn't care about me even before that."

A sudden knot in Ember's throat hurt. She grappled with the intensity of Will's burden. She felt his defeat, his embarrassment.

"That's not true. I never got to meet your parents, Will. But I know there was never any kind of problem between you and them. You would have told me. Serpio has lied and made you believe it. Don't."

Clutching his body as if to hold it together, Will backed away a few feet, bumping into a worktable stacked with weird tools. He stayed, flattening his torso tightly up against it. "That's easy for you to say. You can't possibly understand how much I went through. I was *tortured*. And brainwashed! Most of the time, I can't tell what's true and a lie anymore."

How awful that must be, Ember thought. He didn't have his parents to help. Wee, his dearest buddy, wasn't here yet. And if he didn't even remember any of them?

She was Will's only trusted friend right now. She would have to be the reality messenger and his support. She needed to bring him back to genuine reality—fill in the memories, repair the bleeding soul. In Will's current state, though, she was uncertain he would believe what even she had to say. Yet carrying all Will's bulky emotional baggage was weighing her down. One thing Tranquility got right. Negative emotions were denser than the positive ones. And the fear, doubt, and bewilderment Will was feeling were dark, thick, and cloudy.

She sighed and ventured forth with her encouragement. "I mean—I don't know how your parents feel about you being the most wanted man in Tranquility, but they were proud of you. Proud of all you'd accomplished." She crossed the distance between them and then reached out and patted his arm. Behind her, Xander became the green-eyed monster, his possessiveness like an arrow to her concern for Will.

Will conceded a smile, but it was undeniably strained. He picked up a chrome tool from the table and blew dust off it. Cosmic particles reduced to white, useless residue.

Placing her hand over her heart, Ember held his gaze. "You have to go there, Will. In *person*. Right away. Explain. Tell them our story. Make sure they're all right. Afterward, we can bring them here so they can hide with us."

Xander's face unexpectedly melted into sympathetic lines, his eyes narrowing and his eyebrows pulling down in concentration as he talked to Will. "My parents will take care of themselves. You def need to warn *your* parents. Now. With Serpio out for revenge, they'll be jammed up for sure. If they care about you —and I'm sure they do—they're legit upset right now seeing your face plastered on every street corner and news story."

Striding away from the table that had seemed to function as his support, Will walked directly into the center of the three of them. "You're right. They're going to be on Serpio's agenda if they aren't already. I'm ready to do what it takes. We have to have an airtight plan though. I will *not* be captured again!" Will's right hand made a fist, and he slapped his left hand on top of it.

Ember's heart clenched, feeling Will's worry. "You're right. It's risky. But if something happens, I'll be there. Your mission is my mission. I'm not staying behind. I'm going with you."

FOURTEEN

Will's Parents

"SERIOUSLY? You'll go with me to my parents'?" Will didn't know whether to be thrilled or mortified by Ember's suggestion. To be alone with Ember again? It also made him nervous. They'd be by themselves for the first time since he was captured, and the situation would be awkward.

On the other hand, he wouldn't admit it to anyone, but he was terrified to go by himself. The thought sent a quiver up his spine and made him sweat. If Ember didn't go, though, he didn't like his other options.

And when he saw his parents … would he know them? Would they be happy to see him? A voice suddenly drummed in his head, "Your parents do not love you," and a quick mental flash of a metal room sent an electric buzz through his body.

Before Will could fully process any of his thoughts, Kamar interrupted. "Guys, I'm going up top to open the shop. I just got a notification about a malfunctioning Level One C-car. I can't keep the shop closed any longer during business hours. Ember, you work out what you need to do and let me know." Kamar jumped on the lift and disappeared into the ceiling.

Xander was clenching his hands and lowered his voice to a soft growl. "We barely got disguises, and you're already itching to try yours out? Ember, you going with Will is not safe. He needs to go *alone*! They're his parents, after all."

Will's emotions danced between fury and embarrassment. *Going with Will is not safe? What did Xander think? That he would jeopardize Ember's safety?* He would rather die.

Grabbing his arm not so gently, Ember drew Xander a few yards away with a peek back at the topic of conversation.

Even with the distance, Will caught the words. Ember's whisper twined itself around his ears, her voice always like a siren's song. "You can't be that heartless. After all Will has been through?"

Yeah. Throw me a bone.

Some of Xander's words disappeared, but the gist was there. "Look … that he's … not quite right?"

Will made a pretense of innocence, heading in what he hoped was the perfect ruse toward the open cupboard across the room. He did need water, after all. He took off on a trot in that direction and pointed to the cabinet. Approaching the two, he asked, "Water?"

Ember glanced at Will and gave him a thumbs-up, so he continued on past, now hearing Xander, who didn't seem to care. His voice was raised in angry tones, so it traveled and echoed. Not surprising for a place made of stone. Or a person who might as well be.

"Do we honestly want him out there wandering about, making decisions? What if he gets confused? And what if you both get caught? Then it won't matter about Will's parents. The whole house of cards will come crashing down."

A "shhhh" from Ember sounded like a thick rush of steam.

At the infamous cupboard where the door was propped open, Will grabbed a trio of bottles, tucked two under his arm, and turned to see Xander running his fingers through his hair, jerking through a knot at the end of a clump. Will started his return with a slow pace, wondering just how much more awkward this was going to get. On the way, he opened a bottle and drank deeply, keeping his steps slow to catch the conversation.

"There's no way I'm letting just the two of you go," he heard Xander growl. He saw him shake his head with an exaggerated back and forth motion. "Im-poss-i-ble. If you insist on going, then I'll go with you."

"You can't. Someone has to be here to coordinate Phoenix's arrival." Ember faced him directly and rubbed her hands up and down his arms. "Wait. You aren't jealous, are you?"

"Jealous? Of Will?" He chuckled. The right side of Xander's mouth twisted up. "It would be easier to be jealous of Serpio." He nodded in Will's direction. "Look at him. Sadly, he's damaged goods."

As Xander looked his way, Will blinked to confirm his perception. He could swear the disapproval in Xander's eyes softened. Could Xander maybe feel compassion for him? Even if it was more like pity, he'd take that for now. He would have to prove himself. He could not be a victim, but a victor. Taking another swallow of water, he felt it cascade down his throat and envisioned it being liquid strength and resolve.

"That's my point. He's hurting. I can feel his pain and see it. We have to help," Ember countered.

Xander put his hands on his head and threw them up in the air. "Ugh!"

Ember met Will as he approached. "Time to put a plan in place."

Will gave Ember his most charming smile, hoping she'd also feel his most positive emotions, whatever those were. With his feelings as volatile as they'd been, he didn't know what he was feeling anymore. One thing was sure, though. Ember did, and that was weirdly reassuring. She was his true north.

Ember smiled back at him. "Can you remember where your parents live?"

He frowned, wracking his brain, as he chewed on a piece of

rough nail crowning his forefinger. *This is ridiculous. Why would I not know where my own parents live?*

"When we were … together, you told me they lived in White Sands." Ember said.

Then, like a crack letting sunlight into a dark room, confusion disappeared, and he gave up the assault on his fingernail. "Yes! I remember! Where the lowest class lives. I know the address. I'll find it in no time if I'm in the front seat," Will said, his spirits soaring.

"Front seat? Is that a wish? Because it's not practical." Xander crossed the room as he spoke, over to the two patchwork cars Kamar had built, parked on the edges of the interior. "Didn't Kamar say he built these cars just in case he'd need them?" He ran his hands worshipfully over a blue C-car.

"I don't understand the point of those, really. I mean, great hobby and all, but how would he even get those out of here?" Ember cruised over to where Xander was examining the C-car, popping the trunk and peering inside.

"Didn't—didn't—" Will shook his head, trying to get words out of his mouth. "Didn't Kamar say he could make more over time? We could have a whole fleet of these to use."

"Yeah. Over time, Will. That's one of the many things we don't have." Xander glanced at Will, a look he recognized as Xander's disdain masquerading as impatience. "Serpio isn't going to wait until we're all set to find ways to attack us."

Fidgeting with the ends of her hair, Ember said, "We can't be seen in the car. Even in our new disguises, I think it's risky. I don't think they're stopping CommuteCars or business vehicles yet, but if they don't, they're stupid."

Will quipped, "Well, we could always ride in the trunk."

Xander's eyebrows lifted. "Brilliant!" he said without any trace of sarcasm. "Yes, you can. Totally hidden."

The squeak of the lift descending into their sanctum heralded Kamar's presence. He bounded over to them, his face alight with glee. "That malfunctioning car coming in? Good news. I can fix it quick and return it. You can hitch a ride. It has to go back to White Sands, though."

"Perfect!" Ember exclaimed, giving Kamar a high five. "That's where Will's parents live."

Will sat back down in the chair, pressing his hands into the armrests and his heels into the floor as hard as he could. That was the best way he could do a reality check. Otherwise, he was beginning to think this was all a recipe for disaster.

FIFTEEN

Xander's Eureka

KAMAR HAD JUST JUMPED BACK aboard the lift when he called out, "Hey! Almost forgot!" He hit his head with his hand. "Got a brand-new message from Ava—'Cars on the west side will be the first to be repaired.' That means they're now searching one section of the city at a time. Serpio only has so much manpower. Fifty Sciolists are not enough to canvass everywhere at once, so they're concentrating their efforts. But that's a help to us. We know where to start."

"Oh no! No! The west warehouse is where my mom is, and Wee!" Ember swayed on her feet enough that Xander reached out to steady her. "If they get caught …" She leaned against Xander briefly and then stood ramrod straight, her lips pressed together.

Xander gnashed his teeth and clenched his hands. "Phoenix's west warehouse is a priority, then. But if it's crawling with Sciolists? It'll be high-risk. Our crew can't just walk out of there. Or get here on foot."

This latest crapstorm was getting unmanageable, a hurricane he was trying to hold back with one hand. They had made it through so much, but the odds were mounting against them. So many people to move, and no real help. He plopped down on the floor, his head in his hands.

Kamar gave them an apologetic expression. "Look, guys. That car's coming any minute. I'll be back as soon as I can," he added on his way back up.

The familiar whoosh of the lift somehow gave Xander a sense of security, and yet the basement walls seemed to close in the longer they were there. He couldn't shake the feeling of being buried alive in the stone sanctuary. The dimness, the cold, and the lack of doors and windows were creepy.

Ember placed her hand on Xander's head. "The way I see it is this," she said, her voice matter of fact. "I'll communicate with my mom to let her know we can shelter Phoenix here. Xander, you go to the warehouse to make plans. Will and I will go to find his parents."

Although he hated this idea, Xander had to make some concessions. Ember was right, unfortunately. It was the only way to start the relocation, which now was pretty much a full-on emergency. "Balls! Okay. I'm on board."

Unwinding himself off the floor, he stood. He wanted to tear out his hair at the thought of Ember going out of here without him, but he also knew none of them could stay in a protective shell.

Approaching him with her arms outstretched, Ember embraced Xander and then released him. "I know what you're feeling. But this is for the best."

Usually, Ember's affection tied him into a secure superhero persona, but despite the warmth her arms left behind, he suddenly felt lonely in his own skin.

"The first thing is finding out how we can get our people here without them being captured. I have no idea how to do that," Xander confessed. His neck muscles tightened, and an additional unexpected surge of panic assailed him. What if they couldn't get them out? Was Phoenix creating plans of their own to evade the Sciolists? How would that work with all the warehouses?

All of a sudden, Will became animated, talking with his hands as if he were whipping up caffeinated excitement. "We could set up a distraction! Use someone or some information as bait. Draw the Sciolists away from the west warehouse. If only we had some bombs." Will's forehead pulled together, and he pursed his lips. "We did have bombs … right? I'm remembering something?"

"Yes, Will! You're remembering! Wee had bombs, and he set them off at City Hall. You had to have been there at that time." To Xander's dismay, Ember looked like she had just won first prize in a sympathy competition. As she spoke, each word seemed to carry a little light within it.

Will's face brightened, and he tilted his head to survey the ceiling as if the memories scrolled across it like a cinematic movie. "Yeah. Yeah! I was! Feren was injured. Serpio was pissed … but didn't dive under the table like the rest of us. It was weird. He was pissed but not worried for his safety."

"So even then the Magistrate wasn't worried about dying?" Ember's thought, spoken aloud, had suddenly also just crossed Xander's mind.

"There *is* something about him, then. Our Magistrate survived his killing because he *literally* can't be killed. Let that sink in for a minute." Xander's remark generated a shocked silence, as if, indeed, the reality fairy had transformed Will and Ember into deaf-mutes.

"Well, we have to figure out how to kill him! He's a danger forever if we don't." Will brought his hand to his eye. At first, Xander thought he was maybe wiping away a tear but then saw Will was trying to subdue the tic that had started again.

"Agreed, Will. But right now, we've got to be people movers."

Killing Serpio was still Xander's life-long goal, but in the meantime, he rolled up his sleeves, ready to get to work on the warehouse transfer. He knew, though, that the effort would be more brain, less brawn. It was a matter of outfoxing the Sciolists.

As if Ember could hear his thoughts, she said, "It's going to take too long to figure out how to use bombs. And they're only a distraction, not a way to transfer people." She grabbed her hair with her hands and brought it around to one side of her shoulder, as if changing it up might switch on more ideas. "We need to brainstorm other options."

As usual, Will watched her, the longing in his eyes making Xander feel embarrassed for him. He had a mad urge to throttle the guy, but also a compassion for everything he might be feeling. This guy had pretty much lost everything—his reputation, his girlfriend, his Status, his memories—and that was okay for someone as cavalier as himself. But for Will, it had to be devastating.

Will's fainting spell earlier weighed on his mind. *Was it physical or mental?* he wondered. He didn't want to make a big deal about it, but keeping an eye on Will was going to have to be a priority.

Before Xander could ask Will if he was still feeling okay, Kamar's lift shimmied down. "Got the car. It only needed one part replaced. Easy fix. Have you solved all our problems?"

"Yeah. *All* the problems. Of course," Xander replied with his customary snark. If only. "Actually, we made decisions. Ember and Will plan to leave to save Will's parents from whatever Serpio's cookin' up for them. You and I will mastermind the west warehouse exodus." A glint shone in Xander's eyes. "Kamar! You have these junkers—and the trackers are disabled, right?"

Kamar rubbed his chin. "That's why I built those bad boys," he cracked, gesturing to his creations. "GPS-free and painted for higher Status. Less scrutiny if it's a Level Fourteen and above."

"I can take it to the warehouse, then," Xander said. "I'll join them, and we'll plan how to move everybody."

"The purple car here is ready to go. Even if the Plauditors catch it, which they probably won't because it's off the radar

completely, you can drive it back here, and it will virtually disappear. No one will know where it went."

"Like Serpio's dead body transport vehicle. It's not tracked. It
only shows up infrequently on someone's camera," Will volunteered, immediately looking as if he'd surprised himself with the
comment.

Xander pointed his finger at Will, nodding. "Right!"

"It does get reported, though," Will warned.

With his hand on his toolbelt, Kamar reminded Xander,
"Don't get too excited. This could be a real disaster, you know.
All it takes is for someone to officially 'notice' a car has no
tracking device, and we're all in trouble. The whole mission
could fail. Miserably."

"It's a chance we have to take," Ember said with the
demeanor of a chief executive. "I'll connect again with my mom
and let her know Xander's coming."

Kamar rolled his shoulders and drew his mouth into a
straight line before wincing. "You'll leave before Will and Ember,
Xander. Are you ready?"

"I'm ready!" Xander blurted, rubbing his hands together.
"Get those cars ready to roll!"

SIXTEEN

Ember's Goodbye

AS IF HE were choosing a car for himself, Xander wandered over to where Kamar's reconstructed cars lined the far walls of the basement. Ember could hear him running his fingers across the sides of the vehicles, making silly squeaking sounds before he stood to admire the most modern bright purple one. With its sharp angles and V-shaped hood, it was the epitome of a teenage boy's dream.

Will had found a rubber ball and was bouncing it against a wall across the room, its rhythmic thump comforting. She hoped it was just as therapeutic for Will as it was for her.

Ember sat down smack dab in the middle of the basement floor in a crossed-legged position to conjure a connection with her mom. This time, she buried all her doubts about her ability and was easily able to perceive her mom's "channel." She focused until the conversation in the basement dimmed and the surrounding emotions receded, opening her mind to only what was inside.

"Xander's coming soon," she conveyed to her mom. *"He'll be working with you to get everyone here somehow."*

Satisfied with her mental message, she made her way over to Xander. He wasn't quite all set to go—he had no disguise on his head yet but wore the uniform for the shop, which would define him as legit when he ventured out. Immediately, she noted his self-assurance tangled up with regret. Knowing him as she did, she knew he could hardly wait to leave and yet was conflicted at leaving her behind.

"Shouldn't you—" Ember started.

"Get my wig and mask on," he supplied as he made a straight line to where his gear lay on the adjacent worktable. Taking them in hand, he returned with a grin that quickly turned into a somber tightening of his lips. "You know I'm coming back. I refuse to believe this trip will be disastrous. But right now, I hope you kiss me like it's for the last time."

Leaning into him, she wrapped her arms around his neck as he bent his face to hers. The kiss ignited an inner heat, a slow burn that turned her legs to rubber and launched her pulse into overdrive.

Breaking off the kiss, she asked, "When are you leaving?"

"In a minute or so. Kamar's finishing some things upstairs, and then we'll roll the car onto the platform, and I'll be off."

Xander slipped his mask over his head, tucking the edges of the neck under his mechanic's uniform and adhering it to his face. The mask was high-quality silicone that felt and fit like real skin, so he was able to move his mouth to speak, although he kept patting the lips to firmly hold them in place.

Each time one of them said Kamar's name, it was as if he was programmed to react on cue. The lift descended, and there was Kamar leaning over the railing, already barking instructions. "Flip the switch on in Purple over there. Get it lit up."

A smile burned bright on Xander's face, and he sprinted over to power up the polished, plum-colored sedan.

Will motioned to Ember and cried, "C'mon!" as if she needed an invitation, their steps pounding against the floor like last-place track stars.

Instantly, a low rumble indicated vibration, and then the car fell silent, just like a good CommuteCar should. Xander threw his fist in the air. "Running!"

Kamar strode over from the lift, his face alight. The dashboard flashing on his purple dream-come-true car was no rival for his glow. *A real victory for Kamar,* Ember thought. *His cars are going to help save Phoenix.* She wondered briefly, though, if Kamar was going to be jealous that the first run of this car wasn't going to belong to him.

"Get in," Kamar commanded to Xander. Xander wasted no time scrambling into the vehicle and pushing the release button to roll down the window. "Now, give instructions like you did with the MediCar. Without GPS, you gotta tell it what to do. It will only respond to you because you're in the front seat—not our voices, but yours. And it won't talk back to you, either."

"Got it." He looked at Kamar, his eyes shining.

"We're not raising wheels here. Just getting it to the lift. So, tell it to pull out from the wall and turn east, speed of One. When it gets to the platform, tell it to stop." Kamar lightly slapped Xander's shoulder.

"Pull out, Speed One, turn east." At Xander's command, the coupe engaged and rolled into the room, headed for the hoist quickly, even at the lowest speed. Inches from the lift, Xander yelled, "Stop!"

Following closely behind, the remaining trio cheered until Kamar spoke. "Shut it off. The three of us are gonna push it onto the platform."

Ember sucked in a quick breath. The C-car looked heavy. "Seriously?" But she took her position at the back with the others. Several heaves, and Kamar's masterpiece sat proudly on the upward-bound conveyor.

"Now what?" Xander "When I get up there, I can tell it where to turn to go to the warehouse, right?"

"Right." Kamar hopped onto the platform, squeezing himself next to the car. "Up we go. I'll make sure this thing gets out of the shop properly, and then I'll make sure our car for White

Sands is ready for its return trip. Ember, Will, better get those disguises on. You'll be in the trunk, but you'll need to be new people when we get to the neighborhood."

Will cleared his throat. "Yeah, yeah. Okay. See you, Xander, when—when you—we—get back. Safe travels, buddy." He took a breath as he rubbed his hands up and down his pant legs. It didn't take an Empath to see Will become nervousness personified.

Ember blew kisses, each one carrying the weight of the world. Sometimes, she just wanted to be the textbook model of the perfect citizen. "Bye, Xander. Good luck!"

The steel lift began its ascent, and Xander waved at them before closing the window, a conveniently gray-tinted obtuse triangle.

Worry worms crawled through Ember's arteries. She knew her fears wouldn't help Xander, but it seemed she was always watching him go pell-mell into dangerous situations without a second thought. What if it really was the last time she ever kissed him?

As she tried to pull herself together, she realized Will was speaking. "C'mon. We need to get our disguises on, too. Kamar said he wouldn't be taking too long to get everything ready."

Fifteen minutes later, the duo had their new clothes and wigs on, with the exception of their masks. They could put those on later, before they'd have to emerge from the car. No point in being uncomfortable for the ride; they were going to be in the trunk, after all.

Will's disguise turned him into a middle-aged, dark-haired man with a paunchy belly. Ember felt transformed into a woman four times her age, but as silly as they looked, it wasn't humorous. It was coming down to survival.

SEVENTEEN

Xander's Purple Taxi

AS HE PULLED out of the garage, sitting in the deep bucket seat, Xander worried he wouldn't be able to control the car; he'd only had the MediCar and the "death wagon" experience. Not very good training. Then he dealt with a cold, hard fear that sat like a lump in his stomach.

He'd been putting on a show of bravado in the shop, hiding his nerves under a forced self-assurance. Only Ember would notice that his insides didn't match his outsides. For a while, his brain pinged with the truth: everything rested on him. If the pickup wasn't successful, he would be responsible for every single life that would fall into the Magistrate's hands, not to mention his own certain death. Serpio would be done playing games.

But six miles out, Xander began to relax. Once he'd mastered the C-car's dash and its myriad of buttons and tried out various commands for speed, old Purple seemed like a good friend. His fear of discovery began to dissipate. The streets had few CommuteCars. Odd, perhaps, for a workday, but then again, he'd never paid much attention to that. So far, everything was working in his favor.

Kamar's plan was for him to drive the backroads and travel

at relatively high speed. Without the GPS, he didn't know how far he needed to go, but he knew when and where to turn, thanks to the mechanic's final guidance. He stretched his backbone to its full length, and a smile ruffled his lips as he realized the current trek was nothing compared to the adventures he'd already had.

A right on Rapture Road and three more turns, and he'd be at the warehouse. But around the corner, reality slapped him in the face. There, parked on the side of the narrow street, was a Sciolist's vehicle, its broad light bar flashing white and red. Two Sciolists stood outside.

A shiver shimmied up his bones. *Holy Shazz. I'm screwed!* He didn't know whether to gun it and shoot by in order to put them in his rearview mirror as fast as possible or slow down to ease his way by carefully. A sheen of moisture formed underneath his mask, and his palms wept. *If I'm stopped, I have no ID.*

"Speed Two," he commanded the car, noting the immediate heaviness of decreasing speed as its wheels descended to meet the ground.

As he approached, gravel crunching under his tires, he noticed a third person stood in the street, and one of the Sciolists appeared to be speaking to the unknown guy while the other gestured to Xander to keep moving forward.

Looking at the subject they questioned, Xander gasped, a tiny, abrupt intake of fear-tainted air. The person was shorter than he was—and not as good looking, he thought with a shred of arrogance—but other than that, the detainee matched so many of his own physical characteristics: slightly shaggy black hair, a somewhat muscular frame, and dark eyes. The unfortunate individual was, sadly, dressed in white, his Status making him even more of a prime suspect. It was easy to see they thought they had found *him*, Xander Noble, roaming the streets, a fugitive for the taking. He looked more closely, hoping that, indeed, it wasn't a member of Phoenix. But it was not; of that, he was sure.

Although his heart went out to the guy, it was a lucky break, a distraction that would keep the Sciolists occupied as he drove by. He drew closer and gave a gentle wave to the red-caped inquisitors. Only a little farther, and he would be past them all.

But his lack of disturbance was short-lived. The taller of the two Sciolists stepped out into the road and gestured for him to stop. *Holy Shazz. Now what?* He looked down foolishly as if to make sure he was still wearing the uniform from Kamar's shop, a verifiable reason to be in the control seat of a C-car.

He was "just delivering the car back to its place of origin," he rehearsed in his head. Now that he thought about it, though, he didn't want any doubt cast on Kamar, and he wished he'd chosen to wear his awkward costume instead, even if he'd have had to conjure up a story.

Once the car was stopped completely, the Sciolist rounded the front to hover by the side window. Xander addressed the dashboard, "Open the left window." The window squeaked slightly as it rolled down into the pocket, making him wince with its less-than-perfect performance.

"Hello?" Xander addressed the official.

The Sciolist, all six feet of him, coppery hair shining in the midmorning sun, squinted his eyes and greeted Xander with a characteristic monotone voice. "What is your name, citizen?"

"Finlay Apricus." The name rolled off his tongue as if he'd been born to it.

The man eyed the label on Xander's uniform. "Mechanic, Level Seven. You have to manually pilot this CommuteCar, is that correct? Seems odd."

"Car just came in. Its control panel's pretty damaged—"

"Spare the details!" he snapped. "You fix cars. I understand that. Now, sorry to inconvenience you at your job, but we're hunting the fugitives you've heard about."

Xander knew the Sciolist was certainly not sorry, but it was something halfway human to say, at least.

"Of course. I'm happy to help any way I can! But I'm on a tight schedule. I have to get this car back to the Level Fourteen

CommuteCar base. Then there are others waiting. I sure don't want to let people down. It wouldn't be kind at all." He smiled, his teeth hidden partly by the lifelike latex on his upper lip.

"You need to step out of the car." The Sciolist Xander had mentally named Rusty used an animatronic tone.

His mask suddenly felt suffocating, as if some other human was trying to take over his body. *Stall. Stall. Please don't let them ask for my Alt.* "So glad to see you out doing such an amazing job. I'm sure you'll catch those outlaws soon enough." Then, gesturing to his doppelganger, he said, "Is that one of 'em? Sure looks like that Xander fellow."

A buzz on the Sciolist's Alt caught the ginger's attention. Reading the message, his lips tightened. He swiveled to see the other officer beckoning him. "We've been called to assist the Magistrate. Finlay, get on your way. Be watchful, and report anyone suspicious." The agent made a full turnabout and hurriedly joined his fellow soul crusher.

Beyond the nudge to his conscience, Xander felt he'd passed a fictitious test qualifying him for secret agent. He purged his guilt over the poor innocent getting raked over the coals by remembering it was more than just his own skin he was saving. A ragged breath escaped past his rubberized lips, but the tension in his muscles would take time to release.

He commanded the car, "Speed Five." He needed to get out of there. The vehicle lurched ahead, tearing down the street to reach the next turn.

He wasn't sure he wasn't a Sciolist's topic of conversation. His ears burning, he sped down the road on his way to the warehouse. Within what seemed like moments, he reached it, a carrot-colored monstrosity tucked into the furthest point in the Orange Glen section of town.

EIGHTEEN

Serpio's Target

RIGHT AFTER THE Elite congress left, Serpio brushed his hands against each other as if to dust off caked dirt. Talking to the Elite, especially today, was a nasty business. His plans were always easier to implement if he didn't have to convince them he was right. It was too bad the Tranquility Accords had constructed an Elite at all. He would be better off if he could simply make decisions on his own. He'd often written about that in his personal journals.

For the first time since he had reawakened to life, he sat in his designated chair, thinking about all the disasters that had recently occurred. Before he knew it, several hours slipped away.

Even before his "death" in the arena, things had not been adding up for a while. He'd stretched his brain into more contortions than he thought he could, trying to figure out how the fugitives had escaped every situation. *There has to be a mole.*

Is it Feren? She was his top advisor and knew him better than any other Elite, and she had the keys to everything in the city. But her whereabouts during the events in question made it impossible for her to be responsible for the things that had gone wrong.

And then there was Ava. Such a trusted Elite member, he had

allowed her access to the most sensitive information. She'd been loyal to a fault and always respectful and cooperative. Intelligent and his top Medic. His confidante in times of uncertainty.

No, it couldn't possibly be Ava. Not with her dedication to the Accords, her tireless devotion. There were never any signs of betrayal, not ever. It was unthinkable. He could not believe Ava could be so black-hearted as to help the most heinous enemies of his life. Yet …

Ava had been at Xander's crash scene. He had personally tasked her with making sure Xander would not survive his injuries. She had assured him she would take care of it, all the way down to secretively disposing of the body. And yet, Xander had lived— lived to become a real threat and—he spat—Ember's lover.

Ava had volunteered to recalibrate the Alts. And after that? There were suddenly no Alt connections to anyone missing. As a matter of fact, Ava was the one who had delivered food and supplies to the Plauditorium during the hostage situation. She had begged him to do it, as if she were some compassionate angel accusing him of not doing the right thing.

Was it then at the Plauditorium that she enabled the rebels and the Plauditors to evade capture?

And Ava was in a position of power within the Elite, having the ability to listen and persuade. As a trusted Elite, no one would ever suspect her of espionage.

She was somehow everywhere the turncoats were, and those were just the situations he knew about.

His blood boiled as he thought of her betrayal. He wanted to rip her eyes out, but then she would miss seeing all the things that were to come.

The question was whether to arrest her legitimately or get rid of her some other way. Having Ava "disappear," however, would stress the Elite, and he needed them focused and ready for fights ahead. There was much he planned to ask of the Elite, and Ava would serve well as an example to the others to keep their loyalty in place.

Now that he saw the trail, it should be easy to find evidence. Not only would he bring her to justice, but he could squeeze vital information out of her.

A quickening in his chest accompanied an intoxicating thought: Ava would know where Ember was! He sighed with satisfaction and breathless anticipation, his inner being already burning with the passion he stored away for the little redhead. His plan to have her completely under his control once again made him giddy. This time, she would be his.

He stood and walked with purpose over to the mirrored wall in the chamber. Once there, he straightened his shirt collar, running his fingers over the creases, and made sure his suit buttons were secure. No thread could be out of place. Just as nothing in Tranquility should ever be out of place.

Should he punish Ember when he found her? As much as she deserved to be disciplined for running away and conspiring with the others, he would never cause her harm. She was too valuable for that.

He tilted his head as he took stock of himself in the mirror.

The others would be brought to justice, just like Ava would be. Tranquility would not tolerate traitors. He loved how he had almost killed Xander and Will, the uniqueness of the scheme, and how the Elite embraced the project. How clever he had been to manipulate the Elite into the fight at the arena. And it had been so easy. If he could do that, he could effortlessly persuade them to do other things to his liking.

The fact that he had failed in the end merely spurred him on. He was ready to ignite his imagination again for an ultimate showdown.

Admiring his hair and facial features made him smile before he began to pace, his attention focused on the decisions he must make.

Serpio wasn't sure what he wanted most. To expose Ava? To capture Will and Xander and mete out punishment? To repossess Ember and be free to do with her what he wanted? Or to get his journals back to keep his secrets safe. The list of goals and needs multiplied each day, and it was making him crazy. Barely a moment went by when he wasn't feeling a quiver in his stomach or a prickling of the scalp, an unease like a monster reaching out its claws.

On his OmniCom, he clicked the button to summon his top Sciolists, who were busy stopping pedestrians and C-cars in the western quadrant of Tranquility.

He had only to tell them what to do. "Leave your location. Arrest Ava Validus immediately. Bring her to City Hall."

The OmniCom lit up, the voice of Esryn answering, "Affirmative."

"You'll have to track her. She's already left the meeting today. Contact the Plauditorium to find out where she is on the radar. Have the Plauditors look for unusual movement to and from odd places at the same time. And if she's not at home, take advantage of her absence there. Check your Alt for what I'm sending now—the emergency key code and a Pelagus seal for official documentation to search her home. Look for anything that ties her to any of the criminals on the run, specifically camera footage, signs of guests staying there, extra food, any odd activity for a Medic. And look for my private journals! They have not yet been recovered and contain highly classified information."

"Certainly, Magistrate. If she resists?" Esryn pressed.

"I don't expect it, but if she does, spare no effort to bring her in." After all, pain had a purpose.

NINETEEN

Will's Retrieval

"WE'RE READY," Ember assured Kamar.

Will wasn't sure how "ready" they really were, but there was no putting this off any longer, although they'd both opted to postpone wearing their masks until they arrived at Will's childhood community.

Just getting on the lift and being upstairs again triggered Will's anxiety, but seeing that the shop's immense metal door was shut to the outside gave him a sense of security. That, and Ember was there. She made him feel solid.

A few moments later, he and Ember climbed clumsily into the trunk space of the white CommuteCar. Models fit for White Sands were small, so assembling themselves inside was an ungraceful challenge.

They faced each other, with Ember curled up under his right arm.

As the vehicle rolled out of the shop and its wheels lifted into the undercarriage, Will blew out a breath, his lungs almost bursting from unconsciously holding on to the air for so long. His soul warred with itself as his distress over the mission clashed with the exultation he felt being alone with Ember.

Alone and physically close. Close enough to breathe her scent and practically hear her heartbeat.

"Will," she said. "Your aura is yellow."

"Is that bad?" He wondered for a split second if being in love with an Empath was more stressful than pleasurable. If only he could hide his feelings, just once.

"Sometimes yellow shows that you're balanced, but lemon yellow, like you have now, is the color of fear. The fear of losing something."

"I can't deny it. There's a lot at stake here. My parents …" He wanted to just leave it at that and not discuss his worries and the whole yellow aura thing. Fear? Yes. He had lots of it for himself and for his parents. He also feared never having Ember as his own again.

Ember reached out and gave his shoulder a squeeze.

In spite of his worry, right now, he had Ember all to himself. She might already know what he was struggling with, but it was his chance to see how *she* was feeling about *him*. And about Xander.

He swallowed. "The past few weeks have destroyed everything I ever knew. It's a good thing I'm not being monitored by City Hall. My stress is making me sick inside. It colors everything I do. I'm worried everything I had is lost—my Status, my career, my security, my parents … but most of all, you, Ember."

There. It was out.

The object of his affection lowered her eyes before returning her gaze to him. "You haven't lost me, Will."

His pulse quickened. "What?"

"I know things are complicated. You went away and came back to find I'm with Xander. I—I'm sorry about that. Really. I hope you can forgive me. When I thought you'd gone to the other side and I was alone—I fell for Xander. Hard. I didn't want it. Didn't plan it. It just … happened. But it had nothing to do with you. I didn't stop caring about you. Not really. I knew that the minute you looked at me in the arena." Her eyes misted, and a sad smile crossed her face. "But what I feel for each of you is different."

Will grasped at the fragment of hope flaring in his heart. "Different? What do you mean?"

"You're my first love, you know? An innocent love. I know it's only been a short time since we were a couple, but it seems like it's been a thousand years. When we met, I was a different person. I couldn't stand on my own two feet without you. It didn't hurt that you're all kinds of hot and sweet. So, I have this affection for you and a little bit of—" She bit her lip. "—a lot of—chemistry. It's like a schoolgirl crush kind of thing. But with Xander, it's high-level mutual respect with a fire underneath. It seems more authentic and more … physical?"

"So, let me get this straight," Will said, trying not to allow anger to flesh out his words. "You like me. A lot. But not enough to continue whatever we had before. I lost out to a brash bad boy you want to have sex with. Is that right?"

Ember closed her eyes, whether from shame or frustration, he didn't know. "That's pretty blunt, and that's not fair. You're oversimplifying this. Neither one of us is the same now as we were then. I still love you with the heart of my former self, and I always will, but neither of us is the same as we were a few weeks ago. To jump back into a relationship that has been dragged through a crapstorm wouldn't be a good idea, even if Xander wasn't in the picture. But he is, and even we're taking it one day at a time. Who knows if any of us will even survive what's to come?"

Grudgingly admitting to himself that much of what she said was true, he stayed silent, his mind a cavern of his own special torment. Why would Ember want him again anyway? He was certainly a shadow of his former self. A shell-shocked victim who actually fainted for no apparent reason. Hell, he could scarcely keep his hands from shaking or his heart from trying to run out of his chest at the tiniest disturbance.

Nevertheless, the determination and strength he had always

had would not allow him to give up. He was still deeply in love with Ember, and he would try every possible option to win her back.

He boldly reached out and ran his fingers through a tendril of her hair. She did not shrink away, but placed one of her hands over his. Her hand was warm, soft, and comforting.

"Could you let me try? Try to win you back?" Will's voice was a whisper.

"All's fair in love and war. I can't promise you that anything will change, but I am here. I will always be here." To his surprise, she tilted her face to his and kissed him softly. "A kiss for luck and for all you are."

Before Will could recover from the curveball she just lobbed, the C-car slowed and came to a stop.

Kamar's muffled voice boomeranged unintelligible words that could only mean they had arrived at White Sands. They slipped their masks on, but there was little time to make them perfect. A couple of quick bangs on the trunk was Kamar's signal to hustle.

Trees and shrubs were few and far between in White Sands, a concrete jungle of a neighborhood that no one cared to beautify. But in spite of his memory lapses, Will had brought to mind the one lonely tree just outside the back gate of his parents' home, a broad pine tree with glistening needles that he had never had a fondness for. Until now.

Sure enough, the tree's boughs swallowed them up as they scrambled from the trunk. Enough cover for them to slip underneath and unlatch the gate at the back before they were under a white aluminum canopy that served as the upscale design of the Level One cracker box homes.

They didn't have to look back to know their ride was already gone. They were on their own. They would have to rely on Will's parents' ability to call up a car for them to return.

With a sharp knock and no need to worry about locks in a

poor community like White Sands, Will pushed open the door to the tiny dwelling. "Mom?"

The interior was creepily silent, save the dripping of a faucet and the hum of the crappy KoolKrate; dim and shadowy, the only relief was the reflective white of the walls, empty of the Status-awarded "artwork." Something was wrong.

Although his parents had only a few tables and chairs, none except the small dining table were upright. It was as if a tornado had ripped through the interior. Family pictures that had sat proudly on a small credenza lay smashed into pieces. A shredded piece of white clothing lurked on the floor, the obvious souvenir of a high-level struggle.

Will held his palm over a small panel on the wall that activated the light fixture overhead.

"No! No light!" Ember scolded.

A swipe again, and it was off. But the illumination showed what they might have missed. Someone had smeared a twelve-inch-long cardinal streak across the inside of the door they had just entered. Blood also decorated the floor in polka dots of dark crimson. None of it was fresh.

Will felt his head grow light, as if it were a balloon finding its way to the sky. He swallowed, covering his mouth with his hand in hopes of slowing the insides of his stomach from revolting. "Ho-ly Shazz," he managed to whisper, his throat constricting with every syllable.

Covering her mouth with her hand and swaying slightly, Ember said, "Oh, Will. Your parents …"

Will couldn't stop his cheeks from burning. He moaned, "What have I done? How could I let this happen? We're too late. Now who knows where they are or what's happening to them?" Will crossed his arms to hold back the trembling in his hands.

Ember's eyes were like moons in the dark. She reached her arms around Will in a hug. "We will find them! There has to be a clue here somewhere."

Although he was grateful for Ember's warmth, he felt even more bereft when she released him. "Yeah," was all he could say.

For the next twenty minutes, they searched in the half-light. "I found … I found some hair." Ember held a clump of hair she'd pulled from the carpet. "Whatever happened, they didn't go willingly."

Will finally turned over a picture of himself with his mom and dad and gazed at it longingly. The photograph was certainly not a clue, but as he touched its surface, he somehow felt like himself. Just like the tuft of hair Ember held in her hand, tufts of memory wafted into his mind like a collage. Warm. Happy. Secure.

He walked the few steps to place the photograph on the dining table. There, against all odds, sitting perfectly in place on the table's surface, was a five-inch-long rock, about three inches high, with beautiful marbling of pink and silver swirls. Turning the semi-polished rock in his hands, Will wished the lump of granite could tell him something. Some clue—some information. He was as useless as the rock itself and, save for the few memories, just as brain dead.

Somehow, the stone felt good in his hands, a solid connection to his parents. Examining it more closely, he noted the silver running through it. Silver in a Level One home? No. It was only tin, of course. Couldn't even be aluminum because that was a more in-demand metal, used for the dome itself and to make things like the overhang outside the house.

With one more tumble of the rock in his hand, he dropped it back on the table, where it made a rough clunk as it made contact with the chipped laminated tabletop. All at once, he felt a unique sensation, as if only his brain was on a roller coaster in the plunge. Will picked up the stone again, and his eyes shone as brilliantly as the stone's silver.

"It's possible they only took Mom and that Dad's at work."

"You think that's possible?" Ember wondered if Will had just been granted some psychic ability.

A rush of energy polished his words. "When I was a little kid, I never wanted my dad to leave the house each morning to go to the quarry. So, through my whole childhood, each time Dad left for work, he placed this rock on the dining table as a guarantee that he would be home each day for dinner. Even after I moved out, he kept up the tradition. It marks his place at the table."

"Oh, Will! That's so great you remembered! I'm proud of you!" Ember gave him a spontaneous hug but let him go quickly. But the mask Ember wore couldn't hide her smile.

Will pressed his lips together, the mask's protest making a light squishy noise. "We have to find out if my dad's still at the dugout."

"I hate to say it, but if Sciolists took your mom, they wouldn't just leave your dad."

"I know. That's what I'm afraid of. But what choice do we have? We have to find out." Will clutched at his clothes before smoothing them out again. The tic in his right eye began a new bombardment. At this point, he wished he could simply disappear, never to discover what horror had happened to his parents.

"Agreed. But getting to the quarry? We have no transportation. We can't walk … and it's so dangerous!"

Will paced for a few minutes, caught up in his own misery. They had disguises but no Alts. No way to contact Kamar or anyone for that matter. What a disaster this was becoming. He lobbed meteors of potential disasters around in his brain. He finally righted a chair and sat, the tic in his eye more bothersome than ever. Then he noticed Ember had retreated a few steps away with her back to him. *Great. Now Ember is probably thinking I'm a problem. She's not even talking to me.*

A hand clap, like a three-beat mini applause, interrupted his dejection. "Will! I connected with Mom. I told her we were stranded. She's relaying a message to Kamar."

Of course! He watched her concentrate with her eyes closed, thinking how weird it must be to communicate only inside your head. Leaving the chair, he stood next to her, as if by being close he could hear the words.

"He's coming back! He just grabbed a C-car and is on his way!"

His knees buckled slightly; this time, not to faint, but to accommodate the relief that flooded his body. "That's incredible! What would we do without Kamar?"

"More—what would we do without my mom?" Ember said, her gratefulness so extreme it was almost tangible.

"Or you," Will added. "You're what holds everything together. Like glue."

"I've been called better things," she responded.

"Yeah? I'm sure that's true. But that explains why you'll never get rid of me, either." Will touched her on the arm.

"What? Why?"

"I'm part of that everything."

TWENTY

Ember's Stunner

EMBER DROPPED her eyes to the floor, embarrassed that Will thought she could hold him together. That was a tall order.

The moment passed when Will left his self-confessed dependence behind and went to peer out the shades in the back window. "We'd better be ready the minute we see a car outside."

"I've never been out to the quarry. What's it like?" Ember envisioned something like the pits of hell being ravaged by a mechanical machine resembling a steel creature with a giant mouth.

"It's noisy. If you listen, you can hear it from here. I haven't been there in a long time. When I was a kid, it was exciting, but as I grew up, the racket got on my nerves, so I didn't want to go with my dad anymore."

"What does your dad do there? Does he dig or work underground?" *That would be hard and dusty work,* Ember thought.

"No. No one does the digging. It's all automated, just like cars. Dad does a lot of analysis. He uses drones to map the mine areas and checks the mineral samples. It's actually not very physical. As long as he uses the data correctly, mining is easy. All the metals and minerals we use come from there. To keep resources from running out, there's a recycling plant, too."

Will craned his neck and then lifted the blind.

A flash of light across the curtain and the rough sound of wheels on the ground sent Ember's heart racing.

Sure enough, Will confirmed it. "Let's go."

As before, a white car sat beneath the tree camouflage, its fans whirring quietly. Kamar didn't have to tell them what to do; the trunk was open.

They dove inside, this time not finding it as awkward to pile in. The trunk's lid immediately shut, and they were plunged into darkness, save for a narrow pinprick of light illuminating the interior where the lid met the car's body.

"How far is it?" Ember asked.

"Not far. The powers that be intentionally positioned the quarry near the most undesirable neighborhood. Hence, the White Sands name, too."

"Good to know it's a short ride." Ember shifted and jiggled around in the narrow space, releasing her elbow from where it wedged under her hip. With that, the C-car lurched into forward motion. "Gah! Kamar!"

Will fidgeted by pulling up his legs. There was not enough room for him to fully stretch out. The extra padding around his stomach complicated their positions. "These masks and this added stuffing are hot. I already hate it."

"If you feel as awful as you look, that's bad." She giggled. "From beauty to the beast."

"I sort of remember that story," Will said. "Someone must have read it to me."

"Your mom, maybe?"

"Maybe … It's so frustrating that I can't remember. Serpio did a real gut job on my headspace."

Will suddenly frowned; Ember felt his emotions abruptly change from confusion to something far darker.

"What is it?"

"A memory. I don't know if it's a real thing."

"Memories are real, Will."

With a slight head shake, he tapped his rubberized lips with his fist. "I'm not sure, but I think my parents might have been in trouble before today."

"When?"

"When I was with Serpio. He ..."

The car slowed and came to a sudden stop. They had arrived.

* * *

MOMENTS LATER, they stood looking at piles of dirt, sand, and carved-out tiers. Dirt roads circled the area, winding in and out around equipment and mounds like some type of primitive maze. Clouds of dust generated from the digging machines suffused the air for a moment, until an adjacent giant steel fan sucked its particles away before new crushing activated a second round. Looking up, Ember viewed long, steel troughs and what looked like suspended railroad tracks fifteen to twenty feet in the air, obviously for transporting rocks or the minerals they contained.

Ember heard yelling back and forth among the workers, accented by backhoes scraping through the dirt, and then more yelling, this time directed at them.

"Hey! You! You can't be here on this property!" shouted a middle-aged man dressed in a dust-covered magenta uniform. The dull gray hair hanging out of his helmet was straggly and streaked with fuchsia accents. Walking briskly toward the two, the worker lowered his voice to a Tranquility-approved but assertive tone. "This is a restricted job site. We don't allow visitors."

Will spoke up, but the words stumbled awkwardly from his lips. "We don't want to be here, but we need clearance. We're looking for someone."

The quarryman's eyes swept over him and then Ember.

"Sorry. I don't want to cause you distress, but this site's prohibited for visitors, no matter what brings you here. And with fugitives out there, we can't be too careful." He then stared at them as if they were beings from another planet. "As a matter of fact, you could be rebels. You could be that girl—what's her name? I'll have to report this." The employee pushed his sleeve back to reveal his Alt.

"Wait!" Ember reached toward the guy's arm. "Please. We need your help."

"I can't help you. Sorry. Have to report this. As a matter of fact … you do seem like you're hiding something." He drew up to Ember, and before she could stop him, touched her face. "Why, your skin—it's not real. What the heck is going on here?"

Ember jerked back, her heart leaping out of her chest. "Please. Don't report us. This is a matter of life and death."

Will took a step forward. "We're looking for a worker here. His name's Jack Verus, and he's my dad. Would you happen to have seen him today?"

"Yeah. I know Jack. He's a great guy—one of the best around here."

Ember gasped as Will pulled off his mask. "Look, he's my dad. And he's missing."

Ember wanted to evaporate off the planet. What was Will thinking, revealing himself?

"You're one of them, those—You've been in the news! Will Verus …" The man took a step back, the realization hitting home. "But you're *Jack's* son?"

"Yeah. I am. And he's missing. My mom, too. I think they're in danger. I have to find them, and I mean you no harm. Please, can you help us?"

The man looked them up and down once more, as if he was trying to make up his mind whether to help or report them. "As a matter of fact, I haven't seen Jack today. Figured a sub was probably in for him." Finally, he said, "Follow me. I can see what's up." He called out to another worker, "Jeb! Watch my space?"

"Thanks so much, Mr.—" Ember began.

"Keep it simple. I'm Garth."

"I'm … Jane."

Dusting his pants off with his hands, he strode toward a small, corrugated metal building the color of sand a short distance away. "Here's headquarters. If he's here, they'll know where he is."

Inside, the place smelled stale, mixed with a weak blend of grease and metal. Garth walked past clear-walled rooms with robots inside manipulating what looked like metal pieces. A giant sign with "Caution: Live Extraction" in bright yellow and black could not be ignored. Its message made Ember shiver, wondering what they would be removing that needed an alert. Flashing lights attached to poles cast an eerie glow as they turned a corner toward a desk where several men and women sat in front of monitors, almost as if they were Plauditors. It was easy to see they were keeping an eye on the operations outside.

Garth approached the desk. "Hey, Dixie," he directed to a thirty-something female with drab blond hair and dramatic eye makeup. "You seen Jack today?"

"No. He didn't check in this morning."

Garth frowned before ironing out his forehead with his hand. He tapped the desk in front of the woman with his fingertips. "Okay, Dix. Thanks for your info."

With a shake of his head, Garth turned to them. "I'll walk the place with you, but we probably won't find him if he stopped coming to work. Instead, maybe you'd better hit up the Plauditorium for information."

Will shook his head. "Yeah. That can't happen."

Ember was more determined than ever to grill Garth for information. "Is there a place that Jack might go to—to hide?"

"Hide? From what?" Garth challenged.

"Maybe he needed some time to himself."

"Ha. Maybe." Garth motioned for the two to follow. "I can't be gone from my post much longer. That'll be it for my morning break. But I'll give you a short tour. Who knows? Maybe Jack will turn up somewhere. If not, better check his house and see if he's there. Just a thought."

Ember and Will exchanged meaningful glances.

He directed them to a small, black four-seater vehicle without a roof, structured by steel tubes arranged in the shape of a tiny, standard C-car but without any enclosure on the sides or front. Ember felt she was stepping into a giant bug that had magically morphed into a steel clone. It had tires, but eight metal bars acted like a cage over them and forked out over the sides resembling spider-like legs.

A touch of a button, and the buggy peeled away to traverse the quarry site, one dirt road at a time. Ember held on to the pipe that arched over her seat as they zigged and zagged from what looked like one dirt pile to the next.

At each stop, Ember and Will craned their necks, searching for Jack. The smell of fresh earth, clouds of dust, and the grind of equipment made the tour a miserable experience. Ember held her nose to keep from sneezing, knowing the result would be disgusting within her silicone mask. She shook out her "hair," too, the grit somehow settling into every nylon strand.

Garth called out to workers in the field to ask if they'd seen him, but a shake of the head always followed.

Finally, they pulled up to a pile of rocks, but Ember immediately observed they were not like the other organized piles they had seen. These were large stones and haphazardly jigsawed into an unsystematic heap. Just past the stone "wall," Ember could see a gap, an open hole at the top about a foot wide.

Sure enough, Garth pointed and commented, "This here's the entrance to a mine, but we haven't gone in there since the rocks fell down on the front a few days ago. No one even suspected a problem."

"Why'd it collapse, then?" Will sounded more curious than worried, but Ember knew otherwise.

"Mines cave in from lots of possible causes—leaks of poisonous gasses or explosive natural gasses, dust explosions, collapsing of mine stopes, mining-induced earthquakes, flooding, or mechanical errors from malfunctioning mining equipment. Use of improper explosives underground can also cause it."

Ember sucked in a breath and put her hand on Will's arm. She whispered, "I feel emotion coming from that mine."

"Did you say something, Jane?" Garth asked.

"No. Just talking to Will here. I said, 'It's interesting about the mine,'" Ember deflected.

"It's an issue. Our excavators and backhoes can't enter this area. Not until we know what the cause of the collapse was. That's gonna take some time. With the city in a dome, well … we have to be cautious." Garth's Alt chimed. "Ah. Tour's over—gotta head back. Sorry you didn't find Jack."

Before Garth turned the all-terrain buggy around, Will said, "You mind if we do some investigating on our own? We'd love to tell him about our visit when we do see him. Maybe we could put something in his locker as a surprise."

"You'd have to have permission from the head honcho to wander around on your own. It's dangerous. You need a hard hat and more protective clothing." Garth looked at Ember when he said that; her clothes were silly in a place like this.

Ember closed her eyes briefly. Desperation and sadness drifted into her consciousness from the mine. Pain, too—so severe it was as if her heart strings were cut to the quick. The emotions were tearing her up. They could not leave without finding out what was going on.

"Look, I know you have to get back to work. But is there any reason why someone might be still inside the mine?"

"Inside the mine? Well, no! It collapsed in the middle of the night. Luckily, no workers were here." Garth sounded a little irritated at this point, and he checked his Alt briefly and took a breath.

Will leaned forward from the back seat. "My dad is missing, and you didn't check the mine. Shouldn't you?"

"You're not serious. You think Jack's in the *mine*?" Raising his eyebrows, Garth pulled his head back. "That would be bad. Like I said, the mine's been closed up for the last four days."

Ember kept pushing. "Garth, you have to help! This might be a life-or-death situation.

"I don't know how we'd get him out if he was. Like I said, we can't get machines in there. Sometimes accidents can't be prevented here." With a glance at the heavens and a whispered counting backward, Garth seemed to be practicing a guided stress reliever. He'd turned into a Tranquility puppet, doing his best to avoid a negative situation.

Ember began freaking out, and she knew Will was about to burst at the seams. "Could you trust us to stay here while you go get some other workers now? You could bring human detection equipment at least. That's a start."

Garth ceased his zen exercise long enough to say, "Hmm. I can do that. I still doubt you're gonna find Jack. You realize the odds that he'd be in there, right?"

Will answered, "Yeah. The odds aren't good. If he isn't there, that's great. If he is, we can't wait another minute. You can be a hero, Garth, or you can be a failure."

With the idea that the tour had now become a possible rescue mission, Garth reverted to holding the company line. "I can't leave you here, though. It's against the rules. We'll all drive back to headquarters and then bring the others with the Passive Infrared Sensor."

"No. *We* stay. You go. Hurry up and bring the sensor!" Ember was adamant, surprising even herself with her forcefulness. Her gaze directed at Garth, she felt as if her eyes would bore through him. She needed time to figure out what her empathic radar was telling her. And Will was becoming a basket case beside her, now fidgeting and breathing short, shallow breaths. He couldn't lose it in the presence of a bunch of other people, not to mention that the less people they came in contact with, the better, for their own safety.

"If this is a wild goose chase, I'm gonna get my butt in a sling." Clearly ruffled now, Garth took deep breaths again and nodded. "I'll be back as quick as I can. Remember, even if we detect something, there isn't much we can do."

Garth spoke a command to their bug-like transportation, and Ember and Will jumped out, breathing the dust left behind as he drove away.

"Someone is in there, Will. I'm thinking it's Jack. What's scary is I'm getting way less emotion than I was even a few minutes ago. It's waning—barely there. And I feel more than one person."

"What?" Will blinked rapidly.

Not answering Will, Ember picked her way toward the top of the heap of rocks before them. A wave of helplessness crested over her as she surveyed the disaster. Several of the stones were oversized boulders, surrounded by a cascade of medium-sized stones gathered together so tightly they appeared fused. The enormous weight of the rock pile alone would require large machinery to move. Dangerous. Insurmountable. Yet filaments of emotion drifted through the rock, faded as the remnants of drifting smoke.

Then she saw it. A hand. Unmoving at the back of the pile, it jutted out from under the pile of rocks. Covered with dust and streaked with blood, it was as lifeless as the stone. Holy Shazz. She could practically smell death lurking alongside it.

Will stood behind her, running his hands through his hair and breathing heavily. He hadn't seen the hand yet, and already, she was aware he needed the physical comfort of a hug, but she had to abandon his needs. She couldn't be warm and fuzzy, and she needed to shield Will from what appeared to be a horrifying end for his parents, if indeed it was them under the avalanche.

Her frustration became an unmanageable adversary. How in bitter hell were they going to rescue people buried under rubble?

"What are you seeing? And feeling? Anything?" Will asked as he climbed up from rock to rock.

Instead of answering, she reacted. She kicked a small rock near her feet and watched as it pinged against another and rolled back to her once more.

Hopeless. Everything was hopeless. She grabbed the rock with her hand to lob it, but before it left her palm, it suddenly decomposed, sending bits of shattered stone, micro pebbles, and sand through her fingers. As she turned to see Will's reaction, she tried to close her open mouth, but the shock of what had happened kept her gaping.

Will grabbed her by the shoulders and shook her. "Ember! You can move the stones! You have the power! The auto shop basement wall. It wasn't a fluke!"

"I don't—don't know how!" Ember cried.

"Yes, you do. I have faith in you. Grab those bigger stones and see if you can move them."

Ember gritted her teeth and began to climb the pile, using the larger rocks as stepping stones. She placed her hands on the heavy boulders around her, putting pressure on the surfaces. To her amazement, each one fell apart like a cookie crumbling. With every stone, her confidence grew. She could do this! One rock after another, she sent to a dusty death, increasing her speed and angling for the gap that began widening at the top of the pile.

"Great job!" Will called out.

The time stretched into a fifteen-minute interval. She wondered how long it would take Garth to come back but worked away, finally disintegrating a jumbo-sized boulder. Sometimes, depending on the pressure she used, she could move large rocks away as if they were mere feathers. This was Kamar's power, she realized, but she was now, somehow, in possession of it.

Finally, she had cleared enough away that she could lean her upper torso inside. "Hello?" she called out. "Jack?"

Nothing.

"I don't hear anything, but I know people are in there!" She let out a huge breath.

"Shazz! Thank the stars you could clear the way! What can I do?" Will paced back and forth, at times placing his hands on his head, desperate to help. Moving one small rock at a time, he threw them aside.

Ember made a decision. She wanted to pull these people out before anyone else arrived. "I'm going to open this up! Just be ready to help when they emerge." It would take more work to allow herself or Will to go down or get the ones inside to come out. She wiped the sweat off her forehead; it wasn't that it was hard, really, but the speed and the tension of the moment made her weary.

Rock by rock, inch by inch, breath by breath. She at long last fully uncovered a body. Jack? "Is this your dad?"

"Oh!" Will rushed forward. "Dad?" Will scrutinized the man's face as if concentrating would bring certainty back.

Although she could feel his father's emotion, it was barely perceptible. Ember knew Jack was close to death when his feelings dipped to nothing and then emerged again in a miniscule trickle. The man's horrible condition suffocated his aura to a thin, faded outline. Covered in cuts, bruises, and dried blood, with his face swollen and pale, Jack looked more like Frankenstein than a real person.

Will reached for his wrist. "There's a pulse!"

Together, Ember and Will carried Jack out past the mass of rocks.

"There's someone else in there," Ember said. She could feel the agony, the sorrow and desolation radiating from down under the rocks, again ebbing away. "Will, help me."

Finally, there under more rubble, was Will's mom. If Ember thought anyone could be in worse shape than Jack and survive, she was wrong. Marina was barely breathing. Her wispy aura pressed tightly to her body was washed out, with barely any color. The woman was hanging on by a thread.

Ember looked around, frantic. Marina was far too fragile to even try to move. A shout from beyond the rubble was a welcome sound. Someone was coming.

TWENTY-ONE

Will's Reunion

"HELP! WE NEED HELP!" Will shouted. He looked at Marina and then looked frantically around for who had answered his call for aid.

Ember yelled, "Here! Here! Help!"

Footsteps pounding, two strangers rushed to Will's side, followed by a dozen quarry workers who came running, surrounding them and craning their necks to see what excitement was developing. Squawks and hollers of reassurances, typical of Tranquility folk, salted the scene.

Obviously not understanding the situation, a hard-hatted woman dressed in royal blue dungarees and matching work shirt looked them over. "Are you hurt?"

"No! No—we're not. Look!" Will motioned toward where his dad was. "Come—it's bad! Two people are injured and barely alive. In there." Will motioned to the duo to follow him into where Ember had created an opening.

Another employee ran forward with a cylindrical black object about two feet long. *A sensor*, Will thought. Garth had sent for that.

The responders hurried behind, each dropping to their knees, their faces grim, as they came upon first Jack and then Marina.

"Call a Medic!" the blue-clad woman screamed to her companions. "These people are critical!"

The woman's male companion, a Level Four, punched what looked like a code into his Alt. "Ruby, let's move 'em further away. We don't know what to expect from this heap of rocks. Which is why *no one* should have been standing around here."

"Sorry," Will said as he followed. "We really were just waiting—"

Ember hesitated. "We were with Garth, and then he … left … and then we heard cries for help."

"Garth should not have left you here! I don't know what he was thinking," the woman groused as she moved with lightning speed. "You," she directed to Will and Ember, "stay back. We're in charge now."

The two workers carried Will's mom and placed her on uneven ground laden with small rocks. The Level Four knelt and checked her pulse. Her face pale and her body listless, Marina looked like living death. "This woman will need to have immediate attention. She has a pulse, but it's weak. If they've been under there since the collapse, they've had no food or water for at least three days. I don't know what this lady was doing in there at all." He shook his head. "I hope my sensitivity and mercy to this woman boosts my Alt readings today. I'm sorry I can't be sad for her." As he spoke, he checked his Alt. Satisfied, he continued to hold her wrist and stroke her arm.

With Ember by his side, Will, visibly sweating and pressing his lips together to keep them from trembling, huddled around Marina. He dropped to his knees. His mom could die. After all this. After everything he'd been through, he couldn't stomach the pain of that. If it was true and his parents hated him the way his brain said they did, he would never have an opportunity to make it right. He stared at his mom's face. His head jerked up when Ember spoke.

"There's a good reason we're here after all," she said, her voice brassy. "We can watch her while you get Jack moved. She shouldn't be left alone." Ember was adamant, and her eyes flashed a challenge.

Will stood up and gaped at Ember. *She's so bold,* Will realized. *In spite of her depth and empathy, she is no easy mark, no naïve child. Behind that beautiful and girly exterior, she's as tough as nails.*

In all the hubbub, Will thought he would burst out of his skin. He wanted to tell his dad he was sorry for whatever he'd done to make them hate him, but it wasn't the time or place. In fact, Will's mind blurred with confusion. The whole goal of finding his parents was to get them to safety at Kamar's place. They couldn't allow a MediCar to come and take Marina and Jack away, especially if they were victims of Serpio's schemes.

Then, the Level Four worker, still kneeling at Marina's side, narrowed his eyes, looked at Will, and stood up, towering over him. He pointed a finger. "Hey ... I recognize you. You're one of the guys the Sciolists are looking for. A traitor—and a murderer! Not a good time and not a good place for you! Excuse me." He took a few hurried steps away, looking back over his shoulder and eyeing Will once more.

Images of what could happen flashed through Will's mind— a swarm of Sciolists coming to arrest them. They would have no chance with not even a vehicle of their own. He couldn't tell from the expression on Ember's face, of course, but he knew what she was thinking. They were now totally screwed. All of them. He met Ember's eyes.

I have to stop this. He remembered his work as a Plauditor, how he would be the ambassador of optimism, a job that used to come easy to him but had since been buried under the wreckage of Serpio's treachery. With a nod to Ember, but more of a forti-fying resolve for himself, he jogged, following the Level Four.

"Umm ... I'm sorry. I didn't get your name," he managed to spit out, his voice cracking. *Ugh. Got to do better than this.* The words then tumbled out of his mouth like the letters wanted to crush each other. "Hey—I think you want to help. But I only want you to give me a chance to tell you my story before you report me. I wonder if, once you hear my story, that you would better understand this whole situation." He paused and took a breath. "And haven't you heard? The Magistrate is just fine—perfectly fine. Perhaps you're wrong about me, and then what would happen to our rescue efforts here? Would you rather help Jack, here, or give him grief? And I'm here to help my dad, Jack. If he could talk, he'd tell you I'm no criminal." Will patted himself down and held out his palms. "You may have noticed I have no weapon or anything."

To Will's surprise, the man was looking down and appeared preoccupied with a half-buried object in the ground. He picked up a piece of something that shone brightly in the ebbing light. Turning to Will, he held it up.

"Name's Matus. Thanks for asking. You seen one of these before?"

Will stared at the object, but it didn't look like anything special, but also not like anything he'd seen before. It was a small cylinder, no larger than Will's pinkie finger. He walked closer to examine it for himself. It had markings on it but no lid or base that he could see. "No. That's not a fragment of what you mine here?"

"Nope. It's an explosive device—banned years ago. I've only seen one once, and that was in the museum. Whatever happened here … don't look like it was an accident." He paused to scrutinize Will from head to foot. "You go ahead. Be a help to your dad over there. I'm putting in a call about this whole 'accident.'" He waved his hands around as if to encircle the entire mountain of rocks. "Frankly, I don't care who ya are, as long as you didn't plant this thing."

"No. I didn't! And no sane person would," Will added, knowing without a doubt that Sciolists had planted that thing and deliberately caved in the mine with it.

"Well, son of Jack, whoever you are, you'd better attend to your dad over there." Matus pocketed the device and turned to look over the horizon, shielding his eyes from the afternoon sun.

Will's insides buckled with relief, and he ran back to where he'd left Ember and his parents, his footsteps churning dust up in his wake. They'd still have to get out of there, and fast, before someone else got too righteous.

"That Level Four give you problems?" Ember glanced his way and whispered as she knelt at Marina's head, right where he'd left her.

"I took care of it." He saw the question in her eyes turn to admiration and chose to enjoy the moment. There was no time to fill her in anyway.

A siren pierced the air.

"Looks like more help is on the way," Ember said, and he couldn't decide if she was happy or worried about it.

A pale blue MediCar arrived, stirring up clouds of dust behind it. *Shazz!* Each new person on the scene could turn them in at any moment. But his parents needed help! If only he and Ember were both invisible! Instead, he turned and walked several feet away and pulled his mask back down over his head, making sure every wrinkle and fold adhered to his skin. He'd rather attract strange looks from the people already gathered there than risk being recognized again.

As he returned to Ember's side, he heard her in conversation with Ruby as she continued to sort through the nearby rubble. "Look, when the MediCar comes, we're going to go with these people. We can't leave them."

She's still working the moment, trying to figure a new way out.

As soon as the tires hit the ground, a black-haired woman dressed in gold metallic scrubs scrambled from the front of the vehicle.

The Medic demanded details as she rushed over. "What happened to these people?"

Ruby answered, giving quick details, including how no one would have known about the victims if the visitors hadn't discovered them.

The Medic knelt and waved a device over Will's mom's torso.

"Dehydration. Low pulse rate. Lacerations and bruises. Both arms look broken." Turning to Jack, she did the same, simply saying, "Ditto. Probably punctured lung. These folks will need to go directly to the hospital. They need a Medela treatment immediately."

Will felt his heart tighten into a knot. His parents would go away in the MediCar, and then they'd be vulnerable to danger again. He had failed to protect them.

But when he looked at Ember, he saw her eyes glow with an inner light, but not like the fireball she was earlier. She was like a bubble ready to burst. *What the—?*

"We'll go with you," Ember said to the Medic.

Will sniffed in surprise.

At the sound of Ember's voice, the medical practitioner's head turned sharply, and her eyes widened. She stood. "Of course. That would be the most compassionate thing to do. Having sympathetic humans nearby drastically helps the healing process."

Will watched, fascinated, as the Medic transferred his mom and dad into the vehicle using a device that moved their bodies like magic from the ground to the ambulance. A little, white, rectangular, remote-like instrument did what two grown people couldn't. It levitated the bodies and then moved them through the air and into the car.

As soon as the patients were in the MediCar, the caregiver got to work using the Medela, holding the instrument about eight inches above each body. The pulsing light delivered a shower of healing energy. After about fifteen minutes, the attendant sat back, satisfied. "That's the best I can do for now, but it should help."

The onlookers gathered around the outside of the vehicle until a supervisor gently told them to return to their jobs.

The angel of mercy waved goodbye to the quarry workers and called out a gracious thank you but invited Ember and Will to sit in the back with the patients. Within minutes, the MediCar was streaming out of the quarry.

To Will's utter shock, Ember pulled off her mask.

Her uniform sparkling in the sun from the MediCar's moon-roof, the Medic chuckled with unrestrained delight, declaring, "Ember! I didn't recognize you! Great job! If it weren't for your sweet voice, I wouldn't have known you at all."

"Thank the stars for that! So good to see you! I want to give you a hug!" Then turning to Will, Ember said, "You can take off your mask. This is Ava, our very good friend. She's been our savior more times than I can count. And once again!"

"Ah, Will! So glad we meet again under different circumstances. You look a lot different in that costume. I absolutely did not recognize you." Ava smiled.

The remark reactivated a scene in Will's mind's eye. He had met Ava before! She had been there with the Magistrate during the bombing, but at that time, he had no idea she was a Phoenix sympathizer.

"I do remember you! And yeah. I'm on the poster for the 'ugly dad' contest in this getup. Good to see you, Ava. And thanks for rescuing us and my parents."

Ava sat up straighter in her seat. "I had no idea what I was going to find today, only that the emergency was reported as serious. You were a surprise."

"They'd probably still be buried under that stone if Ember hadn't been here. You should have seen it. She liquefied those boulders. No way a machine could have done it; it would have hurt them even more."

"Ember did *what*? Moved the stones?" Ava's loud and pointed questions threatened to wake the unconscious patients.

Ember fidgeted and looked out the window into space. "I … did. I met Kamar, who can do that, too. And once I touched him, I could. I don't know how or why."

"That's mind-blowing. You might want to be careful with that," Ava chuckled. "But it's definitely good to know." Then, she got serious. "Will, I have no doubt that your poor parents were put in that mine out of sheer spite. Serpio has no heart. He would make sure that your family suffered. So, here's the plan. We can't take your parents to the hospital, but they need more treatment. We have to make it look real, so I'll be driving the MediCar to your parents' house first. Then we go to Kamar's. I can help there. Then the MediCar goes back to the hospital. If I can, I'll get some serums, and you'll push a ton of liquids. I know this is a hard choice, but if you want them protected, they're going to have to go to Kamar's with you."

"Are you sure they're going to be okay if you don't take them to the hospital?" Will persisted. He gritted his teeth and closed his eyes, knowing Ava couldn't guarantee anything but worried especially that his mom was at death's door. He trembled as he felt a panic attack coming on.

Ember reached across and put her hand on his arm. "Yes. It's all we can do."

When Ember noticed Will's quiver, she took both his hands in hers. "We *will* get through this."

Now that the reunion celebration was over, Ava was all business. "I'll report this to the hospital as a non-serious event where I discovered the victims didn't need hospitalization and could be returned home. The good news is that none of you, including Marina and Jack, are wearing Alts, so none of you can be tracked."

Ember put her right hand in the air and tilted her head. "Shh," she said. "I'm hearing my mom …"

The occupants fell silent, waiting.

After almost a minute, Ember's lips danced around a smile.

Will prompted her. "Well?"

"I told her we were going to Obviators and that we have Will's parents. But the best news? She knows someone with special powers who's a healer. She's sending her our way."

TWENTY-TWO

Xander's Bewilderment

ALTHOUGH THE SCIOLISTS' questioning rattled Xander more than he wanted to admit, he finally shrugged it off. He parked about a half block away from the warehouse, smart enough to know a C-car of any type stopped in front of a food surplus building would not be wise.

Off on foot, he took the back alley as he skimmed along the building next door, an unmarked structure he assumed was some other storage facility. Several people passed by, causing him to shrink into the building. *Why didn't we do this at night?* He inched along and reached the back door of the warehouse.

After the secret knock, the door opened slightly, and he squeaked through. Nearly tearing his uniform when the door closed like an elevator on steroids, he tripped over Jasper flattened up against it.

"Shazz, Jasper! So good to see ya, buddy!" Xander clapped Jasper on the back and then gave him a bro hug. He tore the mask off his face, grateful for the freedom.

"Seems like for-ev-ah!" Jasper replied. "You good? You look good."

"Ah ... you know me. Always good." *Well, not so true,* Xander

thought, *but close enough. Ember and Will are out there somewhere …*
He wiped the sweat off his forehead.

Not-so-fond memories of the warehouse roared back: floor-to-ceiling rows of stacked food boxes, ugly but functional overhead light fixtures, concrete floors, and settled dust, the smell of recycled cardboard … What was heaven before when they escaped the Plauditorium was now an unexpected prison.

He witnessed the startled reactions of the warehouse residents as he entered. His arrival had momentarily stopped groups of them in their tracks, almost as if they were directed to engage in some strange tableau. A group of three were attempting to open a dusty can by cracking it against a primitive bench. Another couple were hugging. Five more sat in a circle on the warehouse floor, where one was poised to toss a tiny piece of something into a container. A game? And while they weren't as filthy as the REMS of The Outside, the uniforms they wore were striped with dirt, and the odor of unwashed bodies hung heavily in the air.

Their worry finally broken by the realization of who had entered, the people began to move once again.

Within a few seconds, Xander was crushed by a crowd of twelve, including Wee and Talesa. The west warehouse boasted a very fine crew.

"Great to see you again." Talesa gave him a quick hug. "I'll bet leaving Ember was hard." Her face, wreathed in a smile with a contrasting sympathetic frown, was enough to make Xander wish she was his own mom.

"Yeah." He found himself choking up, as if the devil himself was pressuring his windpipe. He turned to find a dark giant in front of him. "Wee! You holdin' up okay?"

"Ya know I am! How's Will?"

"Yeah … out with Ember trying to warn Will's parents and bring them back to Obviators. I hope they're doin' okay." He tried loosening the neckline around his uniform, as if that would relax him. It didn't. "Will's been struggling, though. We're keepin' him together."

In a warning tone that Xander found amusing, Wee said, "You'd better! He's still my bro." Wee extended his hand, initiating a bro handshake; he slapped Xander's, and they both pulled back with a bent elbow and a fist.

Clapping his hands, Xander announced, "No time to waste. We have to get out of here. Plans—right now! Then three other warehouses to go, with a very alive, powerful Serpio."

"Couldn't believe when we got the info on our Alts that Serpio was *alive!*" Wee's face become a grimace, his eyes blinking like malfunctioning traffic lights.

Wee wasn't the only one who reacted like the sky had just rained stars, points catching all the way down.

"We got to see the announcement—loud and proud--came across the news into our new headquarters, which has a monitor. Serpio is alive. Will's spear went through him in the fight at the arena. But he did not die." Xander shrugged his shoulders. "I can't explain it. No one can. And like I said, we've no time to waste."

A clamorsome uproar ensued that settled down bit by bit as the old news struck anew until little gaps of silence poked through.

Xander started, "Look, we're gonna be—"

Behind him, someone growled. *Angst over Serpio does that to people.* But something about the sound brought him up short and shot pins and needles of terror through him. He sensed a presence—an unnatural movement that made the hair on his arms stand up and rattle his spine.

Hot breath seeped like rot across his neck before a second bellow crumbled the crust of his demeanor. He wheeled around and gritted his teeth as he struggled to shut down the inexplicable horror he was feeling.

His sanity had left him. Xander shrank back, his face alive

with terror and panic. A Greelox crouched to his left, its head moving from side to side, snarling at the group. Its mouth dripped with blood and saliva, its scaly back slick with a mucous-like sheen. It growled, then roared and made a small but calculated leap toward him.

A yell tore from Xander's throat, and he put his hands up, desperately wishing for a weapon before he ran from the creature as fast as he could. "Get back, everybody! Jasper! The rifle! Quick! Shoot, shoot, SHOOT!" His chest vibrated with the intensity of his heartbeat. Sweat broke out on his forehead, and his panic knocked the breath from him.

But instead of shrieks from the group around him, he heard laughter. What the hell was happening?

He blinked, and the Greelox was gone. A man stood in its place.

"What the Holy Shazz just happened?" Xander put his fingers to his forehead before bending from his waist and catching his breath.

Some of the tribe continued to laugh, while others approached him, comforting him with pats on the back and assurances that everything was okay. He wondered if he had stumbled into some alternate universe where people had become unhinged and creatures materialized before his eyes.

He slowly made his way over to where the "Greelox" had terrorized him.

The stranger spoke. "What you saw just now was an illusion, courtesy of yours truly."

"What the—! What the hell?" His pride was shattered by the way he'd just been fooled.

The Phoenix tribe chuckled louder, confusing Xander even more. Wee especially guffawed. "Hilarious! Glad I didn't miss this!"

He turned his full attention to the stranger, a forty-something-year-old man in a silver jacket and matching pants. His hair, too, was silver, as if he'd just been processed through an aluminum foil factory. "I'm Dorian."

From the back of the group, Talesa moved in beside him, and put her arm on Xander's shoulder before releasing it to move away from Xander and closer to the Greelox man. "Dorian here is an Easterner. He's amazing. Our plans for survival just improved with having him."

Dorian stepped forward and gave Xander the Phoenix hand signal. "I know you're flummoxed. I can convince anyone that something is real or not real, and you won't remember it, either. That's my gift." Dorian's blue eyes sparkled.

"What?" Xander said, feeling more stupid and mystified than ever.

Wee slapped Xander playfully on the back.

Dorian tipped his head forward. "When you first walked in, Xander, I told you to not notice me, that I was just a face in the crowd. Then I told you to see that in my place was a Greelox."

The astonishment on Xander's face made the crowd chuckle again, but Xander realized they'd all had demonstrations of Dorian's special talent before he'd arrived. "You're a real show-piece. I'm glad you're not a Greelox." He grinned. "Great to meet you." Xander's mind was already spinning with the possibilities and help this would offer them. In fact, this changed everything.

One thing he had to find out first. He turned his attention to Jasper and Talesa. "Have you been in contact with the other warehouses?"

"Yeah. They've reported more than a few close calls but were able to escape detection. They're waiting for plans from you once they found out you were safe." Jasper's words were sobering.

So much depends on decisions I make.

"Okay. So, we brainstorm." Xander gathered the entire group together, fully aware now of Dorian's presence in the mix. Still freaked out over the Easterner's instant transformation, he continued to watch Dorian out of the corner of his eye; he didn't want to be caught off guard again. "We need a way to get *everyone* to Kamar's at one time. Don't know if that's doable. We're talking about sixty-plus people."

Talesa smiled at him, much like the Cheshire Cat. Tipping her head toward the illusionist, she said, "Dorian is perfect for our warehouse. I sent an Easterner to each warehouse and chose them specifically for their abilities that I think can best help everyone evacuate."

"What? You just tell them, 'Go here?'" Xander knew the remark came out as sarcastic, but it wasn't. He just really wanted to know.

Drowning each other out, the entire group crackled with questions.

"Let me explain." Talesa moved to the center of the room and climbed up on a couple of empty pallets so everyone could hear. The crowd gathered around her, finally sitting as if it was story time. "These Easterners been underground a long time, waiting for an opportunity to use their gifts. By virtue of their hidden lives, they're already on our side. But it wasn't quite so cut and dry. I had to communicate who I'm with, that we're in hiding, and why. I told them it was risky, that they'd be exposing them-selves if they're discovered. I impressed on them that we really needed their help, and I let them know what they were to do. It was a lot of mental work."

Xander, who'd stayed standing, was so relieved that he could have kissed Talesa. "Who are the people, and what are they like?"

"Oslin can camouflage. He blends into his surroundings and becomes invisible." Talesa waved her hands through the air as if trying it herself.

Oos and ahs punctuated the air.

"That's great, but how does that help the others?" Xander envisioned an invisible Easterner herding the very obvious ducks in a row behind him.

"I don't know how, but he has a field he controls with his hands." Talesa put up her hands, opening and shutting them.

"It's allowed him to remain virtually unknown in the city for years. As for our situation, all he has to do is extend the field to cover the people with him."

Xander smirked. "Sweet. Wish I could've been in line for that one."

Uncontrolled babbling rippled through the group. Sounded like others yearned for the invisibility ability, too, especially right now.

"Then there's Red." Talesa gave Xander a sly smile. "He has a sense when danger approaches and also has super strength. It's enough to do serious damage. He could easily kill someone without trying."

"Like, he can smell a Sciolist a mile away and then turn him into pulp?" Xander guessed.

"What kinda name is 'Red'?" Wee called out.

Talesa kept her focus on Xander. "Maybe not a mile, but soon enough to divert. And 'Red's' a nickname. It stands for Rage, Engage, and Destroy, but he has red hair, too. I met him one day when I was waiting for my CommuteCar. He's quite a character." Humor touched Talesa's lips.

"That's two. Who else?" With each description, Xander's mood lifted.

"Glad you can count," Talesa teased. Chuckles spread through the crew. "The last is Lotus. She produces light. Her body becomes like a neon sign. Her light can be so bright it can be blinding."

"Whoa." Xander said before he played the devil's advocate. "Doesn't that attract a lot of attention?"

"It can, but she's had years of practice to control her talent."

"Damn. I can sure see why these people have hidden themselves. They're not just freaks. They're *super* freaks. Hate to say it —I understand Serpio's paranoia." Xander folded his lips shut.

Talesa nodded with bobblehead energy. "Makes Ember look tame, doesn't it?"

Tame? He wouldn't call Ember's talent tame. Not based on

what he'd seen. Xander weighed whether he should share Ember's experience with Kamar's wall and decided it would be best if Ember told her mother herself. Not his job to be the messenger. "Yeah."

"I say there's not enough of 'em," Jasper stated. "Wish we had an army of Easterners."

"You could get your wish. This is only the beginning." She winked before redirecting the conversation. "Each Easterner should be already headed to a warehouse. Dorian is here, and the others are where they're supposed to go."

Xander tangled his brow in the muscles of his forehead and asked, "How do you know?" before realizing how stupid his question was. Of course she knew. She had telepathy.

"It's something you don't have to worry about, Xander. We can trust them."

Xander gazed off into space for a moment, trying to picture how, even with the Easterners, a mass exodus could work in a city where cameras and eyes were everywhere.

One of the Plauditors interrupted Xander's mind movie. "We've discussed ideas, Xander. Each plan has multiple risks, so we've tossed 'em all. We're more like prisoners than ever."

Xander crossed his arms in front of him. "No, we're not! We may need protection right now, but we're a *force*. Don't underestimate yourselves. I have a great idea, but Dorian and the rest of our Easterner friends are going to be key." He paused for effect, his eyes boring into Dorian's. "We're gonna board the Maglev."

Xander's words were met with a combination of laughter, shaking heads, and raised eyebrows, with the exception of Talesa, who looked thoughtful, and Dorian, who put a finger on his lip, clearly contemplating the possibility. "That could work … maybe," Talesa offered.

"I see where Xander is going with this," Dorian said, standing up and raising his voice. "Let's not brush it off so fast."

"Thank you, Talesa, Dorian," Xander said, emphasizing their names, as he reached across and put his hand on Talesa's shoulder. "One of the best things about the city is the Maglev. It's super-fast, stops close enough to every warehouse, and is full of people in transition. Once you're on board, you'd of course separate by whatever Status your uniform represents, so we'd be scattered all over the train. Plain sight, I know, but too typical for alarm. Your faces are not famous—not like mine. And like I said, the Easterners become our insurance. With their talents, all who are with them should be safe. For our group, it's Dorian. He'll convince anyone on board, including any Sciolists, that there is nothing unusual about the passengers on the train."

A murmur went up among the cluster of listeners. A few shook their heads, but most of them were expressing excitement.

Wee waved his arms as if flagging down a speeding car. "Hellooooo. What about cameras, Xander?"

Xander chuckled at Wee's overdramatic demonstration. "What are they gonna see? Only people gettin' on the train."

"True. But I say we need more help—more insurance. I can enter the Plauditorium as a repair tech." Wee patted the insignia on his stolen uniform. Sure enough, it read "Halcyon Tech."

"It may be riskier to connect than to hope for the best. What if someone recognizes you and asks questions? You're not ordinary looking." Xander looked up into Wee's face, far above his. "It's not like your uniform disguises you."

"You forget—I know how to get into the Plauditorium from the tunnels underneath. I can come up using Serpio's hidden lift and go directly into the control room. It won't be hard to find the electronics panel for each section of the surveillance equipment. It's all labeled." He pulled a tiny vial from his pocket and held it up to the light. "This is acid. Should burn up any wire filaments for the cameras to work."

Dorian and Talesa started talking at the same time, Dorian quickly stopping and allowing Talesa to continue. "I think if Wee is willing to take the risk, this could be a great thing. But," she cautioned, "you could be caught. If you are, you'll be tortured for information. You know that. You'll be a marked man, if you aren't already."

Wee took his index finger and drew an X on his forehead. "I'm ready to take those risks. If not, what are we all here for?" Wee looked around at each face in the group. "If we're not willing to die for this cause, we might as well give up now. It isn't gonna get any easier."

Xander felt the weight of those words. "I'm still …" Wee wasn't just Will's friend anymore; he was his, too. He'd been a partner in their escape and had almost died with him. The risks built a skyscraper in his head, but he had to admit Wee was right. Anything to take observation off of them would be important. He pressed his lips together. "Okay. But you better make this work."

Wee grinned. "I'll do my best."

"Long before we leave here to get on the Maglev, you'll take the purple car I arrived in to the Plaud. Finish as fast as you can and drive back to Obviators. If you're stopped on the way, you're going to have to explain why you're not wearing the car repair shop's uniform, but I'll trust you can do that." Wee was creative, but Xander hoped he wouldn't need to be. "And thanks."

"You got it."

Talesa patted Wee on the back. "We can protect Wee and ourselves if we also plan a big scene. A diversion. If Sciolists and Plauditors are busy trying to stop a catastrophe, that gets us even more invisibility."

Xander beamed. It was as if all of Phoenix shared one brain. "We talked about this at Obviators but decided it was better to strategize here."

All eyes fixed on Wee once more. Xander said, "You have acid. Any explosives tucked away?"

"I don't, but a fire can work just as well." He grinned, his teeth flashing white against his dark skin.

Xander raised his hand. "All in favor of using fire?"

Strangely, all but Wee raised his hand, who warned, "We have to be careful. We don't want innocent people to die because we're lighting things up."

The enthusiasm of the group withered.

"Wee's right," Talesa stated. "It has to be somewhere logical and out of the way. No neighborhoods can be threatened."

Xander could hardly contain the meteor racing through his chest. "I know exactly where."

TWENTY-THREE

Will's Apology

THE MEDICAR PULLED into the open garage at Obviators just like any other vehicle in distress would, but Kamar immediately shut the door the moment the emergency vehicle rolled in. Then he pulled an elsewhither wire from the GPS to scramble its current location.

The first moment after exiting the car, Ava grabbed the Medi-Car's portable Medela and crawled in the back of the car before unleashing its magic. She gripped the Medela's box-like fixture with its purple and red beams and held it a few inches above Marina first and then Jack, moving it back and forth, all along the length of each body.

"This is not a full treatment. It's meant to buy time, to allow the body to begin the healing process. Their bodies will respond to the healing lights, but unfortunately, these guys should have a complete, on-the-bed Medela treatment, one with all the bells and whistles. But it will suffice for now. We'll hope for the best." Ava's face reflected her serious tone. She paused before whispering, "I have to tell you, Will, it's touch and go."

"I understand," he said, wishing he could hide his misery under his mask. But his face wrinkled with concern. With a series of spluttering palpitations, his heart seemed to be trying to decide if it should keep beating. Will moved closer to his parents, and although both of them were unconscious, he encouraged his parents to hang on.

After what seemed a never-ending treatment, Ava, Will, and Ember transferred Jack and Marina from the MediCar on hospital stretchers to the back of the shop and onto the open elevator, where Kamar joined them to descend into the safety of the basement.

Ava instantly surveyed her new surroundings but wasted no time making comments about Kamar's safe room. "We need to get these patients settled. That air mattress over there is going to work just fine for Marina. It's too bad Jack will have to be on the floor."

Kamar interrupted, pointing at the cars along the back wall. "You're welcome to use the backseat in one of those."

Moments later, with help from everyone, Marina and Jack were settled. Jack, covered in blankets, lay in the back of an unfinished silver creation that, when complete, would be a clone of the most popular Level Seventeen C-car model in the city.

Ava fidgeted. "I'm here to help, but I can't stay too long. I can be tracked if someone is interested enough." She turned to Ember. "I'm hoping the healer is on the way?"

Ember nodded. "I hope whoever it is gets here fast."

His distress showing up in drops of sweat on his forehead, Will lingered by his mom's side. "Can't you find out when the healer is coming? I'm worried."

The look on Ember's face transformed into one of earnest encouragement. "If my mom said someone is on their way, they are. Right now, we just need to take care of your parents and not clutter up Xander's mission with questions for my mom that she maybe can't answer."

"Right." He glanced over at his dad and then sprang to standing. "My dad's making some noise." What he heard was barely audible—a moan or a sigh—but he was hopeful Jack was coming around. He rabbited over to arrive at his dad's side, Ava and Ember tracing his footsteps. "Dad, I'm here." For the first time since the rescue, Will saw his dad's eyes really focus.

"Will? I can't … believe it." Jack struggled to get the words out, stammering.

"Yeah." Will lifted Jack's head, raising a bottle to his mouth. "Drink."

The water splashed out a little, dripping onto Jack's clothing. "Gonna … drown me."

"Nope. You just need to get it in your mouth," Will quipped before becoming serious. He put his hand on his father's head. He couldn't hold back the tears springing up in his eyes or the guilt straddling his heart. "Dad, I'm so sorry I wasn't there for you. I should have been protecting you."

"No … you're … here."

"I know, I know. But before. I should have been in touch, helping you and Mom. I met Ember and then …" He trailed off, not knowing how much to dump on his dad. Yet, he needed to explain.

"Met …?"

"Umm … met a rebel group." He stopped and glanced up at Ember and Ava standing to his right. "I learned terrible things about the Magistrate, Dad. Things you don't know. My entire life changed. I got caught up and then learned you were in trouble. But it was too late." Will hung his head, bits and pieces of memory striking his head like shattered glass.

"Tried to keep you … out of trouble," Jack said in a tone that suggested an attempt at humor.

"I had to stand up for what was right. But then Serpio kept me prisoner. He wiped and poisoned my memories. I thought you and Mom hated me. But you don't, do you?"

Jack responded, "No, of course not." This was adamant. Strong.

"I was finally able to see that Serpio lied. I hope you can be proud of me, whatever you hear about me. I'm trying to be a hero still, but just in a different way. You haven't been around the recent news maybe, but I escaped from Serpio. I'm in hiding. Sciolists are searching for me for attempting to assassinate the Magistrate."

"You ..." Jack started but closed his eyes. His breath became ragged, as if Will's words had sucked his breath from his body. A full minute passed. "Your ... friends? They're protecting you?"

"Sort of. Well, we're all in trouble," he admitted, swallowing hard, becoming aware of Ember's hand on his shoulder. "But that's a really long story. I hope you know I'm gonna try to be a better son for you, though. I'm trying to get my head on straight again."

Jack reached out with a shaky hand and gave Will's arm a faint squeeze. "I know you'll always ... make the correct choices. We brought you up right."

Will stood up and nodded to the girl beside him. "This is Ember. She's—she's a good friend." He wanted to say Ember was the one he'd been seeing that caused him to disappear from his parents' orbit even before his capture, but he couldn't explain the situation to his dad in a way he'd understand. Heck, he didn't even understand it himself.

Jack peered at her from under heavy lids. "I must not be dead. I can see how pretty she is. Nice ... to meet you."

"Glad to meet you, too. I'm so happy we found you and could get you out of that mess at the quarry." Ember smiled and took Jack's hand.

"I don't remember much." Jack coughed, his voice raspy.

In that moment, Will's emotions shrunk the world down to only the three of them.

He hadn't even been aware that Ava was behind him before she spoke. She stepped into the inner circle. "I'm Ava. I brought you here, but we haven't been introduced." She leaned over and touched Jack's shoulder.

"You—you're Elite..." Jack's words faded out as he tried to put up a hand to thank her.

Will could see all the speaking was tiring his dad. "Don't try to talk. Just rest." Will propped Jack's head and gave him more water.

Kamar's voice echoed into the room. "Hey! I picked up a hitchhiker," he yelled.

Sure enough, when Will turned, he saw a lady on board the lift with Kamar. Her fair hair was shiny even in the dim room. Dressed in basic, tight pants and a short-sleeved, hip-length plain shirt, the turquoise color labeled her as a Level Thirteen.

"Are you the healer?" Ember called out.

"Got to be. Just in time," Ava assured Ember and smiled at the woman, who moved with quick steps.

"I am!" she answered, her voice tinkling like tangible golden sunshine in a jar.

Will raced across the room to meet her and led the newcomer directly over to where his parents lay. He winced as his eyes swept over them again, the impact of their injuries hitting him anew.

"My name's Reselda," she crooned in a buttery tone, gathered her hair, and magically tied it into a knot to get it out of the way.

Will felt his heart take an elevator ride to the bottom floor as he uttered the words,

"Over here is my mom. She's been unconscious since she was pulled out from the rock pile."

Reselda beelined toward where Marina's body lay atop the air mattress on the floor in the middle of the room and set to work. She pulled a cloth from her pocket and a vial of liquid, which she used to wash dirt from Marina's face and limbs. With a separate cloth, she cleaned Marina's lacerations.

Ava assisted, and Will wondered how he could be so fortunate to have such amazing people right when he needed them.

Ten minutes later, Reselda said, "Now, we can begin the treatment."

She rubbed her palms together so hard and fast Will thought she would generate fire. She placed both hands directly on his mother's wounds, starting with a cut on her forehead that had bled up into her hair, matted with the rust of dried blood.

As he watched, the gash miraculously melted together like wax under Reselda's hands. It was as if she sewed it together, and yet there was no longer a visible wound or even a scar. Will's jaw dropped. Never had he seen anything like this before. A simple touch could do that? Ember was bent over her shoulder, her lips parted, looking ready to burst with questions.

A second lesion on Marina's shoulder took longer, but Reselda lightly rubbed the skin on both sides of the tear, and it fused just as the other had. Three more wounds sealed, and then the most brutal of Marina's wounds were no more.

Reselda closed her eyes and took each of Marina's limbs in her hands, encircling them between her palms. She exerted gentle pressure, moving her hands along the length of all of them. "I can feel broken bones and deep contusions."

"What are contusions?" Will asked. The word sounded dreadful, like "confusion," but he knew it wasn't a thinking problem.

"Contusions are bruises under the muscles. It's not as serious as a break, but deeper in the body," Reselda explained. "All of it hurts, and it's not easy to heal."

Will was afraid to ask. "But can you fix it?"

"Yes. It's not instant. It will take some time. I'll be going back and forth from your mom to your dad for a while. Then we must allow them to rest so the healing can take place."

Will let out a breath he didn't realize he'd been holding. "Thanks." It came out in a whisper.

Reselda smiled with the warmth of the sun. "She should be coming around soon. Keep an eye on her while I go take care of your dad." The healer rose and started toward Jack.

Ember, already on her feet, trailed after her. "Can I do anything to help?"

"You can help me with the cleaning. That has to happen first. As you saw with Marina, it can take a while to wash off the grime." Reselda pulled several more folded cloths from her pocket and handed them to Ember, along with a bottle. "Here, sprinkle this on the washcloth. Rub it on your own hands first to clean them from any germs and dirt."

With Ember, Ava, and Reselda all working, they finished the entire scrub down in five minutes, and Reselda moved over to administer healing to Jack, who seemed more alert by the minute. Ember tilted her head to the side and watched with round eyes as the miracles continued.

"He's less damaged than Marina," Reselda assured Ember. "He won't need as much work."

"I appreciate it," Jack said. "My wife would disagree, though. She'd say I need *lots* of work."

Will glanced their way. His heart swelled hearing their amusement. Ember's face was bright as a star.

After making her patient swallow more water, Reselda stood. "I'll be seeing to Marina again. Would you two stay with Jack?"

"That's why I'm here," Ava answered, checking Jack's vitals with a metal object she took from her pocket.

"I'll be happy to." Ember rose to her feet. "Thank you. This could have been the end of them." She seized the sudden private moment as Reselda turned to go. "And Will—Will is—"

Reselda looked at her closely and lowered her voice. "What about Will? Is he injured, too?"

Ember shifted from one foot to the other, her tone confidential. "No. Well, not in the same way. He's suffering from mental trauma. Is there anything you can do for him?"

"I can't heal the mind or the heart, only the physical." She hesitated, looking into Ember's eyes. "But I have a feeling you can give him what he needs. I can tell you are strong. Truly listening and trying to understand are the best ways to help your friend, but too much sympathy will not allow him to do what he himself must do. And touch helps healing, no matter whether it is physical or mental. You don't have to be a healer to make it work. It has its own magic." Reselda smiled and gave Ember an unexpected, all-embracing hug before releasing her. "See? A hug will always help emotional healing."

Ember smiled back, her face aglow, before she swayed on her feet and put her hand to her head. "Oh ..."

"What is it?" Grabbing her shoulders, Reselda steadied her.

Like a coin that had spun furiously before tapping slowly to a finish, Ember regained her equilibrium. "I'm okay ... I think." She blinked and put a hand on her chest, asking Reselda, "Did you feel something just then, or was it only me?"

"I didn't. Maybe it's all the stress. What did you feel?" Reselda reached out to place her hand on Ember's forehead.

Ember stepped back. "Like an electric current passed through my body. It—it burned and made me dizzy. I've never had stress do that. And it certainly wasn't that magic you were talking about. Or if it was, I'll pass."

TWENTY-FOUR

Serpio's Sciolists

SERPIO GLANCED REPEATEDLY at his OmniCom. He hadn't heard anything from his Sciolists for almost two hours. He should have been questioning Ava at City Hall by now, or at least know what was taking the search effort so long. He pinched his nose and squeezed his eyes shut.

He paced and then sat, drumming his fingers on the table in front of him. He could hear his own breathing; it had grown heavier and louder as he mentally berated his Sciolists for taking too much time to complete a simple task. His red-caped agents were being spread way too thin. Trained to pick up emotional resistors rather than to fight crime, the force was ill-equipped to deal with the latest challenges. There were real insurgents out there right now, bent on his destruction. The time had come to recruit additional Sciolists to question citizens in their cars and on foot, search the city's nooks and crannies for rebels, and assemble a Sciolist army to fight back.

It had been a long time since he'd had to gather new apprentices, but it was easy enough. He recruited new members—always men—from the bottom ranks of society. Level Ones were not happy people, and Sciolists were not happy people.

In fact, the training took the last smidgen of any emotion they possessed, smashing and reshaping it all into mere obedience. Sciolists were merely task-masters—ready to serve and not intelligent enough to question. Those he inducted were eager to join and considered themselves privileged. And, in fact, they were. Their standard of living was on a par with a Level Twelve once they were part of the unit.

He would double the force—take it from fifty to one hundred. He'd start the process today and float it through the Elite tomorrow, although having to usher the request through the Elite Council would be like having sharp stones in his shoes.

The need to move forward fueled his impatience. Caving to his frustration, he decided to contact Esryn rather than wait another second. But before he could, his Omnicom buzzed with vibration, and a Sciolist's monotone voice patched through.

"Magistrate, Ava Validus has been located but is on a medical mission with a MediCar. We know MediCar transport cannot be interrupted under any circumstances. Instead, we have finished sweeping her home, gathering what we could find." There was a pause. "Unfortunately, we found nothing out of the ordinary."

"You found *nothing*? Did you question her domestic assistant?" Serpio clenched his teeth and massaged his temples.

"The servant was cooperative and reported no suspicious activity. We accessed camera replays. Nothing unusual. No sign of Verus, Noble, or Vinata. No REMs. None of your journals. She only has ten cameras in place, sir. Several of those cameras are disabled, but we checked the tech logs, and all webcam suspension procedures were approved a few weeks ago."

If what he suspected was true, Ava had to be harboring actual people or have left some telltale sign behind. How else could the fugitives be in hiding? Yet he also knew Ava was smart, and she wouldn't leave any breadcrumbs behind for discovery. Disappointment built a fire in his chest. "Did you check all the drawers, cabinets, and storage?"

"We almost tore the place apart." A slight hesitation yawned before the word "Spotless."

Serpio saw the modest mansion in his mind's eye. When Ava returned home and went inside, she was observant enough to tell immediately there'd been someone there. And the servant would inform her right away that Sciolists had paid her a visit. Best to use the element of surprise. "Wait for her inside. When she comes home, you will arrest her then."

"Very well, sir." The clipped words were the last before the call ended.

At the computer on his desk, Serpio scheduled a new meeting for the next morning with the Elite. And instead of being a member of the council, Ava would be sitting in custody.

TWENTY-FIVE

Xander's Plot

"YOU SEEM PRETTY certain about the fire's location. What are you thinking?" To someone who didn't know him, Wee's booming voice could sound intimidating. Good thing Wee was like one giant puppy. Wee towered over Xander's six-foot frame by a good foot, which made Xander always feel small.

Before his answer, Xander looked up at Wee and then out at the others gathered around. "The genetics lab is the perfect place. We all heard. They're starting to gather DNA from citizens. Without the lab and its equipment, they won't be able to process any of it. Plus, destroying Inventum eliminates all possibility that information on our Easterner friends can be used against them. I say that's our target. We set fire to the lab—it knocks that out and gives us our distraction at the same time."

Talesa's smile was so broad it almost split her face. "That's Serpio's pride and joy, too. He's very protective of it. You're a genius. It's perfect."

"Agreed." Then Xander threw his head back and chuckled, realizing his answer addressed both comments. "I mean, yes, it's perfect. We set the fire during the Revelation Celebration. With the party going on, the fire, and its effects, we'll be safer moving people. Agreed?"

A sing-song chant started among the group. "Fi-ur! Fi-ur! Fi-ur!"

"Who's up for setting the fire?" Xander would have loved to do it. In fact, he died a little inside when he realized he wasn't going to be able to volunteer. He had been the conductor of the almost literal "Underground Railroad." Working with Dorian, he alone had to oversee getting the groups back to Obviators, and this time without being in a tunnel.

Talesa held up her hand. "It will be hard enough for Wee to get safely to the Plauditorium. The more of us we send out, the greater the risk for both capture and a failed plan. I hate to say it, but we need to have inside help again. We need Sciolists. If Sciolists went to the lab, that wouldn't be weird. They're above suspicion. And we know Ava has two Sciolists on our side. We met them. Remember, Xander?"

"Yes. I remember." He flashed back to the moment he'd met Ava's converts. He and Ember had rescued Talesa from her prison Outside and used the food cart to travel back through the tunnel. At the end, two Sciolists stood where they opened the door to enter the city. He had thought they were doomed. But luckily, those were Ava's recruits, and they were only there to help them.

Xander cringed thinking about putting Ava on a pivotal point again. Out of everyone he knew, next to Ember, Ava was the most special to him. But Talesa made sense. The Sciolists could go under the guise of checking things out, maybe even report the fire after they'd set it, and no one would be the wiser.

"That's the best plan. You all game?"

A buzz of affirmation swelled throughout the group. One by one, hands went up in agreement.

"Okay," Xander said, putting two thumbs up. "It's settled. I'll be the one to communicate, but I'll have to use an Alt from someone here." Half the group immediately volunteered theirs by extending their wrists or slipping their Alts off and making the motion to hand them over. "Uh, Jasper. It makes more sense that it would be yours. At least Ava knows you." He reached out his hand.

Jasper shook his head. "But it's not me on that Alt, Xander. It's some guy named Rush Profectus."

"Yeah, but your picture is you. She'll know." Xander reached out again, and this time, Jasper handed over his Alt.

It took Xander only a minute to use the Morse Code app to send Ava a message: "Moving Phoenix to Obviators via Maglev. Tonight 8:00 p.m. during street party. Need fire set at Inventum Therapeutics for distraction. Can your Sciolists set fire?—X."

He watched the minutes tick by on the Alt as the group began to fidget. The little group was in high spirits, but he noticed a few of them using their Tranquility techniques to calm themselves, such as breathing or mantras.

Finally, Ava's message came through, the Morse code a godsend.

"... - .. .-.. .-.. / .- - / --- -... ... .- .. .- - --- .-. ... .-.-.- / .- .-.. .-.. / .- .-. . / --- -.- .- -.-- .-.-.- / ... -.-. .. --- .-.. .. ... - ... # ..-. .. .-. . --..-- / -.-- . ... .-.-.- / .. # .-... .-.. / -- . ...- --. . / -.-- --- ..- / .- / -.-. --- -. ..-. .. .-. -- .- - .. --- -. .-.-.- #" Xander's app translated "Still at Obviators. All are okay. Sciolists—fire, yes. I'll message you a confirmation."

All are okay! Thank the stars Ember made it back safely! He exhaled, realizing with the breath how much he had pushed his worries about Ember to the back of his mind. He'd had to. His love for her could cause his absolute downfall if he let it consume him. He sighed. The burden of leadership was a bright curse in so many ways.

But Ava? Involved with Will's parents' mission? *That wasn't in the plan.* He not only was left to wonder why, but he mourned his lack of being in more than one place at a time and for having Ava put herself at risk for them. And yet, he knew that if she was needed, Ava would have it no other way.

Xander clapped his hands to get the group's attention. "We're good to go on this course. Ava's Sciolists will set the fire. We'll board the train during that time. Dorian, we need to talk logistics."

Dorian turned his attention to the rest of Phoenix. "I'm confident I can trick anyone who sees us to ignore us. That's not hard. The problem will be once each person is on the train because each of you will be in different places depending on your borrowed uniform's Status color. If everyone sits according to their Status, no one should check your Alt for points, but if they do, your Alt will betray you if it is scanned. We don't know if Sciolists are stopping people on the mass transit or if they are just concerned with private vehicles and pedestrians. There are only fifty Sciolists for the entire city, and I imagine they're being spread rather thin. We have to hope for the best. We know we can't stay here. So, we go for it."

"Sounds like a plan." Xander checked the time on Jasper's Alt once more before looking in vain for Jasper to return it. His disappearance made Xander frown, wondering if Dorian was playing tricks on him again.

Dorian then began to draw people dressed in the same color aside in small groups, and started explaining how and when they were to board the train.

A half-second later, Jasper appeared from behind a section of nine-foot-high stacked cans. "What do you want me to do with these journals? I'd just as soon burn 'em, but no one claims they've read anything in there that's useful." Jasper held out three books in a stack. "I've kept 'em safe, but I've hauled 'em around for too long. They need a more permanent place to go."

Xander reached out and took them. "Thanks, Jaz. They're so valuable. The more we get into Serpio's head, the more we'll know how to fight him. And they're evidence against him, so we have to keep them secure until we can present them to the Elite. Any luck getting some of his entries out to the people of the city?"

"Sadly, no. We've not been able to come and go, you know. We've made some copies, but that's about it." Jasper appeared cowed, putting his head down. It was clear to Xander that he didn't want to disappoint his friend.

Xander gave Jasper a playful hit on the arm. "Well, what are we waiting for? We can't leave until nighttime when the party begins. Let's grab a few people and read."

"Um, Xander?" Jasper paused, as if weighing his words. "I'd like to help, but I can't read."

Jasper's statement blindsided Xander. *Jasper can't read?* Although he'd never thought about it, REMs who lived on The Outside often hadn't done well at anything before their exile, especially not formal education. He himself had been lucky; his own parents had pushed his education, even though they were disgusted with his behavior.

Recovering enough to hide his surprise, Xander said, "We don't need everyone to read. Only a few. Your job is still the keeper of the journals! That's the most important thing of all." He looked at Jasper keenly in the eyes, his tone serious. "I'm still gonna need you to guard these journals with your life."

"Huh. Okay. I hope I can still do that job and not die trying." Jasper grinned, the slightly crooked teeth a testimony to a rough life.

"Can you find me two other people who can—want—to read? It's an important job, and I know you'll find the best few." He handed two of the books back to Jasper with a nod. "Maybe Wee to start?"

As Jasper went off to gather volunteers, Xander drifted off to an area away from the group, a journal tucked under his arm. He longed for a chair but made himself as comfortable as he could on the floor. Then, he opened the cover and began to read.

Every log was numbered, just like the first journal Ember had stolen. Strangely, unlike that one, he found little of anything incriminating in the first ten pages. The journal seemed more about the Magistrate's daily life and was full of self-praise. Serpio detailed how he'd solved this or that problem and described over and over how keeping Tranquility the happiest place on earth was his whole reason for living.

In one surprising entry, he discovered that Serpio had an overwhelming love for cats and owned a white one named Sugar that he kept in a room of its own, decked out with cat-themed furniture and an attendant to meet its every need. Xander shook his head. Who knew?

Then, he poured over another page, one with a poem entitled "To A Mother I Never Knew."

To a mother I never knew,
From a son who desperately misses you.
There were so many times I would imagine you,
But you would never appear.
And there were so many times I would cry for you,
Tear after tear.
I have even begged for you,
On both knees,
To please come save me, Mama,
Please, please, please.
And even as the years passed by,
I would never lose hope,
Because it was hope
That kept this little boy afloat.
I would daydream about the moment
When I would finally meet you,
And how I would cry and be speechless
Just to finally see you.
With my own two eyes,
Exactly how I had dreamed,
Angelic and beautiful
And as loving as you seemed.
I've learned that sometimes love
Is so much harder to show than to say.
That's how I know you truly loved me, Mama,

Because you're not here with me today.
I can only imagine
The selfless love that it took
To say goodbye to your child
And take one last look.
To let him go,
In hopes that he can live a better life.
The pain must've felt
Like a dull serrated knife.
I miss you every day, Mama,
And I hope to see you soon.
But if not,
Then I'll see you in my dreams tomorrow afternoon.
Written by Serpio Magnus,
Transplant #1505

Wow. Serpio didn't know his own mother? He'd been a Transplant —adopted out. If so, he didn't have a regular childhood. He was given away because of the one-child law.

Xander had never had one microscopic sliver of compassion for Serpio, but seeing into Serpio's heart like this made the monster almost human. Almost.

He felt an unnatural chill go up his back. Although he'd been raised by his own parents, he, too, had parents who had given him up. Not because he was one too many, but because he had failed them. And he'd had to live with that and be alone. Totally alone. Apart. His eyes welled up, and he shook it off, disgusted with himself for the emotional violation.

Then, he turned the page and sat up. The entry began with the words "I am immortal."

TWENTY-SIX

Xander's Find

THE WORDS JUMPED out at Xander as if they were a herd of Greeloxes in a stampede. "I am immortal."

Xander began to read, his eyes wide and his heart racing.

Many, many years ago, before I was born, our experiments with DNA in Tranquility were necessary. The scientists did remarkable work preventing diseases and healing those who had them. From there, it was an easy trick to allow parents to request certain characteristics for their children before they were born. Many of these requests were granted.

However, once the CRISPR techniques were successful, the researchers repurposed their research to enhance human life. Using radiation on infants, they tried to enhance certain characteristics. Infants as young as three months old had injections to modify their DNA. As they grew, these same children exhibited extraordinary superpowers. They became a new breed—individuals with special talents.

The names of those transformed infants, the first of those experiments, became classified. Those infants, the first subjects of radiation-based DNA practices, are now all at least forty years old. Some of them abused their powers and began to show superiority to others. Others have had issues with their mental health, their minds deteriorating into insanity or depression. This could not stand. Sadly, many of them had to be eliminated, as they could easily overthrow the government and take control of the city. I have taken it on as a special assignment—to make sure these individuals do not threaten our city.

Because the mutations were genetic, they could be passed down. One baby was born and fortunately died before it could grow up. It had freakish features and scaly skin and did not want its mother. The Elite then issued strict instructions that none of that group should have children. Without a doubt, generations of children could have been affected. Mutant children would be very distasteful. No one with a child like that could ever be happy. The children, too, would suffer great misery in their inherited struggles.

The Greelox Outside are a testament to what can happen when science goes haywire.

Although the idea of enhanced humans had its merits, the Elite determined there was too much risk involved. The program was terminated.

This gives me such distress as I, myself, was one of those experimental children. The Magistrate at the time, Augur, gave extra incentives to families who would give up their children for scientific study. Each child had to meet certain criteria, and my adoptive parents were thrilled that my blood type and DNA were already perfect for this specific experiment.

I am profoundly different. My special power is singularly unique. As one of the last children to be entered into the program, I was given the most intensely purified DNA—what they termed the Infinity Protein. It comes from blood and other creatures and is labeled CID 2034. With it, I will never die from any wounds, illness, old age, or trauma. I would live forever unless I—"

Xander turned the page. But when he did, he gnashed his teeth. The sentence was left unwritten. The following entry was all about a celebration for the Elite.

"No!" he yelled. *No wonder Will couldn't kill Serpio!* He put his hands on his head and tilted his head back to gaze at the ceiling in distress. The mystery of Serpio was solved—and yet was only beginning.

TWENTY-SEVEN

Ember's Evolution

WITHIN A MINUTE of feeling the bizarre dizziness and surge of magnetic power, Ember stabilized. *I really should drink more fluids,* she reasoned. Yet the incident bothered her. She was used to feeling other people's emotions and even being overwhelmed by them. Seeing the auras was commonplace, too, so it wasn't that. It was almost as if Reselda's aura had caught fire and then melted into hers.

"Are you sure you're okay?" Reselda kept asking.

Ava's eyes creased into worry as she looked her way.

"What's goin' on?" Kamar, who had been a silent observer tucked a good ten feet away, approached and entered the conversation. "I leave for a minute, and everything goes crazy."

Ember gritted her teeth and said, "Grrr, guys! Yes. I'm telling you, I'm fine. But you're the healer. Do you sense anything wrong with me?" *Just double-checking,* she decided. If in case there was something like exhaustion gone wrong. Or maybe Will wasn't the only one with PTSD.

Will tipped Kamar off. "Ember got dizzy. We don't know why."

"I'm starting to think there's something about this room," Kamar replied.

Reselda pantomimed using a pair of binoculars over her eyes and panning Ember's body as she chuckled. "You're quite healthy, as far as I can see. Do you want to join Will for a while?" Reselda raised her chin to motion toward the son bent over his mother's body. "Kamar can help me here with Jack if I need it."

Across the room, Ember saw Will's murky glow and felt his depression as he sat with his mom. "Yes. I think I'm needed … to look after Will. Thanks for letting me help out here."

"Of course. And remember what I said." Reselda gave her one last pat on the back.

As she drew near, in spite of his discouragement, Will greeted her with a smile. "He doing okay?"

"Yes. I think he'll be fine. Reselda says he's not in as bad a shape as your mom. She's almost finished with him, and then she'll attend to Marina again."

Ember knew the trauma of having a parent sick enough to die. Her mind shifted back to the moments in the hospital room as her mother slipped away—the way the grief consumed her until she wanted to die herself. She knelt next to Will and put her arm around his shoulders for a quick hug.

"Thanks," he breathed. "That helps."

Reselda's advice about physical touch had just been confirmed.

Will reached out and placed his hand on his mother's face. "She's always had the softest face."

Will's fingers trailed gently over Marina's cheek, and it was suddenly as if he woke Sleeping Beauty. Marina's lids fluttered open, and a slight frown creased her forehead. Her cool blue eyes blinked again as she focused on her son's face.

"Oh …" she moaned.

"Mom, you're awake! Finally!" Will gasped before locking shining eyes on his mother.

"Mmm. Will …" Marina whispered.

Will's hands trembled, and he pressed his palms to his eyes before murmuring, "Shh. Don't talk. You're safe." Will glanced at

Ember and smiled, his relief so powerful he probably could have danced. "You're rescued and beginning to heal. This is Ember. She's...very special to me." Will reached for Ember's hand and squeezed it.

Ember blushed and, with a soft smile, said, "Wish we were meeting under better circumstances, but glad to meet you. So happy you're coming around." With her free hand, she clasped Marina's.

But an angry, swollen gash on Marina's arm held Ember's attention hostage. And, it was almost as if she couldn't take her eyes off it. She withdrew her hand from Marina's, rubbed her palms together, and gently encircled the wound with her fingers. A surge oscillated through her hands, and she felt the fleshy tissue move beneath her touch. Like it did with the rock melt, the substance she warmed changed. A rush like molten lava traveled through her hand, radiated up her arm, and settled into her chest.

She tried to yank her hand away, but her muscles locked and tightened. No matter how much she strained and pulled, she couldn't separate herself. It was as if she were bonded to Marina with massive superglue. Her face contorted with a full frown that grabbed her lips and bent them down.

"Ember! What's wrong?" Will was now no longer the joy-filled boy, his frantic glances darting from Marina to Ember in a panicked race.

"I can't … move." The sense of heat and paralysis increased until blotches of red roared up her neck and across her face.

"Reselda! Ava! Kamar!" Will shouted. "We have a problem!"

Just as Reselda and Ava clambered up from Jack's side to meet the new challenge, Ember's body relaxed, limbs becoming fluid. Her joints rubberized, and her shoulders slumped. With the change, she immediately disconnected her hand from Marina's, placing it on her own chest instead. She held up her other hand as a stop signal for the others.

Although aware that her heart was still racing, she called out a lie. "I'm okay … now." The heat, too, began to evaporate as if it had simply been a temporal sunspot in an irrational weather pattern. Maybe she really was okay … Concentrating on her breathing, she slowed its shameless rampage. "I don't know what that was, but it's over."

At some mumbled words from Jack, the others returned to his side, although with hesitation. It seemed the whole group wanted to split themselves into pieces to attend to everyone's needs.

Ember's body's response scared her. This was the second time within the last hour she'd had severe body reactions. She wondered for an instant if Serpio had a way of reaching into her soul and slowly killing it. She wouldn't put it past him.

Across from his mom's body, Will gazed at her with a weirdly fixated stare, as if she'd triggered another psychotic breakdown.

"Will? You okay?"

The two humans beside me are equally broken.

"Yes. Fine." The look refocused and became settled.

She hated how all the attention had immediately shifted to her. Marina was the one needing everyone's support and assistance. If she touched her again, though, she feared another inexplicable fusing.

She'd seen Marina's aura grow brighter, though.

What had she done exactly? She'd felt her own aura overlap with Marina's and energy had flowed out. Her super empathy allowed her to feel Marina's struggle and pain. To touch her again would draw the same sort of effort. But could she help Marina more?

Taking a deep breath, she placed her hands around Marina's wrist—right atop a place where a deformed bulge stuck out. For sure a broken bone. As her fingers touched Marina, the woman's pain and brokenness seeped into her. Almost against her will, her eyes shut, and she felt a change, again finding herself tethered to Marina, space and time falling away. When she opened her eyes, Marina's aura looked like iridescent glass, and her wrist was straight! Bruises and lacerations had faded away, as if by magic.

Ember slowly pulled each finger away, defying the stickiness that bound her to Marina, and it was as if her aura had shrunk down, tightening around her, and then rebounded afterward.

Marina blinked her eyes and sat straight up.

Will gasped out, "Whoa. Mom … you have serious injuries. Lie back down. We're trying to help you."

Marina huffed and sat up straighter. "Well, I'm perfectly fine. Look at me." In wonder, Marina shook out her arms and showed them her palms as if they were proof of perfect health and then reached out and fiercely hugged her son. "I love you, and I've missed you so much." When she released him, Marina craned her neck to see around them, and her eyes became king-sized. "But is Jack—is Jack okay? I need to go help your dad. Please."

Will called for a second opinion. "Reselda—Ava! Can you come?"

Ava beat Reselda to check on Marina's situation. "Marina, let me take a look at you, all right?" She felt her forehead and then looked unsuccessfully for the gashes on her arms.

Reselda also then knelt next to Marina and placed her hands above her body. "I'm feeling the energy." Reselda's brows knitted together before her lips bent in a smile. "She's definitely much better." She examined Marina for her gashes, which had completely disappeared, and felt along her limbs. "I wouldn't have thought she'd be so much better. But she is. Marina has made a complete recovery."

Ember's eyebrows shot up. "What? I mean, that's great, but I don't understand."

Will turned slowly to look at her and pulled her in for a hug. When he released her, his eyes flashed with stars. "*You* healed her, Ember, I'm sure of it. There's something really crazy going on with you."

Reselda, too, gazed into Ember's eyes, as if she could see

through to her soul. "You definitely have the gift of healing. I have a feeling I've passed it to you, although I don't know how." She shook her head but smiled.

Ember hugged herself, allowing her fingernails to dig into her skin to reassure herself that this whole thing wasn't one of her supernatural dreams, another so-called "gift" she'd have to manage. What would this new gift mean for her future?

TWENTY-EIGHT

Ember's Magnetism

EMBER KNEW there was no sense in arguing with Will and Reselda. The evidence was mounting. First Kamar's power and now Reselda's. Just as she always had with emotions, she was somehow attracting other people's talents. She wished she knew why. What was it about her that did this bizarre thing? There was no rhyme or reason to it, except to say she was a magnet for other people's wacky DNA.

Will put his hands on her shoulders. "You're amazing! And now we have two healers."

Reselda continued to look at Ember with the awe afforded to an enchanted being. "Ember is more powerful than I am. Look at what you were able to do."

Marina stood up and hugged Will and then Ember. "I feel perfect. Thank you all for rescuing me."

"Would you look at that," Kamar said, wonder frosting every word.

"This is great news, Mom." Will gave his mom an all-encompassing hug. "But, Ember, now my dad needs you. Let's get him back on his feet, too." Will was already moving in that direction. The group followed, their spirits high.

Although Ember hated the feeling of her aura contracting

around her like a spider's web, she would endure the bizarre discomfort. It was time to help Jack. She seemed to fall deeper into a mindless state this time around, but within minutes after she laid her hands on Jack, he was alert, and all signs of his injuries were gone.

"You should feel better now, I think. Do you?" Ember said as she continued to experience the constricting sensation from her effort.

"Thank you, Ember. You're a real angel," Jack said as he stood up with the speed of a ten-year-old. "Will, you better hold on to her."

Ember blushed, the heat rising from her chest into her face. Will deflected and caught Jack's eye when he said, "Wait 'til your boyfriend comes back. He'll be freaked."

The embarrassment over her relationship with Will in front of his parents was taking too long to fade. "Um, yeah. That's Xander. You haven't met him yet. He'll be surprised, for sure." Ember hadn't thought about Xander since the whole mission with Will and his parents began. She frowned, wondering why her mind hadn't been in both places at once.

Ava's voice pulled her out of her befuddlement. "It's past time I left. Already, this has been a risk, but I wanted to help as much as I could."

A chorus of dismay rang out in response, but Ember was the one who reached out and gave Ava a hug.

Moisture threatened Ava's eyes as she patted Ember's shoulder. "Whatever you do, stay safe. Until later …"

"I'll try," Ember said, her hug like a promise to seal the deal.

When Ava had said a final farewell, Kamar followed Ava across the floor and onto the lift, peppering her with questions all the way.

Ember's work of the last few hours had consumed and depleted her. She was exhausted from the heavy emotions alone, but the healing zapped her energy as if an all-powerful vacuum had sucked the very life from her. The talent might be a gift, but it also required every shred of vitality she had.

Her goofy disguise, too, begged to be replaced with the basic, ill-fitting mechanic's uniform. She excused herself and ducked behind one of Kamar's junk heaps. Peeling off each piece of the impossible-to-love clothing, Ember wished she could do the same with every doubt, worry, and burden. As she huddled behind the car, she savored a moment to herself, although she shivered until her teeth chattered at the chill feathering her body. She'd never get used to the nippiness of their refuge, but the constant fear of "what ifs" in the back of her mind intensified her quiver.

With a sigh, she stuck one leg at a time into the mechanic's jumpsuit, strangely grateful for it. Although it hung on her body like a tablecloth, she celebrated the awkward but floppy comfort of the Obviator's jumpsuit.

A moment later, she emerged to jokes flung to her from across the room about her drowning in green clover or looking just like a leprechaun with her red hair and kelly-green suit.

With every step to join the group still gathered around Marina and Jack, Ember's limbs grew heavy, and as much as she would have loved to chat with Will's parents and communicate with her own mom, her eyelids fought to stay open, and her feet were bricks.

"If you all don't mind, I'd love to lie down a bit—that is, if you don't need the bed, Marina."

Marina put her arm around Jack's waist. "I don't need the bed, thanks to you all. Take some time. You all deserve to rest, but especially you."

Zigzagging over to the nearby air bed, she rolled onto it, murmuring an illogical "thanks" to the mattress for its comfort. In an instant, sleep overtook her, and she could no longer hold her spirit within her body. It escaped to the ceiling, her tether to the earth dissolving as a dream unfolded.

Dark clouds gathered on a distant horizon and then moved in her direction. She saw herself standing on a rooftop and watched the plume of darkness from a distance as one cloud swallowed another, one by one, forming a giant mass of menacing gray. Lightning pierced the billow before thunder pounded out a rhythm that sounded like Morse Code.

As she tried to make out the message, she floated off her feet and into a narrow bed covered in red sheets. Blood. The linens were soaked with it. Surrounding her were several computerized machines, most as small as shoeboxes, and they blinked out her name in colored lights. Her arms were bound with wire and attached to the bed.

A dark shadow slowly crept across her body. The shadow carried a sensation of a high-powered magnet pulling on every vein. Her breath caught as she sank into a coma.

In the distance were voices—but not ones soothing her. They were frantic yells and curses, sounds of a clash, and what she was sure was Will's voice: "Ember! Ember! Ember!"

A sharp intake of air jerked her awake. She sat straight up, her eyes wide and her arms tingling, recoiling, as if the dream had been reality. She covered her face with her hands, reimagining flashes of it, a tear falling sideways down her face.

It had been a while since her dream premonitions had manifested. *Another talent that's a gift and a curse.* This vision had been dreadful, but she knew as certain as her own name that the nightmare had a message. Now it would be up to her to figure it out before it came true.

She crawled off the air mattress, foolishly checking it for red sheets, and stood up. Will, his parents, and Kamar were sitting in a circle in the middle of the basement, their voices rising and falling with conversation and periodic laughter. Smoothing her hair, Ember approached, pasting a smile on her face.

Reselda greeted her. "There's our new hero."

Will's face glowed with a happiness Ember hadn't seen since they'd left the arena. A sweet steadiness colored his words. "Hey. Did you get some rest?"

She felt a shaft of sunshine in her soul as she saw Will being Will. His parents were a calming force.

"It was … good to sleep." She cast her eyes down, not wanting to give anything away.

Wrong place, wrong time to dump her fearful forecast on everyone. What she had to share would be just for Will—and for Xander, of course, once he got back. They and her mom were the only ones who knew about her chimeric warnings.

Jack ran a hand through his tousled brown hair. "We were talking about the mine collapse while you were sleeping. And what we've been through lately. Will came for a visit with the Magistrate … Then we were struggling with having food, although Will had promised to return to help. We understand now that Will was having his own crisis."

Doing a double take, Ember cast her gaze on Will. "You saw your parents when you were with Serpio?" She closed her eyes, her sympathy for him making her heart sink. "You were already being played."

The corners of Marina's mouth bent down and then up. "I know my son. He was doing the best he could. But we were starving because our Alt points were dropping for no reason at all. Then the Sciolists came. They told us we were going to be counseled. Jack and I refused to go, but they seized us and instead took us to the mine at night. They tied us up inside. We got out of the ropes, but as we tried to get out, the mine caved. I'm guessing some type of explosive."

Kamar shook his head in disgust. "Had to be all Serpio. Wait 'til he discovers you're not in the rock pile."

"Hopefully, he won't," Jack replied.

"Don't bet on it." Will stood and stretched. "Nothing gets by him. I know him well."

With Will's statement, Ember noticed the eye tic was back. If only she could turn back the clock on that. Or touch and heal. She had powers that didn't behave at all.

TWENTY-NINE

Ava's Curveball

AS AVA RODE the MediCar back to the hospital's parking garage, she could have soared like a bird. The adrenaline of rescue, although intoxicating, could not compare to being an integral part of the entirety of the rebels' operation. At the time, she had never dreamed that a bizarre, malevolent roll-over of a secret city transport involving Xander and Wee would ultimately thrust her deep into Phoenix's lair. That fateful meeting had set off a chain of events that transformed a personal mission into an attainable goal. She no longer conspired alone. And the crew of rebels had spun love knots around her heart. No matter what, she would champion them.

Her Alt pinged with a morse code message from Xander: *Set fire to Inventum*. She smiled, her affection for the Outsider bubbling within her. It took her no time at all to whip out a consenting response to him, followed by her Alt's immediate cryptic command to the two Sciolists loyal to her and the cause. *Set fire to Inventum*. Done.

Eyes darting from place to place, she took in the scenery and noted the citizens dribbling in or out of the hospital. She had to be on her guard; spies and Sciolists could be anywhere.

With her hand, she shielded her face from the afternoon sun, and spotted her limo waiting at the hospital's Elite space at the curb, like a patient friend. She sauntered over to it, humming both from joy and from a need to appear unhurried and natural. All her moves had to be typical of a normal day on the job.

Once inside the car, she relaxed. An automatic greeting and scented, cool air massaged her senses. She reclined her seat, knowing the programmed command of "home" would carry her to a place of safety. Her work of the day was complete.

After the limo pulled safely into the garage, Ava threw open the door to her residence, eager to see Evangeline, her domestic assistant, who was always ready with a cheerful smile and a cool drink at the end of her long day.

Instead, the hallway's floors shone, lonely in the remaining rays of sunshine dusting them from the skylight overhead. In sudden dread, she clenched her teeth before the word Evangeline left her mouth as a question.

From the corner beyond, two Sciolists stepped out, one from either side of an adjoining room. A storm of nerves ripped through her belly to form a congealed mass in the bottom of her stomach. Her lungs grabbed whatever oxygen they could find as she gulped for air.

As the shock buzzed through her limbs, Ava shrunk back, forcing a protest from her throat. "You—you have no right—"

The words of both Sciolists, spoken together like a chorus, bounced back. "Ava Validus. You are under arrest for conspiring against the Magistrate."

THIRTY

Serpio's Accusations

"WE HAVE Ava Validus in custody, and she is properly secured in interrogation room one." Serpio's OmniCom lit up with Esryn, his Sciolist's, voice. "I will be in the room making sure she is properly secured."

Finally! One of his goals was half met. "Thank you, Esryn. Make sure you remove her Alt. I want her to have no way to communicate with anyone. Store it in the prison locker. I'll be there soon."

Truth be told, he would glide in there within the next five minutes, but he didn't want Esryn to think he was overeager. Trusted Sciolists were one thing, but Sciolists were also judgmental, even Esryn, his most tried and true Sciolist. He ran his fingers through his hair in front of the mirror on the opposite side of the room.

He opened the door from his office and walked with his most dignified posture down the hallway, then stopped before entering room one, the windowed examination room. He gathered his thoughts and his breath and pushed the button to enter. He gave a brief nod to Esryn as a signal that he was dismissed.

"Hello, Ava," Serpio chirped as if greeting her at a social event. "You must be surprised to find yourself here at City Hall."

In a chair facing him, she looked at him as if he were scum on the sidewalk. Ava met his gaze without flinching. "I am indeed, Serpio. I'm Elite. You could have chosen a much more comfortable place." Inconceivably, she gave him a bright smile before acid hit her tongue. "What are you thinking, tying me up like a common criminal?"

Serpio's eyes sparked with fire as he stepped forward, positioning himself a mere foot from her. "You seem to be popping up in all the wrong places."

"What's that supposed to mean? I've been wherever you've asked me to go."

"Yes. Very convenient. In the Tower with Tranquility's Continuum Spectrum. At the Plauditorium with supplies. At the crash site with Xander Noble."

"I can't imagine why you would accuse me of something so terrible, Magistrate. I live only to serve you and the people of our city. What evidence do you have that I am working with the outlaws?"

He sighed, acting the part of someone who had to do something distasteful, such as watching a worm crawl across a dinner plate. "I've analyzed all the possibilities." He ran his right index finger over each digit of his left hand, as if he were ticking off four different discoveries. "There is no question. You are the one aiding the traitors in our city." He prided himself on keeping his emotions in check, his voice level.

"This is something you've imagined up in your head because you have failed to capture them." Ava gave him a look layered with forthrightness and hypocritical purity.

Her audacity, while dressed in innocence, triggered a wave of heat within his chest, and his body tensed in response. "There is no way these children have slipped through my fingers on their own. They're not smart enough for that—and they have no resources." He stared her down. "I looked at all the times they have eluded our efforts." He leaned forward, placing his hands on the table in front of him. "Noble didn't die in that roll-over accident. Why? Because *you* saved him!" He pounded his right fist into his left palm. "Then you lied to me when you said you'd transported the bodies to the Kelasts."

"Two other Medics were at the scene. I had to assist them. Or should I have told them you simply wanted Xander dead?"

Serpio sniffed. "I trusted you to *manage* it."

Ava went on, "In spite of the assistant Medics' efforts, they told me the victims did not survive, just as you had hoped. I drove the bodies in the MediCar to the Kelasts and washed my hands of it. If they were somehow alive afterward, it was from some unlikely miracle. Perhaps like the one that happened to you?" Again, the fake sincerity. She blinked her light brown eyes, never once showing any signs of deception. She shrugged. "My job was completed. I went from there to the Plauditorium, yes, but only dropped off the supplies *with your approval*. I'm sure you've checked the GPS logs?"

Serpio fumed internally at Ava's reference to his miraculous resurrection but wasn't going to give her the satisfaction of a response. Nor could he refute the GPS data. He had checked the logs personally, both on Ava's Alt and on the MediCar. When he'd seen nothing to use against her, he was livid. If he was right about Ava, she had covered her tracks well.

Glancing up at the camera blinking in the corner of the room, he smirked. He had to allow the camera to film the interrogation for the Elite. It was part of the agreement when the Elite voted to allow the questioning. But no matter. He could easily alter the footage afterward.

"*Where* are the traitors, Ava?" Serpio pulled his lips back in a wolfish snarl.

"I don't know. I'm telling you—"

"You *do* know! Who. Else. Is. Helping. Them?" Serpio's words were bullets.

"Last time I saw Ember, Xander, and Will, it was in the arena! And Ember was with *you*. If they ran off, I had nothing to do with it. I wasn't the one who threw the spear."

Serpio's head drew back, and then he dropped his voice to a whisper. "Will is mentally ill. But you! I've given you everything —position, power, and responsibility. And how do you repay me? By being a traitor! Sneaking around—supporting criminals! Now you must make amends. GIVE ME THE INFORMATION! And if you don't, you will do it when I force it out of you in the Tardis Obitus room, where Will Verus had to go. You've put the entire city's safety at risk."

"No!" she screamed, jerking against her restraints. "It's *your* safety that's at stake. Your need for power and control is what puts this city at risk. Will won't ever forget what you did to him! You're a fraud. You've corrupted everything!" Ava's almond eyes sparked with fire, and her tongue spewed cinders. "Your threats don't scare me, Serpio. No matter what you do, you can't get information from me about things I don't know! The Elite won't tolerate your methods, either. You'd better be careful. They are watching more than you think."

"You're a *backstabber*. That's all they need to know." He clicked his OmniCom, summoning the Sciolist back into the room. While he waited the half minute until he arrived, he didn't acknowledge Ava at all.

He addressed all his words to Esryn. "Place her in the holding cell," Serpio instructed. "I'll be back to see her tomorrow after the gala."

Serpio turned on his heel and set off in the opposite direction, eager to begin his preparations for the party that would make him a god.

THIRTY-ONE

Xander's Exodus

THE JOURNAL HAD BEEN a bombshell and drew Xander up short. If Serpio had genetic modifications, the information could maybe be found in the genetics lab. And he had just pulled the trigger on torching the place. Shit.

He scrambled to his feet and sought out Jasper. He'd have to let Ava know that it wasn't a good plan; she'd have to call off the Sciolists ordered to ignite it.

He'd also lost track of time. *How long have I been buried inside the Magistrate's head?*

His eyes darted about the warehouse. So many damned obstacles in the place. The pallets and shelves of food formed walls of plastic and tin.

"Jasper! Where are you?" Xander called out, his delivery awash with something close to panic.

"Hey, over here!" Jasper ambled out from behind a pallet of canned macaroni and cheese and smiled as he approached until he saw Xander's expression.

"I—I screwed up. We can't set fire to the lab! Look what I found." Xander held out the journal and read the last two paragraphs to Jasper.

Jasper's eyes bulged, followed by him scratching his chin. "So … what?"

"We don't know Serpio's DNA formula—and there's no way to kill him unless we find out how to reverse it. There are resources at Inventum that won't be anywhere else. If we burn down the lab, we're screwed. Give me your Alt. I have to tell Ava not to go forward with the burn."

"Whoa, whoa, Xander. You gotta share this with everybody first. You can't just make that decision yourself," Jasper replied.

"Gah!" Xander slapped his face with his palm. "What time is it?"

"Five-thirty," Jasper said as the digits appeared on his device. "Only two hours 'til the street party …"

"Help me get everyone together! We need another meeting." He suddenly felt the separation from Ember. Why couldn't she be here for this whole thing? Without her, the very air he breathed seemed to lack warmth.

Xander yelled out, "Phoenix! Front and center! We have an issue!"

"I'll round 'em up." Jasper scurried away, on a mission to collect all of Xander's disciples.

Xander kept shouting at the top of his voice, hoping there was no electronic surveillance that had been missed.

"Come! Everybody—come!" He wanted to help by running around finding everyone from wherever they were in the approximate eighty thousand square feet, but he had to stay in a central place.

Small groups—some in twos, some in threes—began to emerge. With the stacks of provisions towering to the ceiling, he never could anticipate where the people would come into view until they came around a corner. Luckily, in less than three minutes, the group was assembled around Xander.

"I thought I was a genius—and I am." Xander grinned and paused, his face once again serious. "But my idea to set fire to the lab is no longer a good plan," Xander explained. He held up the journal. "This is what I just learned about our fearless leader." He read aloud from the start, where the journal described Serpio's immortality formula.

When he finished sharing the entry, there was a moment of stunned silence. And then the racket of chatter hit him like a wave. For a small group, they could sure make noise.

Xander tucked the stunning journal under his arm and then turned to Jasper. "Hey, I still need these put somewhere so they're not left behind. Can you find a sack or two somewhere? You've taken good care of these. As you can see, they're important."

Jasper grumbled but did as he was told.

"Okay, okay, everybody!" Talesa cried. At that, the tribe quieted.

Talesa moved over to stand beside Xander. "If Serpio does have his immortality through DNA like he says, there is no way to reverse it," Talesa stated. "But if there is something he needs or can't do without, we need to know. Knowledge is power. I say we stop the burn."

"That's what I think," Xander echoed. "We didn't figure on needing the lab, but that has changed. All in favor of aborting?"

The little party called out a dozen yeses.

"Good. Now, where instead?" Xander's mind had been whirring as he'd waited for the group to come together. "Maybe the Kelastium. Except for the Kelasts running the place, people in there are already dead."

"Great idea, Xander," Wee said. "But the Sciolists—won't Serpio wonder why those Sciolists go to the house of the dead?"

Dorian, remarkably silent throughout, ventured, "Serpio will be busy at the party. He won't have his finger on every pulse. I say that's a good alternative."

With fist bumps throughout the group as his answer, Xander pressed, "Now, give me your Alt, Jasper. I need to message Ava right now!" Grabbing the Alt, he immediately began punching in, "Abort Inventum fire. Instead: Kelastium."

As if dusted with endorphins, he felt the euphoria of relief. He wiped his brow, confident he'd avoided making a mess of their future needs.

Spinning the Alt's wristband on his fingers, he turned to Jasper. "I'll hold on to this for a while to wait for Ava's reply." He slipped it on his arm, knowing his bolstered emotions would rocket the points for Jasper, AKA Rueben Lucio, according to his Alt.

Dorian addressed the squad next. "If all goes well, we leave here in ninety minutes. I'll be in front, but you'll stay in a group and walk on foot to the Maglev station, only a block south of here. I know that's a lot of people in a group, but it shouldn't arouse suspicion. It's going to be dark, but you won't have to hide anyway. Anyone I see coming toward us within fifty yards won't see you because of the mind trick command. You board the train, and I'll speak to the conductor. He will then not check your Alts. You'll go to the appropriate car for your fake Status. We'll be collecting all the other members of Phoenix as well as Easterners at three other stops along the way. Do not talk to anyone, but please smile. You'll get off at the Rainbow Ridge station. At that point, we walk straight to Obviators. It's close. Any questions?"

"I'm worried about walking out of here in a group. You're sure we won't arouse suspicion?" one of the former Plauditors said, his voice strained.

"Have faith. It's not like I've done this a million times, but it's guaranteed," Dorian replied.

"And the cameras right outside here are still blacked out. No one's ever come to fix 'em," Wee assured everyone. "Remember, I'll be your second insurance plan." Wee winked and actually sounded excited. "The second shift of Plauditors should be coming on right before I arrive."

Xander's talent for details kicked in. "Oh, Dorian … we all had our Alts' GPS shut off. Ava did it through the Continuum. Is there any way to cancel out yours?"

Dorian bunched his mouth in a pucker, thinking. He cocked his head. "I could speak to the Alt with a command to disengage. I'll try it." He held up crossed fingers. "Alt, I do not need the GPS on. Turn it off permanently."

A plinky voice responded, "Yes. GPS disengaged."

"How's that?" Dorian spawned a genuine smile.

"Not bad," Xander said.

Checking Jasper's Alt on his wrist, Xander fidgeted. Still nothing from Ava. She knew enough to be watching for messages. Not one to panic easily, he told himself he was nervous because the stakes were so high. Everything had to go as planned. It would take only one fail, and the whole house of cards would come crashing down. Yet, Ava had never let them down before. He would wait.

THIRTY-TWO

Serpio's Preparations

SERPIO DRESSED himself in his gold lamé tux and noted the time on his OmniCom. Two hours had passed since his encounter with Ava, and he could put that behind him to concentrate on the upcoming party. As he looked into the mirror, his black eyes twinkled in competition with the glitter of his apparel. Underneath his jacket, his shirt gleamed with lurex stripes and was accented with a gilt, flowered tie. He straightened his tie, smiled at himself, and stepped into his polished shoes. He would make quite an impression.

Coming back from the dead was a dramatic and unprecedented feat. Feeling powerful and supernatural, he smoothed his clothing, thinking of all the good he was doing for the city. All the citizens of the city would renew their love and respect for him, and perhaps he would even charm some new women.

At that, he thought fondly of his visits to see Talesa, who was imprisoned in luxury in a bunker located Outside. He was so proud of himself to have thought of that option instead of killing her. Talesa could live and be of service to him, and he could also pursue a relationship with her daughter. He truly had a perfect situation.

After the party was over and he got Ava's information, he

could indulge himself in a visit to Talesa. He sighed. So many good things awaited if he could get the fugitives brought to justice and close the door on the whole unpleasant mess.

Tagging the voice app on his OmniCom, he spoke: "The limo now." Since the explosion of his beautiful vehicle not too long ago, he never allowed the car to come early. There was too much risk.

While he waited, he decided to practice his speech. It would be a huge moment. He rubbed his hand on the mirror to wake it up.

"Dear citizens … it is wonderful to see you tonight. I hope this gala makes you extremely happy—happy to see your Magistrate is still with you. I know I am happy—happy to be alive and well after Will Verus, loyal Plauditor turned assassin, nearly killed me."

The mirror's AI voice interrupted. "Your speech should not mention negative things. You must leave Will Verus out of the message."

"Ah, yes. Of course. You are right, Imago," Serpio responded before trying again. "I know I am happy—happy to be alive and well after this challenge to our fair city. We might never know how the universe works, but in its vast wisdom, it saw fit to give me a second chance at life. I give credit, too, to the Medics who came to my aid immediately and, through life-saving measures with their skills and the Medela, were able to stop me from bleeding out, revive me, and heal my wounds."

"What are the names of the medics, Serpio? You should acknowledge them," the mirror advised.

Serpio cringed and then raised his fist to the man in the mirror. "I will not acknowledge Ava Validus."

"That is your choice. I am simply recommending it. If she saved your life or was present at the time, you should mention her as well as the others. It will leave your citizens wondering if you do not."

He sighed but thought for a moment. Ava's downfall would

be all the sweeter if he mentioned her as a hero now and a villain later. "Very well. It could be a good thing, after all. That's all for now, Imago." He did an about-face, danced down the stairs, and left the mansion.

THIRTY-THREE

Will's Move

WILL NOTICED Ember put one hand to her head and close her eyes. Headache? Weariness? Confusion?…Him?

Was he causing Ember too much grief? Should he ask her?

His guilt roared its ugly head again. She didn't deserve having to worry about her own struggles *and* his. Yet, as hard as he tried, his trauma always rose to the surface.

But the triumph in her voice cut through his doubts. "I just heard my mother's voice! She said, 'All warehouses moving out via Maglev. We have Easterners, and we're coming!'"

In celebration, Will ran and hoisted himself up onto a workbench a few feet away to sit among raggle-taggle parts of things he couldn't identify. "That's great news! Sounds like everything is good!"

Will folded his arms in front of himself. *They're all coming soon.* The minutes were now ticking away on a fast track. *Xander will be back.*

Ember wandered over to where Will reigned king of the table, leaned against the table's edge, and twisted her hair, a nervous habit Will found endearing. "Yeah! She says they're all coming on the train—even the ones from the other warehouses. I don't know how they're managing that with so many, but I'm sure they have an airtight plan. They have other Easterners helping them, so maybe they're making it work."

Across the room, Kamar tinkered with the ugly, patchwork car but stopped to give her a thumbs-up. "Son of a sewer rat! That's one way to move a lot of people. Sure wish I could be a fly on the wall. I'd love to see it happen."

Reselda sat in a circle with Will's parents, where she seemed determined to keep a close watch on them. A glint touched her eyes, and she smoothed her shirt, as if the gesture to make her clothes perfect would transfer to the mission at hand. "If there are people like me, I can't wait to meet them."

Jack shook his head in confusion. "Sorry, I obviously missed a lot. What's an Easterner?"

"A person with a power like Reselda and Ember," Marina said. "I had to ask, too. It's bizarre and a bit hard to understand, but Kamar explained that these people have always been in the city, but they've hidden their talents."

"They've been able to heal people? Just like they did with me? Why wouldn't we know about them?"

"Not just healing. Other…things." Will glanced Ember's way, noting the deep frown between her eyebrows.

The paleness of her face and the way she gripped her fingers signaled some anxiety. He got the impression that Ember would rather not share her story. Even the parts he could remember would be mind-blowing. He would respect her privacy; she should be the one who should confide all she'd been through and how she'd discovered her powers. After all, her mom's "death" was a story in itself.

"That's amazing. I've lived my whole life and never knew people like that existed." Jack gazed at Ember with an expression akin to adoration.

With his most gentle touch, Will reached out and wrapped his hand around Ember's arm, meeting her eyes. Her shoulders slumped, and she pinched the skin at her throat.

To the others he asked, "Will you excuse us for a minute?"

As they walked away together, Ember in step with Will but unsteady on her feet, she asked, "What is it? Are you okay?"

"That's what I want to ask *you*." Will kept up a fast pace, drawing her away from the others, until they were behind one of Kamar's other vehicles. He whispered, "I know you, Ember. I can see you're freaked out." Will hoped she would be honest with him. He wanted to comfort her.

Ember came to a halt and stepped closer where she could face him. "I had a dream," she stated flatly.

Wrinkling his brow, Will looked down into her face. His thoughts ping-ponged against his skull. A dream was no big deal…Yet this was troubling her?

"I dreamed of shadows, clouds, lightning and thunder, and a bed that I was lying on, draped in red sheets. The red dripped off them. People were fighting—I could hear them but couldn't see them. And then…at the very end…*you* were calling out." Her voice trembled, and she swallowed before saying, "You sounded like you were in pain."

Although Will wanted to dismiss it—it was just a dream, after all—he brought himself up short. A memory surfaced from the depths of his brain: *Ember's dreams are prophetic.* "I was calling out? What did I say?"

"You yelled for me as if you were hurting. But I don't even know why. All I heard was your voice. I didn't see why you were in danger." Ember twisted her hands together so tightly that Will thought she'd wring blood from them.

"What does it mean?" Will persisted, dropping down off the table to stand next to her.

"I don't know! That's the rub. The dreams are lifelike. I feel like I'm there. But they're mysterious, too—only just clues to what will occur. One thing's for sure. These things will happen. They always do. It's a second sight. There's a real bed like that somewhere, and when I was lying in it, I wasn't moving. And I'm worried that red bed means I'm going to die, and—"

Will felt the color drain from his face and tried to control the tingle in his fingertips.

Ember kept talking, but the words faded into nothingness. *DIE? This was a prophecy about her own death?* An icy sting whipped down his spine. *Oh, oh NO! Ember's dream couldn't mean that, could it? A blood-red bed could be anything...*

He reigned in his horror, breathing steadily to quell the anxiety in his spirit, robbing the words of their power with his breath by letting each word go like balloons into the sky. "Holy Shazz, Ember. That's not going to happen. I won't let it!"

"This is a warning to me. I'll have to watch for signs that this will happen. And I need to save you! Maybe from your post-traumatic stress, or maybe from mortal danger. I don't know...I don't know! But now I'm never going to let you be far from my side." Ember turned and put her hands on Will's arms, gripped them, and tightened the pressure with each word.

Will's breath caught, his heart fluttering. He mirrored her move, placing his hands on her arms. Then he pulled her tightly into his chest and held her. She didn't resist, seeming to want the comfort of a hug. As he felt her warmth, her heart beating in rhythm with his, and inhaled her unique, familiar scent, he strained against her. *Paradise.* He knew he shouldn't be feeling this way. She wasn't his. Not anymore. But he couldn't help it.

The electricity between them was palpable, and the more he held her, the more he wanted her. He slowly pulled back, just enough to look into her eyes. The soft, amber glow of the faint luminescence overhead danced in her irises, like golden candle flames. Without a word, he leaned down, wanting desperately to kiss her, but stopped.

In a purposeful effort, he separated from her, knowing he needed to save himself right at that minute.

She gazed at him, her mouth parted and her bottom lip quivering, her eyes wandering over the outer outline of his body, as if measuring the flare of his aura. Then she closed her eyes and took a step backward. "I need to keep you by my side, Will. I know you need me, and I can feel your pain. It rips me up inside. But we can't do…this. It's too confusing."

Although he felt responsible for hanging his pain all over her, a shaft of hope ignited within him. He put his hands on his head and looked up at the ceiling while slowly spinning in a circle. "What does that mean, you get confused?"

Will felt his heartbeat measuring the seconds of silence as Ember stood frozen and speechless.

"I get overloaded with your feelings and then mine. It's not fair to me. I can't fight them off."

"So, what are you saying? You're a victim here?"

Again, the silence stretched out, quiet as each breath he took.

"I'm worried I've got feelings for you when I shouldn't. And I can't be torn back and forth like this. It's not right for anyone."

Will went from the chill of the Reaper to a fire that ripped through his heart. Replay the words…*Feelings for you. FEELINGS FOR YOU?* "You have feelings for me? Like…like what you told me before, right?"

She didn't answer but looked up at him with doe eyes before lowering her gaze and taking a hesitant step back.

Will took a half-step forward. "Look. It's easy. If you have feelings for me, those are real." He took another half-step forward but did not touch her. Instead his eyes grew wet. "You can pick me. I *need* you, Ember. Xander—he's fine on his own. But I'm not. At least not right now. If you'll give me your love, I can get past all that happened to me. Then I can be everything you need. I promise you that. And I'll keep those clouds, lightning, shadows, red beds, and whatever else comes your way from harming you, to the best of my ability."

He took her arm and pulled her close to him, all the while listening for a protest. When none came, he tilted her face to his and kissed her lightly. Sweetly. Her sigh when he drew back triggered his pent-up desire. He drew her in a second time and then, backing her up to the wall just beyond, pressed himself against her as tightly as he could and kissed her hard, his tongue dipping into her glorious, glorious mouth.

THIRTY-FOUR

Xander's Unease

SIXTY MINUTES TICKED BY, and still no word from Ava. Something was wrong. Ava had never hung them out to dry like this.

He was helpless to stop the burn at Inventum. The knowledge stung.

Nevertheless, a fire was vital. They had to have every Sciolist and city agent caught up with the crisis. His mind machine-gunned 'what ifs' as he paced the floor. What if Ava or her conspiratorial Sciolists had a delay or a mishap? What if she couldn't even order a fire at all?

Phoenix was gathered, ready to exit the back door, but quietly chattered and joked, especially at their lack of showers and the normal lives they had left behind.

But at last, everywhere around him, Alts lit up with messages accompanied by upbeat electronic music announcing the party had begun in the street outside City Hall. Once the fire started, Xander knew the party would be moved inside for safety. Even better. Citizens who couldn't attend because they didn't have the required Status could now be watching on their home screens, which would help, too.

But still, they waited. The way they figured, they'd hold off until after they received an alert about the fire. An emergency alert would be immediately obeyed; at that point, people would have to return home, and they could move with the crowds, just part of the citizens seeking to follow their leader.

He chafed at the slog of time, seconds sucking his life away. Although the friendly prattling and camaraderie of the group usually buoyed him up, even that became an irritation, a razor cut to his nerves.

Then Alts lit up red, and the fifteen shrill alarms that followed shanked the small talk. A hush blanketed the group as an automated command instructed, "Citizens, this is a fire warning. Take shelter in your homes without delay."

Xander slipped his ugly mask on, rubbed his sweaty palms on his pants, and shut his eyes. It was time.

Dorian stood in front of the group, and Xander brought up the rear.

With a nod between them, the Easterner opened the door, and the group slid out into the darkness, where shadows formed and deepened into thick, inky pools. To Xander, the night amplified every sound and swept its charcoaled dust onto anyone's rose-colored glasses. Creeping through the streets, it was difficult to see anything at all. From what he could tell, though, there was no sign of anyone.

Xander was not surprised. He glanced up at the scarce streetlights, grateful they were dim, amber flickers in this part of town where buildings were distribution centers, rarely places for workers, and especially unpopulated at night.

A high-pitched horn pierced the air, followed by another louder blast. At last—fire crews on their way to Inventum. The group whispered to each other, lightly clapping backs and pumping fists in the air. A twinge of regret twisted Xander's stomach, but he celebrated the sounds of the sirens.

All Sciolists, the fire department, and city officials would be consumed with the blaze on the outskirts of town. Far enough away from City Hall, it would capture the attention of both the responders and the citizenry, who would be warned to stay inside and out of the way of danger.

Xander smiled, knowing so much of the threat to them just deflated. And just maybe the lab could be saved—at least enough that they could access it for answers later.

Yet Xander was full of angst. He was sure of Dorian but had no idea whether the other Easterners were equipped to do what was needed. With the hope of the two major distractions of the fire and the party, plus Wee's disabling of the Plauditor's cameras, he told himself that was enough.

A barely discernible scent of smoke wafted his way. He frowned, as the smell reminded him of the clearing Outside where bodies were burned. This time, though, the acrid assault on his nostrils wouldn't be because people were being cremated. All the same, his eyes watered, either from the smoke or the memory it conjured.

Ava's silence continued to gnaw at him for every minute that went by. And he missed Ember. The separation made him uneasy.

No one spoke, and their footsteps were light. Yet his heart galloped. Up ahead, Dorian's silver glimmer leading the way down the first block behind a furniture storage warehouse. A cross street was the first break in the protection of the building.

A few people here and there drifted past his line of vision. Good. They were not the only people out. Each appeared in a massive hurry as Alt warnings continued to go out about the fire. The citizens would only have a limited amount of time and leniency to get to their residences before they would be picked up by a city official for their own "protection."

Dorian motioned to the group with his hand to slow down before a Sciolist walked across their path from the other direction. *What the—!* The breath left his lungs, only to return when he heard Dorian speak to the man. He could hear nothing but the word "here," but the Sciolist paused in his tracks and then continued on, his cloak blowing in the evening breeze, a lone wolf still seeking his prey.

Scampering across the open road, they gleaned safety on the other side, where an automated metalworking plant took up another two blocks, and continued down the dimly lit alley beyond.

One more block, and the Maglev station would be in sight. But first, they'd see the end of the industrial complex. They'd have no choice but to traverse through a park adjoining a neighborhood of Level Nine homes. The homes in Mint Meadows had large windows on their fronts, facing out toward the park.

The park closed at dusk for safety. Anyone present or using it at this hour would be violating the law. Each blade of grass squeaked under their feet, while the chains on the playground swings sang of their lonely plight in the breeze. Their motley crew of workers would be more than a freak curiosity in the night, even in an emergency. Xander held his breath, hoping no one decided to report them.

A small pony in a backyard nickered as they walked by.

A front door just past them opened, and a woman with frizzy hair in green pajamas edged out onto the stoop. "You hoo! You there!" she called, her tone one of those overly eager saccharine voices Xander hated.

Xander rolled his eyes. *A busybody on alert.*

Her eyes protruding wide in an artificial display of concern, the lady took a moment to smile at them; the harmonics in her speech pattern had a birdlike quality. "You're awfully late getting home from work, aren't you, folks? I'm very concerned you're walking about. There's fire in the city! I'm just about to go out back and check on my horse, Brighty. Don't want the animal to get frightened. Then I'm right back in. There was an announcement earlier that people are not to be out. Not out at all. You'd better get yourselves home soon!"

Dorian stepped forward toward the woman and spoke, his words soft as a caress. "Your horse will be fine. We know about the fire and are heading home. You will no longer be concerned for us. You will go into your house and not remember we have passed by."

She stood silent, blinking, before scratching her head and retreating inside.

The lady's threat dragged the energy from Xander's body, and their walk suddenly seemed endless.

Finally, up ahead, the station's lights burned into the night. "What time is it?" Xander asked Jasper.

Jasper whispered back, as if he were seriously going to be overheard. "Eight-thirty. Maglev should be by in five minutes, according to my Alt's info. Perfect timing."

Xander nodded. Until they got on that thing and got the others as they went around the city, he would be a basket case. "Hey, gang," he said out loud. "Be alert up ahead. Remember, even with the fire, Sciolists could still be checking Alts and collecting DNA. Space out and couple up."

In abbreviated groups, they climbed the stairs onto the translucent platform at the station. Colored lights began blinking along the Maglev's track, the multihued illumination directing passengers to where their appropriate car would be positioned for boarding. That meant the train would be arriving in less than a minute.

Were other city folk on board? Xander strained his eyes to see if there were faces in the windows. There … there were. They would blend in! His heart swelled with relief.

Suddenly, out of the shadows came a cheerless voice. A Sciolist stepped out from behind a black kiosk. "Stop! Before you board the train, I will check your information. If I suspect you are a rebel, I will collect DNA by order of City Hall. Then you get on the train."

Before Xander had a second to respond, Bixby rushed out from the cluster. He snapped, "Hel-looooo! There's a *fire*, and you're being a bastard. We're gonna miss the train!"

The group, now no longer separated as they prepared to

board the train, clustered behind Xander. Giving them all a once-over, the scarlet-clad agent drew his Stinger from beneath his cloak and addressed the group. "You are not from a specific site, I see, but many." Flicking Bixby's collar with the tip of his weapon, he challenged, "Why is that?"

Xander smirked. "Party after work. Or is that not allowed?"

"If you were too far away from home, you should have sheltered at the party," the Sciolist countered.

"With all due respect, now that we've left, we can't get inside our homes without the Maglev," Bixby argued, his blue eyes looking more like lead. "Let's get on with it."

Jasper raised his right fist. "If the air's that bad, don't ya need some sort of mask yourself?"

"My safety is not your concern. But *your* safety is my concern. Show me your Alts. I must report your identities to City Hall."

The Sciolist showed no signs of backing down. Restlessness rippled through the team.

Xander stepped forward. "You're out of line. That's an invasion of our privacy. You're causing us distress. That's a sin in the city—or didn't you know? We've done nothing wrong except try to get where we need to be."

"Your happiness is not my job. It's yours," the Sciolist scoffed. "Show your Alts. NOW."

Bixby, Jasper, and another Plauditor extended their arms as if to comply, but their hands became rockets, pummeling the Sciolist. Each thud seemed to echo into the night.

A collective gasp rose from the group. Xander barely mouthed, "Stop" before the Stinger, its tip crackling with an electric pulse, connected with Bixby's shoulder.

"Holy Shazz! Ugh!" Bixby cried.

With the exception of Xander and Dorian, the crew flew into action, swarming around Bixby, who had dropped to his knees with a groan.

Dorian dashed to the Sciolist's side and commanded, "You will now let us pass. You have no further need to question or detain us, and you will ensure the Maglev's schedule is in place until it has made a complete trip around the city and returned here. Once we are gone, you will not remember this encounter. You will nod that you understand."

With a bow that would be incomprehensible otherwise, the official answered, "Of course."

Xander almost burst out laughing but held himself together. He turned to Dorian. "If he's so agreeable, let's get his Alt, too."

Dorian's eyebrows stretched toward his hairline as he smiled. "Sciolist, you have no need for your Alt. You will turn it over to us."

The Sciolist appeared dazed, his face showing even less emotion than the typical Sciolist would exhibit. He nodded, unstrapped his Alt, turned it over to Dorian, and, like a robot, stood, his arms at his side, simply watching Phoenix board the train.

Xander and Jasper helped Bixby, who was groaning and holding his shoulder. Walking him to the highest Status car in the train, Xander and Jasper made sure he wasn't going to faint from the burn.

Once settled, Bixby rubbed his shoulder and finally grinned. "That was a shocker," he joked.

Xander could tell the pain still radiated from the blasted weapon, but Bix was doing a great job sucking it up.

After he left Bixby, Xander made quick use of the Sciolist's Alt, passed it through the Signetworks, the point collector just inside the door, and hurriedly made his way to his assigned level's car. As he went, he glanced around and saw the others had already scattered throughout the train; they had followed his strict instructions to wave their Alts across the Signetworks and then make their way quickly to their own Status sections, joining dozens of other upstanding citizens. He settled himself and buckled in, his kelly-green Obviators's uniform blending into the surrounding wall and upholstery colors, and grinned as he saw Talesa sitting several rows ahead. She turned and gave him a smile. She was a steadying presence in the face of the chaos and madness.

Earlier, a grand debate over using Alts to board the Maglev had pissed Xander off so badly he could hardly see straight. A knowledgeable Plauditor finally screamed that the Maglev wouldn't even function without the wrist devices being processed through the system. The M was programmed until the number of passengers it counted climbing aboard were strapped into seats. He felt stupid he hadn't known about the Maglev's system, but he hadn't exactly been someone who had ever followed the rules.

In two seconds, the train shot out of the station. It occurred to him that the Signetworks would register a Sciolist on board. Not too shabby.

As always, the ride was a blur. He barely blinked before the magnetized, high-speed shuttle arrived at the next station. They had put everything into place as carefully as they could. What could possibly go wrong?

THIRTY-FIVE

Ember's Reaction

WILL'S kiss had set Ember ablaze. After unreservedly and enthusiastically drowning in his kiss for a good twenty seconds, she shoved him away.

"Will! Stop! This is not okay." She couldn't wrap her head around her feelings. The last thing she needed was this ridiculous heat between them.

Will nearly lost his balance as he bore her physical rejection. His face flushed a deep pink, as if humiliation had dyed him the color of a day-old strawberry sucker. Then, locking eyes with her, he forged a rueful smile before he said, "I apologize for the surprise. I won't apologize for the kiss. But kissing you told me everything I needed to know. You do have feelings for me. And they're exactly the same as when we kissed the first time. Definitely not brotherly, and definitely not just friendship."

Ember's chest rose and fell in rhythm with her heartbeat in what felt like cardiac G-force. She needed to control her breathing before she could answer him, which was good because she couldn't gather her thoughts, much less know what to say. She couldn't deny the chemistry she felt, and he knew it.

Taking a deep breath, she said, "That was … unexpected." She broke eye contact and looked at the floor. "I'm obviously not quite … over you. But I'm not suddenly going to jump into your arms. I'm in love with *Xander*!" The last statement came out in an angry rant, and she glanced over at the others across the room to gauge whether they were reacting. They appeared not to be listening.

Will grinned, excitement spilling over into his eyes. "Not quite over me. I can live with that. For now. I'll wait until you figure everything out. In the meantime, I'll be respectful of your relationship with that—with Xander. I promise I won't kiss you again until you ask me to, but I'm going to fight for you. Just as much as I'm fighting for freedom against the Alt and Serpio, or anything else worth pursuing."

Her heartbeat finally slowing, Ember had no more words. She was disgusted with herself for her weakness and her disloyalty to Xander. She turned her back and walked with a fierce stride toward the chair, where she sat down and crossed her arms, refusing to look back at Will to see what he was doing, although she felt his emotions gripping her hard even from twenty feet away.

But not just his devotion and desire. She felt and internalized the grief and trauma he was trying to leave behind. Where his spirit had been damaged, she felt a gloom that was alive. Like sharp talons, they dug into her heart and brain until she nearly fainted from the poison. Ember wished she could separate herself from the blackness in Will's core that spilled into her own soul, oil on water.

Marina, who had been staring into a steel plate on the opposite wall and trying to comb her hair with a shop-worthy wire brush, turned around as she witnessed Ember's stomp parade. "Is everything all right, Ember?"

"Yes. I'm *fine*!" she yelled back before zeroing in on Kamar looking intently at his Alt. She made her way over. "Any news from anyone?"

"Just got a city warning about a fire. Looks like Ava put a plan for distraction into action." He held up crossed fingers.

As best she could, Ember shook off her scattered emotions. Nothing like a revolution to put things in perspective. "What's it say?"

"Only that all people need to stay inside due to air quality. Once the blaze is out, the emergency air purifiers will activate to clear the smoke and pollutants."

"That's awesome. Nothing from Ava?" Ember thought she'd have communicated something about a successful car repair—something so Kamar would know she was in the loop.

Kamar shook his head. "Maybe she didn't think the communication risk was worth it. We'd know soon enough that a fire had been set."

"And the street party? Is it still on?"

"We can see for ourselves." Kamar spoke into his Alt. "Tranview." He waved his Alt in the direction of the screen on the opposite wall.

The screen flared to life, the words "LIVE IN PROGRESS" continuously scrolling along the bottom of the display.

Ember witnessed a stage where various rainbow hues of smoke shot upward and then diffused through the air, creating a dense cloud of iridescence. Music played in time with each vapor's release, an anthem she'd not heard before. The theme crescendoed to a climax. Stepping out from a haze now laced with shimmering, cascading golden flecks was Serpio Magnus himself.

The crowd around him went wild. Screams and cheers washed the venue with noise. A chant began, accompanied by stomping feet. "Ser-pi-o! Ser-pi-o! Ser-pi-o!"

"Oh!" Ember couldn't help but gasp. The sight of her nemesis, whole and healthy, smiling out at a horde of applauding supporters made her blood run cold. As he took a bow, she put her hand to her forehead.

She glanced at Kamar, only to see that during her all-absorbing focus on the screen, Marina, Jack, and Will had gathered behind her. Immediately, she realized that her blood running cold wasn't so much just hers. Will's presence felt like a glacier, his aura, suffusing much like the smoke on the screen, was turning a deep gray. The sight of Serpio celebrating his comeback from the dead had turned Will into a pale shadow.

She took one step rearward, directly in front of Will, her back touching his chest. He was trembling. When she grabbed his hand, she felt as if she was connected to something very, very dark.

The extent of Will's distress soundly registered with her. *He's not just suffering PTSD. He's damaged down to his soul.* His grip grew tight, his fingers lacing with hers with an intensity born of acute distress.

Marina glanced in Will's direction. "Son, are you okay?"

Will didn't answer, but swayed on his feet and put a hand to his head.

Serpio spoke, his smile a slice of summer. "Citizens of Tranquility, I am most grateful for your support. I stand before you today, incredibly lucky to have survived the attack on my life. I owe my continued existence to our incredible Medics, Ava Validus, Felix Mellifluus, and Henry Prudens."

Kamar scrunched his eyes shut and snickered. "Ass. At least he mentioned Ava. I assume she's there in the crowd."

Ember strained her eyes to see but instead gasped. A gloom, cold as a tombstone in the night, bore through her. A second later, Will collapsed in a heap at her feet.

"Will!" As he fell against her, she tried to catch him, scrambling to regain her own balance.

The entire group gathered around. Reselda knelt and slowly moved her hands down Will's body and urged Ember, crouching by his side, to do the same.

Marina looked as pale as Will. "He's fainted, right? Oh, my poor boy …"

Kamar took off to get water, and Jack leaned over to slap Will's face lightly in the hope it would bring him back.

"This is the second time he's fainted. It's the sight of Serpio." Ember repositioned herself where she could stroke Will's hair.

Jack shook his head. "That's all it takes? Just seeing Serpio on the Purview? What's he going to do when he sees him in person?"

"Jack, grab his feet and elevate them," Reselda ordered. Jack quickly hurried to follow her command.

Kamar returned with water and a cloth. He wet it and placed it on Will's forehead.

Putting her hand on his chest, Ember felt his heartbeat. It was steady. The bleakness she felt moments earlier was ebbing some. "Will. We need you to wake up. Will!"

No response except for Will's shallow breathing.

Ember placed her hands on Will's head and closed her eyes. She felt his pulse under her fingers and the softness of his hair. *Oh, Will … you need to come around.* Without another thought, she bent her head and kissed him gently on his lips. She sat up again and stroked his head once more.

As if by magic, his eyelids fluttered, and his aura glowed white. He moved his head from side to side. "Uh … what happened?"

Marina answered, "You fainted."

"Shazz. Again?" Will struggled to sit up.

Jack put his hand out to slow his son down. The pallor from his own brush with death returned to his face, along with a worried frown. "You think you're okay?"

"Yeah." He glanced at Ember, then at his dad, and finally back to Ember, where his eyes rested on her lips.

Something fluttered in Ember's chest like bird wings as Jack helped Will rise to his feet. Will's emotions clashed with hers—a mixture of relief, fear, and confusion. She lightly touched her fingers to her lips and blushed, suddenly sorry for how she'd roused him. *Why did I do such a mushy, impulsive thing?*

As she stood, she rushed her words to cover her embarrassment. "You're okay enough to watch the rest of the party? You could sit down …"

Will's nostrils flared. "No! Don't—I'm fine. I am going to get past this. So sorry, everybody." Will clenched his teeth, balled his fists, and separated himself, planting his legs wide.

Ember felt his anger at himself as if her arteries and veins were tied to his but turned her attention to the screen.

Serpio had been shaking hands and smiling, greeting Felix Mellifluus and Henry Prudens, who had both stepped up on the platform.

"No sign of Ava," Ember voiced, still looking at Will out of the corner of her eye.

"Felix, Henry—thanks again. But medical intervention, as you know, is not enough! My miracle proves that one's mindset can absolutely and totally contribute to healing and defying the odds. As you can see, I am healthy, happy, and ready to resume all my responsibilities as your humble Magistrate. We will have no worry or negativity tonight—only celebration."

The crowd cheered. Spring-loaded, brightly colored streamers shot into the air, popping, one after another. Tranquility's anthem played. People hopped up and down along with the beat of the music, throwing their arms into the air.

Serpio bowed, allowing the crowd to revel in the moment. Then, he straightened and asked for the crowd's attention. At the hush, he spoke. "Due to a fire south of here, we will all be entering the City Hall auditorium so as to avoid inhaling smoke during the party. We have appointed Plauditors for your security to direct you into the building. I will see you all inside Halcyon Hall." He retreated from the platform and disappeared from view.

The partiers turned to one another and babbled, clearly disappointed in the disruption. However, Plauditors scattered throughout took charge, forming groups based on Status and leading them into the adjacent building, a mere thirty feet away.

"How were they able to spare Plauditors? They're short-handed already, right?" Jack's face crumpled with his questions, but he directed his inquiry to Will.

"Those in the Plauditorium are doing double duty for sure. The party's the focus for Serpio right now. He'd be willing to leave the surveillance in favor of parading himself." Will wiped an inordinate amount of sweat from his forehead.

"Seems counterproductive to me," Ember said, stepping closer to Will's side and squeezing his hand. "If he's concerned about where we are, you'd think close observation would be a number one priority."

"Bottom line," Kamar interjected, "he's clearly not frightened. If he can survive anything, what is a certifiable threat to him, really? He wants to capture you guys, yeah. But not at the expense of his own glorified moment in the sun. He's just postponing the hunt, that's all."

Ember exhaled, hoping all the anxiety that she was feeling, along with Will's, would simply blow away. "That works in our favor, then."

Distant sirens, scarcely audible from within their stone basement, nailed down the moment.

Kamar's eyes tightened at the corners. "Serpio has eyes everywhere. He knew immediately when that fire started. That's another reason why he pulled the Plauditors for the event. All of the city's fire crews will be on the scene, but scores of Sciolists will be there, too, to investigate and arrest anyone lurking nearby. He's going to assume the fire's the work of Phoenix. What else would it be?"

Xander's out there in that mess, Ember thought. All it took was one false move, and he and the rest of Phoenix would be captured or worse before they got there. A pang of fear struck her chest, dead center. Although Will's hand still trembled, she dropped it. Instead, she shut her eyes and sent a mental message to her mom.

"What's happening?"

The beloved voice came back. *"We are okay so far. On the Mag and coming. Your Xander is fine! We have Easterners helping."*

"Hey! My mom says they're on their way back! They really are coming on the train." Ember smiled a little unsteadily. It was good news, but scary. "She says they have Easterners with them."

"Those superpower people suddenly popping up like mushrooms?" Jack shook his head, but his face creased with a smile.

"I can't wait to meet everyone." Despite her enthusiastic remark, Marina continued to keep an eye on Will. "These are all people you know, right?"

Ember wasn't sure if Marina was addressing the group or just her son, but she answered. "I know them all, and Will knows many. All except the Easterners, of course."

Refocusing her attention to the screen, Ember noticed the cameramen had followed the crowd of partiers inside the building, leaving behind the multicolored lights and metallic streamers that hung between the avenue's light poles and monumental burnished urns that hemorrhaged blue roses.

The cameras panned to the inside, where the decor was similarly elegant and festive. Spotlights lit the walls with golden light reflecting on the glassy marble floor tiles. Thousands of crystal beads hung from the ceiling, catching the light, and a holographic eighteen-color rainbow spanned the length of the room.

Reporters interviewed guests about the Magistrate's miraculous recovery and the ball itself.

Partygoers collected exotic drinks and finger sandwiches from highly decorated, self-propelled utility carts. A DJ blared dance music from hidden speakers, each song's lyrics about celebration, every tune especially dedicated to Serpio.

In spite of the exaggerated, nauseating gushing of the invitees, Ember marveled at the clothing—so many metallic gowns and tuxedos in shades of copper and silver, and a flush of gold, accented throughout with some of the Status colors just below those levels, indigo and purple. Five levels of Status. She observed Serpio again working the crowd, his chivalry and smiles on full display. Too bad the chivalry was fake and the smiles insincere.

A moment later, a Sciolist approached the Magistrate and whispered in his ear. Ember watched as the Magistrate's skin faded within seconds to an unearthly white. Serpio put his hand to his chest as if pushing the lungs to rise and fall. A sheen of sweat gathered on his forehead. As he tried to wipe it off with trembling fingers, the assisting Sciolist pulled a handkerchief from his own pocket and offered it. With a shake of his head, Serpio walked off the platform. He bridged the twelve feet to the back of the room with steps of lightning speed before leaving the auditorium.

"Look. Serpio's rattled. Not hiding it well either." Ember leaned forward to get a better look. The cameras, however, backed off and swiveled to recapture the frivolity of the crowd.

"What's happening?" Kamar had seen it, too.

"A man who can come back from the dead shouldn't be afraid of anything." Jack inclined his head sideways, his statement more like a question.

Will's trembling iced into a stiff, soldier-like stance. "Whatever it is, I sure hope it's in our favor."

THIRTY-SIX

Xander's Souvenirs

SO FAR, so good. No Plauditor, Sciolist, or Maglev conductor had toured the train to double-check Alts or ask questions since they boarded. Xander hoped, with the injunction, the singular city official who normally rode on the Maglev and kept things in order had long since left his post. Xander wanted to breathe a sigh of relief, but he could not relax. His nerves were drunk with adrenaline.

He felt the tug of gravity slowing the Maglev to a stop. *Already at the next station,* he thought. He couldn't wait 'til he could peel off his mask and walk around in Kamar's protected underground room. In the meantime, he was ready to greet the next group of Phoenix.

Xander hugged himself with his arms as if to ward off anything negative. People got on. Familiar faces and the multi-colored uniforms of Phoenix made him dizzy with relief. A few other hopeful stragglers with no association to Phoenix, including a young mother with a child, were lucky enough to follow the group onboard. He watched them all begin to find their places, a number drifting toward the sliding doors between the cars.

As soon as Red boarded, Xander recognized the new Easterner, with his flaming red hair, but what really stood out was his fashion sense. Red's clothing, although the simple white of a disgraced level, looked fresh and fashionable—a short-sleeved viscose shirt with a diamond mesh texture on the upper section, accented in the middle with a stripe of three color blocks, all shades of white. His polyester pants clung to his legs.

Xander locked eyes with Red. "I'm Xander," he said simply. With a further nod to Red, he then looked out the window, trying to act nonchalant but failing. He turned to watch more people come aboard.

Then he saw red. This time, not the Easterner, but the color. His thirty-second it's-gonna-be-all-right pause ended. Xander stiffened. What in the hell was a Sciolist doing boarding the train?

But of course he knew. The previous Sciolist would have been confused and unable to execute his orders, but that didn't preclude another from stepping up. Serpio would never allow passengers whose IDs hadn't been verified to board the train. The search for the rebels was the Magistrate's primary goal.

From under the crimson hood, the henchman's beady-eyed glare swept across the Maglev's passengers. In a loud, stoic voice, he addressed the group who had just boarded, along with the rest of them. "Esteemed citizens, you are following orders to get to your homes, precisely what the Alt warning instructed you to do. However, this route leads directly past Inventum, where the fire is burning out of control. For your safety, you cannot remain on the train. This route is off limits until the fire is out and the smoke is blown from the dome. Each of you must disembark. You will shelter at this station's building until the all-clear is given."

Subdued cries of dismay rippled throughout the train car before the travelers began to stir and collect their things. Passengers pasted on smiles and enthusiastically called out words to the effect of "Thanks for caring about our safety." A citizen of the city would always turn an unfortunate incident into something they could be positive about. Couples and trios hurried toward the way out, babbling about how grateful they were to have a secure place to go.

Xander refrained from rolling his eyes. Instead, he sought out Red, who was seated a few rows in front of him. Xander stood as if he, too, were obeying the command. They needed to appear compliant. As he did, he nodded and motioned to all his fellow Phoenix seated nearby to stand and signaled a "follow me" to Red.

They followed the Sciolist at a distance as the caped bastard continued toward the back section of the train to deliver his message.

Groups of average citizens headed to the exits and disembarked. He briefly felt sorry for them. *Such unfortunate sheep, obedient no matter what.*

His Phoenix group, a scattered few he recognized in the next car, stood as well. However, Xander's eyes, burning with a warning, met theirs, and he gave a micro shake of his head. He hoped it was enough to convey that they should not move.

Sliding alongside those leaving, but going the opposite direction, he and Red kept their distance from Serpio's weasel, avoiding detection, all the way into the last car of the train. Unfortunately tangled in the crowd near the doorway, they grabbed on to a railing to separate themselves from getting carried right out with everyone else.

There, he caught the Sciolist's attention. As Xander stood aside politely to let the remaining few pass, he gave the sallow-faced intimidator a little bow of acknowledgment.

"Continue to the exit and disembark!" the henchman commanded, addressing Xander. "That is an order!"

In his most honeyed tone, Xander said, "Just waiting for all the others, sir. That's the Tranquility way." He almost snickered as he said it, but he really needed to get innocent people off the train. Things were about to get real.

"Get off the train. Now!" The Sciolist's command was frosty like hardened snow.

Xander didn't move a muscle, just penetrated his enemy with an insolent stare.

The Sciolist drew his Stinger out from under his robe and touched its electrified tip to the metal doorway.

The door froze in the open position, preventing the train from engaging its magnetic pull on the tracks.

Spittle flew from the Sciolist's lips. "You are *resisting*? Unacceptable. And futile. The Maglev will not move."

Red's hair bloomed into what looked like porcupine quills. He rose like a cobra, turning fully to face the Sciolist. "Our journey will not stop here. We are entitled to get to our homes, to safety, where we are *happy*." Red's voice smoldered, the irony of its tone lost in the moment. His scowl, though, could blister even the toughest skin.

Xander took note of the muscles on Red he'd overlooked before. Outlined by protruding blue veins, the Easterner's biceps pulsed as he flexed his arms.

The Sciolist put his hand up, his words clipping the air. "Inhaling smoke will harm you. There are also toxins in the air. Chemicals from the DNA lab. This is for your safety. Safety and happiness go hand in hand."

Xander tapped his foot. The train delay wasn't a good thing. Sweat beaded up on his upper lip. The longer it took, the more risk there was of getting everyone to Kamar's. Why was Red holding back? It took all of Xander's patience not to stand up himself to confront the Sciolist.

Red smiled, sweetness now lacing his words. "We'll take the risk. We stay." At that, Red struck out with lightning speed and grabbed the Sciolist's arms. The force of his grip squeezed the Sciolist's flesh like a latex balloon under pressure. Red struck the Sciolist's face with his fist, a full knock-out punch that swiveled the man's head to the side before it dropped forward like an overripe fruit. Then, he fell to the ground in a crumpled heap.

Red kicked him to the side, saying, "I told you we were staying, jackass."

Their remaining crew's gaping mouths resembled fish gulping for air. Xander himself stared in wonder. Awestruck, he decided then and there he would never in a million years want to be on Red's bad side.

"Congratulations, and thanks, Red." Xander bumped fists with the Easterner. "Is he—is he dead?"

"No. Just whacked silly. I'm gonna throw him out the door." Red picked him up as if he were a dollop of dandelion fluff.

Xander put his hand out. "Wait." He gave Red a smug look. "That's a valuable disguise. We need to get his clothes. Undress him. Kind of creepy, but it has to be done."

"Disguise, yeah. Creepy? Well, he ain't bad lookin'." Red winked.

Xander would have never imagined buff Red leaned that way. He chuckled. "Enjoy."

A minute later, they had the Sciolist stripped down to his flaming red underwear, the abominable uniform wound into a bundle. Xander pocketed Red Riding Hood's Alt for safe keeping, too. Having that alone was of incalculable value.

Red easily picked up the nearly naked man and heaved him out onto the train platform. Xander swallowed hard as he saw how far Red was able to toss him with minimal effort.

Then the Easterner wrenched the Sciolist's weapon from where it impeded the Maglev's door from closing and shoved the Stinger down into the center of the clothing roll.

When the door finally shut, the train launched full throttle.

"Good to go," the wild-eyed Easterner stated, his hair beginning to relax into a straight, natural shape. He moved down the aisle, exiting through the gangway to the next car.

As much as Xander coveted the Sciolist's Alt for information, he remembered it could be trouble. It had GPS. He got up from his seat and began searching for anything metal he could wrap around the Alt to block the location signal. He realized it may not completely do the job, but he had to try. His eyes settled on a shiny metal abstract T mounted on the wall. To his delight, simple screws attached the item to its panel.

He returned to where he had just stashed the Stinger, turned it on, and melted the screws and swath of the T's edges. Continuing to use the weapon as a forging tool, he was able to soften the metal enough to make it bendable. In less than a few minutes, he had molded a few three-inch-wide bracelets that he could attach over the top of an Alt.

Satisfied, Xander returned the Stinger to the clothing roll and settled back into his seat, this time wearing the Alt with its protective device. With that, Dorian riding in the front, and Red in the back, they had their own security detail.

He glanced over to where Red throttled the Sciolist moments before. Xander hugged the bundle of scarlet clothing to his chest before setting it down carefully on his lap, hoping that, if the Sciolist survived flying through the door, he wouldn't remember a damn thing.

THIRTY-SEVEN

Serpio's DNA

A PALE-FACED SERPIO hyperventilated behind the door closing behind him. The party raged on, but the Magistrate almost collapsed before he pulled his Sedo from his pocket, inserted the mouthpiece between his lips, and inhaled. Supporting himself against the wall, he closed his eyes, allowing the dispenser's green vapor to work its magic.

It did nothing to calm his panic. The Sciolist's announcement pounded mercilessly in his mind: *Inventum and all its contents have been destroyed beyond recognition.*

Inventum. The DNA lab.

Anger and grief surged through him like a live wire to water. His nostrils flared, and his eyes searched frantically for anything nearby he could heave across the room. At a loss, he paced.

His bodyguard Sciolist for the evening, Caspian, reached out, his arms flailing in the air as he failed to slow down his leader's movement. "Magistrate, sir. Do you need further assistance?"

"No," Serpio snapped. "I need a full-scale investigation into the fire! This … this disaster is monstrous—beyond cataclysmic." He wiped his face with a handkerchief he pulled from his pocket.

"Good news, though, Magistrate. No lives were lost, sir, and the crews are working hard—saving as much as possible …" Caspian twisted his hands together.

Serpio bared his teeth and glared at the unfortunate messenger. His voice echoed in the hallway. "I don't *CARE*! I don't care if anyone died. Humans are dispensable! The work inside is not!" He stomped his feet, and his face became redder by the second. "The DNA lab must be salvaged! Find out who did this. NOW!" His voice shattered the quiet, rumbling, trembling, dangerous.

"Yes, yes, sir. Of course." Caspian blinked as the words battered him and took a step back. "Please forgive me for not being attuned to your concerns."

A vein pulsed in Serpio's face. Drawing in slow, steady breaths, he tried to control his tone. "Because of this … this catastrophe, we will be unable to process DNA of any suspected traitors. Our entire operation for acquiring and categorizing blood identity is ruined. Even if we rebuild, it will take months —years, maybe." Serpio paused; he could not bring himself to say out loud the words burning holes into his brain: the Infinity chemical solution for his immortality was *gone*. His precious supply had dissipated like smoke in the night. Without his quarterly injections, his life was identical to any other individual's.

And who knew what else was lost and could be needed? The thought was like a steel wool massage on sunburned skin. He wrung his hands and reached for the Sedo again.

His mind splintered into a thousand different directions, grasping for any shred of reassurance. At last, he clawed on to a realization: nothing had happened to the scientists from the lab. They would know what to do. They would figure this out, even if they had to go to the ends of the earth, as indeed they might. Somehow, he could once more obtain the elements he needed for the formula. A ghost of hope cheered enthusiastically in the depths of his mind.

His resolute spirit emerged again. However, time was of the

essence. Once he was due for an injection, he would have to have it.

"Sir, will you be returning to the party?" Caspian stood by patiently, his arms crossed behind him.

"No. I've made my appearance." As if to emphasize his decision, he took off his jacket and handed it to Caspian. He began to move down the hallway, anxious now to address his newest crisis.

Caspian draped the expensive jacket carefully over his arm and followed Serpio down the hallway. "Will you be contacting Esryn to begin the fire investigation, or shall I do that on your behalf?"

"I'll take it from here. You are dismissed."

THIRTY-EIGHT

Will's Idea

WATCHING SERPIO EXIT THE PARTY, Will foolishly prayed that a hideous monster lay behind Serpio's exit door and could shred the leader into tiny pieces, making him incapable of regenerating.

Until the man was dead, which was a very remote possibility, Will would be a slave to the emotions Serpio stirred up in him.

His mom had been watching him from her position in front of the Purview. She approached him with her hands outstretched, as if to hug him but she held back. "Will, son, are you okay now? What terrible things happened to make you so traumatized?"

Will cast his eyes down, embarrassed. "I'm not ready to share all that, Mom. Thanks."

His mom continued to fuss around him, as if she were trying to dust him off, before she enfolded him in an all-encompassing hug, rubbing his back in an attempt to comfort him.

Ember backed away, giving him space he didn't need.

"When you're ready, we're here." She released him and wiped a tear from her eye.

Standing just behind them, his father said, "Will, a word?"

He stepped away, heading for the unoccupied chair sitting in the middle of the room, and waited for Will to follow.

Feeling more self-conscious than ever, Will obeyed, tagging after his dad.

"Sit down." As soon as Will sat, Jack planted a hand firmly on his son's right shoulder. "I know you've been through a lot, and I'm not sure if you realize how proud of you I am."

Grimacing, Will brutally shoved his hands in his pockets, the only way he could hide a part of himself. "*Proud*? Why? Right now, I feel like a failure! I turned my back on you and Mom, got caught, lied through my teeth, became a criminal of our government, and now I can't even keep my emotions in check. I'm mentally scarred—can't even remember all the pieces of my past. I've lost my Plauditor position, too, and I'll never have that again."

"Ah, son. Your mom and I couldn't be more pleased with the choices you've made. A lesser person would have given up long before you did, betraying others to save themselves. You did not. Instead, you endured great pain and sacrifice to do the right thing. And your heart—your heart is what really matters. The love and courage you've shown shines through. You don't have to be anything or anyone but who you are." Jack threw his arms around Will and clapped him on the back.

"Thanks, Dad." Will's eyes grew misty, and he blinked hard before any tears could escape. He let go, profoundly grateful for the devoted support of his parents. He couldn't believe how Serpio could have duped him into believing his parents didn't love him.

Just behind him, he felt a presence—Ember. Then, her warm hand was on his arm. "Feeling better?"

Will gave her a weak smile and a quick side hug. "Yeah. Thanks." Will shook out his hands and stretched his fingers, putting to rest the now familiar trembling. "But now we need to find out why Serpio's not his usual fake, charming self." He rose from the chair, movement somehow more calming than sitting.

Still in front of the Purview, Kamar waved his Alt in front of it, and the screen went black. "We won't know by watching any more of that," he stated. "Ha. Just got a bump in my Alt points for turning it off." He glanced at his Alt again. "It's past nine, a long while since Xander's been gone. Any word from your mom lately, Ember?"

"No, and I don't want to start communicating. I don't want to interrupt the mission in any way. Who knows what they're in the middle of? I'm just trying to stay positive." Ember chuckled. "Xander has never let us down. He's someone to count on."

Will felt the sting of jealousy. *He's out there saving the world like a superhero, and I'm here just taking up space.*

Will dredged up every shred of leadership savvy he possessed. "I know not everyone's here, but we can be making plans—be proactive. What can we do now to be ready to roll?"

Ember nodded emphatically. "We need Ava's help. Kamar, have you heard any more from her?"

"No. I sent her a couple of messages. Maybe the references to auto parts I used weren't clear." Kamar scratched his head and studied his Alt.

Jack, who had been guzzling water since his return to health, stopped drinking to remark, "If she can't answer because it's too dangerous, you need to give her some space."

"I'm worried. If only we could Morse her Alt. I know Ava. She'd find a way to get in touch with us. And as Will said, we're wasting time. Ergh," Ember growled.

A light on the far wall turned green as Kamar turned his attention to his Alt. "There's a car coming in up top. Maybe it's Xander!" Kamar jogged over to the lift platform, jumped on, and rose up into the ceiling.

Xander? Back already? The Outsider hadn't been gone long enough for Will to make things right with Ember. Will's disappointment made him feel like a wilted weed in the sun. At least, though, they'd have news, he told himself.

And Xander was one thing. But what if it was someone else

arriving up top? Someone sent by Serpio … someone who had discovered their whereabouts … or a Sciolist! A car coming in wouldn't necessarily be a good thing … And why weren't there any cameras down here to see what was happening up in the shop?

Sweat broke out on his upper lip as he pondered escape routes, realizing there were none. He felt the blood rise to his face as he thought about protecting Ember and how he would manage it. Never mind that she had become a strong, independent woman; his sense of chivalry would command any amount of sacrifice to defend her.

His mind far, far away, he lost track of time, his reverie broken by Ember's voice. "The purple car!"

There was Kamar, descending on the lift, indeed accompanied by the purple car. No spies. No threat. No doom. Will's relief was so massive it formed physically as a buzz at the back of his head.

Kamar yelled out, "Hey—not who we expected. But apparently, you all know him."

Once the car was safely parked in its space, an enormous guy climbed out. At first, Will squeezed his brain. *I know him, but how?*

The man on a mission jogged over from across the room. Enthusiasm powering his Loyalty hand signal, he gushed, "Will!" as he threw his arms around him and lifted him up off the ground. "How are you, buddy?"

A cloud formed in Will's brain. He concentrated, trying to separate the cloud into something that made sense.

Kamar, following up behind the giant, laughed at the spectacle. "Looks like you know Wee quite well."

"Wee?" Will asked the question as if he were lost.

"He does!" Ember verified. "Best friends."

"We've known Weeford since Will was five," Marina said, embracing him. "Good to see you."

Wee reached out for Jack's hand, but Jack wrapped him in a hug and clapped him on the back.

Wee initiated a vaguely familiar handshake, but Will found he had to follow it in slow motion. The cloud lifted. Now Will recognized his friend, but it was as if Wee were a person from another life, another time, long ago.

Wee launched a hearty bro hug. "Buddy, you gave us all a scare. But you're okay?" Wee seemed to sense a detachment, his smile tight as he rubbed the back of his neck.

"I'm okay, yeah. Just … yeah." Will radiated embarrassment.

Releasing Will, Wee looked around, his eyes shining like brass buttons. "This place! It's a-maze-ing!"

"Thanks," Kamar replied, pride leaking from his smile. "Never dreamed it would be a headquarters."

Wee's eyes continued to roam the room, finally settling on Reselda. "And you are …?"

The woman left her place where she was sitting atop a spare tire. "Reselda. I'm what they're calling an Easterner. My talent is healing."

Wee gave her a grin and the Loyalty gesture. "That's epic! I met another—Dorian—before I left. How'd you end up here?"

But before Reselda could answer, Kamar got down to business. "We need news. What's happening?"

"You know Xander's using the Maglev to get Phoenix here, right? And Easterners are helping, but the group wanted extra security. You don't want facial rec and possible sightings of the most wanted when dozens of our people are boarding mass transit. So, my job was to get in and out of the Plauditorium to disable some of those fancy cameras. I left the warehouse some time before Xander and the others started their mission."

Ember shot Will a look of alarm before twisting her hands and pressing her palms together. "You went alone to the Plauditorium? Those people walk the line. That was a huge risk."

Air burst from Wee's lips. "Yeah. Plauditors are saints. I

couldn't go in there claiming to be one of them." He pointed to the label on his uniform. "I went in from the underground. Barely there long enough to even sweat. I'm sure they were pissed off that their cameras went out, but I wouldn't know. I was long gone."

Was it a million years ago when I was a Plauditor? Unlike the others, only Will understood how dangerous Wee's task was. Although Plauditors were highly esteemed, they were fundamentally narcs. They saw everything; they were trained to. Words trembled on Will's tongue. "True definition of a Plauditor —someone who puts others above himself. And that's you, Wee."

Wee cast his eyes down in an act of modesty. "Nothing you wouldn't have done."

"Do you know … Was Xander doing okay?" Ember asked a little too eagerly.

A pang of jealousy reared up and coated Will's tongue in bitterness. He turned to Ember, not able to resist making a comment. "I'm sure Xander's loving the challenge."

Will's subtle jab caused Wee to wince. "Hey—he's doing a great job organizing and leading the operation, and that isn't easy. He communicated with Ava. He told her to set a fire at Inventum for a distraction."

A muscle twitched by Will's eye. "Ava's setting a fire? That's risky—too risky for her."

Wee's words tumbled out in a rush. "Not her. She ordered a couple of Sciolists to do it—ones she said are on our side. By the time I got to the Plauditorium, the fire was already burning. I could hear Plauditors yelling about sending the fire department, so they'd seen the fire on the monitors by then. Great timing, because there was a flurry. I found the circuits for the Maglev and doused 'em with acid. I made sure the cameras onboard would be cut off, too." Wee held his chin up, pride shining in his eyes.

With her mouth in an O, Ember shared a flabbergasted look

with Will before he pinched the bridge on his nose to absorb the crush of intense information. After its release, Will took in a shuddery breath. "Glad you got out safely and were able to help with the whole mission." He cuffed Wee on the shoulder.

Wee shrugged. "Time will tell."

THIRTY-NINE

Xander's "Ghosts"

XANDER FOLDED the Sciolist's confiscated cloak into a bundle, secured by the ties that pulled its hood around a person's neck. He slid the Stinger into the center of the bundle, where it couldn't be easily seen, and braced himself for the Maglev's next stop. A computerized voice and bell tones announced, "Next stop, Utopia Center. You will have five minutes to exit."

Five minutes for people to enter also, Xander thought. *Not much time.* But maybe the transfer would be as smooth as the Maglev coming to a stop.

The door opened to reveal a male whose brown, crew-cut hair was streaked with purple. The man wore a completely see-through purple, high-collared tactical-style mesh vest. Plum-colored trim zigzagged across the front with half-inch-wide matte straps. His jean-style pants had two stripes of the trim's color above the knees. Accented with a reptilian leather, his mid-calf tall boots sported undone laces and were splayed open. Wide-set amber eyes and a fair two-day stubble gave him an owlish face. Once inside the door, he seemed to take stock of the people inside.

Unsure of whether this was the Easterner he was expecting, Xander stayed quiet and observed the man carefully. He didn't seem to be leading any group, so he stood up from his seat to see if there were others coming in behind.

Xander blinked and did a double take. Individual people he recognized as Phoenix began to appear in front of him, validating their Alts on the Maglev's system as they came through. A second later, each disappeared into nothingness.

Now Xander was sure. "Oslin!" He approached and gave the Easterner a fist bump. "Xander."

"You're Xander?" The man tilted his head, examining Xander as if he, too, had winked in and out of existence. "How can I be sure?"

Making the Phoenix gesture, Xander said, "This signal."

Oslin grinned and copied Xander's movements. "Got it."

Xander resisted the urge to touch Oslin to see if his physical presence was as solid as he appeared. "The … people. They're all here but invisible?"

"They are, yes. I can make them visible, but why? Better for safety to keep them concealed. I'm visible to you only for your sake."

Xander whistled before he tilted his head and scratched it. "Ah. Well, congrats for getting here safely." The train launched from its standstill to its high-speed motion forward, a brief soundless jolt that caused Xander and Oslin to gently sway. Xander sank back down into his chair.

Oslin found a seat across from Xander's and sat down. "Just so you know … I was completely cloaked as I walked to the warehouse. No one saw me enter. Or leave."

Xander nodded his head. "Do you have limits I should know about?"

"I have to be careful that I don't disappear when someone's watching. The Magistrate would never stop looking for me." He looked out the window, craning his head a bit to take in more of the world outside.

"I've never understood why Serpio wants to eliminate you just because you have special talents. Why doesn't he seek you out for what you can do *for* him?" He tapped the armrest with his fingertips. The question had bothered Xander ever since he had heard Ember and Talesa's stories.

"Because each one of us is so powerful. He'd really have no control if I used my talent against him, like I'm doing right now. He'd never know if I stood right behind him with a knife to his throat. Same with any of the others. That's why he's had so many of us killed. When he got a hold of that first list, he made sure they were eliminated. But luckily, except for the names he got his hands on initially, the remaining records were sealed. Serpio would have to search for us, or something would have to tip him off to who and where we are."

Xander knew firsthand about that list—the one he, Ember, and Ava discovered. The "gold journal," a digital record of people who had been DNA experiments. He let that information skim over him. "But Serpio can't die. Did you know that? He's bulletproof. So, you're not really a threat."

"Yeah, I noted recently that our Magistrate defied death. But believe me, it's not all about Serpio. If I used my skills, I could kill the entire Elite or every Sciolist that ever walked if I wanted to. Any person alive. I could cause enough chaos to send our Magistrate into a tailspin. And that, of course, is why I'm here now. You and the others are the perfect fit for me." A small hole in the upholstery of his seat caused him to frown.

Xander's slow smile lit up his face. "You're the ultimate weapon, then."

Oslin looked up. "Yes. As long as I'm not near any high voltage."

"Isn't the Maglev high voltage?" Xander glanced around.

"Nope. Runs on magnets, not voltage. I do have to be careful, though. In fact, at one point during our walk toward the station, the cloaking failed. We moved away quickly, and I was able to cloak us again. I glanced around and didn't see anyone watching, but I'm sure the Plauditorium cameras picked us up."

"Hopefully, we have someone working that out for us. Any idea what caused the problem?"

"No. I can't see things underground, so who knows if interference came from there? Could be we had to cross by the power plant on our way to the Maglev." Oslin's brows were knitted together in a knot.

"You got here without being stopped. That's good news. And I don't even *hear* anybody from your group," Xander confessed. "It's like they're really not there at all." It was like Oslin's power created living, breathing phantoms, and the whole idea was enough to creep him out. Real humans were there looking at him, inhaling the same air, maybe even farting. And he couldn't sense any of it. "Ghosts," he murmured. A shiver involuntarily ran down his spine.

"Not ghosts. Ghosts exist in their own time, and they're never free. Hopefully, our people—these faithful—will make sure we are." Smiling, he flashed the Loyalty hand gesture.

Xander managed a semblance of a smile. "Free? One more stop, and we'll be one step closer." His words had no bearing on what was happening in his brain. He thought about getting off the train, walking the entire group to the warehouse. It was one thing to have fifteen people at a time—a whole other thing having sixty. They were definitely not home free. "How many people can you hide at a time?"

"As long as people can huddle together, I can generate a field with my hands enough to hide maybe thirty. But that's a guess. I've never done it before. Never needed to."

An experiment at a time like this? Far from comforting. Details … he needed details.

"You generate a field?" Xander couldn't conceptualize how that would be done. He held his own hands up and looked them over, sure that Oslin's didn't look any different.

"It's complicated. I can't explain it exactly. I have to concentrate, envision it happening." Oslin relaxed, putting his magical hands in the back of his head and leaning back in his chair. "Who's our next wingman?"

"Not wingMAN. WingWOMAN. Her name's Lotus. All I know is she's brilliant—brilliant in a beam-of-light kind of way."

"Isn't that going to hurt rather than help us?"

As was often the case, Xander steadied his apprehension with sarcasm. "Lightning can either kill you or create energy. Either way, it's an adrenaline rush."

* * *

FIFTEEN MINUTES LATER, the train cruised into the last stop. But this time, when the door slid open, three Sciolists stood there. Without hesitation, they stepped into the train.Xander's heart dropped to his knees.

Great. If only Oslin could make these guys disappear for real. A frantic examination showed him, though, that Oslin was the one who had disappeared. *Thanks a lot, Easterner.* He'd have to resist these ass-kissers himself and hope some benevolent god smiled on him.

He patted the bundle in his lap. The Stinger inside was reassuring.

A Sciolist with black hair, olive skin, and dark eyes stepped further inside. Waving his Alt in front of a speaker on the wall activated the PA system, which he then used to announce his business. "I am Officer Dreyfuss Rector. I have orders from the Magistrate. I regret to inform you, passengers, that this train is operating against City Hall orders. For some reason, the Maglev is still running, although a previous order was issued. You are headed in the direction of a large fire at Inventum. For your safety, you cannot go further. As of this minute, the Maglev is officially offline. The main switch has been turned off. Prepare to disembark. You will take refuge in the station until the all-clear is given. We'll be evacuating passengers from all six cars of the train."

Xander cringed in his seat, ready for the confrontation to come. But Tranquility's red-caped parasites looked right past him. The second Sciolist pointed at a mother and her child. "You both—let's go."

What the—? He realized then that Oslin hadn't deserted him but had cloaked him. He exhaled, fighting the urge to yell, "Hallelujah!" and then realizing it wouldn't have been heard anyway.

With that, the officer waited for the little family to stand and walked them to the open door. "Please exit the train, and a Plauditor will greet you there." The Sciolist's eyes followed them as they disembarked, and then signaled his fellow Sciolists to proceed with the rest of the evacuations.

Xander gritted his teeth. In moments, the rest of their undisguised group would be ushered off the train. Or they'd be recognized and arrested. *I have to do something.* In a rush, Oslin's words came back to Xander: *If I used my skills, I could kill the entire Elite or every Sciolist that ever walked if I wanted to. Any person alive … he'd never know if I stood right behind him with a knife to his throat.*

Xander pulled the Stinger from the wadded robe in his lap and stood. He activated the switch on the end of the pole and heard its satisfying crackle.

Xander lunged forward, jabbing the tip into Dreyfuss's chest. His breath knocked from his lungs, the Sciolist cried out, pressing his hands to the wound. He staggered, surprise and searing pain haunting his face. As he blinked rapidly in confusion, his eyes darted about as he tried to find his attacker.

Xander relentlessly struck Dreyfuss again and again as he cracked the pole's length across the officer's head, flinching as the rod made contact. Dreyfuss fell to the floor, crashing against the steel seat frames on his way down.

Xander turned just in time to see a second Sciolist collapse at the end of the aisle. Although Xander couldn't see Oslin, he knew the Easterner had approached his subject from behind, thrusting him to the ground. Xander flew down the walkway, charging ahead with the Stinger in his hand. A second's hesitation had him worrying he could hurt Oslin instead, but the Easterner suddenly appeared, scrambling out of the way for Xander's attack.

A strike. Then another. The Stinger's tip found its target, carving a mark through the Sciolist's face and ripping the flesh from his cheek. A horizontal swing of the weapon hit the Sciolist squarely to the skull, the thudding sound like a ball to a bat at high speed. He fell, as if in slow motion, his head lolling to the side.

Xander feinted to the left, stepping backward. "The third one went that way!"

He pivoted to see Oslin reappear and extend his hand, moving it in a circle. "I just made you visible, but I can cloak you again. He gestured toward the back. "We'd better go find him. Any Phoenix in that car won't be hidden."

Xander expelled a breath. "They should be all right. Red's there, another one of … you. He's a human bomb. Nobody is gonna get anywhere with him."

Oslin slapped his knee. "Well, gobsmack and blast!" He raised an eyebrow. "I'll look forward to meeting him. Now, what do you want to do with these knuckleheads?" He gestured to the two cardinal carcasses lying on the floor.

"We could throw 'em off the train, but they'll talk—give away too much. We strip 'em down, take their clothes and Alts, and use the Stinger. Our first act of war—eliminating the enemy." Xander was already kneeling, pulling off the first red cape.

Oslin eyed the miniature lights that lined the ceiling, twinkling out the colors of each car's Status level. "Think those have wiring?"

Xander looked up. "Yeah. What are you thinking?"

"We need that to bind these guys up." He used a Stinger's hot tip to open a hole in the ceiling, where he pulled out yards of the coveted microcircuitry.

A shout from behind them heralded Red, who had the third Sciolist laying across his back. He was out cold.

"Red!" Xander stood to greet him. "This is Oslin. Oslin, Red." The two bumped fists.

Xander grinned and addressed Red. "We got two—you got the third. We're going to have to eliminate these guys."

Red unloaded his inert rider unceremoniously onto the floor.

Within several minutes, Serpio's policemen were down to their briefs. Xander pulled the Stinger from where he'd had it hidden and turned it on. A straight line down the middle of each of the Sciolists' chests, and they were dead.

Xander stood above one of the bodies, one foot on each side, his guilt like an ice pick to his chest. In all the battles of his life, he had not ever had to kill anyone, and the weight of the carnage hung on him like a steel-studded anvil. He wanted to both sob and celebrate, knowing it was the first of casualties to come. A revolution would not be without suffering. His eyes met Oslin's, who stood opposite of him.

As if he could read his mind, Oslin put his hand on Xander's shoulder. "Do you not want to live in a real world? If you do, death's a reality, not pretend."

Xander nodded, and then Red tossed each one of the Sciolists out the door of the train.

Taking command of his senses once again, Xander realized they were at an impasse. He groused, "This train's offline, thanks to those panty wastes. Who in the hell's gonna turn it back on?"

FORTY

Xander's Eye-Opener

"THAT'S NO PROBLEM AT ALL." Red laced his fingers together and flexed them.

Xander's chin lift and furrowed brow decorated his response. "You know something we don't?"

"No. You already know. My talent is strength. I'm gonna push this train until it engages. Piece of cake."

Oslin chimed in. "Wouldn't it be better if I just get off and go find the switch?"

Xander reasoned, "We've burned enough time as it is. We can't afford to go searching for the controls. They probably need a special key anyway."

Red pointed his index finger in Xander's direction. "Exactly. All this train needs is propulsion. The major principle behind its operation is magnetic repulsion. The wheels are down right now because it's stopped. Once it achieves speed, the tires retract, and levitation begins. The train's superconducting magnets have already been cooled during its use. As long as those are still cool, the train will move."

Xander stood there staring at Red for a full fifteen seconds, his mouth open. "Yeah. Whatever. As long as it works."

"If you're off the train, how you going to get back on?" Oslin challenged.

"No worries. I have the speed. But enough talk. Let's go." Red headed for the door and jumped out onto the platform.

Moments later, Xander could cross that worry off his list. The Maglev was moving again. In less than four minutes, they'd be at the last station. He sank into a seat, but he wouldn't be there long.

Oslin settled into his seat and began looking at the messages coming in on the Sciolists' Alts. "Xander—getting the inside scoop on everything here. Look."

Over Oslin's shoulder, Xander read incoming messages. They scrolled across the screen like a news bulletin banner. "Revelation Celebration moved indoors due to fire … Fire at Inventum out with major damage … Suspects still on the loose … Magistrate withdraws from party …"

"Wait. What's that?" Xander paused to wait until the words recycled across the screen. "The Magistrate withdraws from party to assess Inventum damage."

"You guys have anything to do with that fire?" Oslin turned to glance at Xander over his shoulder.

"Yep. A friend of Phoenix's helped get it set. An Elite, believe it or not. Hope it means you're safer than you were before. Serpio can't sweep the city with DNA collection if there's no way to analyze it. That's the good part. It was set as a distraction, but it buried all the data about DNA with it."

"Good call." Oslin bumped his fist with Xander's over the top of his head.

Xander groaned inwardly, remembering how much the decision had come back to bite them in the butt; they would probably never find out how to end Serpio's immortality now.

Removing the metal covering from the Sciolist's Alt on his wrist, Xander watched the same words dance across the screen. Xander never dreamed they'd have access to one of these things.

A wish-come-true, knowing everything that went on within Serpio's circle.

Then he gasped. "Ava Validus, an Elite member, is in custody at City Hall ..."

"Shit! Shit, shit, *shit!*" What fresh hell was this?

Startled by Xander's forbidden language, Oslin stood up and faced the leader of Phoenix. "Problem?"

"Yeah. Big problem. I told you who arranged the fire. That was Ava, our inside mole and loyal friend. She's in custody! She's not only the best ally we have, but she knows *everything.*" Xander clenched his fists as his mind raced with the worst-case scenarios. "No wonder I couldn't get in touch with her!"

"What will they do to her? She's Elite. They can't do much without evidence. It's Tranquility, after all." Oslin spoke quietly, but there was a curious edge to his comment that struck a chord with Xander.

"Yeah? That's what Will Verus thought when they took him. After that, Serpio tortured him, and he's still not right." Xander touched his head with a finger, then squeezed his fists. His nails cut into his hands.

Although they would be frantic and in no position to help Ava, he had to let Ember, Will, and Kamar know about Ava's situation. He left his seat and plopped himself down next to Talesa. She raised her eyebrows.

"What is it?" Talesa asked.

"Ava's in custody."

Her body tensing, Talesa squeezed her eyes shut. "I'll let Ember know right now."

"Thanks." Xander wished he could already be working some miracle to get Ava. But for now, the communication had to be enough.

He made his way back to his seat just before the Maglev pulled to a stop, and the door slid open. He didn't even question how the train was operating with only Red to move—and stop—it. His worry about Ava now overshadowed everything.

He prepared himself to see Sciolists once again outside.

Instead, standing just outside the open door was a woman in lavender clothing with shiny, white hair streaming down over her shoulders. An intense gaze revealed large eyes the color of blue sky until she blinked; then he realized they were lavender like her clothes. Another slow blink, and they were green. She stepped on board and gestured to the crowd behind her. Xander had overlooked them, so taken was he by the woman's appearance.

"Come," she said to the group.

Xander looked beyond her and saw no Sciolists. A relieved sigh passed through his teeth.

The fairy-like woman cleared her throat. "I'm Lotus, in case that's not obvious. And you are Xander, which *is* obvious," she said.

"Brutally obvious?" Xander tilted his head. He knew he was famous, but …

"Description fits. Your swagger's hard to miss." Lotus tossed her colorless tresses but did not smile.

Xander cocked an eyebrow, unsure if that action was visible with his mask. "Is there anything I should know about your special talent?"

"My gift is not one you want to experience, so when I tell you to get out of the way, you'd better move."

Although he stood in the aisle leaning against the row of seats, Xander noticed the train began to race away from the station, and the door slid closed. "Noted. What exactly is it that you do?"

Lotus sidled up on the other side of the aisle and spoke across. "When I sense a threat, my DNA causes my entire body to produce laser light brighter than the sun. Problem is, it can blind anyone in my path."

Talesa had told him this about Lotus. At the time, he didn't admit to Talesa that one of his few fears was of being blinded. A surge, like a tiny, electrical shock, pricked down his arms and then passed. He recognized it as temporary horror. "Is it—is it permanent?"

"Can be. Depends on how long a person is stares at me. It doesn't take long. And for those who look at me, it's like staring directly into the sun close up, so it's not usually tolerated. It doesn't cause them pain; it's just too bright for any human being's eyes to endure. For me, it's weird. I can see right through their bodies, like an X-ray. You know, skeletons and all that." Lotus's face had the quiet of a calm lake, her emotions impossible to read.

"Good … to know," Xander replied, almost shutting his eyes in a self-protective response. "Can you turn it on and off at will?"

She looked at him from under her lashes, guarded, and hesitated before answering his question. "I can, but it's taken some self-training. At first, I would light up at any threat, big or small. I've learned over time to concentrate on inconsequential things if I feel my body warming up. Or I can free up my brain to accept the threat as it is so I can be prepared to meet it."

Xander wanted to keep asking questions, but he could tell she was not the type to share all the tiny details.

"What's the story?" Lotus looked around, her iridescent eyes taking in Oslin and the empty-looking train car.

"Lotus, meet Oslin. His gift is cloaking. That's why it's like a ghost town in here. Red, another one of our new Easterner allies, is out moving the train because some Sciolists turned off the switch." When he saw Lotus looking around to find the Sciolists in question, Xander simply said, "They're no longer here."

Lotus nodded.

"Dorian's in the front car. He uses the power of suggestion." To his own ears, Xander sounded like a message on repeat every time a new Easterner came on board. That these Easterners had never met was a miracle in itself.

"I see." Lotus smiled for the first time, her lips gently curling up.

Xander glanced up at the monitor fixed to the wall, showing their route and where the next stop was. "Six minutes to the next station." Although it didn't compare to all the other trauma he'd been through, the Maglev journey felt like it'd lasted days instead of minutes.

He let the news about Ava sink in again, his anguish like a white-hot fire in his chest. There was only one thing to do, and that was to save her.

He spent the next leg of the journey watching the announcements fly across his stolen Alt. They didn't change until he saw "Magistrate launching appraisal of fire. Esryn to head up the investigation early tomorrow morning ..."

He would not sleep tonight. With some trickery, someone from Phoenix would have to get to the lab as soon as possible to see what, if anything, was left. They needed clues to Serpio's DNA. If all was ashes, they'd have nothing to go on. He closed his eyes with something close to prayer, hoping against hope that he could salvage anything that could be used against Serpio.

FORTY-ONE

Serpio's Setback

THE CELEBRATORY NIGHT DRAGGED ON. Serpio was eventually calm enough to return to the party, but his heart was no longer in it. Instead, it was a dead weight in his chest. Even the adulation from his citizens could not erase his panic. His smile was an effort, as if his lips needed a crane to pull up its corners.

The only bright spot in his thinking was Talesa. After the party ended, he'd jump into his Vectura, the unique compact vehicle designed only for trips to the bunker where Talesa Vinata lived as his personal prisoner.

There, he would enjoy hours of caressing her body and letting go of the tension of the last few hours. She would be his physical release.

He glanced at the time: ten o'clock. In one hour, the party would end, and curfew would descend upon Tranquility.

He clicked into his OmniCom using the icon for the Vectura.

A voice responded. "Yes, Magistrate."

"Vectura at eleven sharp."

"Very well, sir. It will be waiting."

Serpio signed out and inhaled. The air suddenly smelled a little sweeter. He caught a glimpse of himself in an illuminated, gilded mirror on the wall. He looked good—his suit sparkling in the glow, his face tanned with a burnished sheen, and his shoulder-length hair shiny black. Talesa should find him very desirable.

To his surprise, the Vectura app lit up yellow on the OmniCom's black face, demanding a new conversation. "Yes?"

"I'm so very sorry for this communique. A problem, Magistrate. The food distributors at the Alimentum Agency have just reported to me that the meal unit has been sent to the bunker multiple times over the last four days at the proper times. It has returned from several trips with the provisions still in the carriage. The cart's indicators have shown some type of blockage in the path."

Serpio gasped. "Did you say FOUR DAYS?" His voice exploded, raw and accusatory. Saliva caught in his throat; he choked on its web. "Why has no one reported this to me?"

The voice over the OmniCom was honeyed. "They tried to figure out what the problem was. At first, the food was dispensed, but the dash indicator on the cart showed a blockage on the track. Because this was unlikely, they thought the cart was broken. The next time, they sent a brand-new unit. It came back also with a failure light, with all the food intact. We checked the mechanics, including the arm that drops the food into the window. No issues. When they were ready to send out a person or a camera to check the bunker's receiving window, you … died, and the whole city was in an uproar. The manager was very apologetic just now and offered to deliver the food personally because he didn't know—"

"There is a PERSON waiting for food! She has nothing unless it comes from Alimentum!"

Serpio spoke slowly, enunciating each word. That was the only way he could maintain control of his tone. "This mistake does not help the prisoner to feel happy, healthy, or secure. You should have sent an Alimentum rep out immediately when the first delivery came back." Inside his chest, his heart had gunned into overdrive, the beats pounding against his ribcage.

For the second time that day, bad news strangled his self-assurance.

"Very much agreed, sir. I will be sure to have the person in charge relieved of her post."

The Magistrate seethed and spat out new orders. "Now, I want food immediately put onto the Vectura. I'll deliver it myself when I go. I'll see personally what is going on out there. In only one hour, I will know what it took Alimentum *four days* to figure out."

* * *

FIFTEEN MINUTES after the party ended, he hurried across a broad lawn, waved his OmniCom, and entered an unmarked building painted with precision to create an optical illusion in order to trick the eye. It completely blended into its surroundings. Inside the structure was absolutely nothing except a twelve-foot-wide door similar to a garage door. Normally flat on the ground, this evening, the door was open, looking very similar to an angled roof over where, just inside, the Vectura vehicle sat waiting, its pewter finish almost disappearing into the blackness beyond.

A twenty-year-old male attendant stood to the right, dressed in a gray formal jacket and pants with a turquoise belt indicating his Status.

Serpio nodded toward the vehicle. "There's food in the Vectura?"

"Yes, sir. All set. Do you have any other special instructions?" The young man seemed eager to please.

"No." The Magistrate climbed into the vehicle's seat and waved his OmniCom across the dash, and the Vectura drove into the darkness, its headlights painting the walls with white radiance.

Forty minutes later, deep underground, the vehicle pulled up to what should have been the curved outer wall of the hideout. Instead, what he saw was rubble. *What in the hell happened here?*

Instead of being able to cruise right up to the exterior door, he had to stop fifteen feet away. Although he prided himself on seldom using profanity, it burst from his lips spontaneously. Irregular chunks of concrete stood independently, like a madman's attempt at abstract statue art. Scattered shards of glass from the bunker's windows looked like diamonds in the headlights. Clearly dynamite or something like it had demolished this secret haven.

"Son of a *bitch*!" He climbed from the vehicle, tiptoeing and picking his way through the debris.

The interior of Talesa's sanctuary seemed to mock him as he surveyed its once luxurious amenities, now in a ramshackle state. He tiptoed among the glass splinters that littered the floor, looking for any clues as to what had happened or who could have done this, inhaling a smell of burnt plastic mingled with the damp smell of the underground, somehow irritating his sinuses and making him cough.

"Talesa?"

He gaped at furniture, now destroyed and broken into jagged pieces. Small mounds of white stuffing lumped in miniature wads lay among the debris like snow. What items survived in their entirety were stuck in odd places, as if they'd been rearranged by a schizophrenic.

Seeing nothing to hint at the cause, he headed into the kitchen area, thinking perhaps faulty wiring or a gas explosion was to blame. But only shadows pooled across the countertops, as if abandoned in another life. A corner of the Koolcrate's door stayed loyal to its frame. The only signs of life were the ants that had already found a way in, forming a parade of mini investigators seeking sanctuary.

A morbid silence hung heavily amongst the ruins, and strangely, no blood.

Could his prisoner be buried under the wreckage? Or …

hiding? He jerked open an intact cupboard door, the closet large enough to hold a person. Nothing. The items inside hung in their places, oddly oblivious to the chaos.

His eyes scanned the chamber again, and seeing a pile of rubble where shoes protruded, he went to work moving the rubble enough to discover the shoes were a misleading clue.

"Talesa?" He boldly called her name again, but it felt false, as if he knew the answer would never come.

Disbelief married red-hot anger. His lips tightened across his teeth, and heat rose behind his eyeballs.

Who had destroyed his prison, and *where was his prisoner*? His pent-up anger flowed into a primal scream.

After a long minute, he climbed back into the Vectura, only to realize he had no smooth turnaround space. Normally, the narrow passageway for the vehicle had a circuitous loop that allowed for the return trip. He pounded on the front console in frustration and sat waiting for solutions. But he was all alone, helpless to even call on a single Sciolist.

His OmniCom's communication signal couldn't reach anyone that far out of the city.

He backed up the auto, smashing the back end of it into the tunnel's side wall and veered back onto the narrow road.

The way back seemed to take forever and was littered with broken ambitions.

FORTY-TWO

Xander's Destination

THEY WERE ALMOST THERE, ready to step off the Maglev. With a flourish, Xander unzipped his uniform and stashed the bundle of clothing, including the Stinger, into his jumpsuit. He hated the bulk, but he needed to have his hands free.

He looked around at the "empty" train as he made plans. Two groups would do it. He, Dorian, and Red would take half the group. Lotus and Oslin would take the other.

"I'm not invisible, right, Oslin?" Xander pinched his own arm, a silly gesture that never would have answered his question.

"You're solid as steel," Oslin answered.

"I need to talk to everyone on the train. Can you undo your spell?" Xander didn't mean to be funny, but Oslin chuckled.

Oslin flicked his wrists, and the car was now visibly occupied —in fact, almost every seat was full.

Immediately, the group babbled and tossed quiet hellos to Xander, looking almost shocked that someone could now actually hear them. Regardless, they remained cautious and careful about making noise. It was the first time Xander had had a chance to acknowledge most of them.

Exposing and using the Sciolist's Alt would be risky, but he waved it in front of the PA system's speaker before covering the Alt's face once more. "Hey, everyone! Xander here. We're getting close to the end. I'll be giving instructions, so listen carefully."

A subdued cheer went up from around him, but it was tangled with unease, much like the vocal sounds made with a gag across a mouth.

With his hands on his hips, Xander continued. "No one's checking for Status seat assignments now. When I say 'go,' if you're seated in the front car for Upper Status, you'll move to the next car down—that's the one I'm in. If you're in the very last car, you'll move to the one in front of yours. Hope you've got that. Now, go!"

Prepared for a flurry of activity, Xander suddenly realized there wouldn't be many entering his car. Only two came with Dorian, former REMs and his best friends. Both were in copper uniforms—fake Level Sixteens. With a half-smile, Xander declared, "The *high-Status* Phoenix!" The irony wouldn't be lost on them.

Jasper chuckled. "You're right about that."

"We ain't lettin' it go to our heads, though." Bixby's scarecrow-like build and haunted eyes made the statement all too real.

Jasper bent down to the floor. Straightening up, he held out a most familiar object—a rifle. "Here ya go. I'll keep one, and you the other."

Grateful Jasper had kept both rifles safe all this time, Xander clapped him on the back. "You rock, bro." Xander reached for the weapon, clasping its length to his chest. He looped its body-hugging thick strap over his shoulder.

There was no way to tell if everyone was redistributed, but Xander launched into his second set of orders.

"Everyone in my car will be with me, Dorian, and Red." Xander stopped and leaned forward, pressing his hands onto the back of a seat. "In case you haven't already met, this is Dorian. He has persuasive mentalist talents. He can and will control any threat with a simple command. Red's outside pushing the train, or we wouldn't even be in motion right now. In a moment, he'll stop this beast, and we'll walk to our destination."

A murmur vibrated through the group as they reacted to the descriptions. Among themselves, a few already familiar with Dorian or Red enthusiastically recounted their own experiences with the person who had shepherded them from their ware-house. However, most of them appeared nervous, firing off questions, fidgeting in their seats, or wearing expressions more indicative of shivers vibrating up their spines.

Xander couldn't blame them. It was a perilous expedition, and they all knew it.

"Oh … forgot to add this—Red can crush anyone or anything that's a danger." Xander allowed a smile to cross his lips. "We'll be in good hands with both of them."

Heads nodding, many held up crossed fingers or displayed the Loyalty gesture.

"One last thing. We're Group One. We leave first."

Xander turned to Lotus and Oslin. "Follow me." Xander made his way down the aisle into the car behind theirs.

Once there, Xander was relieved to see the car was full and his comrades settled. He didn't need the PA system to speak, but his voice boomed out as he leaned against a trio of seats. "You all follow directions well. Now, pay close attention! The next phase of our journey is about to begin!"

The passengers snapped to readiness.

"You're all in Group Two. You'll be second off the train, and you'll be with Lotus and Oslin."

Lotus gave them all a genuine smile. "Some of you have already met me. For those who haven't, I light up. I have a biolu-minescence powerful enough to put someone's eyes out. So, when we get off, I'll walk behind you and blind any threat. And a warning: Do not look at me at any time during this mission. You can be blinded, too. It's unfortunately something I haven't been able to control." Lotus glanced Oslin's way. "As far as cloaking, Oslin, you won't have to make me invisible. That would not only be dangerous for the others, but I can take care of myself."

"I'm sure that's true," Oslin said. "But someone who looks like you shouldn't ever be invisible anyway."

With a nearly imperceptible flicker of her eyelashes, Lotus's face glowed slightly with embarrassment. "You're making me blush."

Oslin winked at Lotus and then launched into directives for the group. "I'm going to need you to grab each other's hands when we leave the train. That's the best way to guarantee you'll all be cloaked when I activate my abilities. It's like you're the current connected in an electrical field. Hang on to each other, and you should be completely invisible."

"Next time we talk, we'll be where we need to be, a secure place where we'll be hidden. We just have to make it there. It's still nighttime, so that's on our side. And the good news is it's roughly only a block from the station." Xander gave them the Loyalty gesture and returned to his car, leaving Oslin and Lotus behind.

Xander could feel the Maglev start to drag. They were slowing already.

Even with the Easterners for protection, his own face was way too famous to test fate. He slid the familiar mask down over his head, annoyed at its discomfort, hot and tight, as it bonded with him like a real, second skin.

The Maglev slowed, sluggish and almost heaving, as if it were a person out of breath. Xander imagined that as strong as Red was, he probably would be panting somewhat, too, after what he'd had to do. At the stop, the door automatically slid open.

This was it. Make it or break it, they would be out there.

FORTY-THREE

Ember's Work

HAVING Wee back with them left Ember both heartened and restless. It was like getting a taste of some sublime dessert but being denied the whole piece. She couldn't wait until the entirety of Phoenix was there, safe and sound. Every pulse of her heart missed Xander's smiles, at moments wondering if Xander wasn't more of a dream than a person. She strained her ears for sounds of the lift.

To Kamar's amusement, she found some rags in the cupboard and towed Will and Wee over to polish the hoods of Kamar's escape cars until they were like glazed glass. Standing to admire their work, they kidded each other about whose sections were shinier.

What she didn't anticipate hearing was a message from her mom, but when Talesa's voice wove its way into her consciousness, she raised her hand to ward off others from approaching or speaking to her.

Although she was already used to the intermittent vibrations of traffic along the street, now it bothered her. It broke her concentration and interfered with the words trying to enter her head. Individual letters piled into her consciousness, and she worked to sort them out. Finally, the message became clear.

"We received info about Ava. It's bad news. She's been picked up for questioning. I assume she's in a holding cell at City Hall, but that's not verified. I will let you know when I get more info. See you soon."

Panic flashed across Ember's face. "Oh no." She reached out and gripped Will's arm but then called everyone together in the center of the room, where they immediately sat in a circle on the floor.

Will's parents looked at each other with questions on their faces; their auras communicated that they didn't know quite what to expect, and Ember couldn't blame them. Reselda, normally calm and serene, fidgeted with some fuzz she had found in her pocket. Even Wee's eyebrows were tents of anticipation.

Ember sighed. "My mom just communicated with me. Ava's in custody."

"Actually arrested?" Will asked as he thrust his hands into his pockets.

Ember put her fingers on her chin, thoughtful. "It was brief. She's being questioned. My mom didn't know if she was in a cell."

Will cringed. "Questioning sounds gentle, but it's not. Serpio does all kinds of things to get information. She's in trouble. *We're* in trouble. If Serpio tortures Ava like he did with me, she could spill everything."

Ember's eyes watered. "I have faith in Ava. She'll never give up what she knows, even if Serpio hurts her."

Will blurted, "You don't know what it's like in that—that place. And until you do, you can't assume anything. No matter how great Ava is, she's only a human being."

As she watched the blood rush to his cheeks, Ember could feel his anguish. Wee, sitting next to his friend, put his hand on his shoulder.

Ember slammed her words into life, throwing her hands out in front of her. "We have to rescue her! Serpio will never let her go, not if he thinks she's betrayed him."

"Whoa—slow down," Kamar cautioned. "You're going to be in grave danger if you try to get her out."

"That's what I thought when Serpio got Will. And it was almost too late by the time he could get free. We can't just sit here!" Ember unmasked her frustration.

"It's dangerous, yes. But it's also dangerous to leave her there." Will's voice cracked, and he cleared his throat. "The longer she's there, the more we're at risk. Serpio has ways of getting information."

"I agree." Ember wrapped her arms around herself as if the chill of icy dread was coming from the outside.

Kamar groaned. "There's no way."

His remark sank into them like a stone, and the group stood, silent, breathing in the decay of disappointment.

Out of the blue, Will's eyes flashed open wide. "The tunnels! Phoenix used tunnels to escape the Plauditorium ..."

"No tunnels connected to this place, Will, or I would've discovered them when I carved this place out." Kamar winced. "Didn't know at the time I could've made a major error."

"Even if the tunnels were there, I'm sure Serpio keeps an extra sharp eye on those now." Ember swallowed hard, remembering their narrow escape.

Will erupted. "But, Ember! Kamar! You guys are gifted, remember? Couldn't you create tunnels going out to wherever you want?"

Ember inhaled, and her eyebrows darted up. She met Kamar's eyes, now the size of dinner plates. "Is that something we could do, Kamar?"

"Umm ... yeah ... A tunnel would take some time, but we've got to try. I can manipulate it. Ember can, too. Others cannot. The walls have Tegrite in them—the hardest rock on earth."

Will whispered, "Tegrite?"

But Kamar wasn't giving any geology lessons. "If we're gonna do it, we have no time to waste. Right now! Let's ... get ...

started!" His proclamation sounded like the chant of an overenthusiastic cheerleader.

"Tell me what to do," Ember said, a nervous vibration creeping into her consent. She flexed her fingers.

Kamar reactivated the screen on the Purview where, moments before, they'd watched a frazzled Serpio. He pulled up a color-coded aerial map of the city that showed buildings, distance, and power grids.

Everyone huddled around the Purview, even Will's parents, examining all the options, pointing out obstacles, and discussing where they needed to change course.

"The route to City Hall has to start over there," Kamar said, pointing to the south wall. "While Ember and I work, Will, you can see my GPS on the screen. If we're headed into any trouble, blow the air horn on that workbench there. If we're deep in the tunnel, blow it at the entrance."

Will gestured to the Purview's city maps. "Looks like you have a great route. Here are the coordinates that'll cut right through to City Hall as the crow flies. No need for detours. You won't intersect with any of the existing tunnels." Will seemed excited, his face radiant with purpose.

Wee put his size sixteen foot up on the single adjacent chair and leaned forward. "Better than that. Kamar can program those coordinates into his Alt's GPS, and it'll guide you as you to where you have to dig."

"I knew that," Kamar boasted, although Ember recognized he was embarrassed for not thinking of it himself.

"Perfect!" Ember's mood lifted. "Thanks, Will. We would be lost without your help." She remembered how Will thrived when he did good deeds for others. This was exactly what he needed in order for his damaged soul to heal.

Ember ran to the cupboard and grabbed water and a few protein bars before heading over to where Kamar stood at the predetermined "entrance" to the beyond. He had already placed his hands on the wall.

"Hey!" Will yelled.

Ember jerked around, startled. "What is it? A problem already?"

But instead of a frown, Will had a smile on his face. "This is gonna be huge. If this works, Ember and Kamar can make all kinds of tunnels for Phoenix. We'd be able to get from one place to another all over the city, and no one would know."

Ember stared at Will at first in shock and then in wonder. "That's brilliant. It would take a lot, but it would be worth it. Kamar?"

"Yeah. Super brilliant. But it'll take incredible labor, and I have a business to run. Closing up the business isn't possible. I get a notification when a car's coming in. But I can work when I'm not working, if you know what I mean."

Ember and Kamar began tearing apart the wall, almost as if they were swimming through water, pushing their hands outward and through the stone. Chunks of mortar from the existing wall crumbled onto the floor, sounding strangely like metal hitting tin. Within a few minutes, a five-foot-wide jagged hole marred the once-smooth surface. The coppery earth beyond peeked through before it, too, broke down into dust.

Using a high-powered vacuum, Marina and Jack cleaned up the concrete and dirt that fell out from their first efforts and then placed it into a TrashVac that sucked the debris from the site to the central trash facility in town.

One thing Ember didn't realize: she might be able to demolish rocks and dirt, but it didn't prevent her from becoming filthy. Her uniform was quickly streaked with grime; her hands were covered in powdery soil. A warm blanket of dust and grease and something vaguely metallic assaulted her nose. It reminded her of how the air smelled after a rain.

Although she had a geological gift, it was still work. The effort it took surprised her. After just two hours of sweat and toil, she felt like a person three times her age. She ached in every joint.

"Kamar, I have to stop, at least for a while."

She hadn't been willing to take a break, knowing that Ava's life—and their position—was at stake. Every moment was precious. Her stomach began a slushy turn at the thought of Ava in the Magistrate's control, but gouging out a tunnel was much more tiring than she'd expected. The effort felt a lot like swimming underwater.

Kamar dusted off his hands. "We should quit for the day. We'll need to find out from Will which direction to go next anyway. Plus, we need food. Those protein bars aren't gonna cut it. And Ember? You need a shower!" Kamar joked.

"But not you," Ember said. Her tone was so straightforward that it took Kamar a moment before he realized she was being sarcastic. "As for more food, I feel sick. Too much anxiety, I guess."

"We made great progress. I'd say we cleared a good thirty yards."

"That's great? At this rate we'll be tunneling 'til I'm eighty." Ember turned around and scrambled toward the basement with Kamar right behind her.

The stretch, though, seemed endless. By the time they'd made it back to the place they'd started, she had congratulated herself; it really was an accomplishment.

With a cough, she emerged from the darkness.

Will watched her come out and showered her with smiles. "Hey! Introducing Ember—champion of the underworld! How'd you do?"

"Getting there." Ember wondered if that were true. She didn't even know where "there" was exactly.

"Hey! Good to see you guys. Did you get to the Earth's core today?" Jack quipped.

Ember hesitated because she was so dirty, but as she walked back into the room, she gladly went palm to palm with high fives with Wee, Jack, Marina, and Reselda.

"If only we knew for sure if your friend is okay," Marina said.

Ember's gut twisted. She felt guilty for quitting when Ava was in so much trouble. She wondered fleetingly if it would also help having the others join in digging. *Without tools, though, it's a waste of good energy.*

She longed for Xander to return. She missed his brash but intuitive leadership. He had to be freaking about Ava, and she yearned to share her worries with him.

But she couldn't help but notice Will. He nearly beamed with an internal light right now, from his head with its shiny blond locks to his toes. He was something irresistible.

What was she going to do? She was torn in half. Two amazing guys who wanted her. She adored both of them. When she was with Will, it seemed right—like coming home to a safe but alluring place where innocence reigned and love was pure. Plus, he needed her desperately to restore the balance in his life.

Xander oozed heat and life and passion; being with him was a little like being near fire but staying just far enough away from the flame to stay protected from harm. Exciting, intense, and seductive, he was an unlikely hero in motion. She was the yin to his yang.

Her internal tug-of-war tormented her.

She needed to decompress. That was it. The digging had been dirty work. Kamar's suggestion of a shower was a no-brainer. Then clean clothes and maybe, by then, some food. Anything to get her head on straight and pass the time.

Her stomach growled loudly. It appeared she was hungrier than she thought.

Standing nearby, Marina heard Ember's belly rumble. "Good heavens, girl. You're hungry! What do you say we find some food? I'm assuming there's food here somewhere? No one can go hungry when there's so much at stake."

Spoken like a true mother, Ember thought.

The group gathered around for food from the cupboard. The provisions were far from great, but they ate what they had gratefully.

Once Ember finished eating, she was determined to get cleaned up. "Kamar, mind if I use the shower upstairs?"

With permission granted, she emerged at the top, stopping by the closet of uniforms for a fresh one.

She reveled in the chance to be alone in safety, enjoying one of life's best pleasures. Immediately, the hot water lulled her into a relaxed state. Inhaling the scent of the coconut soap as she pressed the liquid soap dispenser, she watched the dirt roll off her skin and down the drain. It made her feel human again. She took her time, sudsing up her hair and rinsing it until the water ran clear.

She stood in the shower, thinking about all that had happened in the last few days, daydreaming about how her life had changed … about Xander … about her new powers … and about Will.

When she finally stepped out, she grabbed a towel and squeezed her hair into the terrycloth before rubbing her skin until it shone. Then, she wrapped it around herself and tied it. Luckily, a hair dryer with a domed hood hung from the ceiling. She looked up to activate it, and that's when she saw a window directly above her head. A skylight in the ceiling.

Through it, she could see the inky, night sky, the stars twinkling brightly like a diamond garden. She stared at its beauty, magnified through the glass, unexpected and serene.

What looked like a short steel ladder was attached high up on the wall right underneath the glass. Just below it was a black switch on a small panel with the engraved words "Fire escape."

She grinned, a mischievous thought galloping through her brain like a drunk stallion. A way to get onto the roof? Did she dare?

Yes.

The ladder began to slowly descend until the base hit the floor, and the glass panel pulled back until it was fully open.

Her jaw dropped, and her eyes grew wide.

By now, the rain would be over for the night. She hesitated

only a second before climbing the ladder. Almost to the top, she peered out. Was it safe, or was her adventurous spirit leading her into something stupid?

The rooftop was flat, wide, and secluded. Dense trees, thick as a woven basket, were a forest wall surrounding the rooftop on all sides. No sound, no people. Alone. Her own little oasis. How long had it been since she had a moment to herself?

She clambered off the ladder onto the platform. The nocturnal breeze, only slightly cooler than the day's, bathed her body like a blessing from stars that glimmered, amplified by the city's dome. She breathed in the air, its jasmine scent a remedy for all the stress and uncertainty of the last few weeks.

With a dozen tentative steps, she left the hatchway behind her, the light beneath barely leaking its way out to dissolve into blackness. She ran, kicked her heels, and danced to a melody in her head, feeling something akin to the joy of a bird in flight. Ember gazed at the stars as she arched her back and spread her arms to the sky. Stretching and twirling her way around the rooftop, she pretended she was the featured dancer on Tranquility's biggest stage. No matter that she had never longed for fame. Tonight, she celebrated. Her freedom might be pretend, but she held it close to her heart.

She finished her performance just close enough to the portal to catch the diffused glimmer of the shaft of light from the room below, where the mock spotlight caught her final bow.

Her chest heaving, she remembered that reality waited downstairs. The luxury could not last.

She sighed, closed her eyes, and took a final deep breath of liberty before turning reluctantly to go back below.

When she opened her eyes, Will stood before her, not four feet away.

She gasped and threw her arms across the front of her body.

His face flushed with a glow that rivaled the moon's. "I … you were gone a long time. I set out to find you. I didn't expect …" His bottom lip trembled. "… this."

FORTY-FOUR

Will's Fantasy

"SHAZZ! WILL!" Ember might have screamed, but from the strangled sounds she made, the words seemed glued to her throat.

He wanted to keep drinking in the sight of her, her body highlighted by the moon, the towel leaving little to the imagination.

But he knew he couldn't. He'd frightened and embarrassed her. Will lowered his eyes and turned around, putting his back to her, but his body was feeling the earth move.

Ember found her full voice again but had turned her back, too. "You followed me up here!"

"I didn't! I mean, I didn't mean to. We all thought you'd been gone a long time. I was worried. I knocked on the bathroom door, but no one answered. I waited and knocked again. When you didn't respond, I called your name. I didn't hear anything—not even the water. Then I really panicked. I thought something might be wrong. After all, you've been through a lot … I opened the bathroom door, afraid of what I'd find. No one was there. Then I saw the ladder and the open skylight …"

"Don't you think you're being just a *little* overprotective? I haven't been gone *that* long!" Ember's accusatory question and defensive statement could have been hostile, but instead, she offered a change of tone. The question dripped with tenderness instead.

"I'm sorry—but not sorry. I care about you. I got worried. You're sort of important to me, you know?" Will turned away while shielding his eyes with his left palm and pulled a lengthy sprig of jasmine from the bush next to him. "I'm giving you an olive branch—that's a legendary peace offering. In this case, jasmine. We good?"

Ember turned back far enough to take the tiny bough, although a flush crept across her cheeks. "We're … good. Now, could you go back so I can get dressed?" In spite of her assurance, she still fidgeted, pulling her towel even tighter around her chest and then pushing him away with a savage shove.

He swiveled in a complete circle, jokingly mimicking a show of being wounded by her blow. "Ugh. I don't know how I can make it back without emergency treatment." He stumbled around, clutching his chest, finally bumping into Ember with his goofy antics.

Their eyes met. A slow burn traveled through him, a combination of hope and desire.

His eyes traveled the length of her body. "Ember …" Saying her name inflamed him even more, but he held his ground.

She placed her fingertips on her lips and pressed hard before releasing them to speak. "Your aura … you're taking my breath away."

Will knew his emotions lit her up. She was soaking up every ounce of his runaway hunger and devotion. Before he could think at all, his arms tightened around her, as strong and confident as the self he used to know. He pressed against her as if her every curve and hollow was magnetized to his every muscle, sinew, and organ, hardly believing he had her somewhat naked body pinned against him.

He kissed her then, first tender and then with a sudden, unrestrained intensity. She tasted like mint and magic. His mouth moved her lips apart, sending fierce quivers along his nerves. He felt her surrender. She kissed him back with an urgency that matched his own. A rising current of fever stunned him and left him faint.

He trembled. He wanted to gently lay her down on the rooftop under the stars, gaze at her beauty, and fully claim her as his own. It was taking all his self-restraint not to create space between them to explore her body with his hands. If he did, he would not be able to hold back.

He took a deep breath to ground himself and then another.

This was dangerous in all kinds of ways. He had been away from the basement for too long. The abrupt mental image of Xander seeing them together blurred and then destroyed the moment. For that matter, anyone could come looking for them.

Will separated himself from Ember but closed his eyes before putting his hands on her shoulders and turning her away from him, not daring to look at her again.

She began to turn back around. "Will—"

Will's face was fierce. "Don't. Don't turn around, Ember. I'm going back to the others. I … I want you too badly, and I shouldn't be here. I'm not sorry I got to be with you like this. It was a moment in heaven. But I'm sorry I took advantage of a situation I shouldn't have. You're not mine. Just know I would go to the ends of the earth to be with you."

He backed up and finally turned, quickly reaching the opening to the floor below, all the while wondering if his heart would ever be the same.

FORTY-FIVE

Xander's Return

XANDER MADE sure his mask was in place and jumped for the open door of the Maglev, more than ready to finish the journey.

Dorian stopped him with his arm. "Wait. I'll check it out first." He stepped outside the train.

Although Xander watched him, the delay seemed eternal before he returned.

"Well?" Xander prodded, leaning forward.

"All clear. Except for our friend Red out there."

"Did someone say they saw Red?" The strongman took a step into the car, grinned, and high-fived Xander.

"If you didn't see anyone, that's enough for me. We go for it." Xander clenched his hands and released, the only anxiety that showed. He gestured to the Sciolists lying on the floor. "Red, you'll be coming with Dorian and me."

Xander shouted out to the car's passengers, "Let's go!"

As a body, the group followed the three scurrying across the platform, concentrating on creating silence from their lips to their toes.

"I thought maybe Oslin would make us into ghosts," Dorian whispered. "But I'm glad he didn't. I would find it quite weird."

Xander chuckled softly. These Easterners were a very odd bunch.

Their little tribe hurried, pressed against the buildings, seeking as much cover as possible. No one spoke. The darkness helped, and curfew was now long past.

When they'd walked a good fifty yards with no surprises, Xander became nervous. The silence was too good to be true.

After the Sciolists had confronted them at every station, Xander knew others were simply waiting to be summoned. The plans they'd made to set the fire as a distraction had not taken the caped correctors out of circulation as they had hoped. He glanced over his shoulder, double-checking that the rest of Phoenix followed.

The Sciolist's Alt on Xander's wrist buzzed. He squinted at the words streaming across its face. "Maglev halted. Sixty-five riders on board disembarked: Avalon Station. Probe Team: search two-mile radius."

They're coming.

"Guys, we're gonna be on somebody's radar *soon*." Xander held out the Alt for Red to read.

"If they come, you run, and I'll fight." Red bared his teeth, looking ready for a battle.

Dorian shot Red a cautionary look. "Even if they see us, they may not stop us."

Xander furrowed his brow and raised his eyebrows in an "Are you kidding?" look. "You're far too optimistic, my friend." *No wonder he's a Level Seventeen,* he thought.

Dorian grabbed Xander's wrist and voiced his own command to the Sciolist network on the other end. "Gideon here," he said, winking at Xander. "Already on site. No sign of anyone. The party in question is MIA."

One monotone response came through the apparatus. "Noted." Xander gave a thumbs-up to Dorian.

Dorian gave a final command. "No assistance needed. Cancel the call for Probe Team."

The Alt buzzed. "Noted. Sending two singulars from Insurance Team."

Dorian was grinning. "We do not need back up. I repeat. There are no signs of passengers or the rebel threat. Stand down."

"Heard, received, and approved." Then, Alt silence.

A sound from behind a building, much like the blast of multiple rifles, startled Xander. He stopped in his tracks and glanced at Dorian, who instead increased his speed, and Xander skipped to keep up. Red moved out in front.

"I heard gunshots, didn't you?" Xander's nerves surged with adrenalin.

"Xander, it's just the Emporium, the city's trash disposal. When the trash goes through the main vac, it makes that noise." Dorian gestured toward a gray structure. "That building's the center." He put a hand on Xander's shoulder. "We've got this."

Ahead, a brilliant light swept across a grassy field. Xander sucked in a breath, his muscles tense. *That's not trash.*

"Motion sensors," Dorian explained.

"What's in motion?" Red asked. "We're not even there yet."

"Something else is." Xander gritted his teeth, wondering if other lights would come on as they moved into the streets adjacent to Obviators.

"Just lights, Xander …" Dorian persisted with his reassurance. He continued to walk at a ridiculous pace.

"Wee should've made sure those were disabled when he visited the Plauditorium." Xander knew that wasn't fair; he hadn't thought of that himself. Even so, it was nice to have a scapegoat. "I say we keep to the buildings, even if we have to go out of the way."

"Roger that," Red agreed.

"Of course." Dorian shrugged. He was more relaxed than a sightseer on a summer's day.

"Shazz!" Xander jumped. Another light blinked on as they

hurried past a jewelry store. *Coming closer to the main part of town. Obviators is only two blocks away.*

Then he blinked. Twice. He caught a sudden but slight shift ahead in the blackness. Something was definitely out there, far down the street.

What was emerging from the shadows?

A person, for sure, but not a Sciolist. He would have seen the ridiculous red garb. No … a person dressed in a dark color. The cloak had a cowl like a Sciolist's would. Not black and not gray, but what appeared to be maybe a deep green? This was no Sciolist—or anyone with a recognized Status for that matter.

But that was not all. Xander's attention zeroed in on the bizarre thing walking beside the figure up ahead.

At first, Xander thought it was a dog, but the peculiarity of seeing a dog out at night made him strain his eyes to see better. A faint motion light finally fully illuminated the duo, and Xander drew in a breath. This was no dog with the man; thick and oversized, it looked like a cross between a hippo and a manatee. A pig? *Not in a million years would there be something that weird walking around.*

I've had too little sleep, he thought, rubbing his eyes. Surely if it were real, Dorian had seen it, too. "Dorian … do you see something? What's … who's that up ahead?"

The mind master slowed his steps and narrowed his eyes, focusing on the figures in the street, now coming their way. "I do see a person and … some kind of dog. Maybe they'll just go along their way."

"That's no dog, and they're coming toward us." Xander pulled the gun off his shoulder and then changed his mind. *Way too noisy.* Passing the rifle off to Talesa, he reached into his jumpsuit and ripped the Stinger from the bundle.

The crowd behind them shifted, falling into line single file directly behind the three leaders as if they were a shield. No one spoke, but Xander knew they were all seeing the same thing.

"Better to avoid what we don't understand." Dorian

motioned to a broad building to his right. "There's enough room for everyone to take cover behind that. I can speak to whoever is coming and get him to leave."

In double quick time, Xander herded the Phoenix assemblage into an opportune six-foot space separating two buildings. He and Red both flattened themselves to the building's wall at the corner, where they could still watch Dorian, who simply stood in place, waiting for the mysterious stranger to approach.

Muffled footsteps came closer, along with the sound of a soft snort. Xander wiped salty sweat off his brow, quietly cursing when a drop fell into his eye.

Peering out, Xander eyed the stranger and the beast with him. The cloak was indeed a glossy fabric of deep forest green. He couldn't see a face within the hood well, but when the head briefly turned his way, he was surprised to see it was a woman with olive skin.

The unknown person's four-legged nightmare was on a chain, but the obvious strength of the animal would need much more restraint than that if it wished to escape. *Obviously a mutant*, he thought.

It resembled an immense, overstuffed cat, its back about five feet from the ground, its endoskeleton reinforced with synthetic muscle, for sure. Its mouth appeared almost fused together, but on second glance, Xander decided it was just extra gums, black as tar, that gave that impression. Teeth were visible and pointed, wicked sharp, and, although short, looked savage enough to rip tin. Muscle showed through its rubbery skin, which wrinkled across its chest, hanging in folds. No ears stuck up on the top of its head; instead, three holes marked each side above its eyes. A nose, flattened flesh that gathered in vertical creases down the middle of its face as if it had run into a wall, gave it a repulsive vibe. There was no mistaking the muscle in those legs, which were elephantine in shape, but solid and squatty. Ferocity showed in its eyes, fathomless, like a cave to the soul.

With a calm demeanor, Dorian said, "Hello there!" and gave

the Tranquility salute. In spite of his poise and friendly greeting, he stood directly in the middle of the other's path with his arms crossed.

The stranger returned the salute and placed herself in front of her "dog." "It's past curfew. What are you doing walking the streets?"

The monster by her side growled. Its snarl, along with their conversation, was loud enough for Xander to hear from his position fifty feet away. He cringed at the risk the noises made, wishing the sounds would evaporate into dust; yet he leaned out further, making sure to hear every word.

"I might ask you the same. Who are you? And what is that?" Dorian pointed to the disgusting creature at her hip.

"My name is Petula," she said, not acknowledging his other question. "Who are you, and where are you going this hour of the night?"

Dorian gave her a remorseful look, "Returning home. Had to delay my trip due to the fire. Just properly inconvenient." Then, he fixed his eyes on hers and issued a terse command. "You will go on your way, and I'll go mine. You will forget our encounter."

"Of course. Have a wonderful night." The woman plodded forward, tugging the freakish animal along with her.

Xander observed Dorian standing and waiting, watching carefully as she bridged the eight-foot space between them to go on her way.

Suddenly, with a shrill yowl like that of a banshee, the creature lunged at Dorian, the stubby, two-foot legs obviously not a deterrent to the animal's ability to move quickly. Before Xander could blink in disbelief a second time, the beast hurtled onto the Easterner, knocking him off his feet and to the ground. The monstrosity stood on top of his chest, saliva dripping from its mouth, pointy teeth glistening.

To Xander's horror, the creature tore at Dorian's arm, ripping pieces of flesh off the bone. Blood gushed from the wound.

Dorian screamed. He struggled to sit up, to shove the beast away. "Stop! Stop, stop, stop!"

Turning to the group behind him, Xander hissed a quick order: "Silence! Stay hidden!"

Although Xander could do nothing to stop the noise of the assault from shattering the peace and exposing them to responders, he could thrash the demon attacking Dorian. He burst out from behind the building, the Stinger crackling in his hand. Red, too, charged forward.

Xander's legs pummeling the ground and his weapon slicing the air, with Red at his side, he was primed and ready for action. Mere feet away from tackling the hellhound, the woman reacted.

"Grallper!" she yelled at the mutant biter. "Draw back *now!*"

With a final snarl and unworldly howl, the animal shrieked again but disengaged and scuttled away, its reptilian tail between its legs. The beast settled itself by its keeper's side, as if obedience came naturally to a monster.

"Dorian! What—!" Seeing the blood and chunks of Dorian's arm mottling the street, Xander scanned the area frantically, his heart jumping hurdles in his chest, desperate to find something to wrap around his comrade's arm. When Dorian's eyes rolled back, he knew Dorian was barely holding on to consciousness.

The woman's eyes, wide and yet ghostly, flickered. She hovered over them, her right hand covering part of her face. "I'm so sorry! Grallper's not used to people. He's Inventum property." She pulled the Alt on her wrist up to her eyes. "Alerting Medics now."

Red made a move to restrain the woman, but at the same time, Xander threw out his arm. "No! No, no!" Xander knew Dorian needed medical attention, but it couldn't happen. Their entire operation would collapse in a hot minute.

Dorian's spoke, his voice a whisper. "I need—Xander, sit me up."

Xander put his arm around Dorian's shoulders and carefully

lifted him to a sitting position. In spite of his caution while handling him, Dorian's blood painted Xander's hands.

The Easterner's eyes focused on the woman. "You … will … leave us now. Take that animal away. You will not … report … not … remember … anything."

Petula turned away, her manic minion turning one last time to growl.

FORTY-SIX

Xander's Phase Two

XANDER SAGGED WITH RELIEF, his nerves unraveling like severed coils of barbed wire. He pushed perspiring palms to his eyes, pressing back the frantic spin of his brain, trying to focus on Dorian's injury. Ripping his right pant leg from ankle to knee, he created a makeshift bandage, wrapping it around Dorian's shredded arm.

The bleeding was severe and soaked the fabric, despite its layers.

"Red, can you carry him? Take him. Get to Obviators fast! I'll follow with the others."

"Righto. I'm on it." Red hoisted Dorian up on his back with a gentle heave. "I'll be careful, but I'm running with him." He stopped, worry etched on his face, but in a second, Red had gone.

Xander loped back over to his group still huddled behind the building, where Phoenix threw questions at him like single bombshells. He quickly explained the series of events to the crew, who accepted the news with a resolve he had to admire.

On the other hand, even with the building keeping them in the shadows, he felt exposed, more vulnerable than an insect in an avalanche. His Easterners were gone. It was only him and half of Phoenix.

Resuming possession of the rifle, he narrowed his eyes and scanned back in the direction they had come. The others should be coming, not far behind. If he met up with them, he would have Oslin and Lotus as protectors. Problem was, Oslin's group was cloaked. He strained to see if Lotus had indeed remained visible, but his shoulders slumped. Nothing.

Xander, you're depending way too much on other people. The voice in his head snapped him out of his self-pity. He had always depended on himself for everything—been a total loner up until recently. It was time to get his head back into that space.

"C'mon. We push forward. Break yourselves up into singles, pairs, and trios, but keep up." His tough self-talk added an unintended brusqueness to his words.

A moment later, he found Talesa by his side. Fond of Ember's mom, he smiled at her as she put her arm around his shoulders and spoke. "This has been tough, but keep the faith. You're doing a great job. The other group is only about fifty yards ahead of us. They moved on when we had the incident with Dorian. We can join up and have a little more security."

"How do you—" *Of course she would know where the others were.* Her mind was like a GPS with the Easterners. "How could I forget? Lead on."

With Talesa now at the forefront and mentally communicating with Oslin and Lotus, Xander again checked behind him, glancing at every shadow as a possible threat and making sure all his followers were indeed following. He motioned to them to hurry.

In the space of a minute, they met up with the other group, Oslin suddenly reappearing to greet them and give instructions. "We saw what happened." Oslin quickly made a pass through the air with his hands. "You're now veiled. But this is a very large group. Safest thing to do right now with so many of us is to hold hands. We stand a much better chance of staying concealed if we're connected."

Oslin reached out his right hand for Xander's, and the group followed suit, a multi-pronged octopus led by Oslin.

The bulky group marched along, not near as quickly now with their giant amoeba form. Xander's earlier mind lecture about being independent had become absolutely worthless, but he was happy knowing the odds were again in their favor. He had nothing to fear from lights or shadows.

Trudging past Level Seven businesses and restaurants, he at last got a sense of place. Other than their mad-cap run to the car repair shop and his harrowing field trip with the purple car, he'd not checked out the area. But his heart leapt when he saw the sign for Obviators mounted on a pole and lit with rainbow colors. A couple of blocks, and they'd be there, the mission over. The smile on Ember's face was already in his mind's eye.

Then he stopped short, feeling the accordion snap of the other bodies to which he was connected. His eyes were glued to an alcove in the ridges of storefronts on the street just ahead where two Sciolists stepped out, bantering about something he couldn't make out until they bridged much of the distance between them, when he could overhear the conversation.

He sucked in a breath, remembering he had no reason for dread. The Sciolists could not see them. Not daring to whisper "I'm sorry" to the person whose hand he held, he picked up his pace. *Just keep walking.*

No sooner than the thought floated through his brain, he heard a yell. "What the—!" Both Sciolists appeared confused, their faces blank, their eyes wild and staring.

With a slight head shake, one elbowed the other. "Did those people just … appear out of thin air?"

Tapping his fist against his lips, his partner hissed, "Yessss. Reporting immediately." He wasted no time machine-gunning words into his Alt while his companion thundered, "What trick is this? Some prank? Your actions are suspect, and you are breaking the emergency edict. You will submit to arrest."

The Sciolists moved forward, their Stingers out and crackling with current.

Although he didn't stop walking, Xander's blood froze, his heart growing icicles of terror. *What was happening?* His mouth welded shut with shock, and for once, he was at a loss for words.

Looking frantically in every direction, he saw the problem. They had just walked by a charging station for CommuteCars. Unenclosed, the multiple ports held tubing with enough voltage to service an entire fleet of cars. The hold on Oslin's power had only one restriction. They had violated it.

He felt his hands empty their human connections and, for a split second, saw the terror-stricken faces of the people around him before a handful broke ranks and ran for cover, the Sciolists now yelling profanities and calling for immediate backup.

No, no, no! Holy flaming Shazz! He grabbed at the rifle, caring about nothing now but taking out the threat.

A crisp ray of light blazed behind him, its rapier-like intensity slicing through the night, a supernova at warp speed. His reflexes scrambling, he dove for the ground, his eyes closed, his heart bumping against his ribs.

A silence settled among their ranks, followed by the garbling of voices and smothered squeals. But as Xander slowly got to his feet, the voices that rose above were those of the Sciolists, screaming that they could not see.

Xander turned to find Lotus standing just behind him. "We should go," she said simply.

Xander threw his right arm up in the air and made a motion forward. "Fall in and hoof it! Now!"

The group poured forward, moving independently from one another but converging within a half block, the panicked defectors hiding behind trees running into formation. Grabbing one another's arms and hands, they disappeared once more into the night.

FORTY-SEVEN

Serpio's Penalties

KEYED UP beyond a coffee addict's high, Serpio couldn't sleep. He tossed the blankets off the bed, almost as if it would help him uncover the answers he needed.

An insistent buzz on his OmniCom further destroyed his efforts to settle down for what little was left of the night.

"Yes?"

At first, he found it hard to believe the voice on the other end was a Sciolist. He picked up a frantic undercurrent, a breathless rush of words that wobbled their way to his ear. "Sir, I apologize deeply for the interruption and for the hour. It … we don't know how or what actually happened. Some people in the street were there one minute but disappeared into thin air the next."

He sat up, rigid. Perhaps he had not heard right. "Disappeared? Dis-ap-peared."

"Yes."

"What nonsense is this?" *Is this some practical joke?* But no one would do that, not to him, the Magistrate. "Get to the point. Who was it?"

"A group of people, sir. They … suddenly appeared in front of us. Some ran—then they walked toward us and then … they vanished."

"When was this?"

"No more than five minutes ago. We looked for them—"

He pinched himself, unsure all of a sudden if he had indeed fallen asleep and was dreaming, but he found reality to be absolute. Serpio seethed with indignation and exasperation. Through clenched teeth, he said, "Keep looking. Whoever this is has some sort of technology. Use our GPS to find them."

"We did, sir. Nothing registers on the trackers."

These Sciolists have to be under the influence! But the incident nagged at him. No Sciolist would report to duty that way—not unless they were asking to be terminated.

"Go door to door in the area and beyond. See if there were other witnesses. Find who's responsible. I want this mystery solved. Immediately!"

"Sir, we'll need backup." The voice had regained firmness.

He sighed, clicked off, and sent out an alert. A fleet of Sciolists were now on their way, but he was certain they would discover some type of holographic spectacle. *If this is the rebel group playing tricks …*

He got up, dressed hastily, and hurried through the multiple hallways and doorways to City Hall's prisoner pods, where Ava was confined. Maybe by now she'd have had a change of heart, ready to give him the information he needed. He'd press Ava for answers to the mystery disappearance, too.

Sitting on the floor in the corner, Ava jumped, startled, when he opened the door to her compact compartment. Her eyes, typically fiery, were outlined instead in red rims, the art strokes of salty tears. Her short hair, normally a perfect boy cut, resembled flattened straw. There was no trace of a smile; she had ceased to masquerade any happiness. Although he, too, was bleary-eyed and frustrated, the sight of her discomfort soothed him. He still had the power. He still had ways to learn what he had somehow missed.

"Ava … how are you doing tonight?" Serpio stepped closer, reached out, and touched her on the shoulder.

Ava shook off his hand. "I would ask you the same. What are you doing here at this hour? Was the party not enough entertainment?"

Serpio smirked. "It was highly entertaining. Since I'm still riding high, I've come to offer you a deal."

"A deal? What kind of deal could I possibly want or need?" Ava's eyes shone with distrust.

"I have a list of evidence to submit to the Elite about your double-crossing deeds." He paused, waiting for a reaction. When he got none, he continued. "As you know, a full trial is very rare here, but if you are to be held, the Elite have called for it. So, I have no choice except to bargain, for your sake. Having you stand before your peers and answer questions in a formal Inquiry would be complete and total humiliation for you. It would be painful for the Elite as well. As you know, I try to protect everyone to the best of my ability."

"Your big heart is admirable, Magistrate. Who knew you were so protective of those who defend you?" Ava sounded positively saccharine.

"Well, of course," Serpio said with casual innocence. "I am trying very hard to spare you as well. You can help everyone, including yourself, if you'll provide me with the information I need."

Ava leaped up and came within inches of his face. "And what do you *need*? The entire list of DNA-altered people so you can eliminate them? Increased surveillance? Extra Sciolists? Using Ember for detestable purposes? Torturing Will into obeying? Or is it Xander's boldness that you need? I'll not be able to provide you with any of that, Mr. Magnus."

Serpio curled his fingers and laughed. "I have the best intentions for the city. It's my duty to keep Tranquility peaceful, and to do that, I sometimes need to be unorthodox. That includes finding the rebels and two-faced traitors like *you* in order to restore life to what it was before you all ruined it. And Xander? His so-called courage is false bravado. He covers it well, but he's as frightened as a two-year-old in a skydive." He buzzed his lips, the raspberry showing his deep contempt. "I need to know where they are. All of them. So, the deal … if you give me information that allows the capture of any one—just one—of them, I'll allow you to go free. You'll go to The Outside, but at least you'll have a small chance of survival. If I capture them all, you could be placed in a guest cottage after being stripped of your Status. Otherwise … well, it's anyone's guess." He shrugged but honed his coal-black eyes on hers.

"If I did, you'd kill them. The price of my so-called freedom would be blood."

"I would never harm Ember. She's …" Serpio wanted to confess all the reasons but bit back the words. "She's too important."

"Why? She's no different than all the other humans with modified DNA that you've terminated."

Serpio drew back as if stung. *How does Ava know about my elimination campaign?* He could count on one hand those who knew: the three transport conductors who took bodies to The Outside and two trusted Sciolists.

Ava flexed her arms, and her face ripened into a shade of red. "You think you're so clever arranging "random accidental" deaths and planting poison in the Augur Prize rings. And the coverup of those Augur Prize deaths—all the promotions to top-secret posts that don't exist. I know those people didn't go undercover! They went to The Outside—dead—and then up in flames so they couldn't be traced."

"Ava … Ava. You need psychiatric evaluations right away. You aren't well. You are losing your mind. Is this why you're helping criminals and making up stories?"

And. There. It. Was. Just by accidentally uttering those five powerful words, "You are losing your mind," he'd all but solved his problem with Ava. He would simply present Ava to the Elite as mentally disturbed. This was going to be easier than he imagined.

"You know I'm not losing my mind! My dad knew you were doing terrible things, too."

Ava's dad? Ava's dad … Validus … Drake Validus! The name registered like a sudden siren. Serpio sucked in a breath.

Ava pounced, now reckless with her attack. "Yes! The very person you sent to The Outside years ago for not giving you the complete list of people who were genetically modified."

Understanding dropped like a meteorite shower. Why had he never connected Ava with her father? *She has the same name!* It wasn't like she had even tried to hide it. He had been completely blind, and for no good reason at all, other than blocking the entire incident out of his mind. It had been fourteen years since those scientists at Inventum had refused to cooperate. And then eliminating the people involved without raising red flags had been stressful. He'd pulled it off, but not without a lot of blood, sweat, and tears.

Serpio sniffed. "Poor Ava. Someone has lied to you. Drake Validus was overprotective of the data because he conducted unlawful experiments. As Elite, you're well aware that we can't have people like your father here, especially at Inventum. He had to pay for his crimes. What's important is how you pay for yours. So, are you ready to save yourself? All I need is just a tiny bit of information. I'd rather do that here than in the therapy room. Two to three words are enough to tell me where they are."

"I will not. Those are your three words."

"You're confirming that you do know their location." All of Serpio's suspicions became a shower of confetti. He had indeed nailed the rebels' helper.

Ava pressed her lips together. "Three different words. I. Can. Not."

Serpio blew out a breath in frustration and fury. He was becoming weary of Ava, her lies and, most of all, the long-buried history she'd kept alive. That alone was worth crushing her into nothing.

"Tomorrow, your delusional mental state will be explained to the Elite. They will be as they are—sympathetic. They will insist you get immediate treatment. Of course, in the meantime, they will disassociate themselves from you."

"I am allowed to defend myself! They will expect it." Ava's chin came up.

"I will explain to them that your ... condition ... is much too fragile, that you already begged for therapy in hopes of regaining some of your senses." Serpio raised one brow and then rubbed his hands as if he were washing them in germicide.

Ava's face bloomed red, and her eyes flashed with wrath. "If I go down, your turn is coming, Serpio. The Elite are not stupid."

Serpio snickered. "We shall see. In a few hours, it will be morning. I shall take you to the therapy you need."

He turned on his heel without a backward glance, leaving Ava in the dark.

FORTY-EIGHT

Ember's Buzz

EMBER CONTINUED to stand motionless on the rooftop for another minute. A shiver went up her spine. The stars in the sky above winked at her secret, and the bushes sent their long shadows further across the rooftop like dark omens.

What was I thinking?

The only answer was that Will remained in her heart as if he'd never left.

Her history with him and the way he looked at her ... all the while standing there like a flawless, hot Greek god ... his golden hair lit by moonlight ... his aura flaring with fire ... his chest taut with muscle ... It all made her melt. It was as if both of them had held their breath in some magic spell.

And really ... did she even deserve his love? She had turned away from him and thought the worst of him the whole time he was captured.

She hurried then, climbing back down into the bathroom where the light assaulted her eyes and illuminated her soul. Once there, she threw on the clean uniform and saw the button for the washing machine that she'd missed earlier. The practical things suddenly took control.

Descending into the basement, across the room, she saw

Will's parents asleep, sharing the air mattress that had been hers the night before. They looked so cute snuggled together.

She saw no sign of Will or anyone else, though. A backseat door was open on one of Kamar's cars. Crawling inside, she lay down and fell asleep as soon as she shut her eyes.

Music? No. The dots and dashes of Morse Code made a beeping rhythm just like an upbeat song. She was in a room, the walls painted a pale pink. Strapped to a bed underneath a murky sky shedding rain, she twisted her face away from the onslaught of raindrops, gasping when she realized they were drops of blood.

Someone leaned over her, a broad, black shape. Only a sinister smile showed white against the darkness. She writhed and cried out for help. Screams of pain and war cries answered, followed by Will calling her name. Then Xander's voice ... but she could not make out the words before they faded into the night like dust in the wind.

"Ember ... wake up. Two Easterners arrived, and one is badly hurt." With an apologetic smile, Will shook her awake by jiggling her legs.

She bolted upright and slid herself across the seat. The dream lingered, but she could not dwell on what it meant, not with this emergency. "Where?"

But she saw the victim immediately. Just off the lift, a muscular, red-haired man held an injured man in his arms. Blood saturated his silvery clothing on one arm, both shirt and biceps shredded and gummy with gore.

"Holy Shazz!" Ember ran to them, everyone else in the room already getting supplies. "Guys! Get him to that worktable over there!"

Red ran a hand through his hair. "This poor guy is Dorian. I got him here as fast as I could."

"What happened?" Ember ran alongside, her question almost lost in the shuffle.

With everyone in hyper mode, they soon had the injured man situated on the table.

Red put his hand to his head. "We ran into this creature from Inventum that attacked him."

Ember flashed back to the Greelox she and Xander had met in The Outside. She shivered but had no time to ask more questions. The man would bleed out if they didn't act quickly.

Unwrapping the saturated fabric, Ember swayed on her feet, dizzy with disgust. Moans of sympathy from the people around her, along with the rusty scent of fresh blood, made a sickening scene. Gashes and puncture wounds sluiced trails of sticky slime among jagged, loose pieces of flesh dangling by threads. Dorian was unconscious, his eyes shut, and his breathing shallow. His face bore a moon-like pallor.

Ember and Reselda crowded around Dorian. The healer placed her hands on Dorian's chest. "I'll put the curing here, on his heart. He's lost a lot of blood, and the trauma has made him weak."

Ember nodded. With a deep breath for courage, Ember, too, moved her hands down Dorian's arm, blood staining her palms and fingers. Waves of warmth pulsed into him.

Then a vibrating sensation streamed through her hands. Her healing power was going into Dorian, but she was getting something coming to her as well. She felt the same surge as when she had met Kamar and suddenly panicked. Would her weird absorption cause Dorian lose more energy than he was taking in?

To her relief, Dorian moaned, and his eyelids fluttered. *He's responding.* Ember repeated the movement over and over, each time witnessing the flesh coming together and the bleeding slow. The final pass left Dorian's arm completely restored.

"He's doing well," Reselda announced. "He should be coming around quickly now."

A few more massaging touches, and Dorian sat up, his face flushed with fresh color. "Did I … live?" he asked.

The group, all watching the transformation, erupted in laughter, applause, and high fives.

"Barely." And Ember meant it. She stood, feeling drained.

They had saved the man's life, but she knew it had been a miracle. She glanced from Red to Dorian. "Welcome to both of you. I'm Ember, and the other healer is Reselda."

"Thank you. I wasn't sure …" Red shook his head. "Reselda, you do us all proud." He gave her a grateful hug. "And Ember … the Queen of Hearts! You really must be all that with how you healed Dorian. And you fit your name, just like me. We're both Rusties."

Before she could tell him that she wasn't queen of anything, he came in for an all-consuming hug, his fiery zest a natural fit with his red hair. His personality made her happy like a playful puppy would. But the moment he touched her, she could feel his talent invade her body like a turbocharge to every cell. All at once, she felt invincible—incredibly strong and powerful.

Words stuck in her throat, but she managed to gasp, "Good … to meet you, Red." She broke off the hug, quite certain she'd just inherited Red's ability, but bewildered by the quick transfer and her ineptness in how to use it. Kamar had shown her the way to use her hands, and the healing gift seemed to come as she touched an injured person. Would she suddenly be able to lift a building with a flutter of her eyelashes? She'd better find out. The power, unlike the others, could have terrible consequences. Would she crush someone simply by hugging them? Probably not, because Red had just hugged her, and she was all right. But how did it work, then? All of a sudden, her insides tumbled into each other, and she wasn't sure if she was terrified or angry. She didn't ask for this.

"Um … Red. How do you manage your ability?" She wasn't ready to confess that he had just crowned her Red Number Two. It would be awkward—and then she'd have to explain …

"Manage?" Red repeated, a hint of confusion in his fiery eyes.

She shrugged and looked at the floor, trying to appear nonchalant. "I mean—aren't you dangerous to everyone around you?"

He gave her another curious look. "Mind if I rest?" As he

unfolded himself to sit right there on the floor instead of finding another solution. "Sit down, and I'll spill all my secrets." With a wink, he patted the spot next to him.

"I hope that wasn't a rude question," she began, her Tranquility manners kicking in.

"It's okay. You're friend, not foe. What I do is channel emotion. If I put all my energy into developing anger, I get strong—really strong. I have to be mega careful with that. But with it, I can run like the wind, too. No one can catch me if I do." He put his hands in his lap. "With my Alt, you see how careful I've had to be?"

Red glanced over his shoulder and then stood. Will was approaching from a few feet away.

Will extended a hand to Red, who shook it. "Thanks for being here. I'm Will. And yes, the notorious one," he said with sarcasm.

"I happen to be a big fan," Red replied, giving him a bro fist tap.

Ember stood and pressed her lips together, upset for a moment that Will had stolen the rest of her time with Red. There was so much to learn. But she had captured enough for the moment. Now she could bring her worries about Xander to the surface. "When do you think the others will be here? They must not have been far behind."

"They're coming. Last I saw, they were regrouping and heading out again. It shouldn't be too long." Red smiled and then raised an eyebrow as he glanced from her to Will.

"What time is it?" Ember's eyes roamed the room. *Why isn't there a clock here?*

Red replied, "Too early. Six. No daylight outside yet."

"Then it's already been over an hour since you arrived with Dorian. Could they be in trouble?" The tightness in her chest expanded.

Will slid his arm lightly around Ember's shoulder. "It'll be okay, Ember. Xander doesn't go down easy."

"Ah," Red responded, looking intently at Ember. "Backstory's becoming clear."

Right then, as if Will spoke a spell, the lift swiffed its way down into the room. Ember's heart leapt. There was Xander, surrounded by a crowd of others. Looking like a disheveled street rat, his hair messy, his uniform rumpled, and mask in hand, Xander wiped a smear of dirt off his face.

"Xander!" As she ran, he stepped off the lift, and she catapulted herself into his arms, her hug like an iron vise. "So happy to see you!"

"Me too. I missed you so much." He laughed and kissed her before freeing himself to pan the room for Dorian. "Red got here? Is Dorian …?"

"They're here and fine. Look, Dorian is over there, sitting up, with Red." Ember pointed, her smile brimming with pride.

Xander openly stared at the Easterners before looking back at Ember with his jaw dropped. "Fine? Dorian's *fine*? That's impossible." As if he had to see it to believe it, he made short work of the distance to where Dorian sat, Ember following.

Dorian and Red both greeted him as Xander reached out and touched Dorian's newly healed arm before pulling his fingers away as if he'd been physically shocked. "You're okay? How?"

Dorian glanced at Reselda before fixing his eyes on Ember. "Ember and Reselda cured me. I'm appreciative and lucky. They saved my life."

Xander's pupils, brimming with ardor and astonishment, focused on Ember. "What—how did you do that?"

"Apparently, it wasn't a one-off with Kamar's powers." Ember shook her head, still not comfortable with the weird drawing power she had acquired.

"I go away for a little while, and you morph." Xander chuckled but looked at her with wide eyes.

Ember gave him a look layered with adoration. "I guess you'll just have to stick around to see what I can do." She winked. "So, I didn't get the whole story. What happened out there?"

Red rushed to answer. "Some weirdo met us on the route and had a demon with 'em."

Ember rolled her eyes. "A demon? C'mon, guys."

Xander grimaced. "It was something unnatural. Had to be a genetic mutant."

Dorian extended his finger as if it were a gun and made a click with his tongue. "Exactly. A lady had this creature. Said it was from Inventum—that they had escaped the fire. She seemed to be able to control it at first, but the thing went crazy and attacked me."

Ember put a hand to her chest. "My stars! And the rest of Inventum?"

"Gone," Xander said with a flicker of his eyelids. "The fire—I couldn't stop it before I realized we'd need the lab to discover how to limit Serpio's grasp on eternal life."

Ember's spirit sagged within her. How would they learn Serpio's secret without the lab?

Xander took her by the hand and motioned with his head toward the people dispersed through the room. "C'mon, Em. Time to meet a couple of others."

Talesa suddenly emerged through the crowd, wrapping Ember in a big hug.

"Mom!" Tears of joy welled up in Ember's eyes. Although she was connected to her mom telepathically, she loved being with her mom, something she never took for granted any more.

While Ember beckoned to Will, Kamar, Reselda, Jack, and Marina, Xander called out, "Lotus and Oslin! You need to meet a few more in our Phoenix family." They all quickly introduced themselves to one another, and in a few minutes, they were chatting and joking about their experiences on the Maglev.

Ember stepped back, waiting her turn and sizing up the new Easterners. They each appeared remarkable in their own way.

Like she sensed with Red, she could see and feel that these Tranks had a glamor that made them stand out.

Lotus's remarkable color-changing eyes were mesmerizing. Ember swept her own down over the gal's entire body to check out the first significant female in the group of Easterners. "Hey. Good to meet you. And what is your talent?"

"I glow—brightly enough to blind. I use it only in emergencies."

"Of course," Ember replied before thinking that was a stupid thing to say. She took a few steps back, hoping she didn't look rude. "And how do you light up?"

Lotus laughed. "Very carefully."

Ember took another step back, deliberately choosing not to touch Lotus. If she was collecting these bizarre talents, she wasn't sure she would want to light up like a neon sign.

She turned to the next person, Oslin, who stood right behind Lotus. *This one is a little more guarded,* she thought. Then, she blinked.

He was suddenly gone!

Xander laughed and began calling his name. In an instant, he was there again.

"Want to disappear with me?" Oslin asked, raising and lowering his eyebrows. Although his face was serious, she sensed a tease behind it.

"Sure?" Ember managed to whisper, not sure at all.

"Maybe later. Anyway, that's my talent. Good to meet the famous—I mean, infamous—Queen of Hearts!" He bowed his head before her and took her hand. The snap of electricity hit her quick and hard, almost knocking her off her feet.

Ember dropped her hand, jerking it back into the palm of the other. He looked at her curiously. "Umm … sorry. No offense, Oslin, but please don't use that name. It's Serpio's, and I hate it. I'm just Ember."

Oslin nodded his head again. "Fair enough, Justember."

"And one more thing?" she added before he could turn away.

"Yes?"

"Do you—do you use something to make yourself disappear?"

He tapped his head. "My mind. But I do put out my arms in a sort of swimming motion, especially if there are others I want to cloak as well. Why?"

"I need to know, that's all." Ember said. "Maybe I'll try it out sometime." As she giggled, she hoped the Easterner would find her remark amusing.

She didn't have time to find out.

Xander held up his wrist, shiny metal covering the red-banded Alt underneath barely gleaming.

Kamar gasped. "A Sciolist's transmitter?"

"Yeah. Because I had this, we learned about Ava. I'm ready to rip anyone apart to free her."

Will glowered at Xander before glancing at Ember. "Good for you, but we're already in gear. Ember and Kamar are constructing a tunnel to City Hall. We can get to her that way. Hopefully," he added.

Ember noticed Will's eye twitch and his aura flare. Stress.

Will laced his fingers together and cracked his knuckles. "Ready for Operation Rescue? Ava's got to be miserable and in danger. We've no time to waste."

FORTY-NINE

Serpio's Subterfuge

AFTER FINALLY FALLING ASLEEP, Serpio awoke a few hours later to his servant arriving to help him prepare for the day. At seven, his emotions were already in high gear as he placed three things on the agenda for the day: a meeting with the Elite, a city-wide search for Talesa, and a "therapy session" for Ava. At least one woman who had poisoned his life with her treachery would meet her fate today.

It shouldn't take much to break Ava once she was tortured, and from there, he should have the answers to every other problem. He could find Ember. Discover where Talesa disappeared. Capture the rebels and put them to death, but in a fun way. His body tingled with anticipation.

At nine sharp, he faced the Elite and called the meeting to order. "Thank you for coming to this emergency session today. I appreciate the time you are taking from your busy schedules. The silver lining for this meeting is about providing help for someone in this Elite group who has recognized a psychiatric disorder in herself."

He paused, witnessing the members glancing around to see who was missing and murmuring to themselves.

"Yes, I am sorry to say that it is Ava Validus, our respected colleague and first-class Medic."

Moans and ohs came floating back. He waited, making sure his words would have the desired impact. "Ava came to me last night accusing me of … terrible things. However, as I looked into her eyes and heard her words, I realized she was suffering from some type of insanity."

Again, a murmur rose up from the Elite. He dropped his head and shook it back and forth, playing out the role of the sympathetic supporter. He raised his head and looked at them with a soft, rueful smile. "After talking with her for some time, she confessed to having a great deal of mental confusion. Unbelievably, she wanted to come here today herself to tell you that —" He stopped, rubbing the front of his neck as if choking on the words. "—I, your humble and protective Magistrate, have been killing people and hiding the evidence."

Exclamations of shock and vocal expressions of sympathy moved like a wave across the group. Serpio caught a comment about how Ava had always seemed so level-headed, along with how excellent it was that Ava could get help. "She will come out even better than before" was a phrase passed around.

Feren was the first to stand and be recognized. "My heart goes out to dear Ava. She is such a lovely person. We want her to get well. Perhaps she has not been managing her emotions? Were there no red flags? Nothing that indicated she was slipping?" Feren took a cleansing breath and assumed a preaching stance. "This is what can happen if we allow stress and worry to make a home in our consciousness."

Serpio dropped his head again. "I'm afraid there were no signs. If only we could monitor thoughts as well as emotions. We could then save a person before it would get to this point."

A murmur of agreement passed among the assemblage.

Feren continued to stand. "Is she resting comfortably now? I assume she is at Solace, where some mental retraining could be performed for her. I trust she is in good hands."

"Yes. I am seeing to it personally," Serpio replied. "I'll be keeping you all informed on her progress as I learn about it. Thank you for your time today. I ask you to keep this information private. That is all I needed to explain, but as it is a delicate situation, I desired to see you all in person." He prepared to wish them all a good day and exit as quickly as possible when a fair-haired, elderly Elite woman he recognized as Maribel spoke up.

"What about the fire? Shouldn't we have news of that?"

Serpio nodded agreeably, although inside, he churned. He lowered his voice to a soothing tone. "Yes. I am sorry to say that Inventum burned to the ground. Very little was spared. However, the upside is that no lives were lost, and we can rebuild." Again, a murmur swelled through the crowd.

"How will we process DNA for suspects?" Maribel pressed.

"The DNA collection from suspected individuals will be on hold temporarily. Once I pull our scientists together, we can start gathering resources again. I will have more news after I can speak with them. Be assured that we have not stopped looking for the suspects—it's just that we can't identify them in the way we'd hoped."

A man with jet-black hair named Jared stood and spoke. "Are we any closer to finding the rebels? It seems inconceivable that they're still eluding all our efforts. These thugs are domestic terrorists! Setting buildings on fire? Planting bombs? And trying to kill you, our dear Magistrate. What's next? We must find them."

Serpio nodded his head. "Yes. The problem is that we don't have enough manpower. I agree, these criminals must be found and punished. Our entire way of life is being threatened. But our Sciolists are stretched to the limit. Remember, they still have a job to do—apprehend emotional resistors. I request approval for doubling our Sciolist forces, especially now that DNA identity is temporarily shelved."

Jared turned to the others, putting his index finger up on his right hand—displaying the Tranquility gesture. "A great step forward and a very necessary request, don't you think, my fellow Elite? Shall we all say 'love'?"

Serpio was mystified at how quickly the council joined in, the word "love" echoing around the room in a solid chorus.

"You are a great Elite with a true understanding of greatness. I will begin recruitment immediately and hope to help Ava as soon as I leave you now. Have a beautiful and peaceful day."

Leaving the chamber, he called upon Esryn to begin the selection, which would be a lottery. By the end of the day, Esryn would have fifty new recruits ready to undergo immediate training. Things were definitely going his way.

* * *

IN RECORD TIME, Serpio made it back to the holding cell where Ava sat hunched in a corner. Although there was no way she could have made it out of the holding pod, with its hard-core door and unbreakable glass, she was still cuffed.

Two Sciolists stood adjacent to him, waiting for orders.

He opened the door. "It is time, Ava. Time for you to give me a final decision. Have you even a smidgen of information to exchange for your future?" Serpio knew he was wasting his time; it was going to take a concentrated effort to break Ava.

With one giant step at a time, he advanced until he stood directly in front of her.

"You know my answer, Serpio."

Serpio looked her up and down. He wished he could feel pity, but he did not. She was just another necessary sacrifice.

Serpio stroked his chin. "Very well. A little therapy might help. After all, a mere twenty minutes ago, I assured the Elite that you were already receiving it. They were most compassionate about your situation."

"You're less than human, not allowing me to speak on my own behalf." In spite of Ava's hopeless situation, it didn't quell her anger.

"'Less than human' is not necessarily a shortcoming. I can live with that." Serpio nodded toward the officers. "Arturo and Cabot here will take you to your treatment, and I will see you soon."

Backing out of the enclosure, he trotted merrily back down the hallway, his head bobbing back and forth as he personified a new, frisky foal, took the elevator to the top, and made his way to one of his favorite playgrounds, the silver therapy room.

Once there, he set the controls. No matter how often he visited the place, the smooth, silvery walls and emptiness of it were an antidote for the chaos of life. So beautiful. So simple. He smiled, knowing he would soon have everything in hand.

Sooner than he anticipated, Arturo and Cabot brought Ava, kicking and screaming, into the therapy room, closed the door, and left. Ava was already stripped down. He had allowed her to keep her underwear, a gracious gesture under these circumstances. He smirked, though, at the dainty gold lingerie, much fancier than what he expected for such a plain, boyish woman.

Finally quiet but breathing hard, she looked around and then up, discovering the one-way window from where he observed her. Ava's fierce look in his direction could have melted iron. She paced back and forth, frenzied, but slowed down in seconds when Serpio released mind-altering music into the room.

It was lush orchestration, pleasant to the ears. Meant to purposefully relax her, the melodies were laced with "Ava" repeated over and over. A specially engineered voice, smooth and melodic, lulled the Medic with its slow cadence and rhythm.

"You are entering a relaxed state ...

... your eyes are growing heavy ...

... you are now going deeper and deeper into this beautiful soothing relaxation ...

... every sound you hear causes you to go deeper and deeper into this calm state of relaxation ...

... you will want to lie down and surrender your mind."

Unlike the process he'd used with Will, this therapy was

gentle; he wasn't trying to flip Ava's personality and loyalty like he had with the young Plauditor. What he needed at this point was information. She might be strong enough to withstand torture, and that would get him nowhere. Advanced hypnosis techniques would not give her a choice in the matter; she would literally be under his spell. If he could get her to confess what she knew, he could proceed with punishment later.

His eyes darted to the clock. After less than six minutes, she lay down on her back and slipped into a relaxed state, her eyes fluttering and her body limp.

He chafed with impatience, but it was not time yet for him to intervene.

The artificial intelligence that controlled the voice advanced to instructions. The music's volume lowered. "Imagine yourself being recognized as the one member of the Elite to save the city from the rebels. Your Status will rise, even within the Elite. To do this, you will be eager to give answers to the Magistrate's questions."

A slight curve of Ava's lips and a nod confirmed the suggestion had registered with her. Her breathing deepened. The AI continued. "All your fears and worries are dissolving into the air. When you exhale, you are letting them go. The more you breathe, the more you will feel good about revealing the secrets weighing you down."

Ava took several deep, cleansing breaths, blowing out gusts of air with her lips, as the voice droned on: "You will soon see the Magistrate, but he will appear as a beacon of light. You will not be afraid, but will know he is a powerful friend. He will ask you questions, and you will be honest with your answers. As you do, your hands and arms will light up, and you will see how very illuminating your replies are to the entire universe."

Ava slowly sat up and looked around in anticipation of the Magistrate's appearance. Then, she examined her hands, as if she was already looking for the promised glow from her fingertips.

Serpio took the elevator down and stepped into the room,

bringing a small, plush chair with him. He was filled with enough anticipation that his hands trembled. The seat would keep him together. "Hello, Ava. Are you feeling relaxed?"

"Yes. I feel very calm and peaceful."

"Very good. Tell me about your friends." He looked her in the eye, although knew she was seeing only a glowing silhouette.

"My friends? Samantha's my next-door neighbor. She's so nice. Brings me cookies sometimes. And Cami. Cami's been my friend since I was a teenager. She—"

Serpio reigned in his impatience, but it colored his words more than he wanted. "Not Cami … I need to know about your friend, Ember."

"Oh. She's not really a friend. More like a daughter, if I had one. She's a teen with lots of secrets." Ava put her index finger over her lips.

Now we're getting somewhere. "What secrets? Is she somewhere near by? Somewhere I can talk to her?"

"No. You can't talk to her! She has to hide." Then, with a smile, she held up her arms. "Look, I'm lit up!"

"See what you can do? When you answer the questions, you get to glow." Serpio worked his jaw and redirected the next question in hopes she might reveal more if he sought information on the rebels. "Is she hiding with other people?"

"Yes. She has a boyfriend with her. She loves him."

Ah. Xander, then, was with her; but there was no way all the rebels would be in one place. If he found the two of them, that would be a success. "Her boyfriend … Xander, right? Where is he?"

As she tried to see her reflection in the silvery walls, Ava's face registered disappointment, "My glow … it's disappearing. But I can't tell you. It would put her in danger. I cannot put a person in peril for any reason."

"I'm sure she'd be okay. She has my protection." *Wasn't the hypnosis enough to convince her that he was a strong ally?*

"Ember is someone with strange power. She only needs herself."

He clenched his fists, frustrated. "I already know she is an Empath. That makes her highly sensitive to others. She will need my support and safe keeping." As much as he tried to keep his voice even and quiet, it rose in pitch and volume.

"No. She has what she needs—her own crew. She can also stop time, heal people, and crush rock."

He pulled his head back, stunned, as if hit by an unforeseen blow. Fixing his gaze on Ava, its intensity could have bored a hole in her face. He narrowed his eyes, as if making them perfect lie detectors. But Ava appeared to be wholly under, her eyes closed, her body relaxed, a faint smile on her lips.

If she was telling the truth about Ember, those would be beyond supernatural talents, paranormal even, defying the laws of physics and science. He'd never heard of someone who could stop time. How would that even work? Crush *rock*? Heal people? How would little Ember be able to do those things? How would anyone?

Then realization hit him, like fully seeing the sun after looking at it through a pinhole during an eclipse. Ember had modified DNA—that, he knew. And she was born with it—passed down from her mother in a rare occurrence, as the genetic campaigns were long over by the time she was even conceived. By some freakish coincidence, she had these other talents, and he hadn't even known. She was far, far more than just an asset for Tranquility, where emotions were central. No; she was dangerous. Just like the others—a threat to their way of life.

As if he had tasted something unpleasant that he'd scraped off the bottom of his shoe, he shuddered and puckered his lips.

He took a breath to steady himself before extending his next question, more determined than ever to get a solid answer. "I'd like to see all that. Where can I find her?"

Ava made an exaggerated hand motion, zipping her lips. "I

cannot tell you. I am sworn to secrecy. I can tell no one, not even an angel of light like you."

"I can bring my light to her, as you can."

"She has all the light she needs."

Tired of holding back his anger, he bellowed, *"Tell me where I can find her!"*

"NO!" As if he had intentionally released Ava from the trance, she surged to a standing position and glared at him. She had come undone, and all pretense was gone. Her eyes were icy, her voice glacial. "You will not capture my soul, Serpio. And you are no angel of light."

"You are right. I'm much fonder of darkness. You have chosen to find that out for yourself."

FIFTY

Ember's Faith

ALTHOUGH EMBER HADN'T KNOWN ALL the members of
Phoenix very long, she felt after her time with them that they
were like the brothers, sisters, aunts, and uncles she'd never had.
She circled the room, giving out hugs and getting reacquainted
with her Phoenix family. Will's parents joined in greeting the
fellowship as if they'd been members all along. With a room full
of happy people, positive emotions flowed through her like a
rush of fluttering wings.

She was struck by the moment. Where in the past, she had
isolated herself in hope of insulating her empathic nature, she
realized she had a purpose to fulfill. Life wasn't about her and
how she felt. Instead, helping others with her talents and her
heart was the very crux of happiness. It was the instant she realized who she aspired to be—who she was meant to be. Someone
who no longer fought for herself, but who was a champion for
others.

Ember ushered Xander, Talesa, Will, and Wee to where
Kamar showed off the progress on the opening in the wall. As
they went, they had dug out just enough for what they needed,
making it an economical but uncomfortable passage. Wide
enough for one person at a time, crouched or on their knees, it

was still an impressive feat, the distance already long enough that peering in without a light made a journey to hell look more inviting.

"You should hurry. Ava's got to know we're trying to get to her. Are you ready now, Ember? Kamar?" Will shifted his weight, impatience showing in his shuffle.

Kamar turned his wrist from side to side, flashing it in front of them all like some new-fangled toy. "Uh … someone? I'll need a Morse app on my Alt, assuming we can get a signal under there. Can't communicate otherwise."

Xander's eyes roamed the room until they zeroed in. "Shawney!" he shouted. "Got an Alt that needs an app 'fore Kamar goes into the gap!"

Laughter rippled across the room; Xander bowed, and Shawney hurried to Kamar's aid, adding the code.

That was funny, but Ember pressed her lips together. She didn't have an Alt, leaving her with no communication at all. Should she depend on Kamar's? That didn't sound like such a good idea.

"Xander, if I take along one of those Sciolist's Alts, we can be alerted to threats and maybe even where those red rangers are."

Xander walked up to her, put his arms around her, and rested his chin on top of her head for a few seconds before releasing her and answering, "You're absolutely right. But it's a problem of sorts. If the GPS shows up on Kamar's Alt, no problem. He's expected to be here, and he comes and goes. But a Sciolist's Alt at Obviators? Too weird. Too risky." He held his wrist in the air with the precious Sciolist's Alt on it. "I have it covered so it blocks the GPS."

"It blocks the GPS? You're sure?" Ember looked at it skeptically.

"I would have smashed it by now if it didn't. The other two we took are already smashed into smithereens. But I'll wear it, not you."

Frowning, Ember realized Xander meant to go with her and

Kamar into the tunnel. She couldn't allow it. Ember had seen Xander's bowed shoulders since he'd returned and the way he squeezed his eyes shut and then opened them wide to stay awake. His haggard appearance spoke volumes, cementing her decision.

"A multi-person attack isn't smart. It's better that I go alone with Kamar."

"What? I'm going! I can't just sit by!" Xander ran his fingers through his already messy hair. "This is exactly what Serpio would want. You going there—you'll be dead on arrival." He turned to the others standing behind them. "Ember and Kamar can tunnel, but I'll follow with some of you. No way they're going to get all the way to the end where Ava is and have no protection or backup. We have weapons now—three Stingers and the two rifles Jasper's been keeping. Only two bullets left in each of those, but they're better than nothing."

Kamar shook his head. "Give both of us weapons we can use. We'll get there, and I'll go in and get Ava. When we leave, we'll have to close up the tunnel behind us anyway. We can't leave it exposed. Serpio and his Sciolists will know right where to go to find us. There's no room for a crowd, especially with Ava."

Wee, who had walked to the opening in the wall and peered in, stated, "Kamar's right. Lotsa people … noisy and slow."

Ember's eyes met her mom's. "I have to do this. I'm *going* to do this. I'm terrified, but it's the right thing to do. Along with Kamar, I'm the only one who can do it."

"Ember is strong and smart," Talesa said as she held Ember's gaze. "And I have a feeling she has discovered she can do more than she ever dreamed. She's grown up and is becoming who she really is. That takes courage."

Ember beamed under the encouragement. "Thanks, Mom," she answered as she gave her a quick hug. "But I don't just have courage. I have every power of every Easterner here." She paused, looking at each face to see if they understood. When Xander's eyebrow lifted and Will's brow puckered, she continued. "When I met each one, all it took was a touch, and I'm like them."

A bouquet of auras bloomed in wonder within the silence of suspended breath and hushed heartbeats.

Then everyone spoke at once, peppering her with questions.

"I could sense it," Talesa said, her smile soft, "but I didn't want to be the one to reveal it. You had to do it in your own time."

Ember motioned to gather them all in a group and put her arms around them as they huddled in. "Now you can all stop fussing. I can take care of myself. And Kamar will be with me."

"I'll take care of her," Kamar said, cringing as soon as the words were out of his mouth. "Umm, I mean, we'll stay together."

"We'll be careful. I promise." She turned to Xander. "But it's settled. I'll have my mask. Hand over that Alt, and grab us those Sciolists' weapons."

Even with Ember's assurance, Xander could have conjured up a storm, his eyes flashing, his mouth set at an unforgiving angle.

Ember knew he was worried about her, but his outrage wouldn't change her mind.

Xander glanced at Will in what appeared to be a plea for support, but Will lashed out. "Well? How about helping? Get those Stingers."

Xander bristled but made his way across the room, returning with the electrically charged shafts. Taking the Alt off his wrist, he handed it over. "Keep it covered, and use it only if you have to."

"Thank you." Ember stood on her tiptoes and gave Xander a bear hug and quick kiss on the lips before turning to leave, her passion for the mission now uppermost in her mind.

Xander grabbed her arm and pulled her back, wrapping her up again in his arms and kissing her with a fervor that demanded closed doors. She sank into him, his fire burning its way through her core.

Xander released her. "There. Now you're charged up and ready." He cocked an eyebrow, one of Ember's favorite Xanderisms, sexy as all get-out.

She and Kamar tucked the weapons down into the top of their uniforms, but with Ember's one final look back, Will's jealousy and Xander's worry streamed across her like a billowing thundercloud.

Moments later, with flashlights in hand, Ember and Kamar climbed into their passageway—darkness ahead and a storm behind.

FIFTY-ONE

Will's Words

WILL'S stomach had turned over as he witnessed the kiss between Ember and Xander. Then, he felt bile rise to his throat as he watched first Ember and then Kamar climb into the hole. He closed his eyes and took a deep breath, hoping it would calm his guts, but the stakes were high, and he was already strung out from all the stress.

He glanced over at Xander, who continued to stare at the hole in the wall long after Ember disappeared. At that instant, he empathized with his rival; they were both feeling exactly the same way.

Luckily, Xander seemed to finally shake off his earlier angst and wandered off in search of conversation with a few former Outsiders and Dorian.

Will felt a giant hand on his shoulder. Weeford. "You doin' okay?"

"Hey, buddy. Yeah—just kinda green for a minute." He swallowed back a bitter surge from his stomach. "Great to see you, Wee. We've gotta catch up."

"Yeah, yeah. Have a drink with me? I need somethin' to keep me awake. They got anything here like that?"

Will laughed and shook his head. "Only the basics, but how about water? We can imagine it's Ambrosia." He suddenly felt more settled having Wee nearby.

Grabbing water from the cabinet, they relaxed on the floor just outside the tunnel, Will wishing Kamar's place had more creature comforts. Wee downed almost his entire bottle of water before plonking it down on the cold concrete and hiccupping once.

Will fidgeted, not sure how to tell Wee that much of their past friendship was like cobwebs in his mind. He decided to first talk about the present; perhaps the past would come back to mind as they talked.

"It's terrible about Ava. I mean, I don't know her much, but I know Serpio. She'll be questioned 'til she breaks."

Wee grasped Will's shoulder again and pushed on it. "Ava's a saint. She saved my life. I hate like hell that she's been taken." Wee hesitated before adding, "And you! When you were captured, we were shredded. I ended up running from the Sciolists with Xander instead of you. It killed me. I was worried sick."

"I heard about your accident. You're lucky to be alive. But you're okay, right? No after effects?" Will held Wee's gaze.

"I'm okay, thanks to Ava. But you weren't. I don't know your whole story. Can you share the details, or is it too painful?"

"I don't want to share everything that happened. It's … hard to relive it." Will caught himself tearing up and gritted his teeth to pound the emotion deeper so it wouldn't spill out.

"Bro, I get it. Had to be hell. You were all alone, tryin' to be loyal. Serpio had to have mistreated you to get information."

"Yeah, not for a while. But then …" Will felt the words catch in his throat as the memory of the torture came roaring back. His right hand trembled, and he tucked it underneath his folded legs.

"Remember, bro, we've always told each other everything!"

Wee's big brown eyes were melted chocolate. "But look, if you don't want to talk about it, it's okay. I can respect that."

We've always told each other everything. If that were true—and Will assumed it was—they'd had a great friendship indeed.

His confession then spilled out like the explosion of a shaken soda. "I had … a hard time. I had to lie—to pretend I was spying on Ember for the good of the city. I had to convince Serpio and the Elite I was loyal to the Accords. I couldn't communicate with anybody! I felt so alone, but I gave the best acting job of my life. And I do remember feeling like a lowlife jerk. Then, Serpio questioned my motives and he … he erased most of my memories, convinced me I had no friends and that my parents didn't want me. I didn't know who any of you were anymore."

Wee leaned in. "He messed up your memories? How?" He picked up the bottle from the floor and drained what was left of it.

"A secret room. He called it 'therapy.'" He put his fingers up and did air quotes. "All I know is after that, I was totally devoted to Tranquility and only wanted to please Serpio." Will hung his head. "Serpio will do the same to Ava if we don't get there in time."

"Buddy, it's okay. Are you figuring things out now?"

"Some of my history has come back. Much is still blurry for me. And I'm still messed up from it. Anything that's a threat makes me fall apart or look like there's an earthquake in my bones." He held out his hand, and it was, indeed, trembling.

A host of emotions crossed Wee's face. "You've been through a lot. Unwinding's going to take a while. I'm here for you, though, like always. But I can guarantee you won't need me for long. You're stone, remember?"

Will forced a laugh. "Sure."

"Now for the big question." Wee allowed a slight grin to slide onto his face. "Did you connect the dots with Ember?" Wee cocked his head to the side and raised one eyebrow.

Will shifted his position to buy himself some time. What was the right answer for that question? He stared, unfocused, into the distance before giving his head a slight shake. "I never was able to fully forget her, even with Serpio's mind-altering crap. She haunted me, and when I saw her in the arena, it all pretty much came back. I'm still in love with her, Wee."

"And now you have competition."

Will ran his hands through his hair. "Yeah. Who would have thought?" Then, he quirked his lips. "I've been trying to win her back. I'm hopeful. I think—no, I know—she's not sure of anything."

"You got game. She'll come back."

"Speak of the devil," Will muttered.

Xander sauntered over to them and, with a gleam in his eye, said, "We've been stirring up plans. Next target—the city's main machine."

Wee's jaw dropped. "The Continuum Spectrum? How you gonna get in there? That's shut up tighter than a casket on the Fun Zone's coaster."

Xander burst out laughing. "Perfect analogy. But you forget. We have Easterners. It makes a project like this doable."

"The ideal target for Phoenix—no more happiness points on our Alts. I'm up for it." Will was practically coming out of his skin, but in a good way. Finally, a chance to get in on the action.

"Not sure you should go, Will, because of your ..." The words disappeared before they were out of his mouth. "I thought I'd take Wee and a few others. We don't need many—the fewer of us, the better."

Will bristled. "I *said*, I'm up for it." He stood to emphasize his words. He wasn't going to cower behind his mental vampires or have Xander think he was a handicap. "What's the plan?"

Xander raised an eyebrow, "If you're sure ..." He shrugged. "Okay, then. We'll take both of you, Dorian, Oslin, and Lotus. Once we breach the building, Lotus will use her voltage to burn up the computer. That'll disable all the city's Alt readings. We free the people and give our dear Magistrate something new to worry about instead of chasing us down. Let's see how Serpio fixes that."

Will squared his shoulders and offered Xander a fist bump. "'Operation Blitz the Machine' it is."

FIFTY-TWO

Serpio's "Therapy"

IT WAS time to turn up the heat on Ava. Literally.

Without another word, Serpio left Ava to return to the loft above. Once there, he programmed the ear-splitting music, the ceiling's blistering sunlamps, and the negative messages that would dishearten her until she screamed for mercy. He watched her through the window as he cranked up every single option available to him. If this didn't shatter her self-control, he didn't know what would.

He pressed the final button to activate just as his OmniCom pulsed with light. Damn—a call coming in. His first thought was to leave it unanswered. What call could be more important than his session with Ava? He glanced down at his wrist.

This one.

Serpio's voice was hurried. "Yes, Truss. I've been waiting for your call." His voice took a bitter twist. "In fact, why didn't you call sooner? You know what's at stake." He clenched his fists.

A voice responded. "Magistrate, sir, my apologies. I would have called sooner, but as the head scientist, I needed to see the lab for myself to determine if there was anything that could be saved or remained usable. I regret to say there is not. Only one thing survived, and that was the mutant. The attendant was able to get out of the building with the beast."

Although none of this was news, Serpio tried to compress the clawing panic in his chest. He leaned against the console in front of him. "How about the directions for my formula?"

"I know the formula—not hard to commit it to memory, which I did many years ago. Good news—we can get the pituitary gland fluid for part of the formula from the mutant. The problem is getting the rest of what we need to make it. First, we need—"

"Whatever we need, we get." Serpio's words were barbed teeth.

Truss hesitated in a long pause that streamed over Serpio like the shiver of a dying sun. "It's … not that easy. We need blood from another human subject—someone with the genetically modified DNA from the experiments of years ago."

Modified blood. He almost wanted to laugh at the irony— needing the blood of those he'd executed without a thought.

Then the corner of Serpio's mouth pulled up into a half smile, and he silently threw a clenched fist upward. He knew of such people, of course—Ember and Talesa. All he had to do was find them.

After that, a common medical instrument was all that was needed to extract blood. He shuddered when he thought about how, decades earlier, only a Medic with training could draw blood from a vein. Now, a short aluminum gun called a Lamia would pierce the skin; a small switch would activate a vacuum, pulling the person's blood into a deep chamber attached. It was simple and clean.

"What else do you need?" The optimism of what would be within his reach colored Serpio's words.

"We also need fluid from a jellyfish, but not just any jellyfish, which is difficult enough already because they're pretty much extinct. Officially, Turritopsis dohrnii, a tiny, transparent creature that lives forever because of its regeneration abilities. And then there's a mushroom—but again, not your generic mushroom—one that has special eukaryote cells. We had the mushrooms stored in proper refrigerators and the jellyfish living in specially designed habitats. Now all that is gone—the stores of formula *and* the living beings." Silence again. "I don't know if we can get those again, Magistrate, but we can hope—"

He wanted to shout "too much information!" but he needed every bit of it. Where on earth would he find these things? Certainly not in Tranquility. A thrumming roared through his ears. "Where could these mushrooms and jellyfish be found?"

"As I said, they probably no longer exist. The samples were gathered long ago and—"

"I'll form a knowledgeable team immediately. They will know where to find these things." Serpio tilted his head from side to side, the tendons popping over the bones in his neck. His brain spun with what seemed like fifty thousand scenarios of who would go and where they would travel. It would be a dangerous mission, but all he cared about was getting what he needed. He would raise a selection of competent and hardy people and send them out of the dome and into the unknown.

This would add to his already crowded lists of tasks, starting with his Sciolists. He'd have to start training his new recruits immediately, especially if he was ever going to find Ember.

Once he found Ember, he would get the blood he needed.

And that blood? With her power in it, chances were he could inherit every power she had. The thought intoxicated him.

A bonus would be having the girl back under his complete control. She was both too dangerous to free and too beautiful to resist. His mind played with the possibilities until a voice inter-rupted his daydream.

"Sir?" Truss was still on the line. "The journey … well, it will be … the people probably won't make it back, sir …"

The Magistrate screamed his response and hit the adjacent wall with his fist. "THEY WILL GO, AND THEY WILL FIND THE ELEMENTS!" His voice raw from the effort, he swallowed and took a long, steady breath. "You and your colleagues will set up at Solace. There is a room there—probably several."

"Sir, the equipment was burned up. It—"

"There are items you can use from the hospital and from Solace. Get them immediately. Set up. We only have two weeks before I will need another injection. Start today!" As an onslaught of spiky heat flooded his entire body like venom, Serpio clicked off the call.

He physically and mentally jerked back to the moment at hand.

Ava. How long had he left her?

He turned back to the window and choked on the shock forming a ball in his throat.

Ava lay on the floor, her body limp but curled into a half-moon, her hands across her chest as if to protect herself from the torture leveled on her. Blistered skin looked as red as a Sciolist's uniform, her eyes swollen and pasted shut. Her face was frozen into a twisted scream, her once lovely features squeezed into ugly seams. She did not move.

He blurted out strings of four-letter curse words he didn't realize he knew, aware that he had just rendered Ava impossible to question. She was the key to everything. Everything!

"No, no, NO!" He leaned hard on the buttons, shutting down the system, silencing the electronic abusive utterings, the blast of scorching heat, and the piercing jangle of acid-rock music.

Ten seconds later, he threw open the door, flying to the inert body lying in the middle of the room. "Ava!" He put his hands on her face and patted it. No response. Gripping her shoulders and shaking her, he tried to rouse her again. "Ava!" He checked her pulse. The throb was faint and very, very slow. He closed his eyes in relief; at least she was not dead. Her breaths were tight, small wisps, cobwebs of air. Ava might be alive, but barely.

He had to act. Now.

If she were to survive, he had to get her to medical facilities. And survive, she must. His own life depended on it.

On his OmniCom, he hit the signal for Cabot and Arturo's return.

In the five turned forever minutes he waited, he schemed. *If she regains consciousness, I will have extreme power. Her imminent death would be the perfect ultimatum.*

FIFTY-THREE

Serpio's Save

AVA NEEDED medical attention if she was going to survive. Only a Medela could revive her. Even then, it was touch and go. She needed a Medic. Problem was, Ava had been his go-to Medic. She was the one he called when something needed to be kept under wraps. A moment of indecision throttled Serpio's path forward.

Appearances were everything, even with his Sciolists. Cabot and Arturo arrived to find Ava propped up against Serpio, who sat behind her, cradling her and tenderly touching her head. He looked up and put on a show of brimming tears.

"In the course of therapy, Ava became ill. She needs medical attention. I'm no practitioner, but it appears she has done something to herself. She has physical trauma but is mentally unstable. You will need to carry her—take her in your vehicle to the Solace Institute." Although Sciolists were trained not to ask questions when given an order, Serpio dropped a tight command. "Ask or answer no questions."

Arturo nodded while Cabot answered. "Of course, Magistrate."

Serpio edged apart from Ava, making sure she lay down on the floor gently. He felt her breath as he passed his hand in front of her nose. "I'll be on my way immediately. Ava is a very special Elite member. I will be seeing to her needs personally."

Cabot, the stronger of the two, picked Ava up with great concern and carried her through the doorway, followed by Arturo.

Serpio's trip to Solace was a blur, his brain overstuffed with various scenarios for Ava's survival or demise. He arrived before Ava, giving commands at the front desk. "An Elite, Ava Validus, is arriving. She needs immediate care."

From behind the desk, the Medic in Charge spoke into her Alt. "Prepare a Medela treatment and an Elite room, STAT."

Ava must be protected at all costs! No one could know where she was or that her physical condition was critical. He spoke into his OmniCom. "Esryn, send three teams of Sciolists to Solace. One team should be positioned fifty yards out. The other two, send inside." And Serpio, the immortal himself, was on guard.

* * *

IN THE GILDED ROOM, Serpio sat by Ava's bedside, waiting for an opportunity to question her once more. Although she'd had a treatment, the prognosis was grim. Her face, puffy with fluid, looked round and somehow angelic, her eyes closed but large, her black hair soft and strangely shiny as it lay cropped around her head. Her lips held a pout, full and sweet. Her limbs, though stiff and red, held the secrets of her torture.

Finally, after minutes oozing into a century, Serpio saw a flutter of eyelids. He sat up, his heart racing. He would get answers now.

"Ava, can you hear me?"

The word "yes" came out in a whisper.

His pulse picked up, as he imagined hers did as well.

"Dear Ava. The Medics can save you, but only if you tell me where Ember is."

He swore he saw a faint smile touch her lips, although it could have been an illusion.

Ava's voice, hoarse and bitter, barely reached his ears. "You … have … lost." With that, the flickering of her lashes ceased, and her breath came no more.

FIFTY-FOUR

Xander's "Blitz The Machine"

AFTER GATHERING them in a circle in the center of the basement, Xander addressed the weary group of Phoenix. "You all did an amazing job getting here from the warehouses—kept quiet, didn't panic, and followed orders."

Whoops went up among the pack of them. Many of them put their arms around one another's shoulders and formed chains. Jasper and Bixby hoisted Xander up on Wee's shoulders to cheers and applause.

From high above them, Xander continued his speech. "You are exactly what the phoenix personifies—determination and resilience. No matter what, you aren't willing to settle for less. The phoenix spirit animal teaches that even in the darkest times, there is always hope for new beginnings and that anything in this life is possible when you have the passion of a phoenix. And now we're going to strike out again. This time, we'll destroy the Continuum Spectrum's ability to track us and to collect data on the emotions of Tranquility citizens."

Again, clapping and hurrahs answered as Wee bent over to allow Xander to jump down off his shoulders.

"We may find we can only deactivate the computer temporarily, as the Magistrate will put his repair crews on it immediately, but it will give people a freedom they haven't ever had and prepare their minds for change. It may not be Serpio's final handicap, but it will certainly hit him in the jugular." Xander made a motion like slitting his throat.

Across the room, the blurry whiz of the lift robbed his attention. A Level Four man with an egg-shaped head, squinty eyes, and a small suitcase in hand rode the elevated hoist, along with Talesa. What—who was this? If it weren't for Talesa's grin, his stomach would have dropped along with the lift's descent.

Talesa looped her arm through the guy's arm and piloted him over to where Xander stood, staring. Talesa's spirited voice spilled out. "Everyone! I'm introducing a new Easterner. This is Chester Arete. His talent is making weapons. And while I don't love the idea of using violence against people, you know what we're up against."

Chester nodded at the group, one wisp of graying hair, the only one on his head, flying slightly with his nod. "Greetings, folks. I'm sorry I was never able to join you before. I'm not fond of being noticed. I finally agreed to meet Talesa here where she assured me I would be safe, at least if I smashed my Alt before coming. I overheard the young man here talking about a mission of sorts. I'll be the first to say I won't be joining you on any outings. My only function will be to supply you with weapons you can use. Mind you, they're primitive but helpful."

The introduction was met with cheers and cries of welcome before Talesa drew him away. Xander imagined Talesa would be giving him a quick tour and debrief before asking Kamar for spare parts.

A voice rang out. "Who is going and how?"

A devilish smile danced across Xander's lips. "We'll need Banks for his tech ability," he said, nodding to the Plauditor, "along with Red, Dorian, Oslin, Lotus, Wee, and Will—the Dream Team. Taking a car's too risky without Kamar, so we'll walk. According to the map, it's three miles to Harmony Tower. If all goes well, we can cover that in a little over an hour. Only

Dorian will wear his Alt. His won't track." Dorian nodded to acknowledge Xander's instructions. "We'll hope the simple Tranquility door code app will work on the Harmony Tower entrance. We'll leave after a couple hours of sleep and some food. We know how to get there and what to do when we're in."

The lack of a way to break into the building was driving Xander mad. The place was under heavy lock and key. The only way they'd had success before was Ava. The thought of her sacrifices brought a mistiness to his eyes that he quickly blinked away. "What we don't know is how to get into the building, especially without noise. Thoughts?" Xander posed the question to his team.

"I can easily break the door down," Red volunteered with a grin, "but I can't promise it'll be quiet."

"Lotus, can you melt the lock?" Talesa asked.

Lotus tilted her head thoughtfully. "Yes, maybe. But it could work against us. The metal would warp, welding the door shut. Plus, the flash would be seen for a mile."

Will looked like he'd been given a zombie-inducing compound. The shadows seemed to leap out from under his eyes, and for some reason, his pupils took on a feverish glint. His right arm reached out stiffly. "There's … a password."

"What? How do you know?" Xander pressed.

"I was there when Ava asked for access," Will said. "I can't remember a lot of stuff—but I do remember that conversation. It was right after the bomb went off."

Xander's heartbeat quickened. "Shazz! Do you know what it is?"

"No." Will's head dropped.

Wee propped his arm up with his other hand and held his finger to his lips. "Uh, Xander? I read some stuff in Serpio's journals. Guess he has a cat?"

Xander smirked. "I read that too, Wee. Maybe the cat's name is the passcode? I don't remember the stupid cat's name, though."

Will gave a low chuckle before raising the right side of his mouth in a twist. "That would be weird and not impossible. But what if it's not words? It could be numbers, and there's no way we could figure that out."

The group babbled among themselves with suggestions of possibilities, from numbers corresponding to the alphabet to outlandish number formulas.

Xander shouted above the jabbering of the people around him. "Wait! Get the journals! We can look for clues in there—like the dumb cat's name. Whose got 'em?"

Jasper raised his hand. "I still got 'em. Put 'em in a food distribution bag at the warehouse so I could carry 'em around better. Hang on. I'll bring the sack."

Xander was torn. Would rereading the journals be a waste of time? Or could they be the key to finding the key code? He paced, watching Jasper as he retrieved the bag and jogged back like a well-trained canine.

As he distributed the journals among the group, Xander said, "The subject matter in those little books is shocking, but don't get caught up in that. Look for anything that could be a code. Write it down. We'll take it with us. If nothing we discover gets us in, we'll have no choice but to have Red break down the door."

Will and Talesa scavenged for the shop's handheld digital record-keeping device, Kamar's Quire, a note-taking tool, finally finding it up above in the shop's service bay.

Will spoke into the Quire as half a dozen people called out possibilities from the texts. In thirty minutes, a vast list emerged, documenting everything from Serpio's clothing sizes to his address, his favorite color, the date he became Magistrate, and even a number representing the Status levels all combined, along with fifty other numbers and words that seemed significant. Talesa added her name and her birth date as options, too. Finally, Wee found the name of the cat, which he yelled out, laughing. "Sugar!"

Xander closed one eye and pointed his index finger at Wee. "That was it!" Looking across the group, he raised his voice. "Thanks, everyone. We have enough. Now we get some shut-eye. I'm flat-lining. But two hours, tops, then we go."

Sadly, the floor would have to do for sleeping. He lay down, feeling the cold of the cement climb through his limbs like a vengeful wraith. Still wired from the adrenaline high of the mission, his brain raced through the "almosts" and "what ifs." A mental rehearsal for "Operation Blitz the Machine' had him tossing and turning, wearing a hole in the floor. He worried about Ember, now probably deep into the underground passage they were creating, closer to a heroic rescue that could turn sour. With a sigh, he hoped they'd be discovered by whoever needed them more.

He gazed at the ceiling, nerves tighter than a hangman's noose, until all was quiet around him, save the snores of those in a well-deserved slumber. He thought of Ember and how she didn't even know he was beginning a brand-new operation without her. He thought fleetingly of messaging Kamar with details of their plan, but it would only make Ember anxious, and she had enough to worry about. Instead, he concentrated on her beauty and grace until it calmed him enough that he could close his eyes.

What felt like a minute later, the movement of people around him roused him from his sleep. Two hours had somehow passed, and it was time to set the people of Tranquility free.

FIFTY-FIVE

Will's Window

THE DREAM TEAM gathered in a circle and reached one arm in, their hands one on top of each other's in a show of solidarity.

"Your fate is my fate! Phoenix forever!" Xander called out.

"Phoenix forever! Rah!" the group answered, throwing their arms in the air.

Will felt his hands quake afterward, grateful he didn't experience it during the cheer. *Just nervous energy,* he assured himself.

Xander and Will dressed in Sciolist uniforms for extra insurance. Xander grabbed one rifle, and Will took a Stinger. Will gave one last longing look toward where Ember carried out her rescue mission and then tightened the belt around his waist as if he could somehow pull the girl back into his arms.

It was now broad daylight, but even before they stepped out of Obviators, Oslin had cloaked them all. Thanks to that, Will carried a confidence he barely recognized as his own. Just to be safe, though, he threw his hood up onto his head and snapped his Sciolist's cloak about him as they walked by a group of kids watching a boy riding the latest toy—a pint-sized "flying saucer" that whizzed down the street six feet in the air. The children didn't even glance their way, but their actions brought an unexpected smile to Will's face.

The Easterners took the lead, forming a protective force on the front lines. Banks, too, took the helm of the group, insisting on keeping an eye out for any technology that could betray their whereabouts. Will was happy to have Wee on his right. The guy obviously had been his best friend for a reason; his recounting of childhood memories along the way was like warm fuzzies against his skin.

Xander turned his face and met Will's eyes in a direct challenge. "So … do these memories seem real to you?"

Will tried not to look away. "Yeah, actually. I've remembered my parents, and Wee helped a lot." He threw an appreciative glance in the direction of his friend.

"And Ember?" Xander asked, thrusting his chin up but not taking his gaze from Will's face.

"I remember everything."

A beat of silence, sticky with unresolved angst, lingered like a thick, musty smell.

Will knew he had just lied to Xander. He didn't remember everything with Ember—not yet—but it was coming back. And it was better if Xander thought he had recaptured his history with her. It made him more of a player in the game.

The conversation between the two rivals died at that point, and Will chose to hold his tongue for the remaining miles.

* * *

OSLIN'S CLOAKING had served them well.

Our luck held, Will thought. *No catastrophes. Maybe it's a good omen.* They could hardly believe it when, at last, Harmony Tower stood before them.

While the building itself was beautiful with its octagonal stained-glass-studded roof, the eight-foot-wide, six-foot-tall door was unusually intimidating for Tranquility. It was painted to look like multihued marble using Tranquility's eighteen Status colors. Yet even with a cursory glance at it, Will saw faces and creatures within the swirls—an optical illusion, of course, but unsettling, nonetheless.

Wee fidgeted as if he were bouncing to keep warm and was first to verbalize disappointment. "Anybody see a place to key-in a code?"

Xander ran his hands over the door, inviting the others to do the same, in case of a hidden hatch.

"Nothing here. We seriously screwed?" Banks queried, his tone cautious.

"Wait. There's a tiny window," Will observed. "See?" He pointed to a three-inch pane of glass to the left of the door.

Xander rolled his eyes and scoffed, "That's nice, Will. We don't need a damn window."

Will's disgust for Xander swelled up, but he steeled himself, resisting the urge to lash out. "It's not a window to see out, I don't think. Look. It's got a tiny light above it." He waved his hand in front of it. A dot of illumination twinkled.

"It's a kind of camera or something maybe." Red put his eye up to it. "You can't see in."

"Don't!" Oslin pushed Red away. "You're invisible, but what if it's infrared? High voltage? Radioactive? It could undo your invisibility. Or it could be some kind of alarm. We can't take chances."

Banks made his way closer. "Let me see it." He put his hands up in front of him. "I promise I won't touch it or get too close. But if it is cybernetic, it's got to be there to open the door. Great find, Will."

The group stepped aside. Banks stood a few feet away, staring at it. "It's a reader for sure. Whatever the code is, it's transmitted electronically. We need an Alt." He turned to Dorian. "That's your cue."

"Enter a password, sure. But where do we start?" Dorian tapped on the face of his Alt.

"Just go one at a time. Start with the cat's name," Xander

suggested, rolling his eyes. "At least we might learn if it's letters or numbers."

"Very well." Dorian tapped "Sugar" into the door code app on his Alt and then waved it in front of the glass.

Nothing.

"Try another," Banks urged.

Will illuminated the screen on the Quire and read off five more options, all with the same disappointing results.

Red tapped his foot impatiently. "We're wasting time. The more we fool around, the riskier it gets. I say I just break down the door."

Lotus put up her hand like a stop sign. "No. We seem to be safe enough. Let's try a few more."

Wee crossed his arms and grunted. "We haven't tried Ember's name yet …"

A sour taste polluted Will's mouth, and he suddenly felt unclean. *The Magistrate wouldn't actually use Ember's name, would he? Ugh.* He managed to choke out, "We probably should …"

Xander looked at their faces as if gauging agreement. "We keep trying. Use it."

Again, nothing.

Will knew he was overreacting, but he felt relief. The code was something else. He called out the next option. "1-5-0-5!" *Please, let this be it.*

"What's that number from?" Oslin's puzzled face mirrored the others'.

"Serpio's number from his placement as a Transplant," Xander replied. "A spare kid that had to be farmed out to some other parents. It still bothers him."

Who knew? That explains a lot of Serpio's need to be important. Will's curiosity couldn't be denied. "How do you know it bothers him?"

Xander pulled on his bottom lip. "All in the journal. It's like Serpio's brain on paper."

"Actually a good choice because no one would guess it," Oslin said, tapping his head with his index finger.

Oslin clapped Xander on the shoulder. "How'd you remember that? Impressive!"

Xander shrugged. "It stuck with me because it was pitiful, I guess."

Dorian flashed the new code in front of the cyber reader. The light above it flashed green, and the click and thump of a latch disengaging sounded like a symphony.

Eyes popped, and fists pumped, along with war cries that Will knew weren't heard by anyone but themselves.

They charged in, stopping in their tracks for several seconds to marvel at the interior, a jigsaw of Tranquility's Status colors painted on the walls, and feeling the unnaturally cold temperature, unfamiliar to them in Tranquility. Here, the air smelled stale, as if it never circulated. A round space, it was larger than Xander expected from the looks of it on the stone exterior. About fourteen by sixteen feet, it could have held everything a well-furnished bedroom would have had. In the middle of the room breathed an enormous computer system, its tiny lights winking at them as if to confirm its life.

"Banks! Where's the part we need? Or do we trash the whole thing?" Xander's eyes glittered even in the dim room.

"If we disable all of it, there's no communication." Frowning, Banks examined the front panels, looking for clues. "Here's a control panel …"

"But no passcode. Here we go again," Wee said, his shoulders sagging.

"We don't need a passcode," Banks said. "We're going to destroy it, not access it. But just to see what happens … Dorian, can you wave your Alt with the door code in front of the screen here?"

"Righto." When Dorian's Alt passed across the screen, it lit up.

Several icons glowed on the screen—a gold compass, an orange smiley face, and a white skull.

The group gasped collectively. Will, however, raised an eyebrow. "That's way too easy. What's to keep just anyone from accessing this thing?"

"Maybe no one's tried. After all, this is Serpio's baby. I doubt anyone gets in here unless it's life or death." With several attempts to work the keyboard, though, Banks shook his head.

"What do you think those icons are?" Looking at the screen, Red flexed his fingers, cracking his knuckles.

Oslin's right lip turned up. "Now *that* is easy. The skull's gotta represent anyone who's dead. The compass—that's for sure the GPS tracker system. And the face, well, that's our bingo."

"Yeah, but we can't get into it," Red said, cracking his knuckles one more time and making Will want to throttle him.

"That face is orange. Look at the lights on there. Same color." Banks pointed to the tower with a hundred orange lights that decorated the circumference of the computer terminal. "This has to be the Continuum Spectrum."

Lotus stepped forward. "That's my cue. It's time to shine." She looked at the others, and her lips tightened. "It's not safe for you to be here when I do it."

Will noticed Xander already heading for the exit, calling out over his shoulder for the others to follow. It was almost as if the guy was actually afraid.

"Do it up right, Lotus," Will advised as he followed the others out the door.

FIFTY-SIX

Ember's Intel

EMBER WIPED her hand across her brow and sighed. Her limbs were weary, and every possible snippet and segment of her was streaked with dirt and grime. It was as if her energy had been sucked from her veins. She didn't know how much longer she could keep smashing, mushing, and moving dirt, but they could not give up.

"How you doing?" Kamar asked her for the hundredth time.

It seemed like he needed to be reassured every five minutes, and it was getting on her nerves.

"I've been better," she said, fessing up this time instead of merely replying "fine." "This is hard. I thought this would be easier. I feel like a ditch digger, not an Easterner."

"It's the distance. That's why the basement took me five years. But for now, I have to stop. Sorry." Kamar peered out of eyes rimmed with crud and exhaustion.

"What?" Ember stared at Kamar like he had just grown three heads. She quit shoving dirt and stone aside. "We're almost there to rescue Ava! We have to keep going."

Kamar looked at her with sheepish eyes. "Just got a notification—a CommuteCar's coming in for repair. I'm on the hook to do my job."

Ember hadn't thought about that part—the part where Kamar had an actual business to run. "Holy Shazz! Now what?" It wasn't Kamar's fault, but she wanted to scream at him.

"We go back to the shop, take a break, and I'll fix the car. Then we come back. It's not ideal, but …"

Ember was tempted to take the breather Kamar suggested. But her heart wouldn't let her. "You go. I'll stay. I can keep working, and you'll come back when you can."

"No. I'm not leaving you by yourself. That's lunacy."

"Not if I promise to be a good girl and just dig. If I get to the end without you, I'll wait."

Kamar examined her face as if he could see the word "lie" printed on her skin. "I don't know about that. You seem to have a determined streak that could get you into trouble."

Ember grinned and then laughed. "You're right about that. But I promise I won't dig out of the tunnel without you." She frowned. "I'm not sure how we're gonna do it anyway. Won't destroying the floor of City Hall be impossible?"

"Girl, if you can tear Tegrite apart, you can get through anything." Kamar brushed past her and headed in the direction of the basement before turning to look at her one more time. "You did promise—remember that."

Ember held up two fingers in a promise gesture. "I promise I will not dig through the floor of City Hall without you."

Kamar shook his head. "Well, I'm not leaving you without communication you can actually use. Here's my Alt for now." He unstrapped it from his wrist and offered it to her. "Don't crash my points either." Once he saw his Alt safely on her right wrist, he hurried away, his aura flaring a muddied blue for the anxiety he had just shared.

Ember knew he had no choice. She imagined CommuteCars piling up outside of Obviators in some sort of primitive traffic jam where they sought out a mothership signal from Kamar. The vision brought a smile to her face.

She pressed on with her task, trying not to think about what awful events could happen once they successfully made it to where Ava was.

A buzz and a glow leaking out from under the protective covering on the Sciolist's Alt on her left wrist stopped her movements. She moved Xander's improvised sheath aside and read the words tracking across the screen. "Guardian Team, report to Solace immediately. Ava Validus moved to Solace. Extra protection needed."

The shock hitting her like a metal pole, Ember dropped onto her butt. The walls of the carved-out tunnel around her mocked her as they closed in with suffocating invasiveness.

She choked on the lump forming in her throat. *All this work, and Ava isn't even at City Hall.*

With her arms crossed across her knees, she buried her head as hot tears soaked her sleeves. Kamar's Alt would surely take a hit.

After crying for several moments, Ember stood and squared her shoulders. She would abandon this project and return to headquarters, where she would share the message with Phoenix, and they would make decisions to get Ava.

* * *

EMERGING FROM THE PASSAGEWAY, she dusted herself off and stood there, disoriented for a moment. Her eyes searched for Xander, but her gaze landed on her mom instead. She smiled.

Talesa rushed over and embraced her. "I have good news. You remember Chester? He's the one you were supposed to meet when—" Her mother stopped mid-sentence and slowed to perhaps choose her words carefully. "The Easterner you were meeting when you and Xander were captured."

"Yes. Of course I remember. He's a guy you wanted to make us some weapons. That didn't turn out so well. We never got to meet up." Ember chuckled, although the pain of the memory was still fresh and grazed her laughter.

"He's joining us, and now is a better time than before. Kamar may have parts he can use, so he doesn't have to bring much with him." Talesa's enthusiasm bubbled out before taking a more serious downturn. "We will need weapons eventually, sad to say."

"Mom, that's great. You're working behind the scenes like a pro." Ember beamed at her mother.

"I thought Kamar said you were staying in the tunnel until he returned."

Ember's smile faded. "I wanted to. But then the Sciolist's Alt notified the entire force that Ava's not even at City Hall. She's at Solace."

Talesa's face crimped in concern. "How terrible! That means a big change of plans and lots of lost time." She hugged Ember again. "How can I help?"

Ember gripped her mom back. It centered her. Releasing the embrace, Ember asked, "I should talk to the team. Where is everybody?"

As her eyes swept the room, she observed small groups of people clustered here and there. Some sat on the cold, stone floor chatting. Others at the periphery were checking out Kamar's vehicles, both inside and out. She caught threads of their conversations and their emotions wafting her way—impressed as she was when first seeing Kamar's creations. A couple argued over the lone chair. Another wandered around and kept asking others where the windows were, seemingly craving sunshine. As large as the basement was, its semi-darkness gave new meaning to the word "gray." If they didn't have to be in the basement for protection, the place would be downright depressing.

"Well, you know Kamar's up top working on a vehicle. Most of the group is catching up on sleep, making plans for circulating information to the city, or reading Serpio's journals, which seem to be popular entertainment … Oh, you mean, 'where's Xander?'" A soft, impish chuckle followed.

A smile jotted across Ember's lips but was blotted out when

Talesa answered the question. "Don't be upset," Talesa warned, talking slowly, "but Xander took Will, Wee, Banks, and the Easterners to destroy the Alt system at Harmony Towers."

A gasp tore from Ember's mouth. "Filthy Shazz! He didn't even tell me? What the—"

Talesa interrupted with a finger to Ember's lips. "You had your own mission to worry about. And if something went wrong on his end or yours, you'd be in less danger not knowing what they were up to. He did it because he cares about you and didn't want you to worry. Besides, knowing Xander, did you really think he'd just wait around doing absolutely nothing until you came back?"

Ember let her face dissolve into disappointment and then her insides took a deeper dive. *What if Xander doesn't come back?* His self-assured smile and love were her cornerstones. *Or Will?* She'd left him wondering and incomplete. *What if they all fail— get caught along the way?*

The thought ripped a hole through her heart before she replied, "No. You're right. When did they leave?"

"It's been about two hours."

Two hours … Not long enough for them to be back anytime soon. Designs in her head twisted, writhed, and pivoted into a dangerous idea. If Xander could keep her blind to his actions, she could, too. She grabbed the mask and wig she used earlier and patted her uniform for reassurance. The Stinger was still there, nice and safe.

She would rescue Ava alone.

FIFTY-SEVEN

Ember's 'East'

WHY NOT? She had power now—more exceptional abilities and special talents than anyone else in the world. She could put them to good use and finally bring Ava out of the Magistrate's evil embrace.

The only thing she regretted was having to deceive her mom, but it couldn't be helped.

Although the basement was filled with over fifty people milling about the room and chattering among themselves, Ember focused her attention on Talesa. "Mom, you're not going to worry about me," she said as she placed her hands on her mother's arms and looked directly into her face.

"What? I always worry about you! You're my daughter!" Talesa reached out to straighten Ember's clothes.

"Oh, Mom. I know. I—" she stopped, realizing that her "gift" from Dorian wasn't working at all.

How could she make this happen? Or could she just go upstairs and hope her mom wouldn't miss her?

No.

She knew she'd taken possession of Dorian's power. Maybe she needed to do something special. But what? She racked her brain while Talesa fired one annoying question after another about her work on the tunnel.

Yeah … she was going to have to try some weird stuff. This had to be like hypnosis, what Dorian did. "Mom, hang on," she said, dashing off to a work bench and capturing a chain and small silvery disc with a hole in it.

"What are you doing?" Talesa asked, laughing and staring after her, shaking her head.

"I want to try something." Standing in front of her mom, she attached the chain to the inch-wide metal plate. "Watch the circle," she ordered.

Her mom furrowed her brow, and released two notes of a chuckle. "Okay …"

Ember dangled the orb and allowed it to swing back and forth. "Keep your eye on this."

Talesa laughed again.

"Mom! Seriously! Watch the thing! Keep your eyes on it."

"All right." Talesa focused.

"You want to follow my directions." Ember tried to concentrate.

"I—"

"Don't talk." Ember was determined to make this work.

"What is this all about?" Talesa finally said after a minute.

In frustration, she sighed and hit her forehead with her hand. Ember dropped the metal objects to the floor as her mom's eyebrows shot up. "Only an experiment. I just don't want you to worry about me." Ember turned to slink away, ready to trash her entire plan.

"I'm not going to worry about you."

Whipping around, Ember drew closer. "You're not going to worry about me."

"I'm not going to worry about you."

What did I do?

She thought about her speech. Was it the way she spoke? No

… Her movements? Realization dawned. The way she touched her head?

Indeed. Her mom almost appeared to be expecting more instructions.

I'm making this work!

She touched her palm to her forehead again. "You will think I'm working in the tunnel now."

"You're working in the tunnel now," her mom replied.

Yes! She pulled her hands down in a backward fist pump.

Giving her mom a hug, she felt her mom's love flow back to her in a wave before releasing Talesa and leaving her standing in the middle of the room, a confused look on her face.

Ember made her way to the singular metal chair in the center of the room, which was strangely empty considering the earlier argument. Stepping up on it, she scanned the Phoenix population, checking to make sure that everyone was within hearing distance. Although she worried about those who were sleeping not getting her command, they would most likely sleep through her planned endeavor and would not see her leave.

Another palm to her forehead. "Hey, everyone!" she announced, trying to get the attention of the now dear friends in the room. She waved her arms to attract more notice.

Left behind by Xander's group, Bixby was the first to react. He had somehow found a pair of augmented reality glasses—the kind that allowed mechanics to look at an engine and see what areas of a vehicle needed to be fixed—and was playing with them, extending them out in front of him before putting them on and looking her way from behind the lenses.

"Ember's out of the tunnel!" he yelled. "But she's alone!"

That's all it took for the group to gather around, pelting her with questions about the tunnel or Ava.

She put up a hand. "I don't have time to answer your questions. You will also not remember that I was here. You will continue to think I am in the passageway." She followed her words with the Loyalty gesture. "Say nothing to anyone."

Heads nodded. The Loyalty signal mirrored hers.

As she jumped down from the chair, Ember was exhilarated but suddenly anxious, too. How was she to keep all these techniques straight? And they would just immediately work? She'd have to keep her wits about her.

And for what she was about to attempt, she'd have to use Oslin's cloaking talent to stay safe. But how would she activate *that*?

What did she hear Oslin say? A force field? Using his arms?

Threading her way through her Phoenix tribe, she looked for reactions to her presence—even running to the lift with giant strides and jumping up and down on the metal platform to make noise. Her actions made a ruckus, and people looked her way, curious. But they didn't speak to her. Instead, she heard them complain about the slam of her shoes creating a ruckus.

Then a realization. She told them all to think she was in the tunnel! Not such a good test.

The solid steel of the lift beneath her feet somehow fortified her desire. She tightened her fists, dismissing negative thoughts and the fluttering feeling in her chest. In exasperation, she threw her arms out in front of her and then drew an imaginary box around herself using her hands. The gesture seemed silly, as though she were training to be a humorless mime, but she'd had so little information from Oslin. She remembered the arms were involved. To somehow create a cocoon around herself seemed the most logical action.

With the flick of the lift's mechanism, she arrived in the main shop above. The familiar screech of the platform gliding into place, the rumble of her feet against the steel, and the unforgettable smells of Kamar's shop—electronic equipment and paint—immediately hit her senses. A built-in fan sent wafts of recycled air across her face, blowing her hair into a brief whirlwind of red.

Stepping off, Ember darted behind an open cabinet, surveying the scene of safety signs, workbenches along the walls, and robotic rolling creepers winking at her as if begging to be used. A raised, long strip of textured matting glowed with intense, blue light.

Kamar was circulating some type of bleeping, electronic wand over the sleek hood of a royal blue CommuteCar when he turned and called out, "Who's there?"

Now for the test.

She stepped out.

"It's ... just me."

"Ember!"

Ugh. I'm not invisible at all.

Kamar dropped his tool and came around the vehicle with his palms out in a "stop" gesture and then pointing. "Don't come any closer—those blue mats running under this vehicle are high-voltage conductors charging this battery. I'm testing it."

She stepped back with her fingernails digging into her palms. "Okay ..."

"Is everything all right? I thought you were staying in the tunnel."

Ember wanted to throw something. But on the other hand, Kamar was entitled to know what was going on. She cared about him too much to have him return to the tunnel and try to find her. He'd be entirely panicked. "Yeah. I'm fine, but not Ava! She's not at City Hall. She's at Solace."

"You've got to be kidding me." Kamar's shoulders collapsed, and he groaned before carefully laying his instrument down on a table to his right. The blue lights from the mats dimmed and went out. "Come on in," he gestured. "It's safe now. How do you know?"

As Ember walked toward him, she held the Sciolist's Alt in the air. "Sciolist message. Good thing we found out. Anyway, I thought I'd tell you before you came back down. I didn't want you to hurry, but I also thought you'd want your Alt back." She handed it over and gave him her sweetest smile.

"Yeah ... yeah. I'll wrap up here, and we'll plan what to do.

Ava's still at risk, so we'll have to go there somehow. Go on back down now. I'll turn on the current again once I know you're safely on the lift." Kamar turned back to his work, adjusting his Alt and picking up his tools.

But Ember wasn't going to waste any more time. Concealed or not, she needed to get on her way. She'd figure out the logistics as she went. Now that Kamar's body and attention were behind the injured vehicle, she ran with a speed she'd never possessed before out the open door and into the sunshine-streaked street, making herself more vulnerable than she'd been in weeks.

With a dive into the dense foliage on the west side of Obviators, where the shadows were, she quickly donned her mask. A new face. She peered out but saw only a few people walking down the street a block away. Here in the less traveled area of town, only those who had warehouse jobs trickled along the streets. Still, eventually, she would be in the city's main square, where people intersected one another like rainbow crosswords.

She wrapped her arms around herself and concentrated but still had no idea how to trigger the invisibility. *Think, Ember, think. Become invisible! IN-VIS-I-BLE!* No. Something about using her arms. What was it Oslin said?

A decision—keep to the sides of the buildings and somehow fight off anyone she came across—would be her only salvation. But with the night's remaining moisture, the green grass beneath her feet squeaked like a tightening of giant screws, and the fragrance of the surrounding lavender bushes tickled her nostrils even under the mask. She couldn't afford to make noise! A squeeze on her nose with her fingers squelched her sneeze, and she left the grass for the sidewalk, hoping the cement would be more muffled.

The chaos of the streets with the foot traffic punctuated by cars cruising along gave her a sense of anonymity. Who would even notice her anyway? Nevertheless, her heart pounded in her chest. Her face under her mask was etched with fear and determination. Eyes darting to and fro, she maneuvered her way along, each step calculated to avoid drawing attention, her uniform, fake face, and borrowed hair blending mercifully with the urban landscape. With every passing moment, as she darted behind buildings like a rat in a maze, she inched closer to where Ava had to be. Though fear gripped her, she refused to let it consume her, and she pushed forward with a steady resolve. The city's labyrinthine alleyways and hidden corners became her sanctuary, shielding her as she pursued her path to a harrowing destiny.

To make it to Solace, she had no choice but to venture into the public plaza. A shake shop near the start of the plaza made her mouth water with its glowing pictures of malts of every color. Sunlight gleamed against the east-facing windows of tiny, multi-hued shops, and on tiptoes, she carefully dodged a few slender, sparkling puddles leftover from last night's rain.

Once past, she forged ahead with methodical steps, her skin sweating against the metal Stinger within her clothing. Pushing along the plaza's edges, where the park-like greenery bordered the space, she kept her head down, hoping her reserved demeanor wouldn't attract the attention of a concerned citizen who wondered why she wasn't smiling at people along her way.

A jolt against her torso preceded Ember's tumble to the ground, and tears flooded her vision. She felt her uniform rip on her knee and braved the brutal sting of a fresh scrape.

"Holy Shazz!" exclaimed a matronly woman, restabilizing herself firmly on the marble pavers beneath her feet.

"What happened? Didja trip?" a man's voice stirred the air.

"No. I … I don't know …" Ember answered, her mortification growing into a shadow threatening to swallow her up.

"I ran into something. Don't know what," the woman said, her eyes round. She rubbed her shoulder as she searched the area around her.

Ember blinked and righted herself, calling out, "I'm so sorry, I—"

But the couple went on their way, completely oblivious to Ember's presence. She stared after them. *They didn't see me!*

Elation bubbled up inside of her, and she fought the urge to jump up and down like a child. Now that she knew she was unseeable, she stripped away her mask and breathed a sigh of relief. Using her forearm, she wiped the perspiration from her face. In her head, she began to work out new plans that, up 'til now, were solidly insane.

Her footsteps took on the solid stomp of a soldier's as she marched through the square and down the street. Solace was now a mere block away.

FIFTY-EIGHT

Xander's Dream Team

XANDER and his Dream Team watched the kaleidoscopic windows of Harmony Tower flood with light. Inside, Lotus had unleashed her brilliance in a show of blue-ribbon glory. It was as if lightning had struck within the building not once, but twice.

"Get ready to shift into high gear. When Lotus comes out, we fly." Xander threw his head toward the street, wishing he was already on his way back to Obviators. He suddenly felt chilled, a foreign feeling he couldn't shake off. He danced in place.

But when Lotus opened the door, she instead motioned to them to follow her inside.

A strong, acrid smell hit Xander's nostrils, and he plugged his nose with his fingers. A few of the others followed suit, Dorian and Banks coughing against the odorous onslaught from melting steel, plastic, and electric wiring.

"That's some nasty smell," Wee confirmed.

"What's going on?" Xander asked as they followed her back into the building. His impatience was escalating to annoyance.

Lotus pointed to where a light flickered on the processor, the front of which appeared melted into misshapen tar. "I went full throttle twice—completely melted the outer shell. But I'm not sure I got all the wires. The thing's still lit."

"Ironic that the vile thing belonging to the Magistrate won't die," Banks commented, rubbing his palms together before using a skewer-looking tool he'd extracted from his pocket to poke at a thin yellow wire.

As if the filament had yelled "surprise!" it buzzed faintly, and then fried pieces fell onto the floor. The pesky light on the mainframe's exterior flickered once more and went out.

Wee pushed a charred wire away with his foot, cursing when it stuck to the front of his shoe.

"That's it! It looks broken now," Banks reported, pumping two fists like hammers in the air.

A nanosecond later, Xander's nerves shattered. An alarm splintered the air. He jumped as if he'd been stung. Its stabbing siren, not at all in keeping with Tranquility's peaceful alerts, had him covering his ears and cursing aloud.

Wee and Dorian joined with a louder "Shazz" and dropped to their knees next to a cowering Will and a frozen Banks. Oslin's gasp was drowned out by the noise. Lotus's eyelids fluttered like a hyperactive butterfly before they snapped shut. The alarm abruptly quit, and the distinct, acute click coming from the door was loud in the sudden silence. Xander's eyes widened. *It can't be …*

Red made it to the only exit in dizzying speed, his hair quilled out, yet even his strength couldn't move the mechanism or the door itself. He shook his head and tried again, but nothing happened.

Xander rushed to Red's side. "You can move a *train* but not a *door*? What's the deal?" His heartbeat thrashed in his ears.

"Hey …" Wee and Will said together.

"Got no idea," Red moaned as the others crowded him, pushing and yelling in frustration.

Curse words piled up like a crown on Xander's head. They were in deep. "Lotus?"

"I would blind you all."

Everyone started talking at once. Their frantic voices bounced off the icy, rainbow-patterned walls.

Then, the door clicked with a loud thud and opened, but it held no freedom. Instead, a force of a dozen Sciolists stood inches from the frame, electrified Stingers in hand.

Retreating with fire under their feet to the opposite side of the room, they raced behind a mirrored room divider covered on the front with clear crystal strips of various thicknesses that reminded Xander of falling rain. All eight pressed against the wall behind it. Xander shielded his body, crossing his arms over his chest and turning his torso to the side, thinking they must look like pinned insects on a display board. Caught.

The three Sciolists on the front line advanced at breakneck speed into the middle of the chamber, followed by six others with murderous facial expressions. Their tall, blood-red figures were garish against the soft colors dusting the walls. Staying within the threshold were the remaining three.

"The Spectrum is damaged!" the largest of the main three snapped, thunder in his speech. "Look!" He advanced eight feet across the floor to the melted mass of metal, touching it with his index finger and then drawing back with a jerk, as if the thing could contaminate him.

Xander shared eye gazes with his comrades. Their eyes were like his, bugged out like full moons as they listened.

With the burn of bile in the back of his throat, Xander prepared himself with how to explain their presence once they were discovered. With Sciolist apparel on himself, he could come up with a story that he had already caught the others in the act and it was being handled personally by Serpio—that the new arrivals had no need to be there—that … Turning his body, he put one foot out, only to feel Oslin throwing his arm against his chest.

"Stop!" Oslin mouthed.

Through a refracted space, Xander watched four outraged Sciolists pronounce the Continuum Spectrum's fate. They threw each word like a bomb as they drew together around the mangled black box, examining its remains. "Ruined!" "Wrecked!" "Destroyed!" "The heart of the city …!"

Four others, silent as tongueless serpents, prowled the room, probing. Within what felt like seconds, they methodically scrutinized every nook and cranny, advancing finally to the back … to the team's hiding place.

Behind the ridiculous mirror, ready to be detected, Xander went on the offensive with the plan in his head. "Found them before you even arrived!" Xander yelled. His heart clambered up his throat and strangled his utterance so it came out loud but hoarse. He stepped out, just as he had envisioned.

But he stopped in his tracks.

"No one here. No one here at all," the apparent captain of the Sciolists announced.

No one here? Xander thought, letting the letters party inside his head.

The way the mystified Sciolist toured the room with his arms outstretched in a sweep sent Xander into an emotional roller coaster of both laughter and tears.

Xander tilted his head back, humbled by the miracle reprieve, before he put his left arm across Oslin's shoulders and his right across Lotus's. Each one in turn followed suit, the thunk of arms connecting along the line of the Dream Team, as they realized their invisibility had held.

Matching a rhythm to the sentence and echoing it with footsteps, a Sciolist voice declared, "They must have fled at once."

"Documenting now," another vocalized, droning details into his Alt about the failure of his team.

Once the communication finished, the captain threw his hood over his head, and pronounced, "This mission is complete. We report back to City Hall."

With a formation into a single file, the Sciolists marched toward the door.

Now emboldened, Xander crept into the room to witness the

shameful exit of the red troupe. He smirked as a thought danced in his head.

Just before the last one went through, Xander jerked his legs out from under him, leaving a flustered Sciolist flat on the floor and blubbering about what weird force he had just felt. He scrambled up, a crimson flush staining his face, and studied the ground to determine the cause of his stumble. Finally, with one more backward glance, he hurried out the door to catch up with the others.

Behind him, Will gave Xander a playful slug on the arm, but his words were a scold. "Let's go before you decide to do anything else that stupid."

Xander only grinned.

FIFTY-NINE

Ember's Eclipse

WITH HER SAFETY net of invisibility, Ember made a game of weaving through people, although she reminded herself there was soon to be a very serious challenge ahead. In fact, she had no idea what to expect or how to find Ava, much less free her.

At Solace, she stood, rooted, in front of the iridescent, multi-hued door, chewing a fingernail. It was here where the Magistrate discovered her empathic abilities. And it was here that her life took a turn so severe that she'd had to grow up overnight. She scrunched up her features as her mouth dried up; even her saliva didn't want to enter those doors.

The door slid open with barely a sigh, and the "healing" music characteristic of Solace baptized her ears. A Medic who stood behind the counter and hummed along with the music looked her way but shook her head as if the door opening by itself was something she encountered every day and was an irritation to be sloughed off.

Now to find Ava.

She walked in on tiptoe before realizing how stupid that was. At six feet in, she looked to both her right and her left, and her spirits sagged. Each hallway had a beautiful gate adorned with carved wooden and metal flowers that blocked passage to where all the patient rooms were. And they were locked. She remembered that from her own visit here. A Medic had led her into the exam room the day Ember arrived for her physical exam.

If I use my talent from Red, I can break the gate down.

She quickly discarded that idea. It would lead to a mess and put Solace on high alert. She still wouldn't know where Ava was or even if she was still here. Her lips trembled at the thought.

She would have to make herself known and tell the Medic at the front desk she needed to see Ava immediately. Her mind whispered, *Use Dorian's talent instead.*

Ember cringed when she saw the woman behind the desk jump back suddenly at the sight of a person standing directly in front of her. Her eyes doubled in size, and her hand flew to her mouth. "I'm so sorry. I didn't see you come in," she said, her voice strangely steady and compassionate under the circumstances.

"Didn't mean to startle you," Ember said, earnestness shaping her apology.

The Medic's eyes narrowed and settled on Ember's red hair. A frown creased her brow before the middle-aged woman smiled, advertising a set of polished teeth that still gave the look of a jackal poised to pounce on its prey. "I know who you are. You're the lost girl they're searching for."

Shazz! Shazz! Shazz! The mask and wig burned in the pocket of her dirt-streaked uniform. When she'd decided to abandon the invisibility, she'd forgotten to disguise herself again.

Adrenalin shot through Ember's veins, and with a loud voice vibrating with panic, she pushed on. She pressed her palm into her forehead. "You now realize I am no one you should recognize! I'm a concerned friend here to see Ava Validus. You will show me to her room." She patted the Stinger concealed within her clothing.

For a long minute, the Medic did not respond but stayed stock still and seemed to stare right through her. Ember shifted from one foot to another, wondering if she'd somehow stopped time instead.

Finally, the Medic acknowledged her. "Of course. Right away. She has Sciolists guarding her, though. She's Elite and is very, very ill."

"Very, *very* ill?" Ember repeated. "I know she was brought here for illness, but … just how ill is she?"

"I'm so sorry. I can't give you details." The mousy woman, a Level Ten, offered Ember a deep sigh and a thoughtful expression.

Just to be sure the Medic couldn't evade her demands, Ember placed her palm on her forehead again while clenching her teeth. "You *will* give me details." She needed to know what state Ava was in. *Is she too frail to move? Will Ava have to be healed first?*

"Again, I'm sorry. I don't know anything. Her stay here is highly classified. No one knows her current state except the Magistrate himself." The lady's smile and words were sincere. Ember could tell by the emotions drifting from her.

"Take me to her room!" Ember wanted to scream; precious minutes were ticking by.

"I'll call a porter. I can't leave my station." The desk monitor pushed a call button within the booth.

Rather than argue, Ember nodded. At least she would get there.

A Level Eight overeager, smiling concierge arrived almost immediately. His smile, though, quickly faded. "You're … you're Ember!"

"You don't recognize me!" Ember slung the words as fast as she could before realizing she hadn't activated the gift at all.

But it was too late.

Two Level Sixteen security guards stormed into the lobby from each side of the hallway gates.

The porter must have activated an emergency alert on his Alt.

The Stinger she carried within her uniform called to her. Her talents lay waiting. But panic swirled around her like a vortex and caught her up. Dizzy, she gasped for oxygen. She should run!

The voice within her spoke with lightning speed. *No, Ember, don't run. Stand your ground and speak. Ava's life is at stake.*

She had to make a choice. The right one. A simple command would do the trick.

But before she could open her mouth to speak again, a purple-garbed guard shoved something cold against her neck.

Drowsiness saturated her body as she struggled against a faint. With her sight blurring into fog, she tried desperately to focus, only to imagine her worst nightmare walking toward her.

Before everything went black, she felt a different kind of darkness. The Magistrate had entered the room.

SIXTY

Ember's Quandary

COLD FINGERS WANDERED down the planes of Ember's face, tracing a comma at the edge of her lips.

She blinked her eyes and tried to focus. "Wha-at—" she began when she pulled her arms up from beside her. Like a marionette gone berserk, she thrashed about when her movements were met with resistance.

The Magistrate gazed down at her with his fathomless eyes. *Ugh. He caressed me!* She suppressed the vomit climbing up her throat.

Jerking her head away, she cried, "Don't! Don't you touch me!"

Panic clawed at her insides.

Again, she struggled, but she now clearly saw where she was —still at Solace. Pale pink walls with painted-on flower motifs seemed translucent and steel medical equipment assembled around the bed in which she lay. A fan above her head stirred perfumed air and played an orchestrated melody.

"Ember … I never thought you'd be so easily back in my presence." Serpio uncrossed his legs and smiled. His teeth shone pearly white through his alligator grin, but the dark circles under his eyes told her he'd lately fought a few sleepless nights.

In the tiny room, two bearded men who looked like mad scientists were busy arranging equipment, pulling a few frightening contraptions on silky wheels over to her side.

Again, she yanked against her constraints, this time hard enough; they broke into steel fragments and clattered against the floor. In an instantaneous leap, she was out of bed, knocking the Magistrate off his chair, where he lay in a sprawled, confused jumble of limbs.

She ran.

He rose.

In a mad dash, courtesy of Red's transferred talent, she was down the hallway. Shrieks of shock and frustration wafted from the room. Then she stopped in her tracks, wondering what to do and which way to go. She couldn't leave without Ava. *Where is she?*

Invisible again, she scurried from room to room, thanking the universe that doors were open or unlocked.

A balloon hovered over an empty cot.

A child sobbed for his mother.

A middle-aged man peeked out from under the sheets.

A teen girl polished her own shoes with a nonexistent rag.

None were Ava.

She kept going, door to door, aware of pounding footsteps behind and in front of her. Knowing that no one could see her made her square her shoulders and hurry with a wide and steady gait while still trying to contain her heartbeat within her ribs. *Ava has to be here somewhere!*

"Ember! Where are you, my dear?"

Serpio.

When the Magistrate called her name, his tone sugared and lubricated, her fingers curled into her palms. The voice grated against already frayed nerves. He was right behind her, searching, too, traipsing in and out of patient compartments, but for her. Tossing her head, she sneered. He would never find her.

At the gate back into the lobby, she paused. She should break through, break it down, and bore into the other wing of the clinic. *Ava must be there.* Ember's desperation became a noose around her neck, twisting ever tighter, only to cut off her oxygen. Suddenly off-balance, she teetered into the gate and scraped her arm across its jagged, decorative blossoms.

"Gah! Oww!" She gripped her arm, eyeing the deep grooved gash and watching the blood run down its length, leaving a crimson splotch on the floor.

Behind her loomed her nemesis. "There you are! Ember, you have a new power? Thankfully, I can see you now." Breathing hard, his puffs of air leaving behind a scent she could only identify as rotting fruit, Serpio leaned against her, bridging his arms over her head as if he had become a human cage.

What happened to my invisibility?

The searing sting in her forelimb answered her question. The injury had broken something other than flesh. It had punctured some aspect of her invisibility.

With a grunt, she thrust herself against him, funneling Red's strength into his muscular chest. Serpio cried out with a yelp and fought back, stopping to put a hand over his chest in a protective and shocked fashion. Ember's mind flashed back to the arena, where she witnessed him speared through the chest.

Someone screamed out, "Medic!" and within seconds, a man ran into the hallway.

Blinking light came from somewhere beyond. Robotic voices droned from hidden speakers. "Code Five breach! All security personnel to west hallway immediately. Code Five breach. All security personnel to west hallway immediately."

A half dozen Sciolists streamed from concealed doorways Ember didn't realize were there. Advancing. Converging. Stingers at the ready. She spun, drawing her own.

Lighting her Stinger's voltage, she fought her way through the melee like a banshee, her legs and arms battering the red-caped forms trying to hold her. With heavy-handed strikes and yells, her potent forcefulness and speed brought the small army to their knees, where she pummeled them until all six lay whimpering on the floor.

A-va, A-va, A-va! The name pounded through her like a bombastic pulse, and she pressed her legs into a run.

"Stop, Ember!" Her own name echoed from the floor into the hallway, adding a syncopated beat to the rhythm of Ava's name. "I … need … you to help Ava!"

Serpio? Pleading?

Ember slowed and stopped twenty feet away. She turned to face him—the esteemed leader of Tranquility still on the floor, his clothes awry, his eyes wild, clutching his chest. She'd knocked him around, surely causing bruising, but he suddenly seemed like a wretched, wounded animal, helpless and vulnerable. His emotional state sluiced from his pores, cloudy and black, with bright yellow arcs flashing within. Fear of loss. Hopelessness. And … death? Although even the sight of the Magistrate sickened her, something about his cry for help unhinged her heart.

He did say Ava. Ava needs help.

Do not trust him!

But Ava …

She stood in the center of the hallway, her feet apart in a steadfast, wide stance, her arms up in front of her, karate style. "I need a promise of safety." Channeling Dorian, she commanded, "If I help, you will not harm me."

A copper-clad Medic wearing a name tag that identified him as Jago hurried to assist Serpio but was brushed away with a pointed command. "I don't need medical help. But stay. We'll need a Medic soon."

Despite his denial, Jago helped the Magistrate stagger to his feet. He shuffled forward until he stood a foot away from Ember. With his head slowly swiveling, he glanced around and muttered, "I don't understand …". He rubbed his eyes before seeming to shake off his shock.

One by one, scattered throughout the hallway, each Sciolist

stumbled and wobbled to their feet. With a curled lip, Serpio said, "You are dismissed. Get yourselves put together. Then, position yourselves at the front door. Let no one enter. And next time, don't be such weaklings! This *girl* broke you. Disgusting."

Serpio flicked his hands, and the Sciolists bowed and took leave, their red capes drooping in disappointment, sliding from the vicinity like shadows in the night.

Ember flexed her fingers and narrowed her eyes, staring down the Magistrate, the bane of her existence. *I could easily send this monster into oblivion, and he would be gone.* Then, she remembered. He could not die.

With eyes that were unexpectedly soft, he reached out his arm, palm up. "Ember, dear. If you help, I will not harm you. I would never hurt you anyway, my Queen of Hearts." He leaned in closer and whispered, "I'm in love with you. I've tried to show you that. Your very presence takes my breath away. I will always keep you safe."

Ugh. Her stomach pitched, and her chest burned with his confession. Bile stretched into her throat, and she shivered.

Serpio took a step back but kept his gaze locked on her. "The thing is, Ember, Ava is very ill. The Medics"—he gestured toward Jago—"haven't been able to help her. She is close to death. And you're a … a healer? Ava told me you have developed new powers." His gaze traveled down her body, assessing her, similar to their first meeting right here at Solace.

Ember opened the distance between them, still close enough to judge the Magistrate's words and feelings. "I am. I can heal—if it's not too late. I'm ready if Ava needs my help."

"Yes, of course. Something you should know. She's … lost a lot of blood."

"Take me to Ava. Now." While she wanted to know how and why Ava would have hemorrhaged, she bowed to the urgency of the situation. She would ask no more questions.

Leading the way, but with a hiccupping limp born of the scuffle, Serpio unlocked the gate leading to the lobby and proceeded across to the hallway on the opposite side. "I will take you to Ava."

I knew it! She's over there—furthest from where I was. I hope I can still save her.

With her lips in a line, she followed Serpio, fussing. "Can't you hurry?"

The Magistrate either didn't hear her or chose not to answer.

Jago, walking behind her, his heavy eyebrows almost touching, reached out and put his hand on Ember's arm mere inches from her injury. "Looks like you've had a painful scratch. That will mend. But Ava ..." He shook his head. "Even the Medela couldn't heal her—too great a loss of vital fluids."

Ember remembered Will's parents. They'd lost blood, too, and had been dehydrated. Ava didn't think they could live without what she could get from the hospital. She was able to heal them anyway. But then Reselda had helped, too.

Even people who were severely injured weren't expected to heal themselves in Tranquility. *If Ava needs blood, why didn't they give it to her?* Surely Tranquility stored a supply for an emergency? She'd been taught that O-type blood could be used for anyone ...

As if the Medic could hear her thoughts, he said, "Solace doesn't usually take patients needing intensive care like the hospital. Solace is—"

"I know what Solace is!" Ember snapped. "I don't know why Ava is here."

At Ember's reaction, the Medic's face held a wounded expression, as if he'd just been slapped. He continued his lecture anyway. "Even if she was in the hospital, hospital blood supply —type O—is all manufactured and kept at Inventum—the genetics lab. And you know the building was destroyed, sadly. So, if you can't help, Ava will definitely die."

The corridor seemed to stretch into infinity, but finally, the Magistrate stopped in front of a gold door. He turned to face her and leaned in to whisper, "Don't be surprised when you see Ms.

Validus. Sadly, she is in a coma. I wouldn't have promised you sanctuary if I wasn't in great need of your talents. As I said, this is a last resort."

You would absolutely promise. I used my talent for that, too.

She nodded, and Serpio waved his wrist to open the door. *Shazz. I would have met a locked door!*

She edged closer to the Magistrate, still trying to discern signs of subterfuge. But his disposition read more like obsession and dissatisfaction than deception, and she fought off its negative claws sinking into and under her skin. A cloudy red swirled with blue. And while her ability to feel emotions was razor sharp, her talent to detect deceit? Pretty unreliable.

The door slid open. A tiny gasp escaped Ember's lips. There was her beloved friend, Ava, a sheet up to her chin. Absolutely still. Pale. Except for the monitor to the right of the bed tracking heartbeats, there were no other signs of life. A painful lump formed in her throat, and she suddenly couldn't swallow.

She recalled Will's parents and her own mother's illness and how their state of health had smothered their auras and heartstrings. It was no wonder she couldn't immediately detect any emotions emanating from Ava. She'd need to be inches away before she could detect anything, if they were perceivable under the coma.

Ember's eyes slid to the Magistrate and then back to Ava. "I have to lay my hands on her." Itching to get started, Ember lunged forward from the doorway.

"Wait." The Medic stopped her with his arm. "We need you to do … whatever you do, yes. But Miss Validus needs blood! You have the right type."

"How do you know?" Ember snapped.

Serpio put his arm around her and drew her closer to whisper, "I know everything about you, Ember. You should know that by now."

The lights in the ceiling above brightened, and she blinked to shut out the sudden heat and brilliance, drowning her in exposure. *How could he know everything?* Her hands trembled, but she propelled herself a foot away from him, her strength allowing her to do so with an ant's worth of effort.

"She shouldn't need blood! I can heal her." She ran to Ava with every ounce of effort she had, Red's energy propelling her with lightning speed.

She reached out and touched Ava's arm hanging over the side of the bed and then her face …

Before she could move another centimeter, she felt a prick on her arm.

"You …" Through blurred eyes, she watched the world rapidly fade and go dark.

SIXTY-ONE

Will's Grit

"WE MADE IT!" Will blurted. Home couldn't have looked any better than the inside of Obviators.

A cool, soothing breeze of relief blew away the dense weight of fear and vulnerability Will had carried during the mission.

The ride down on the lift was further marked by lack of warmth. The basement gave the words "cold and damp" new meaning. But the minute they descended into the basement, a slew of questions, back slaps, and congratulations from Phoenix greeted them and warmed Will's spirits.

Crowding around, the rest of Phoenix continued to pelt them with questions. They finally made their way to a spot in the middle of the room. The Dream Team stood in a line, Wee at one end and Xander at the other, leaving Will in the center. The attention and praise, although for the whole team, made Will want to melt into the floor. He'd never been comfortable with adulation, and since his torture, it was even worse.

"It was masterful!" Red assured the listeners, pumping his fists and doing small leaps in the air.

"Cracking good!" Dorian held his arms up in a victory V. After relating the entire story, with some side comments by the others, he concluded, "We almost became the success poster of the day for the Sciolists."

Xander laughed, putting a devilish glaze on the others' remarks. "You should have seen that Sciolist's face when I tripped him going out!" He stripped off his Sciolist's cape, tossing it on a nearby table.

Will smiled, too, but he put his hands in his pockets to hide their unsteadiness. Secretly, he congratulated himself for having the courage to be part of the mission. But even now, safe and sound, his heart was still a manic butterfly trapped in a jar. Where was his courage? He felt like a baby, and shame gathered in his chest. If he ever was caught by Sciolists and not put to death, he would be labeled a lunatic, sent to Solace, and then dumped Outside.

The mission finished, he ducked behind one of Kamar's vehicles to shed his Sciolist's uniform. He felt unclean in it, and he jumped back into the Obviators' uniform with relief. With a red bundle in his hands, he passed it off to Jasper on his way back to the group, who accepted it with a nod.

The familiar miniscule hole in his heart widened as he scanned the crowd for Ember and found her missing. He called out, "Where's Ember? She and Kamar still working?"

"I'm here," Kamar answered, entering the room from behind one of his junk cars. In his arms he carried a spare part. "Just missed you guys comin' in. I'd been up top until I finished fixin' and returning a malfunctioning unit. Saw Ember a while ago, though. She got a message on the Sciolist's Alt."

Xander's head whipped around. "What message?"

Pinching the skin at his throat, Kamar said, "Yeah, it's a big deal. Ava isn't in the holding cells. She's at Solace." Worry floated in his pupils. "I told her we needed a new plan. I thought she'd be waiting at the door for you guys …"

Will's eyes met Xander's—not that they'd ever had any camaraderie, but now they were fused together in confusion and distress.

Ember's mom tilted her head thoughtfully. "I think I saw her, too …" She paused and then shook her head as if to cast a bug from her ear. I'm certain she's in the tunnel—" Talesa broke off, her bewilderment dragging into space.

Xander's mouth worked into a dubious pucker. "Talesa, *you* know Ember. *I* know Ember. She wouldn't stay in the tunnel. Not if it was a lost cause."

All of Phoenix began babbling about Ember. Who had last seen her? When? A crackle of nerves punctuated the debate.

With his teeth baring down on the inside of his cheek, it seemed to trigger Will's feet to shuffle on their own. "Ember's gone after Ava. You all know it. Talesa, send out your telepathy. Find out where she is. Tell her to come back RIGHT NOW!" He hadn't meant to yell, but his panic was wildfire, consuming him, turning his mouth to dry ash and his veins to burnt twigs.

Talesa blinked rapidly before closing her eyes in concentration. She laced her fingers together, as if she could somehow make the connection with Ember more powerful.

The entire room hung suspended. The only sounds echoing through the chamber were Chester's clinking and hammering of imagined, spectacular weaponry.

With a rueful smile that softened a furrowed brow, Talesa splayed out her hands in front of her. "Okay. She's at Solace. That's all I know."

"That's all?" Will practically pounced on her.

"I wasn't worried before, and I don't even know why. But I am now." Talesa clutched at her clothing before rubbing her hands down her pant leg. "I've sent message and after message to her and got no response. It's like I can't get through to her. I hit a brick wall. If she's with Serpio at all, she's in trouble. Even if she does have powers—or maybe *because* she has powers."

"Ya *think*?" Xander sassed. His Adam's apple bobbed with fervor.

Will felt like someone was jackhammering under his skin.

"What are we waiting for? We have to go—now! Especially if Ava's there. They're both in for hell."

Xander's restless energy spoke more than his words. "So say we all!"

Xander's phrase was one Will hadn't heard in a while. It took him back to his very young childhood when he had abandoned it for more upscale slang. There was no doubt Xander was on board.

"Who's going? Other than me, of course." Talesa cast her glance over the people of Phoenix.

Lotus glowed a little before frantically pulling her light back. Except for her eyes. They held fireworks. "All of us Easterners, right?"

"In!" Red shouted, turning to the line and extending his hand out. The other six Exceptional and Special Talented ones slapped their hands atop his.

"I'm going for sure," Will pledged as he straightened his spine and walked to Talesa's side. *If Ember's in trouble, I'm going to be there for her.* That was, after all, what he had promised her from the beginning.

Jasper grabbed Bixby by the arm and stepped forward. "Xander, not without us REMs. I mean, you can't. We're your pack."

Will wondered if having so many volunteers would be a help or a hindrance. With Ember and Ava both at Solace, Serpio would have multiple bands of Sciolists.

"We should have teams," Will surprised himself by saying. "We can go into Solace in waves. Each Easterner takes a group. If the first group's invisible, they won't even see us coming until it's too late. Bixby and Jasper, you wear the Sciolist uniforms. If you stay out front and get exposed, you'll stay safe in the red clothes."

Wee clapped and exclaimed, "Brilliant!"

"Great strategy," Xander conceded, placing his finger on his lower lip and moving it back and forth thoughtfully. "But Lotus acts alone. No posse. She could hurt more than just the resistance." He pulled his red shirt off, and handed it to Bixby.

"Happy to come in last." Lotus flipped her glossy hair and then knotted it up on her head in a quick action that made Will wonder if she had actually tied it like a rope.

Xander peeled off his red pants and tossed it to Bixby, who stood waiting. "Oslin—"

"Yes, Oslin ..." Bolstered by his own ideas and determination to save Ember, Will cut off Xander's words with his own. *No one elected Xander commander.* "Oslin, you're the first group. Who wants to join Oslin's team?"

"I obviously need to be with Oslin," Xander asserted. His eyes locked again with Will's, holding a challenge.

"Great," Will went on, oblivious to Xander's drama.

"I have to stay," Kamar said, regret tingeing his concession. "Cars could come in."

Xander waved his right hand. "No judgment. Most will stay behind, just in case of—" He broke off, not finishing the horrifying implications. He jogged over to where his mechanic's uniform hung from a peg on the wall near the lift and shuffled into it.

Will found his bravado suddenly springing a leak. He took a deep breath to settle the stripped wires lining his brain. "That's a group of four with Oslin, then. Almost flawless." With a nervous sidelong look at Xander, he said, "I'll be joining you."

"I'm with Will," Wee yelled out.

"REMs go with Xander," Bixby said, with murmurs of agreement from those nearby. "We wanna be the first line. Take me and Jasper."

Jasper gave him a thumbs up before putting the red Sciolist cloak he had in his hands around his shoulders. A moment later, he'd dressed himself under the cape.

Returning to the group, Xander gave a thumbs-up. "That's six. Perfect. Sensational Six.

Red stepped up on the chair nearby. "Second surge?"

Another assembly of six joined up with Red, including Talesa, who had hesitated a moment too long to be included in the Sensational Six. "We're Smokin' Six, chappies!"

Dorian swept up many of the people he'd accompanied on the way to Obviators. "I'll take my friends here and anyone else who feels they can trust me. Remember, my words alone can keep you safe." He winked.

Within a few minutes, after drafting Reselda, Dorian defined his group. "Scorching Seven!"

"That's it, then." Xander rubbed his palms together. "Anyone not with a team stays."

"You forgot the most important thing!" a voice called out.

Heads turned. *What 'important thing' did they forget?* A thorn of anxiety stabbed at Will's newfound stability.

"C'mon over here! You need weapons!" Chester, the Easterner of weapon wizardry, gestured wildly. The grin on his face was like a kid who'd discovered he could fly. He picked something up from the table—an odd pipe structure that spewed fire.

Altogether, the revolutionaries thundered across the room toward a worktable laden with bizarre small arms and assorted weapons.

Chester handed over the fire-breathing gun to Xander. "No instructions needed. Just don't aim it at your friends."

Xander gave Chester a quick grin and walked eight giant steps away. As he flicked a switch on the curved pipe at the bottom, a blaze erupted, eight inches of orange and blue. He clicked it off and loped back to the group, his swagger just as much on fire.

"I haven't had a chance to make more of those, but I have about ten of these things." Chester held up another long pipe with a canteen-looking attachment. "A very narrow cannon. But it fires shock waves. They'll pass through people and objects."

"How does it do that?" Wee asked, as he backed up a few inches.

"Does it—does it vaporize people?" Jasper asked, wonder painted on his face.

Chester shook his head. "No. It's deceptive. The shock waves are actually harmless. But it sounds like real thunder is hitting you. Gas from the cylinder of liquid petroleum mixes with air and then explodes. This creates a lot of strong bursts. The gas moves through the cannon barrel and gets stronger until it comes out. People should actually fall down, thinking they're wounded."

"But if they get up ..." Will let his words disappear.

Chester held up what looked like a short rifle—a bright orange-red contraption. "A blast of heat. Depending on how long you hold down the trigger, it can burn a hole in somebody."

"I need that." The words burst out of Will before he knew it.

Chester handed one over. "I guess it's yours, then."

"We're set," Talesa affirmed. Then leaning in, she cooed, "Thank you, Chester. You're a lifesaver."

Xander approached the table and fist bumped Chester before addressing the rebels once more. "We leave both rifles behind for Phoenix here. Who's got the Stingers?"

"I had one," Kamar said. "In the cupboard for safe keeping. Ember had the other."

Will's lungs unfurled. Breathing space. "Thank the stars for that! She's at least got a weapon."

Xander got in the last word. "We leave now!"

SIXTY-TWO

Serpio's Shadow

AT SOLACE, two translucent pieces of equipment lay on the table. The Medic picked up one, a small device that looked similar to a remote control, and explained, "This is the near-infrared vein finder. Once I position this over Ember's arm, I can see every vein as if they've been lit with glow-in-the-dark paint. Then I'll use the other."

He exhibited a round canister with two lancets on the side. It makes a painless incision in the skin, and a built-in vacuum draws blood to the skin's surface and deposits it in the tank."

Like a nervous first-time father, Serpio hovered nearby but kept eyeing the exit as if he expected the zombie apocalypse to commence any moment. Finally, he turned his back and activated something on his OmniCom, but not before he felt the slick film of sweat on his forehead.

"She's completely sedated, sir. Everything's set up for the blood draw, including the bag over on the wall." Jago gestured to an overflow vat mounted on the wall attached to the hose. "Now I'm going to calibrate the machine for the correct amount."

A slight whizzing from the equipment hummed through the

room, reassuring Serpio that everything was going better than expected.

"Good, good. Make sure you get a couple of pints. Most of it will be stored, but we get it now while we can. But make sure Ember is unharmed and feeling no pain."

"Yes. Of course, Magistrate. She's under only slightly—just enough to keep her comfortable and unaware. It will take some time. The vacuum pulls slowly to allow the body to keep from going into shock."

Serpio winced, wiped his forehead, and pasted on a smile. Was it the stress making him feel so unwell? A tiny, gnawing throb, like a second heartbeat, troubled him, and he put his hand to his chest. It subsided after he took a deep, cleansing breath.

He thought he saw a shadow pass by the window, but he blinked, and it was gone.

He tapped his OmniCom and spoke into it. "Esryn. Answer *now*."

This was the second time he'd tried to communicate with his most elevated Sciolist.

Has something happened to Esryn? Unfastening the top button on his shirt, he next shook out his hands, loosening up twitchy muscles.

Time to try his second-in-command. "Aero," he said as his feet continued to thump back and forth on the cold, marble floor.

Silence.

"Aero!" His voice blazed, tart with impatience.

He stopped his pace and studied his OmniCom. Its illumination showed steadily. But something was faulty … had to be. What was wrong with his damn OmniCom?

A dreadful thought cascaded into his consciousness. "Jago! Is your Alt working?"

"Umm …" The Medic looked up from where he finished strapping the HemoTech 3000 to Ember's arm and then down at his Alt. "It's lit but shows the last reading was … well over two hours ago." He transferred his questioning gaze to meet Serpio's.

Over two hours ago. Something—someone—had dismantled the system. Someone wretched. And he knew who it had to be.

Pounding coursed through his ears, at first a mild wave, but one that quickly escalated into a stormy surge. The hammering grew to a roar. He wanted to run from it, but his feet rooted themselves to the floor. As if someone was pulling his muscles and veins through his skin, they strained to bursting. He swiveled to punch a pillow, and although he wanted to put his fist through a wall instead, a wafer-thin, rational thought overrode the urge. But even baring his teeth didn't stop Serpio's dry heave as he frantically looked for a place to empty the contents of his stomach.

Jago ran to him, putting a hand on Serpio's shoulder. "What? What is it? Are you okay?"

Nostrils flaring, Serpio deeply inhaled the lavender-scented air of the room, mentally vowing vengeance. His stomach quieted enough to seethe, "I'll be fine. Get back to Ember! GET. THE. BLOOD!"

SIXTY-THREE

Xander's Offensive

THANKING the stars for Kamar's Frankenstein vehicles, Xander and teams of Phoenix made their journey to Solace in mere minutes. The sun had drifted behind the buildings in its lazy afternoon decline, starting to create shadows among them. With their eyes peeled for danger, they all marveled at the sudden lack of Sciolists on the streets. Whether that was good or bad remained to be seen.

A block away from Solace, Xander climbed out of Kamar's purple car, which he'd nicknamed "Legend." Five others followed, their movements on fire as they landed their feet on the white asphalt, calling out encouragement, eager to get their mission underway.

A yellow CommuteCar whizzed by, rustling the sunflowers and daisies that lined the street, the occupants within waving and smiling as if they were in a parade, the sounds of the radio inside blasting an upbeat tune that could be heard through the closed windows.

Xander squinted his eyes on the lookout. Phoenix's second car, a silver vision of lightweight fiber-plastic, pulled up and parked behind theirs, its rough construction marking the air with an unwelcome screech. It parked beneath a giant tree with monstrous limbs that hung down to embrace the vehicle. Not the perfect camouflage, but it was better than nothing. Red's team alighted and joined Oslin's, where they joined hands to cement their invisibility.

Xander tapped his foot on the stamped concrete beneath his feet to shake off the nervousness he felt. He knew in his heart that this would be a confrontation like no other. If Serpio had Ember, her destiny hung in the balance. His heart withered and died each time he thought about Ember being anywhere near the Magistrate. And Ava … she had put her life on the line for them. She didn't deserve any pain in life, much less Serpio's horrifying abuse.

But they had a team that was ready to do what it took. To fight. To rescue. And to kill if anyone got in the way. With the annihilation of the Continuum Spectrum and the chance to skewer Serpio's schemes, this was the turning point they'd dreamed about.

The third, final car, a coppery sedan, pulled up in front of Legend, and Dorian's team spilled out and immediately joined hands with the others as they began their short march to Solace. The scrape of their shoes and an occasional lighthearted insult marked their passage.

Still thirty feet out, Xander issued orders. "Okay, here's the plan. I'm sure there are Sciolists in that place. Dorian's team—distract them. Use your thunder guns. Make noise. Get them to follow you a good ways from Solace—as far as you can."

Oslin warned, "I won't be nearby. Don't go *too* far out. Can't guarantee you'll remain invisible. In fact, you probably won't," he added with a grimace.

"I can always tell those Serpified morons where to go." Dorian's lips twitched as if he hoped for the experience.

The group quickly nodded in agreement, each of them showing confidence in their abilities and their weapons, and they began to move down the road, not in a straight line, but instead like a giant amoeba.

Xander called out orders. "Red, after we get inside, if you don't see any Sciolists, your group will come up close to the building. You make a human chain, passing communication to and from Talesa, who'll be outside."

Talesa smiled and gave him a thumbs-up. "I'm info central for Easterners."

"Can you tell me where Ember is in there?" His mind spinning about the logistics, he didn't want to play hide and seek with Ember's location, and Talesa was his GPS.

Talesa nodded toward one side of the building. "Easy. She's in the west wing—the furthest away. If she moves, though, I won't be able to let you know."

"Fair enough. Hey, Lotus, can you get on top of the roof?" Xander pointed to the front of the facility, where vines wandered up through open stuccoed squares.

"Yeah. I know what you're thinking," she replied, tilting her head and narrowing her lavender eyes as she shuffled along at the center of the group. "I can flash Morse Code. I'm communication for the others."

"Yep." Xander tried to make eye contact with each of their faces. The plan was looser than a gossip's tongue, but each would have to do their best.

* * *

"WE COULDN'T HAVE BETTER cover than Solace's shrubbery," he stated as he took his team behind the nine-foot-tall blooming hedge that surrounded the building. The greenery shrouded them with limbs of lush leaves and soft white flowers that perfumed the air. "Not that we need it," he said with a smirk, remembering he wasn't visible anyway, "but insurance never hurts."

Now thirty feet from the building, grass crunched under his feet. He eyed Will on his left, who caught Xander's gaze and nodded. Appearing strangely stable with an upright posture,

Will carried one of Chester's heat guns, holding it close to his chest.

To his right was Oslin, crouched in a modified squat, poised to spring up at any second, a Stinger in his grip. The sweat under Oslin's armpits bore witness to the Easterner's lack of enthusiasm for another battle, one that might not end well.

Up ahead, there they were—Sciolists. Crimson figures stood in position, resembling a swarm of bloodthirsty hornets, their garish uniforms a warning of the power they held. Xander spotted at least ten of them, fanned out, on guard, not fifteen feet from the entrance. Trained for Removal. Trained for rebellion. Trained for resistance.

Xander's warrior yell, silent to even the trees around them, signaled Dorian's team. At a cul de sac near where they'd left their cars, they activated their thunder weapons. Sounds of heavy explosions echoed back to Solace, but the hubbub definitely reverberated into the city. His very bones vibrating from the racket, Xander allowed himself a chuckle as he heard the rumble.

Alarmed by the sudden commotion, just as they'd hoped, the Sciolists rushed away toward the source of the noise, yelling their way through the foliage.

The front of the building, its alabaster exterior flecked with chips of Tranquilian color, now stood unguarded, save for one Sciolist who'd stayed behind. His eyes darted back and forth as if he were watching a rubber ball zigzag past him.

With Xander's arm windmilling, the Sensational Six advanced at a run. Oslin tore off the skin on the sentry's back with the electrified tip of the Stinger he carried, and the Sciolist fell down, writhing and crying out for help. *He'll be no problem.*

But instead of bursting through the door that should have opened automatically like welcoming arms, the entire team slammed up hard against it.

Locked! *Of course.* Xander gritted his teeth and then yelled an obscenity.

Just when he thought he would implode from his frustration, Red flew out of nowhere, blitzing to Xander's right. "Move back!" the Easterner shouted, throwing his body to bulldoze the door.

Xander shuddered at the sudden cyclone of chaos as the door twisted inward and cracked, the steel frame groaning a cry for help as it gave way with the clatter of a hundred cymbals descending from the sky. Sides of the door's frame tore into fragments, leaving swirling dust behind in its wake. Glass shards blasted across the floor's polished tile while shimmering splinters showered overhead in a crystalline torrent. The destruction stretched into the lobby like the aftermath of an earthquake. Xander gritted his teeth as he gaped at the ruins of bent metal and kaleidescoped glass. Undaunted, Xander dashed through, his team alongside, envisioning them to be moving in slow motion, like the heroes in a film.

Jasper and Bixby stood on either side of the blown entrance, holding their weapons in a ready position. With invisibility protecting their communication, Jasper shouted blow-by-blow snippets about the rebels' status. The communication chain would stay informed.

For mere seconds, Xander scanned Solace's sickeningly plush interior.

Five Sciolists jumped into action, all running out of the gaping entrance hole, frantically seeking whatever upheaval had demolished it. The caped adversaries spun, feinting right and then left, multiple times. Hollering gibberish, they sputtered and struggled to find the right words for the impossible.

They're like mice in a maze, Xander thought.

Clearly puzzled, they wielded their Stingers like swords, slashing the air and jabbing wherever they thought they heard noise. His Phoenix gang eluded the prods and plunges with the grace of ballerinas.

A Sciolist with a star embroidered on his cloak, clearly a commander, and a craggy face only a mother could love cued up his Alt … or tried. He spoke into it with an authority born of small power, then shook his head and his wrist as if to wake things up. He turned to the nearest colleague and rasped a command, "This Alt is malfunctioning. Use yours. Report immediate breach!"

The other spoke into his, and only silence talked back. "Dead, sir. Rampant fail?"

The captain paced back and forth. "We stand our ground, then. Go—go in person. Let the Magistrate know of the problem."

Beneath his protective shell, Xander grinned. It was just too good.

He watched the Sciolist head for the west wing. *Ah. So Serpio is there also.* Things just got more challenging.

At the gate, the disciple held up his wrist, only to hang his head in disappointment. The Alt wouldn't open the gate. He returned to his team as a paragon of disappointment.

Xander yearned to strike them all down but leaned on Phoenix's ability to stay undercover. Best to just move on down to where Talesa said they would find Ember.

"To the corridor, now!" Xander had already begun to travel in that direction, dodging the unwitting Sciolists and leaving them to wonder why, in all their searching and striking, they still hadn't found the threat.

Followed by Will, Wee, Red, and Oslin, the Outsider maneuvered thirty feet to a gate at the entrance to the hallway. Red simply bent the metal posts with his hands, releasing the lock's grip. Xander frowned and gritted his teeth, worried the noise from the bowed frame would tip off the Sciolists from the lobby.

Racket outside their protected shell was audible.

Their reprieve was exactly two seconds.

Motioning with his hands, Xander demanded his team flatten themselves against the wall.

After yelling for backup, the bewildered Sciolists, convinced they had finally found the danger, charged into the hallway. Still not discovering the threat there, they blew past.

Now, follow the mice.

Along a long, dimly lit hallway wide enough to mimic an alleyway, Serpio's disciples shifted position, paused to listen, and brandished their weapons at various places along the way. They passed seventeen closed doors of various colors that checkerboarded the passageway.

Eventually reaching the end, they spread out in single file, five feet apart and weapons at the ready. The tall one with the craggy face stood militantly in front of the last door.

Gold. *Ava has to be behind that door.*

With Xander's command, the six Phoenix counterfeit ghosts lined up, each assuming a position across from a Sciolist. One on one. Man to a man.

Red met Xander's eyes and then was the first to strike. With one fluid movement, he picked up the Sciolist under his arms and threw him against the opposite wall. The Sciolist's violent scream and thud seemed to rock the foundations. Red stomped his large foot atop the guy's chest and twisted his neck—a twenty-second slaughter.

In the same breath, Oslin jabbed his fully electrified Stinger deeply into his opponent's chest. With a gasp of surprise, the Sciolist crumbled to the ground, blood gushing from the mortal wound and pooling on the floor.

Will took on another Sciolist four feet away, the click from his thermal gun the last sound before he shot a blistering scorch from the Sciolist's head to his toes. The heat ruffled in waves over his target. The flesh on the enemy's face melted like a wax candle as he screamed, trying to touch his features with fingers webbed together in a glob.

Wee grabbed the ankles of his subject—the smallest Sciolist— picking him up by his legs and turning him upside down. With a high-pitched shout, the Sciolist made a valiant attempt to thrust his Stinger into Wee's leg, but Wee dodged the pass and hung him by his feet from a rack on the wall.

"Now maybe you'll quit hanging around!"

The Sciolist's curse-laden response faded into nothingness as the fight raged on.

Alongside the others, Xander concurrently struck out with his flame blaster. The sizzle of flesh drew a pitiful yowl from Xander's victim, who dove into full-on defense mode and swung his Stinger through the "empty" space. Xander sidestepped him with a leap. The Sciolist lunged, shoving his Stinger at whoever was attacking him.

With a crack and a pulsing volt of power, the pole struck Xander across the middle with the force of what felt like the fury of a meteor slamming into the earth, propelling him through the air in a violent tumble. Xander's breath dissolved.

I will not be beaten.

Gripping his middle, he rose and parried, again firing ginger-blue flames. The smell of the Sciolist's burned flesh seared his nostrils. He stepped back—one, two— preparing to continue his assault, when the Sciolist fell forward, the Stinger in his hands plowing into Xander's side.

White-hot pain radiated through Xander's body, and he gasped before his lips launched a spine-chilling caterwaul. Blood drained from his ribcage like juice through a sieve. His head spun, and his legs gave up beneath him. As he crashed to the floor, his hands lost their grip on his weapon, and he clutched at his ribs in panicked agony, feeling liquid warmth leave his body.

I'm dying.

SIXTY-FOUR

Will's Wishes

WILL WATCHED Xander cry out and collapse to the floor, gushing blood brighter than the cloaks of his enemies. It pooled on the marble tile, a fierce reminder of the brutal reality of a revolution, staining the pristine surface with its vivid and ominous hue. The sight of Xander's lifeblood spilling out in such a violent and final manner left Will reeling, his mind struggling to comprehend the suddenness and brutality of the scene before him.

In that moment, he knew he would never forget the sight of that crimson pool, nor the sound of Xander's anguished gasp.

The pandemonium of the skirmish could have awakened the dead, but to Will, Xander's fall displaced the rest of the noise, as if it were the only sound in the universe.

Xander, the Invincible.

The realization of the catastrophe rained down on the Phoenix friends like shattered glass in a freeze frame. Marked by gasps and the pounding of heartbeats, they began to rush to Xander's side but stopped short.

A new swarm of Sciolists entering from Will's left flooded the corridor. Fifteen more assailants. The drum of their footfalls hammered through the building and through Will's gut.

Pulse spiraling, skin sweating, limbs trembling. *What happened to Phoenix outside? They couldn't stop them?*

With his little squad, he turned to meet the onslaught. Barely battered by the first offensive, they struck out with fresh vigor. This time, however, the enemy outnumbered them. With Phoenix still concealed, though, they brought a heroic, surprise assault. Preemptive kicks, slicing weapons, and burning flesh drew blood and coppery, putridly sweet smells. Cries and yells bounced against the corridor's shiny walls.

Will had his weapon raised when the sought-after gold door sprung wide open, light spilling out into the hallway like the sun exploding through the clouds, revealing two prone, motionless bodies. White sheets and freakish contraptions. Haunting music and long copper hair draped over the side of a table …

Long copper hair. Ember?

A sharp movement barely within his peripheral vision seized his attention and sent a shiver shimmying up his back. He ratcheted his spine and swiveled to aim his weapon. With an impulsive click, the heat shot out before he realized his target was a mere Medic caught in the wrong place at the wrong time.

The window beyond the lifeless bodies flared with what resembled lightning as bright as the glow of a meteor. *Lotus.* And then Will recognized thunder guns firing, one after another. Phoenix was fully present outside the door.

The Medic yelled, "Don't! Please don't hurt me! Don't … touch me! I'm leaving! Just—" He ran from the room, his hands in the air, his eyes twice their size, and bolted past Will.

In the Medic's shadow, Serpio Magnus shambled out, holding his chest, his glittering eyes narrowed to tiny slits, his body stiff with anger as he expelled a taut breath. With a scan of the men littering the floor and the fracas at hand, his gaze instead rested on Xander. His mouth curled into a smirk.

"Of course you'd come, you lovesick snake! Too bad you're far too late—and too dead." He kicked at Xander's inert form, forcing another gale of blood to burst from Xander's wound.

What? Serpio sees him! Will pressed his knuckles into his eyes. Exhale. Inhale. Exhale.

Will crouched and dodged the haphazard blows of the Sciolist in front of him with a twist and a jerk, harnessing the fighting experience he learned from the arena. The buzz of the Stinger as it whipped through the air riveted Will's concentration.

But his attention wavered to the decision he had to make. Ember was in that room! He could see her—her body prone on a table, tubes connected to something—something awful. *Is that blood … bubbling out and running down the wall?* And Ava? He didn't know. All he knew was there was another helpless person there.

Rescue them—get them out—but how? Two unconscious bodies …

He blocked a punch from his assailant and ducked again, but too late. A savage gash in a zigzag shape appeared on his arm before he even realized he'd been hit, so focused was he on getting into the room. He turned his head as if he could hear anguish beyond the door, and the Sciolist's fist crashed across his jaw, bending his face in the other direction.

He reeled backward, clutching his chin and making a move toward the door down the hall.

"Ember … Ember! Ember!" he bellowed, his heart in his mouth, suddenly realizing she couldn't hear his cries while he was within Oslin's shield.

But there—in the way—was Serpio, his most feared tormentor. Knees weakening and dizziness threatening to force him into a faint, Will fought the tide of terror welling up inside his chest.

"You! Will Verus!" The Magistrate now saw him, too. Something about an injury made invisibility evaporate?

Abandoning his Sciolist opponent to his comrades, Will advanced on the Magistrate, trembling, his entire being hardened with hatred. *I won't be able to kill him.* The thought threatening to drown him in the deepest part of his soul, but he could mutilate and hurt Serpio, give him payback for all the misery.

Using a full-on muscle-bound charge straight into Serpio's chest, Will plowed him down onto the floor and allowed his entire weight to force him flat. He flinched at the sound of his own fists cracking against the Magistrate's jaw as he struck with all the pent-up energy born of long suppressed fury.

A groan of acute pain from the Magistrate only fueled his efforts as Serpio's face, gooey red and doughy, crumpled further beneath Will's fists, the man's teeth dripping blood as his lips ballooned into a clownish mouth.

With a colossal lurch, Serpio hurtled his oppressor off his body and turned the tables, launching himself on top of Will's upper torso hard enough to knock the wind from him. A garland of stars whirled in Will's brain as he struggled to regain his breath. Finally, a rush filled his lungs, and Will struggled to roll out from under the Magistrate's heavy form, a muscular weight thirty pounds greater than his own.

"Quit, scum … while you can," the Magistrate hissed. "Nothing … you do … will kill me."

The air was thick with the odor of blood and sweat. It taunted him with its stink of defeat and memories. His own stench, a combination of fear and wrath, sucked the life from him.

As the fog of defeat gathered around him, a yell of triumph echoing from the hallway beyond burst through the air, the unmistakable Phoenix rallying call. "LOYALTY!"

The whoop threaded itself through the desperation that tore through his veins. Its bolt of spirit somehow drove his arms into an explosion—enough to catapult Serpio off his body to an area a few feet away. Serpio's frenzied scream couldn't suffocate the thumping rhythm in his throat that took shape as a chant: "Loy-al-ty, loy-al-ty, loy-al-ty."

He buried his hand in his uniform and jerked his weapon from it. As if it were a blinding light, the heat left the gun to bore into Serpio's face like a flaming sword, blasting the Hades-hot current directly into the immortal's face and holding it there until Serpio's eyelids swelled and his screams were silenced by the fusing of his lips.

Still wishing for a way to finish him off, Will hurled himself away from the devil on the floor.

The loyalty rap morphed into a new form. Xander, Xander, Xander …

Will flew to Xander's side, placing his head on his chest to check for a heartbeat. Heartbeat? Slow, feeble. Breath? Yes, but faint. Xander was dying.

Xander—his constant pain in the ass, a detestable rival he couldn't shake—his condition gruesome beyond words. Paler than his fair skin had ever been, as if death had given him a ghostly kiss, the REM's eyes were shut, his limbs splayed out at unnatural angles, blood soaking his clothes in a sticky, red bath.

Get Ember … or help Xander?

He turned to see the others battling on, most now visible and fiercely doing their best to fend off so many Sciolists. Hot mucus and tears streamed down Will's face. His eyelid jerked, and his fingers twitched. The despair of a no-win decision threatened to break him in two. He couldn't leave Xander … could he? If they got Ember out and Xander was dead, he would have her love, perhaps. But she would be inconsolable and never forgive him for leaving Xander to die.

The battle raged around him, the weapons clashing against warrior cries. He rapidly threw his thermal gun into the front of his jumpsuit. With a swift inhale, an immense groan, and a Herculean strength he pulled from somewhere deep in his soul, he bent, heaved Xander up into his arms, and ran.

SIXTY-FIVE

Will's Run

STREAMING DOWN THE BATTLE-STREWN HALLWAY, Will weaved and dodged the Sciolists as his comrades protected his run. Around him, drops of blood flew, and the crack of weapons against bone made him cringe. The drive to the end had his back aching and his arms straining with effort. Xander was heavier than anything he'd ever carried, and he would have sworn he had an elephant in his arms. In his head, all he could chant was *hurry … hurry.*

Bursting into the lobby, he yelled at the top of his lungs for help. His grimace turned into a grateful purse of his lips as he saw Bixby still standing guard.

"Bix! Send help inside!" To his sense of urgency, the words seemed to fall out of his mouth like leaves lazily falling through a reluctant breeze.

Bixby threw the Loyalty gesture in response, calling out to Talesa, "Lotus needs to flash a code! All Phoenix inside!"

Will wobbled on his feet as he saw Phoenix casualties lying outside the entrance, a half-dozen strewn across the grass, ironically separated by flower beds of roses. Heaving from the effort of Xander in his arms, he stumbled into the open air of the exterior courtyard. A shaft of sunbeam shot out from behind the trees, an orange flash measuring the lateness of the afternoon.

Reselda knelt over one of the fallen, a Plauditor he'd met on his first day of work. The man's arm dangled from his body, and the healer quickly shook her head as she jumped up at Will's frantic hollering.

His head practically swiveling off his neck, Will glanced around, looking for safety. Xander was *visible*, and unless Sciolists who may still be in the area thought he was already dead, they would finish him off in a brutal way.

But there was no time to waste. Will laid Xander down on the lawn just outside the steps to the now non-existent door. A rustle in the bushes a crow's flight distance beyond made his blood run cold, but he couldn't allow himself the worry.

Reselda's terrified cries scraped the air around them. "No! Xander!" In the space of thirty seconds, Reselda leaned across Xander's limp body, resting her entire torso on top of his, her clothing absorbing fluid leaking from the wound. Will's frown dissolved into a glow of hope.

"Is he … will he …?" Will wiped the sweat and grime from his forehead and then shoved his hands under his armpits to keep them steady.

As she separated from Xander, Reselda moved her hands across the wounds with her eyes closed. "I've got this. I'll do the best I can. Go—go do what you need."

Without a backward glance, Will coerced his legs into a sprint. He hoped his spirit would carry him forward, as exhaustion and anxiety threatened to cripple his effort.

Ten—twenty—thirty—forty yards, and he'd be back. Back to the gold door and Ember.

He rocketed into the hallway, bouncing against the gate's steel sidebars on the way in.

What he witnessed made his heart lurch with an unnatural cocktail of celebration and dismay. At least six Sciolists were down on the floor, not moving. But Oslin and Red still clashed with the rest, fighting their way toward the gold door on the left, but at more than fifteen feet from it, they were far from gaining ground. In the middle of it, Wee lay on the floor, grimacing, holding his right leg, and crying out from pain.

"Wee! Others are coming! Can you hold on?" His best friend … The tightness in his throat choked off a swallow. His desperation was like a bungee cord pulled tight against his soul.

"Uh … huh," Wee murmured, his ebony eyes filling with tears.

From a distance behind him, he heard the footfalls of his family—the Phoenix family—coming on his heels, balancing their lives on a thin razor blade of conviction.

Where is Serpio?

No longer in the hallway …

Lurching along through the hall, Will felt the whip and burn of a Stinger across his back as he evaded the final Sciolist in his way. Instead of slowing his pace, the blister fueled him with renewed purpose. All he could think about was getting to Ember.

He swept into the room.

Just inside … Serpio.

His nemesis blocked out everything like a cloud over the sun, but a click of his mind's camera captured two beds beyond. Ember and Ava were there.

Will stood frozen for a nanosecond, and the air shifted as the Magistrate em his eyes upon him, his malicious presence casting anxious designs on Will's psyche once again.

A mere glance at the Magistrate's damaged, warped face and webbed fingers caused Will to gag. His skin appeared saggy, waxen, and sticky and reeked of animalistic bile. Sucking up his distaste, Will averted his eyes, saving the contents of his stomach.

Now he looks exactly like the monster he is.

A Sciolist supported Serpio, who staggered on his feet and clamored toward where Ember was fifteen paces away.

"No you don't! Keep away from her!" Will's voice tore from his throat.

Straightaway, the warlike din in the hallway shrank to a discordant fragment that sounded dreamlike in Will's brain and stirred up whispers of his instability. The room's ominous quiet was disturbed only by Serpio's shuffle and a faint dripping—subtle as a shadow's footfalls but loud enough to force his eyes past the bed where Ember lay. Blood overflowed from a translucent bag, which then trickled down the wall and left a garnet puddle on the gilt-colored slab.

Will was no Medic, but the bag of blood on the wall, brimming over, told the story.

A random fact from Plauditor training scrolled across his mind like a news ticker. A loss of two liters of blood results in death.

His heart catapulting out of his chest, Will pulled his thermal gun once again from within his uniform. He made a mad sweep to his left, which placed him directly in front of the duo, blasting them with heat before the Sciolist could even fumble for his weapon. Flesh melted like ice cream left in the sun too long. With an anguished cry, the Sciolist fell, followed by the Magistrate, who resembled a gruesome dancer performing an awkward pirouette.

In that instant, two Sciolists invaded the room, steamrollering their way inside, with screeching cries from the hallway and the tussle of bodies failing to jerk them away and wound them.

The taller of them scrutinized him for a snug second, sneering, then jabbed with his Stinger but missed, sending Will several feet in an evasive tumble. He slammed into shelving on the wall to his left, knocking over a trio of large bottles that slivered into bits when they hit the floor.

Grabbing a long piece of the shattered glass, his fingers bled as he pushed himself up from the dive. Will's nerves converged into a missile, jetting up his back before scattering like wild beasts throughout his arms and chest. His mouth turned dry as dust, his arteries steel, his pulse rocklike. But he would not give in, no matter what. He would rather die than surrender his only chance.

As the two devils approached again, Will readied himself for the inevitable clash. The first attacker lunged forward with his Stinger, but Will deftly dodged the strike once more and countered with a stab from the shard of glass, followed by a swift kick to the groin. He was down. The second attacker landed a blow to Will's back using the blunt end of his Stinger, and Will wheeled back around in a pivot, drawing his heat gun from his uniform's pocket. With multiple shots of hell's fever on the Sciolist's face and chest, the fighter flopped to the floor like a writhing fish and then was still.

His throat lurched with a hard swallow, and he steadied himself before a wave of light-headedness threatened to take hold. But he could not flounder now.

With his teeth baring down on the inside of his mouth, he barreled across the room to where the last vestiges of sunlight danced from the windowpane to light up the ginger hair of the girl he loved. "Ember! Ember, Ember!"

The pallor of her face was the first thing he noticed. A feeling of déjà vu christened his senses; Xander had looked just as ghost-like, just as lifeless. But Xander had breath. Ember lay motionless, her respiration spellbound, with wasted tears on her eyelashes.

A monitor on the wall behind her tracked her vitals. Numbers and sporadic, tiny blips were the only signs of life.

His ears buzzed with dread. His skin blotched with its typical pink-when-anxious hue. Nausea curdled within his gut.

He sucked in quick bursts of air before dizziness hit his brain, and he gasped before whimpering, the salt of grief springing to his eyes. What Ember lacked, Will made up for. There was no calming himself as spots invaded his vision, and his hands shook uncontrollably. *C'mon, Ember. Breathe!*

After what felt like forever, a breath came from Ember, but it was more suitable for a mouse. He laid his hand over her chest to feel her heartbeat, only to question whether it was there at all. His own chest thumped with palpitations, and his entire body tingled with dread.

As despair terrorized him, he pushed his palms into his head. What should he do? What *could* he do?

A thought fell from the universe. *Put the blood back into her body!*

Just as the words, warm with comfort, settled into his consciousness, the Sciolist he'd left by the doorway somehow rallied and, at a speed rivaling a serpent's strike, scrambled toward the blood bag on the wall.

"No!" Will yelled.

But it was too late. The Sciolist ripped the pouch from its anchors, cradled it in his arms, and limped with astonishing speed toward the door.

I have to get that blood! Will was a streak as he pushed every muscle into motion. He tackled the Sciolist from behind, pulling him forward in a feverish grapple for control. Both toppled over, Will's adversary knocked senseless when his head crashed against a table full of medical equipment.

When the Sciolist went down, so did the blood. It soaked the front of the agent's uniform before spilling onto the floor, running in rivulets, shiny and harsh, as if it sought to escape on its own.

All was lost. Disentangling himself, he pushed himself up and finally stood.

Despair. Wrath. Disbelief. Plenty of that. He bent and vomited, mixing fluids in a vile hybrid.

Think, Will. He pounded his head with his fist. Could he find other blood? The lab was gone—this mental hospital not equipped. His own? He would give Ember his entire heart if she needed it.

But the thought was impractical and impossible without

help. And he had no idea whether his blood type matched hers. Minutes ticked away.

Ava? He rushed to where Ava's body lay a mere six feet from Ember's. Could Ava's blood be the salvation?

Glancing around, he scrambled for a device to hook the two together. He leaped to the cabinets for supplies, finding a new bag and hose.

A couple of devices lay on a tray next to Ember. He would have to figure it out.

He reached across to grab Ava's arm to somehow connect the two bodies, concentrating with all his might on how that might happen. But to his shock and dismay, Ava was cold. And not just slightly cold. A stone had more warmth. No breath. No color. Putting a fist in his mouth to stifle a scream, he reeled, dizziness threatening to pull him into a place where dreams lived.

SIXTY-SIX

Will's Antihero

WILL GRABBED on to the steel girders along the bottom of Ava's mattress to save himself from a nosedive. Using every ounce of strength he possessed, he brought his Tranquility training to mind and delivered oxygen to his brain with a breathe-and-hold pattern. In … Out … In … Out … In … Out … Stable.

Through the open doorway, sounds of battle still roared. What was happening out there? Then, he rubbed his eyes, confused. He thought he saw a supernatural being slide into the room.

He must be dreaming—or dead himself.

"Xander?"

"In the flesh!" The hallucination tornadoed into the room but stopped when his eyes blazed, emotion fueled by the sight of the bodies lying about like misfit puzzle pieces.

Will blinked, but it was certainly Xander. And right behind him was Reselda, who nearly tripped over Serpio's body and pressed into the space beyond to rush to Ember's side.

"How'd you—" The air suddenly reeked of both death and miracles. Again, the noise beyond faded into another space and time in his head. He was never so glad to see someone in his entire life, and it took all his restraint to not run and hug his long-detested comrade.

Will pointed to the floor, and his words quavered. "Ember might be dead. She's lost too much blood. There's no more of it."

A string of curse words shot from Xander's lips. "Ava?"

"Dead." *Even the word itself sounds lifeless,* Will thought.

Will swiveled to address the healer. "Reselda?" he begged, anguish marking a frown between his eyebrows.

"I'm trying." The woman had already placed her hands on Ember's chest. "How much blood has she lost?"

Will picked up the depleted bag from the floor. "More than this."

Reselda hung her head, still moving her hands along Ember's torso. "She needs blood. I can't restore that much fluid. And I can't give her mine. If I do, I can no longer heal."

"I could—" Xander started.

"You can't. You're barely back from the dead yourself," Reselda warned as she listened for Ember's breath. "And we don't know your blood type."

Will paced in the tiny space between Reselda and Xander as his hands trembled from his unwelcome personal earthquake, and he put them in his pockets to quell their rebellion.

"Argh!" His cry blended into the sounds of thunder guns and screams from the hallway, the conflict hazarding threats of invasion into their space.

Time, too, was the enemy.

As if they all had the same thought, their eyes converged on a point on the floor.

Serpio lay silent, six feet away, but the body still breathed.

"He's got to be a match," Reselda stated. "If he wanted Ember's blood, maybe it was for him."

"I don't know why he'd—" Will started as he joined Reselda and couldn't resist touching Ember's cheek with his finger, wishing with all his might that his love could heal her.

His black hair defying gravity, Xander cried, "Let's do this!"

Will and Xander, on either end of Ava, gently and reverently lifted her down from her resting place. They picked up Serpio, his lanky form like a dummy, and placed him on the table instead, with Xander rearing his head back in disgust as he took in the Magistrate's mangled face.

For another precious minute, they bantered about how to hook everything up but soon found the Lamia, the device that suctioned out the blood. Moments later, Serpio's blood flowed into Ember's body. Xander stood on one side of Ember, Will on the other with Reselda, who moved her hands along Ember's motionless form during the procedure, imparting strength into each of her limbs.

Five minutes stretched into ten, then twenty as the team seemed to breathe as one, waiting for Ember's breath to join with theirs. The entire world hushed suddenly, as if it, too, held its breath.

Out of the blue, Oslin, his body red-soaked and battered, his fingernails scraping along the entrance to their tenuous sanctuary, hung against the doorframe by his arm, a smile leaning on half of his mouth. "The enemy … is neutralized."

The trio exhaled in relief, joined hands, and raised them up.

As if Ember could still feel their emotions, the monitor showed what Will decided was an increasing heart and breathing rate. At least it seemed to show more peaks, more life.

When her eyelids fluttered, Will smiled. "Look! She's responding!"

Now they would wait. Ember's recovery would add to the triumph of the day.

SIXTY-SEVEN

Ember's Love

HER SENSES, although as dull as a murky pool, told Ember to react. She tried to sit up, but her body tugged boulders through its veins, weakness on a collision with gravity.

She struggled against the tide of listlessness, pushing her eyelids hard to open them to no avail.

She thought she'd opened her eyes. Hadn't she?

No. She had tried, though.

Well, no matter. She felt the lavish love of both Xander and Will seeping into her psyche. And she knew Reselda was there, too. A healer. Maybe she needed that.

She had no idea what had happened after she had restored Ava. She … did, didn't she? Cure Ava? Although she remembered touching her, it was all a blur.

A warm hand. Xander.

A breath. Will.

With a sense of peace enfolding her like a soft blanket, she surrendered to the feeling and to the devotion around her.

It was good to be alive.

She was, wasn't she?

Afterword

I hope you loved reading *Bleeding Out* as much as I did writing it. If you have a minute, I'd love to hear what you liked (or didn't like) about this book.

Indie authors like me depend on readers like you to post reviews. You don't have to write much, but I would appreciate feedback through wherever you purchased my book.

Thank you so much!

Acknowledgments

Kudos to my enduring and gracious Escondido Writers Group for their critiques and encouragement during the writing of this book.

Also, a million thanks for my family for their patience and feedback throughout the last year and a half while I immersed myself in the world of Tranquility.

Special thanks to my editor, Victoria Basnuevo, for her suggestions and corrections.

And applause to my cover artist, Miss Nat Mack, who continues to impress me with her talent.

To God be the glory!

About the Author

Tanya Ross is a former educator, wife, and parent of two. She has been the facilitator of the Escondido Writers Group for several years and has sponsored local book fairs to benefit fellow authors and the community. She is an accomplished writer who has won a plethora of awards for her series, and who hopes to inspire others to reach for the stars. Follow her on social media and check out her website at www.tanyarossauthor.com

www.ingramcontent.com/pod-product-compliance
Lightning Source LLC
Chambersburg PA
CBHW050606170726
48283CB00001B/133